THE QUIET
INVASION

Also by Sarah Zettel

Reclamation
Fool's War
Playing God

Available from Warner Aspect

SARAH ZETTEL

THE QUIET INVASION

ASPECT®

WARNER BOOKS

A Time Warner Company

Aspect® name and logo are registered trademarks of Warner Books, Inc.

Warner Books, Inc., 1271 Avenue of the Americas, New York, NY 10020

Visit our Web site at www.twbookmark.com

Ⓦ A Time Warner Company

Printed in the United States of America

First Printing: February 2000

10 9 8 7 6 5 4 3 2 1

Library of Congress Cataloging-in-Publication Data

Zettel, Sarah.
    The quiet invasion / Sarah Zettel.
        p.   cm.
    ISBN 0-446-52489-1
    1. Women scientists—Fiction.   2. Venus (Planet)—Fiction.   I. Title.
PS3576.E77 Q54 2000
813'.54—dc21   99-051756

This book is dedicated, with deepest thanks,
to my spiritual big sister,
Dawn Marie Sampson Beresford.

Acknowledgments

The Author would like to thank Timothy B. Smith for his expert technical advice, Laura Woody, who knew about the yeast, and Dr. David Grinspoon, whose *Venus Revealed* she consulted frequently during the writing of this book. She would also like to thank Betsy Mitchell and Jaime Levine, whose patient work made this a better book, and Karen Everson, who was there for the crisis.

THE QUIET
INVASION

CHAPTER ONE

"This is Venera Control, Shuttle AX-2416. You're clear for landing. Welcome back."

Hello, Tori. How are you doing? thought Helen from her seat in the passenger compartment. She liked the fact that the shuttle pilots left the intercom open so she could listen to the familiar voices running through the landing protocols. Overhearing this final flight ritual made her feel that she was really home.

I just wish I was really home with better news.

She bit her lip and settled a little further back in her crash-couch. Helen was the only Venera-bound passenger this run. She'd flown from Earth in the long-distance ship *Queen Isabella*, which now waited in orbit while the shuttles from Venera ferried down supplies and equipment that had to be imported from Earth.

Helen stared straight ahead over the rows of empty couches. The ceiling and front wall of the shuttle's passenger cabin were one gigantic view screen. Venus's opaque, yellowish-gray clouds churned all around the shuttle. Wind stirred the mists constantly but never cleared them away.

She strained her eyes, struggling to see the solid shadow of Venera Base through the shifting fog. Despite everything, Helen still felt as if she carried the bad news with her, that nothing could have changed aboard Venera until she got there and handed the news over.

I'm not there so it's not real yet. Helen smoothed down the indigo scarf she wore over her stark white hair. *Arrogance, ar-*

rogance, old woman. This last trip should have finally put you in your place.

She really did feel old. It was strange. Even in the modern era of med trips and gene-level body modification, eighty-three was not young. She had never felt so old *inside,* though. She'd never felt calcified like this, as if something in her understanding had failed, leaving her standing on the edge of events she was unable to comprehend clearly, let alone affect.

The shuttle's descent steepened. At last, the cloud veil thinned enough that Helen really could make out the spherical shadow of Venera Base—her dream, her life's work, her home.

And now, my poor failure.

Even with self-pity and defeat swimming around inside her head, Helen's heart lifted at the sight of Venera. The base was a gigantic sphere buoyed by Venus's thick CO_2 atmosphere. Distance and cloud cover made the massive girders and cables that attached the tail and stabilizers to the main body of the station look as thin as threads.

Venera rode the perpetual easterly winds that circled the planet's equator. The shuttle matched Venera's speed easily, and the navigation chips in the shuttle and the runway handled the rest. The shuttle glided onto the great deck that encircled the very top of Venera's hull. It taxied straight across the runway and to the open hangar.

The shuttle jerked slightly as it rolled to a stop. A moment of silence enveloped Helen. This was no tourist shuttle. There were no attendants, human or automated, to tell her it was okay to get up now, or to make sure she claimed all her luggage, or to hope she'd enjoyed her flight and would come again soon.

Instead, the hissing, bumping noises of pressurization, corridor docking, and engine power-down surrounded her. Helen stayed where she was. As soon as she stepped out of the shuttle, it all became real. The transition would be over. Her illusions would no longer shield her. Helen found she did not want to abandon that shelter.

"Dr. Failia?"

Helen started and looked up into the broad, dark face of the shuttle's senior pilot. What was his name?

"Yes?" She pushed herself upright and began fumbling with the multiple buckles that strapped her to the couch. *Name, name, name . . .*

"I just wanted to say, I know you're going to get us through this. Everybody's with you."

Pearson! "Thank you, Mr. Pearson," said Helen. "We'll find a way."

"I know we will." He stepped aside to give her room to stand. Helen did not miss the hand that briefly darted out to help her to her feet and then darted back again, afraid of being offensive. She pretended to ignore the awkward gesture and retrieved her satchel from the bin under her couch.

"Thank you again, Mr. Pearson." Helen shook the pilot's hand and met his eyes with a friendly smile. *P.R. reflexes all in working order, thank you.*

Then, because there was nothing else to do, she walked down the flex-walled docking corridor.

Bennet Godwin and Michael Lum, the other two members of Venera's governing board, were, of course, waiting for her in the passenger clearing area. One look at their faces told her that the bad news had indeed flown far ahead of her.

Her hand tightened around her satchel strap as she walked up to her colleagues.

"I take it you've heard," she said flatly. "We lost Andalucent Technologies and IBM." *There, it's official. I said it.* The last shards of her comforting illusions fell away.

Ben Godwin was a square-built, florid man. Every emotion registered on his face as a change of color, from snow white to cherry red. Right now though, he just looked gray. He opened his mouth, but nothing came out.

Michael, standing beside him, glanced briefly at the floor and then up at Helen's eyes. He was a much younger, much leaner, much calmer man with clear gold skin. He wore his black hair long and pulled back into a ponytail. The gold ID badge on his white tunic proclaimed him the chief of Venera's security. "They took the University of Washington with them."

He spoke softly, but the words crashed hard against Helen. "What? When?"

"About an hour ago." Ben ran his hand over his bristly scalp. "We tried to get them to wait to talk to you, but they weren't—"

Anger hardened Helen's face. "Well, they'll have to talk to me anyway." She brushed past the two men. "We can't afford to lose their funding too."

Helen did not look back to see if they were following her. She just strode straight ahead into the broad, curving corridor that connected the docking area to the rest of Venera. She ignored the nearest elevator bundle and started down the stairs instead. She was not waiting around anymore. She'd been waiting on people for months on Earth. Waiting for them to tell her they had no more money, no more time to wait for results, no more interest in a planet that would never be amenable to human colonization or exploitation.

Helen kept her office on the farm levels near the center of Venera's sphere. Full spectrum lights shone down on vast soil beds growing high-yield cereals and brightly colored vegetables. Ducks and geese waded freely through troughed rice paddies that also nurtured several species of fish. The chickens, however, were penned in separate yards around the perimeter. The chickens did not get along with the more peaceable fowls. Quartz windows ringed the entire level, showing the great gray clouds. Every now and then, a pure gold flash of sheet lightning lit the world.

The farms had been meant to give Venera some measure of independence. Acquiring good, fresh food was vital to the maintenance of a permanent colony, and from the beginning, Helen had meant Venera to be a permanent colony.

Old dreams died hard. Venera might have actually had real self-sufficiency, except for the restrictions the U.N. placed on manufacturing and shipping licenses.

Old fears died hard too.

Helen's office was an administrative cubicle on an island in the middle of one of the rice paddies. She knew people called it "the Throne Room" and didn't really care. She loved Venus, but she missed Earth's blues and greens. Setting up her workspace in the farms had been the perfect compromise.

Helen kept a spartan office. It was furnished with a work desk, three visitor's chairs, and an all-purpose view screen that currently showed a star field. Her one luxury, besides her view, was a couple of shelves of potted plants—basil, oregano, lavender, and so on. Their sweet, spicy scents were the air's only perfume.

Helen dropped herself into the chair behind the desk and tossed her satchel onto the floor. It was only then that she became aware that Michael and Ben had in fact followed her.

"Who'd you talk to?" Her touch woke the desk and lit its command board. She shuffled through the icons to bring up her list of contact codes.

"Patricia Iannone," said Ben, sitting in one of the visitor's chairs. "She sounded like she was just following orders."

"We'll see." Helen activated Pat's contact and checked the time delay. Four minutes today. Not great for purposes of persuasive conversation, but doable. Helen opened the com system and lifted her face to the view screen. "Hello, Pat. I've just gotten back to Venera, and they're telling me that U Washington is pulling our funding. What's the matter? You can't tell me the volcanology department has not been getting its money's worth out of us. If it's a matter of being more vocal about your sponsorship or about allowing your people some more directed research time, I know we can work out the details. You just have to let me know what you and your people need." She touched the Send key, and the com system took over, shooting the message down after the contact code, waiting for a connection, and a reply.

Helen swiveled her chair to face Ben and Michael. "All right, tell me what's been happening since we talked last."

So Ben told her about some of the new personnel assignments and promotions and how the volcano, Hathor Montes, was showing signs of entering an active cycle. Michael talked about a rash of petty thefts, an increase in demands on the data lines caused apparently by the volcanology group gearing up for

Hathor's active cycle, and a couple of in-stream clip-out personas trying to get themselves inserted onto Venera's payroll.

"Now that would be all we'd need," muttered Helen. "Handing out extra money for a couple of computer ghosts."

As she spoke, the desk chimed. All of them turned their attention back to the view screen. Helen's stomach tightened. The star field cleared away to show a fashionably slim, young-looking woman with beige skin and a cloud of dark-blond hair, worn unbound under a pink scarf.

"Hello, Helen," she said soberly. "I was expecting this. Listen, there are no complaints about the publicity, the facilities access, about anything. The problems are application, opportunity, and resource distribution. The comptrollers have decided our people are going to have to be content with St. Helens and Pelée for a while. The industrial research spillover is contracting, and there is just not enough to go around right now." Her expression flickered from annoyed to apologetic. "There's no more after this. Anything you send is going to my machine. I'm sorry, but there is nothing I can do."

The stars faded back into view. For a moment, Helen met Ben's gaze, but she looked quickly away. She didn't want to see what he was thinking. *We could have done this,* he was thinking, *if you'd been willing to do it small. If you hadn't insisted from the beginning on a full-scale base where people could live and raise their children and make a lifetime commitment to the study of this world.*

She pressed her fingertips against her forehead. That was what he was thinking. That Venus was, at most, four weeks away from Earth. It wouldn't have mattered if people had to come and go. Venera could have been made small and simple and then expanded if things worked out. But, oh, no. Helen Failia had her vision, and Helen Failia had to push it through. Helen had to make sure there were children like Michael who could lose their homes if the funding ever collapsed.

"There is a way out of this," said Michael. "There has to be."

"What?" Helen's hand jerked away from her face. "Michael, I'm open to suggestions. I've just spent four months scavenging the whole of Mother Earth for additional funding. It's not there."

"Well." Michael rolled his eyes toward the ceiling and then brought them back down to meet Helen's gaze. "Have you tried a com burst out to Yan Su on the Colonial Affairs Committee? There might be some U.N. money we can dredge up."

Ben snorted. "Oh, come on, Michael. The U.N. pay to keep a colony running? Their business is keeping colonies scraping and begging." As a younger man, Helen knew, Ben had been strongly sympathetic with the Bradbury Separatist movement on Mars—the same movement that had blossomed into the Bradbury Rebellion and, for five short, violent years, Bradbury Free Territory. Because of that, he still took a very dim view of the United Nations and their off-Earth colonial policies.

She had to admit he was partly right. Since the Bradbury Rebellion, the C.A.C.'s sole function had been to make sure nothing like that ever happened again. Hence, the licensing restrictions. No colony could manufacture space shuttles or long-distance ships. No colony could manufacture communications satellites, although they were graciously allowed to repair the ones they had. There was a whole host of other hardware and spare parts that either never got licensed or were taxed to the Sun and back again.

Most of the time that didn't bother Helen. She dealt with the C.A.C. through her friend Yan Su, and so far Su had been willing to help whenever she could. Now, though, they were coming head-to-head with the old, frightened public policies.

"You think they want to deal with ten thousand refugees?" countered Michael calmly. "It's got to be cheaper to let us stay where we're at than to pay for processing ten thousand new resident-citizen files."

Helen nodded absently. She found, to her shame, she was not ready to admit that that avenue had been shut off almost a year ago. Maybe she could try again. *Now is not the time for pride,* she reminded herself firmly. *You've begged everybody else. Why not the government?*

"Yan Su helped put us up here," said Michael, more to Ben

than to Helen. "Maybe she can help keep us up here." Ben's only response was to turn a little pinker and look sour.

As little as she liked to admit it, Michael was right. It was time for last resorts. Without their three major funding sources, they were not going to be able to meet their payroll. They could buy some time by laying off the nonpermanent residents and sending them back to Mother Earth, but then they wouldn't be able to complete their research projects and they'd lose yet more money.

Helen looked at the time delay again. Venus and Earth were moving out of conjunction. If she put this off, the time delay was only going to get worse, and she didn't want to have to conduct this conversation through the mail. "Why don't you—"

Movement outside the office cleared the door's view panel. Grace Meyer stood in front of the door with her arms folded and her impatience plain on her heavily lined face. Helen suppressed a groan. What she wanted to do was open the intercom and say, "We're having a meeting, Grace. Not now." But she held back. Grace had proven herself willing to make trouble lately, and Venera did not need more trouble.

"We'll finish in a minute, gentlemen," she said instead. "Door. Open. Hello, Grace," she said, not bothering to put on a smile, as Grace would know it was false. "What can I do for you?"

Dr. Grace Meyer was a short woman with a milk-and-roses complexion. Her lab coat was no longer crisp, and her tunic and trousers were as rumpled as if she'd slept in them. She wore a green kerchief tied over her short hair, which was the same strawberry blond as when she'd moved to Venera fifteen years ago. Grace was a long-lifer. She was actually twice Helen's age, even though she looked only half that old.

Grace nodded to Ben and Michael and then turned all her attention to Helen. "I heard about U Washington."

Helen sighed. "The only thing that travels faster than bad news is bad news about you personally." Ben and Michael did not smile. Ben looked grim. Michael looked like he was trying to calculate the probable outcome of this scenario so he could ready his responses.

"What about U Washington?" asked Helen.

Grace glanced at Ben and Michael. In that glance, Helen read that Grace would like to ask them to leave but couldn't quite work out how. *And I'll be damned if I'll help you,* Helen thought.

"Helen," Grace started again, "there are still sources of money out there. If we shift emphasis just a little—"

Here it comes. "To the possibility of life on Venus?"

Grace leaned across the desk. "You saw my new grant from Biotech 24. That's good money, Helen. The absorbers—"

"Are a complex set of benzene rings with some strange sulfuric hangers-on under heat and pressure."

Grace was a chemist who had come to Venera to help look for the ultraviolet absorber in the Venusian clouds. The clouds were mostly transparent to ultraviolet, but there were bands and patches that absorbed all but the very lowest end of the UV wavelengths. For years, no one had been able to work out what was happening. Grace and her team had isolated a large, complex carbon, oxygen, sulfur molecule that interacted with the sulfuric acid in the clouds and the UV from the Sun, so it was constantly breaking apart, re-forming and re-creating more of itself. Which was fine; it had won her awards and acclaim, and brought Venera a lot of good publicity.

The problem was, Grace was trying to get the compound, which she called "the absorber" for simplicity's sake, classified as life.

Helen got slowly to her feet. She was not tall, but she had a few centimeters on Grace and didn't mind using them. Especially now. She did not need this. "Your absorbers are not life. No funding university or independent research lab we've had on board for the last ten years has said it could be qualified as life, or even proto-life."

Grace held her ground. "But there's—"

"There's one little company that's got more of an existence in-stream than out in reality. It's willing to gamble on your idea this is some kind of alien autocatalytic RNA." Grace subsided just a little, but Helen wasn't ready to. The past months had been too much on top of the past year, all the past years. All the fighting, all the frustration, all the time wasted, *wasted* on stupid, petty money-grubbing and useless personal projects. "I've read your papers, Grace. I've read them all, and you know what? I wish I'd tried harder to get you to leave it alone. You've directly contributed to the image of this base as a useless piece of dreamware. You have cost us, Grace. You personally have cost all of us!"

The intercom chimed again. "What is it?" demanded Helen icily. She needed to take the call. She needed to stop yelling at Grace. She was falling out of control, and she could not afford that. Grace could still make trouble—publicize internal dissension, that kind of thing. There was plenty she could do. Plenty she would do. Helen needed to stop.

"Ummm . . . Dr. Failia?" The screen flickered to life to show a slender young man with clear, sandy-brown skin and thick black hair. Behind him, a floor-to-ceiling view screen displayed the ragged gray cliff, possibly the edge of one of the continent-sized plateaus that broke the Venusian crust.

"Yes, Derek?" Helen tried to smooth the impatience out of her voice. Derek Cusmanos headed the survey department. Actually, Derek and his fleet of drones *were* the survey department. He always did his job well. He had done nothing to deserve her anger.

"I . . . I'm getting some pictures in from one of the drones near Beta Regio that you need to see, Dr. Failia."

Helen's fingers twitched as she tried not to clench her hands into fists. "This is not a good time, Derek. Shoot me up a file and I'll go over it—"

"No, Dr. Failia." Strain tightened Derek's voice. "You really need to see this right now."

Curiosity and concern surfaced together in Helen's mind. She glanced back at Ben and Michael, who both returned blank stares. A glance at Grace produced a shrug and a pair of spread hands.

"All right, Derek," said Helen. "Show me."

Without another word, Derek pushed his chair back so they

had a clear view of his wall screen. Helen heard him give soft orders to his desk to display the current uplink.

The screen's view changed. The gigantic plateau wall receded into the distance. In its place stood a smaller, rounded canyon wall, the kind that typically bordered the ancient lava channels. On the canyon's cracked floor, Helen saw something sticking up out of the ground. Derek gave another order. The view zoomed in.

The new, tighter view showed a perfectly circular shaft protruding from the Venusian ground.

"Oh my God," whispered Michael. Helen just got out of her chair and walked slowly forward until her nose almost touched the intercom screen.

It was not anything that should have been there, but there it was. It was circular. It had a cap on it. Its gray sides glinted dully in Venus's ashen light, and it sank straight into the bedrock.

"This is live," said Derek from his post off-screen. "I'm getting this in right now from SD-25."

"You've done a diagnostic?" cut in Ben. He supervised Derek's "department." "The drone is functioning on spec?"

"On spec and in the green," said Derek. "I . . . I didn't believe what I was seeing, so I sent SD-24 down after it. This is what I'm getting from SD-24." He gave another order and the view shifted again. Now they looked down from above, as if the camera drone perched on the canyon wall, which it probably did.

The capped shaft sat there, smooth and circular and utterly impossible. Even Venus, which had produced stone formations seen nowhere else in the solar system, had not created those smooth lines, that flattened lid.

"Well," said Ben. "I don't remember putting that there."

"Derek," said Helen quietly, "I want you to keep both drones on-site. I want that thing recorded from every possible angle. I want it measured and I want its dimensions and position to the millimeter. We'll get a scarab down there to look at it."

"Yes, Dr. Failia." Derek sounded relieved that someone else was making the decisions.

"Well done, young man," she added.

"Thank you, Dr. Failia."

The intercom cut out and Helen turned slowly around. "Do I have to say it?" she asked dryly.

"You mean that if that's what it looks like—" began Ben.

"We have evidence of life on Venus?" Grace folded her arms. Her green eyes gleamed brightly. "Oh, please, Helen. I'd love to hear you say it, just once."

A muscle in Helen's temple spasmed. "Now is not the time to be petty, Grace."

Grace smiled. "Oh no, not petty, Helen. But you'll have to allow me a little smugness. I've been shouting in the wilderness for years now. If this bears out—"

"*If* this bears out." Ben emphasized the first word heavily. "Venus has thrown up some landscapes that make the old face on Mars look passé." He pushed himself to his feet. "Kevin is on shift. I'll have him outfit us a scarab ay-sap." Kevin Cusmanos was Derek's older brother. He was also chief engineer and pilot for the surface-to-air explorer units known as scarabs, which transported people to and from the Venusian surface. "I assume you're coming down to see what's what?" Ben looked pointedly at Helen.

"Of course," she answered. "And Michael's coming with us." She looked to him for approval and he nodded. His face held a kind of stunned wonder as the implications filtered through him. Helen knew exactly how he felt. If this was played out, it meant so many things. It meant human beings were not alone in the universe. It meant there was not only intelligent life out there somewhere but it had also left its traces on Venus.

It meant money for Venera.

Grace opened her mouth, but Helen held up her hand. "Not this run, Grace. Next one, if it turns out to be more than rocks and heat distortion." *Keep up the patter, Helen. You do not know what's really down there. You only know what it looks like.*

Somewhat to Helen's surprise, Grace just nodded and stepped aside for Ben as he hurried out the door. Helen did not, however, miss the purely triumphant smile that spread across her face.

Can't blame her, I suppose. "If that's what it looks like," she repeated out loud.

"If that's what it looks like, all our old problems are over with, and we'll have a set of brand-new ones," said Michael. "But ohmygod . . ."

Helen touched his arm. "I quite agree. Go grab your gear, Michael, and tell Jolynn and the boys you won't be home for supper."

"Yes, ma'am." He snapped a mock salute and hurried out the door.

Grace and Helen faced each other for a long moment. "Well," said Grace brightly, "I think I'll go reorganize my files. I think there's going to be some new work coming in." She left, and the door slid shut behind her.

Finally alone, Helen reached up and untied her scarf. Her long white hair fell down around her shoulders. She combed her fingers through it, feeling how each strand separated and fell, brushing her cheeks and shoulders. It felt coarser than she remembered it feeling when she was a young woman. Coarser and yet more fragile, like its owner.

Let this work out, she prayed silently. *I don't care if I have to spend the next fifty years apologizing to Grace Meyer. This could save us all. Please, let it work out right.*

Less than five hours later, Helen, too on edge to remember she ought to be tired and hungry, unstrapped herself from a second crash-couch. This one was in the little dormitory aboard Scarab Fourteen. The scarab itself crawled across the Venusian surface, following the signal output of Derek Cusmanos's two drones.

Because it was Kevin Cusmanos's policy to always have two of Venera's twenty scarabs ready to go in case of emergency, heading to the surface had been a matter of grabbing overnight bags and calling on Adrian Makepeace, the duty pilot for the afternoon shift. Kevin said he'd take the board down himself, but he wanted Adrian's experience in the copilot's seat.

Scarab Fourteen was a clone of all the other scarabs owned and operated by Venera Base—a wedge-shaped, mobile laboratory that could both fly and roll. They were designed to take a team of up to seven researchers plus two crew members to almost any spot on the Venusian surface that wasn't covered in lava. Built wide and low to the ground, they were practical but not comfortable. Adrian, Helen noticed, seemed to be developing a permanent stoop and a tendency to walk sideways from all the time he spent in them.

Designing for the heat and pressure of the Venusian surface had proved incredibly difficult. That was one of the reasons Venera floated through the clouds. The surface was an oven. Up in the clouds, the temperature was close to the freezing point of water. Down here, they had to carry layers of insulation and heavy-duty coolant tanks that had to be recharged and refrozen after each trip.

Helen picked her way between the crash-couches, rocking slightly with the motion of the treads until she emerged into the main corridor. Ben and Michael had gone ahead of her and already crowded behind Kevin's and Adrian's chairs in the command area. They all stared through the main window that wrapped around the scarab's nose.

The scarab ground its careful way across the nightside of Venus. Outside, the cracked surface of Ruskalia Planitia glowed with the heat it radiated, creating a quilt of deep reds, bright oranges, and clear, clean yellow. Overhead, the light reflected off the clouds, lending them the color and texture of molten gold being stirred by some invisible hand.

Kevin, a cautious, quiet man, who was almost twice as broad in the shoulders as his younger brother, kept his gaze flickering between the map displays and the window which showed them Beta Regio, a ragged wall of living fire wavering in the distance.

Coming down several kilometers from the whatever-it-was had seemed prudent. They did not want to land accidentally on something important.

As Beta Regio grew larger, the plain under the scarab's treads became rougher. Small, knife-backed ridges, blood red with escaping heat and blurred by the thick atmosphere, rose out of the plain. The closer they came to Beta Regio, the higher the ridges rose, until they became ragged walls. At last, Scarab Fourteen drove down a glowing corridor, following the path carved by a river of ancient lava.

A million similar paths spread out around the various Venusian highlands. Kevin drove the scarab gently over the rocks and swells, guided by the global positioning readout and the signals from his brother's drones.

The lava trail dead-ended at a sharp, smooth cliff that shone a livid orange. Some coal-bright sand rolled lazily along the brilliant ground, brushing against the hatchway set into the living rock.

"Venera Base," said Kevin in the general direction of the radio grill. "This is Scarab fourteen." It was somehow comforting to see he was staring, as was Adrian. *As are we all.* "We have the . . . target in sight. Are you getting our picture?"

"We're getting it, Boss." Helen almost didn't recognize Charlotte Murray's voice, with its undertone of uncertainty, as if she were torn between fear and awe.

Helen understood the feeling. Her own eyes ached from staring at the brightly shining artifact. It was a perfectly circular shaft, about two meters across, that protruded half a meter out of the rugged surface. It glowed red hot, like its surroundings. Its lid had a series of, what?—handles? locks?—spaced evenly on all the sides she could see.

She glanced at Ben and saw his thoughts shining plainly on his face. It had to be a hatchway. It couldn't be anything else. Someone had built it there. That was the only explanation.

She knew he was not about to say any of that out loud, however. It wouldn't do. It was bad science and poor leadership, neither of which Ben would tolerate.

"Well"—she straightened up—"who's coming out to take a look?"

"Dr. Failia, you're not—" began Kevin. Helen silenced him with a glance. He was probably right. It probably was not a good idea for an eighty-something who was behind on her med trips to don a heavy hardsuit and go outside on Venus for a bit of a ramble.

But I'll be damned if I'm staying behind to watch this through the window.

"Right behind you, Helen," said Ben. Michael didn't say anything. He just headed down the narrow central corridor toward the changing area at the back of the scarab.

Helen rolled her eyes and followed, with Ben and Adrian filing after her. As copilot, Adrian's primary job was monitoring, or baby-sitting, any extravehicular activities. The EVA staging area took up most of the scarab's wide back end. Still, there somehow never seemed to be quite enough room for even three people to get into the bulky hardsuits.

The hardsuits themselves consisted of two layers. The soft, cloth-lined inner suit went directly over a person's clothes. This layer carried the coolants circulating in microtubules drawn from tanks which were pulled from the freezer and strapped, along with the O_2 packs, over the shoulders.

Then the pressure shell was assembled. Based on the hardsuits used in very deep industrial sea diving, it kept the user's personal pressure at a comfortable one atmosphere. It was also heavy as all get-out. Despite the internally powered skeletons, every time she put one on, Helen felt like a clunky monster from outer space.

But it was all necessary. The best simulations they had suggested that a person exposed to Venus's surface temperature and pressure would flash-burn a split second before any remaining chemical residue was squashed flat.

Finally, Helen locked down her helmet. The edges of the faceplate lit up with the various monitor readouts and the control icons. Helen had never liked the icons. They were line-of-sight controlled and she found them clumsy to use. Adrian looped the standard tool belt around her waist and stood back.

"Check one, check one, Dr. Failia." Adrian's voice came through her helmet's intercom. Following routine, Helen waved her hand in front of her suit's chest camera. "Reading you, Scarab Fourteen," she said. The monitors in each hardsuit were slaved to the scarab for earliest possible detection of mechanical trouble.

"And we have you, Dr. Failia," replied Adrian, glancing at the wall monitors. "Check two, check two, Dr. Godwin." The routine was repeated with Ben and Michael. Helen leaned against the wall and tried not to think too much about what waited outside. The picture had burned itself into her mind. It was an artificial structure, no question there. She couldn't wait until the rest of the solar system saw it. Good God, they'd say, there was somebody else out here or there had been. Her Venus, her beautiful, misunderstood twin to Earth, housed or had housed intelligent life. . . .

Steady Helen. Remember, you still don't know *anything.*

The checks on Ben and Michael's suits came up green, and Adrian let them all move into the airlock. He swung the hatch shut behind them. The suits maintained pressure for their inhabitants, but the airlock had to equalize the pressure inside and outside before the hatch would open. That meant pumping the room up to a full ninety atmospheres worth of pressure.

As the pump started chugging, Ben turned toward Helen. "Well, it's either aliens or the biggest practical joke in human history."

"If we open it up and a bunch of those springy worms fly out, we'll know, right?" said Michael, carefully bending his knees to sit on a bench he couldn't quite see.

"Would they fly out, under pressure?" asked Helen. "Or would they just sort of pop and bounce?"

"That's one for Ned and the atmospherics people." Michael's hands moved restlessly, tapping against his thighs to some internal rhythm.

There seemed to be nothing else to say. Each of them lapsed into silence, thinking their own thoughts, making their own calculations or dreaming of their own futures. It took about fifteen minutes to pressurize the airlock. Right now, it felt like hours.

But finally the gauges all blinked green. Ben worked the levers on the outer hatch and swung it open.

"Good luck, Team Fourteen," came Adrian's voice.

One by one the governing board stepped out onto the glowing Venusian surface. Helen had never been so aware of being watched—monitored by her suit, overseen by Adrian and all Scarab Fourteen's cameras, followed by her colleagues, tracked by Derek's drones, which sat dormant on their own little treads, a short distance from the target object.

She took refuge in chatter. She activated the general intercom icon.

"Failia to Scarab Fourteen," she said. "Are you receiving?"

"Receiving loud and clear, Dr. Failia," answered Adrian. "Our readings say all suits green and go."

"All green and go out here," she returned. "Except Dr. Godwin forgot the marshmallows."

"That was on *your* to-do list, Helen," shot back Ben. Helen smiled. That had been an early experiment. The marshmallow exposed to the Venusian atmosphere had not roasted, however. It had scrunched up and vaporized. The egg they'd attempted to fry on the rock had exploded.

The memory spread a smile across Helen's face and made it easier to concentrate on the way in front of her. The cracks in the crust could be wide enough to catch a toe in, sending a person tumbling down in a most undignified fashion and wasting time while they were helped back to their feet—if their suit held up to the fall. If it didn't, there'd be nothing left to help up.

Helen dismissed that thought but held her pace in check with difficulty. She did not want to waste any more time. She wanted to sprint on ahead, but she had to settle for a slow march.

Still, they got steadily closer to the target. The closer they got, the more obvious it became that the object had to be artificial. It was indeed perfectly circular. The smooth sides rose about a half meter out of the rock. A series of smaller spheres protruded from it. For a moment, the three of them all lined up in front of the thing, examining it in reverent silence.

"Okay." The word came out of Michael like a sigh. "What's the procedure? Measure it first?"

"Measure it first," said Helen.

Slowly, Helen, Michael, and Ben circled the target in a strange, clumsy dance, recording everything yet again and measuring all of it. Yes, the drones had technically done all of this, but that was the machine record. This was the human record, and they needed it to help prove that this object was not just the result of some computer graphics and hocus-pocus.

The shaft was exactly forty-four centimeters in height and one and a half meters in diameter. A second, apparently separate section rested on or was attached to the top. That section was also one and a half meters in diameter but was only ten centimeters thick. Small, spherical protrusions, each appearing to be ten centimeters across, were attached to the sides of the upper section (like somebody'd stuck a half-dozen oranges there, Ben noted), equally spaced at sixty-degree intervals and attached by some undetermined means. A small circle, eight point three centimeters in diameter, had been inscribed three point six-four centimeters from the outer edge of the top section.

"Well, you're the expert, Ben," said Helen. "Is it or is it not naturally occurring?"

Ben's helmet turned toward her. "You're kidding, right, Helen?"

"No, I'm not." Helen remained immobile. "I want this all for the record."

"Okay, then." There came a brief shuffling noise that might have been Ben shrugging inside his suit. "In my opinion, based on the observations of the previous robotic investigation and my own two eyes, this is not a naturally occurring formation."

"To my knowledge, no one on Venera Base has ever authorized construction of such an object," added Helen.

"Are you going to open it, Helen, or can I go ahead?" Michael asked mildly.

Helen bit her lip. Part of her wanted to call down a whole team to swarm over the thing, analyzing every molecule before they did anything else. She told herself that was the good scientist part of herself. The truth was somewhat less flattering.

I'm afraid: of what we're doing, of what might, or might not, happen next.

"If you want to try, Michael, be my guest." Helen stepped

back, hoping no one realized she was giving in to the private fear that bubbled, unwelcome, out of the back of her mind.

Michael walked around the hatch. He ran his fingers over the small circle set flush against the lid. He walked around the shaft again. Finally, he grasped two of the protrusions and leaned to the right.

The hatch slid slowly, unsteadily, sideways. A huge white cloud rushed out. Michael lurched backward.

"Steam?" said Ben incredulously. "There was water in there?" There was no water on the surface of Venus. Some particles in the clouds, but other than that, nothing.

"No analysis on that," came back Adrian. "Sorry."

"Not your fault," murmured Helen.

The cloud evaporated, and they all bent over the dark shaft. A tunnel sank straight into the bedrock. Their helmet lights shone on the bottom about four, maybe five, meters down. The first ten centimeters or so of rock around the mouth glowed brightly, but after that, it darkened to a shiny black, shot through with charcoal-gray veins. Thick staples had been shoved into the rock just below the glow-line, making what appeared to be the widely spaced rungs of a ladder.

Five sets of eyes stared. Three cameras recorded the ladder. One recorded the doctors as they waited. Nothing happened. Well, nothing new happened.

Helen straightened up and looked at her colleagues. Ben and Michael returned her gaze. She saw the awe tinged with ashamed fear in their eyes and felt a little better.

"All right, gentlemen," she said. "Let's go meet the neighbors."

One careful step at a time, she climbed down into the shaft.

What none of them saw, not with their cameras, not with their own eyes, was how one of the outcroppings on the side of Beta Regio crawled a little closer to the hatchway, as if to get a better look.

Chapter Two

The clouds of Home hung low overhead, pushing thick, yellow fingers deep into the clear. Harvest flies swarmed around them, feasting on spoiling algae or floater larvae. Here and there, a solitary shade darted into the swarm, skimmed off a few flies, and soared away.

There should be a thousand of them, thought T'sha as she watched the tiny bird. *Where have they all gone? Why are the flies winning?*

It was not just the absence of birds that disturbed the day. It was the smell, or the lack of it. The wind supporting her body blew light and sterile. It should have been heavy with salt, sweat, and rich, growing life. The dayside currents never blew empty from the living highlands. Except, today they did.

T'sha tilted her wings to slow her flight. This was not good. According to the reports, the winds had been reseeded with nutritive monocellulars not twelve miles from here. Had the seed been bad, or had the planting failed to take? Had they underestimated the imbalance on the microscopic layers here? If they had, what else had they underestimated?

It might be something else, whispered a treacherous voice in the back of her mind.

No, she chided herself. *I will not believe blasphemous rumors.*

People were not straining the winds right off the highlands to take fresh monocellulars for their homes. There had been patrols. They had found nothing. No one would be guilty of so much greed, so much sin. At least, not yet. Things had not gone so far yet.

At least, they shouldn't have. But winds that were empty of algaes and krills and other nutritional elements were becoming more common. Worse, there was word from the Polars that some of their winds were becoming currents of poison. A permanent migration down to the Rough Northerns was being debated even now if the Northerners could be persuaded to accept such a move.

Below T'sha spread the canopy, bright with its mottled golds, blues, and reds. From this distance, it looked healthy, ready for a casual single harvester or a concentrated reaping. But before too many more hours had passed, T'sha knew she was going to have to go down in there while the team confirmed what she suspected: that there would be too many flies down there too and not enough birds or puffs to clear them out. They would travel deep into the underside between the canopy and the crust and see the canopy's roots withering.

It was just as well the area itself was lightly traveled. She scanned the horizon in all directions and, apart from her own team, saw only one distant sail cluster. Her headset told her that it was the Village Gaith. T'sha reflexively gave orders to send greetings to the city and its speakers.

The rest of her team worked less than a half mile away. Their bright-white kites and stabilizers billowed in the sterile wind. T'sha could almost feel the engineers glancing nervously toward her. She was not behaving as she should. She was not a private person anymore. She was an ambassador to the High Law Meet. Her duties, in addition to making promises on behalf of her city and representing her city to the legislature and courts, included making people nervous. She was supposed to be hovering around the edges of the team, waiting for them to give her the words to carry back to the Meet.

Come now; time to play your part. You want the truth; you need to go collect it. T'sha banked, curving her path back toward her team. *You're doing no good drifting out here sniffing and brooding.*

A waver in the air currents over her shoulder made her

glance back. A new orange kite sailed on the wind. T'sha turned in a tight circle to read the signal lights flashing on its frame. Her bones bunched briefly.

What does D'seun want here?

Like T'sha, D'seun served as an ambassador to the High Law Meet. She respected him as a close reasoner and an even-minded legislator. His birth village had died when he was still a child, but, against great odds, he had risen to become ambassador of his adopted city. She had wished many times they did not hover on opposite sides of every debate concerning the search for New Home. D'seun could only be here to check up on her team. The samples they were analyzing would help measure how critical the ecological breakdown here on Home was and so help determine how much time they had to make decisions regarding the new world.

She considered heading straight back to the survey team. But then she decided that keeping D'seun at a distance from her people might be advisable.

Let them get as much done as possible without him fluttering behind and making suggestions. The circumstances here might not be as bad as they seem.

T'sha fanned her wings, letting the wind proceed without her and waiting for D'seun's kite to approach.

His kite was a pleasant hybrid with sails of orange skin and gold ligaments. Startling green scales dotted the shell-strip struts. Its engine was shut down, and it coasted on nothing more than the power of the wind. D'seun balanced half-inflated on the kite's perches. He raised both forehands in greeting to her.

T'sha spread her forehands in return. As D'seun and his kite drew near her, T'sha stilled her wings and let the wind pull her along so she could keep level with him.

"Good luck, Ambassador T'sha," he said pleasantly, shifting sideways to make room for her on the perches. "Will you join me?"

"Good luck, Ambassador D'seun. Certainly, I will." There was no disagreement between them so great that courtesy could be disregarded. T'sha cupped her wings to lift herself up slightly and wrapped all twenty-four fingers around the kite's perches. Then she deflated herself until her back and crest were level with D'seun's. They touched forehands formally.

D'seun was even younger than T'sha was. The bright gold of his skin sparkled strong and clear in the daylight, leaving his heavy maze of tattoos, both official and personal, in dark relief. His white and blue crest, which marked him as an Equatorial, streamed all the way down to his shoulderblades. T'sha suspected both the crest and the skin were enhanced. Fully inflated, he was only slightly smaller than she was, something T'sha was ashamed to admit she found disconcerting. Even her birth father was only three-quarters of her size.

D'seun spoke to the kite in its command language, softly ordering it to change its drift so they angled away from the survey team's distant sails. Disquiet gathered in the pockets between T'sha's bones.

"What brings you out here?" T'sha asked, deliberately keeping the question conversational.

"I had to call into the High Law Meet to finish some reportings." D'seun settled his weight back on his posthands, leaving his forehands free to stroke the kite's ligaments. "So I was there when the Seventh Team returned."

The Seventh? Oh, no. T'sha's mother had still been a child when ten worlds had been selected as candidates for New Home. T'sha had heard the memories of the raging debate as to whether Number Seven, which had . . . complications . . . , should be included in the roster of test worlds. Ambassador Tr'ena, one of T'sha's predecessors in the ambassadorship of Ca'aed, had lobbied hard against its inclusion. He had lost. T'sha had had to deal with the consequences of that loss.

D'seun, on the other hand, had risen to the rank of ambassador on the strength of what he and the Seventh Team had accomplished on that same world.

D'seun turned his gaze from the kite's ligaments. "The seedings have taken on their candidate. The life base is spreading. We have found New Home."

"They have taken on this candidate." T'sha pushed her muzzle forward. "What about the others?"

D'seun swelled, as if he carried the best of news. "None of the other seedings were successful. It is Number Seven, or it is nothing."

"There are other worlds out there. Millions of them."

"We do not have the time to test those millions."

T'sha strained the wind through her teeth. It held nothing, no taste, no texture, no scent. Empty air. Good for nothing but carrying flies and bad news.

"You came all this way to tell me this? You could have sent a message. I do wear a radio." She tapped the fine neural mesh of her headset for emphasis.

T'sha searched D'seun's stance and bearing, trying to get some feel for what he wanted. Despite his confident size, he was not at ease. He gripped and released the perches with each hand in turn so that he rocked unsteadily. His eyes darted about behind their lenses, looking for something other than her.

"There are things I wished to say to you directly," said D'seun blandly.

T'sha's posthands clenched the perch a little more tightly. "What are they? Do not speak against this candidate world? Do not say that if we must take this candidate, we must approach the New People and tell them plainly what we have come to New Home to do?"

D'seun inflated himself a little bit more. "The Seventh is the only planet where the life base has taken." Light sparkled against his skin and his tattoos. He had several new patterns running down his shoulder—a kite with billowing sails, a pattern of interlinking diamonds, and an ancient pictorial symbol for movement.

T'sha turned her gaze from D'seun's personal vanity. "Did the Seventh Team also report that the activities of the New People are increasing?" Her friend Pe'sen had monitor duty at the Conoi portal cluster. Now and then, he slipped her advance notice of team reports.

"That's all to the good," said D'seun calmly.

"Is it?" T'sha watched the cloud fingers in front of them with their haze of flies. Perhaps some hunter birds could be imported from the higher latitudes. They adapted well and needed little breeding supervision.

"What else could it be? Life must expand. Life helps life." The intensity of his words rippled the air. She could feel them against the skin of her muzzle.

Is that what you believe? Or are you only saying that because you know it's what I believe? With D'seun, this could be a question. She had seen him use partial truths to manipulate speakers and ambassadors before.

"Not all life views the world, perhaps I should say worlds, in the same way." T'sha pointed her muzzle toward the thick, sulfurous columns of haze and rot. "We see this abundance of flies as a danger signal. How do the flies see it?"

D'seun held up one forehand. "Intelligent life understands the void must be filled." That was an old truism, one that had never been put to the test. D'seun knew that as well as T'sha did.

"But filled with what?" muttered T'sha.

D'seun deflated until he was level with her again. "It is a question, certainly."

"No, it is *the* question," said T'sha. "And it is the one we are not asking."

She watched the bones under his skin expand and contract as he resisted the urge to swell up and tower over her. "*You* certainly are."

"Because someone must." She had carefully gone over all the available memories of the New People. They themselves were as hard to see as shellfish in their shells, but their creations were easily found. Their creations existed on three planets and one satellite of the Seventh World system, and one of those planets was Seventh World itself.

What did not seem to exist was any sign of life outside the shells, which was what breathed life into the debates. No good information had yet been acquired about their home world. They were obviously intelligent, but if they were not actively spreading life to New Home, were they making legitimate use of its resources? And if they were not making legitimate use of its resources, what stopped the People from doing so? There were those who argued that a system that already supported life was the best place to move themselves to. It would provide community, knowledge, and resources. D'seun was one of those, although he generally argued much more about knowledge and resources than he did about community.

Until now, of course.

D'seun deflated, becoming small, tight, and hard. "We need a new haven and new resources to ride out this imbalance." He sounded like a recording, running over and over until the feel of his words overwhelmed his audience and they could draw in nothing else.

Remain calm. Remain calm. You are an ambassador now and do not have the luxury of unchallenged opinion. T'sha leaned closer, seeking to draw him out. "Have you considered that contact with the New People will put an end to many questions?"

D'seun inflated slightly. "I agree, but this is not the right time. We must establish life beyond a few building blocks. We must be able to prove to the New People that we are serious about assisting with life's common goals."

Are you just trying this out on me? Why aren't you presenting this to the debate clusters? "But do we know they are common goals? Do we know the New People see things as we do?"

D'seun rippled his wings. "You and yours are too afraid of this thing we do. This is not greed. We need a new home, one where we can organize and arrange the life which supports us, where we can wait out what is happening on this old home of ours."

"I do not accuse you of greed," said T'sha. *Not yet.* "But you are right. Those I support act from fear. I am as afraid of taking this action as you and yours are afraid of not taking it." She leaned a little closer, her muzzle almost touching his. She wanted every word to sink into him. "Fear fills the air around you until you cannot feel what is truly happening to you." She pulled back and let herself swell until she felt her bones press hard against her skin. "We are all afraid. That is why we must question everything we do. We must act on our fear, but we must not act out of fear."

D'seun ruffled his bright crest, raising and spreading its tendrils. "I feel your words. Do not think I am numb. But raising yet more uncertainty at this time could be disastrous. We must be sure, all of us."

T'sha looked down at him. He did not flinch or subside. He just returned her gaze.

At last, she asked, "What do you want?"

"I want to poll your city and its families. I have made a formal request to the High Law Meet. It will be sent to you within the hour."

T'sha's bones trembled. *I should have known this was coming. I should have read it in the way that flies are clustering.* "You question my fitness as ambassador?"

"No." D'seun's reply was easy, simple, and T'sha didn't believe it for a moment. "I seek to eliminate uncertainty in this great project we are undertaking. If your doubts truly reflect the doubts of your families, then it must be widely known."

Anger swelled T'sha until she thought she would float away on the wind. "Then let us set the polling time. But I tell you, D'seun"—she leaned close, making sure every word touched him—"I will not be stilled."

"Neither will the project, T'sha."

Whatever else he had been about to say was cut off by the voice of T'sha's headset vibrating through her ear. "Ambassador T'sha, this is Village Gaith. Help. You must help. I am in rot. You must help my people."

T'sha's wings spread in instant response. "We will be there."

"What's happening?" demanded D'seun.

"Village Gaith. It says it's in rot." She barked a quick transfer command to her headset. "Engineer K'taan!" she shouted for her team leader. "We have an emergency in Village Gaith. They are in rot. Take a sighting and get everyone there as quickly as you can."

Under the sound of her own voice, she heard D'seun give orders to the kite. It unfurled its wings to their fullest extent and reined in its tail. The winds swept it up. Its engines added speed. T'sha made herself compact so as not to add any drag that might slow them down. The wind grew hard and full as it raced across her shoulders, pressing the kite into swift motion.

Another rot. How many did that make since the First Mountain last saw the dayside? How many cities in how many latitudes were dead or dying, and what was the total refugee count? Two and a half million? Had it gotten up to three million yet?

She spoke to her headset, telling it to seek details about Village Gaith. After a few moments, the set murmured back to her.

"Gaith is a Calm Northerns village, with about a thousand individuals from four different families calling it home. Sixty percent of the individuals are children. Individuals are good engineers, have contributed several widely adapted adjustments to canopy balance in recent years, and have raised several excellent surveyors and samplers. Its ambassador is T'nain V'gan Kan Gaith. He has been notified of the emergency at the High Law Meet and is returning now. Its local speaker is T'gai Doth Kan Gaith."

T'gai. Oh, memory. I haven't seen you since I was declared an adult. She remembered T'gai's visits to her parents' complex, his dark-gold skin, and his speaker's tattoos branching out all around his muzzle. He always had some new point of discussion to raise, some new poll to try to start. He was all a speaker ought to be—busy, serious, forward thinking.

How did a rot start in his own village?

She shook herself out of her own thoughts as she realized D'seun was watching her.

"I'm sorry. You spoke?"

D'seun dipped his muzzle. "I was saying this is your latitude. You should warn the cities."

Good, good. Pay attention, T'sha. There's work to do. "Yes. Of course." She commanded her headset to call Ca'aed.

"I hear you, Ambassador," returned her city's deep voice.

"Ca'aed, there's an emergency in Village Gaith. Warn the downwind cities to take quarantine precautions. I'm on my way to assess the damage. I'll have more news soon."

Even as she spoke the words, a fresh finger of wind touched

her. This one was not empty. It was thick with something far too cloying to be a healthy scent. She could see Gaith in the distance—a sphere bristling with sails and sensor fronds. It looked peaceful, but that smell, that too sweet taste . . .

"I have their location, Ambassador. . . ." Ca'aed paused, and worry stiffened T'sha's bones. "I can't raise the village. I hear no voice."

T'sha glanced at D'seun, but he was looking straight ahead at Gaith. It took T'sha's eyes a moment to focus, but then she too saw what was wrong.

Around even the smallest village, there would be a few citizens flying freely about their business, but Gaith was surrounded by a swarm of its own people. They fluttered about the shell and bones like flies without purpose.

It was the sight of panic.

D'seun spoke to the kite. It brought them around to Gaith's windward side. They closed on the village, and T'sha saw that its sails and wind guides were no longer white, as they should have been. Huge patches of grayish-brown funguslike growths disfigured their surfaces.

The smell of rotting flesh engulfed her. T'sha instantly tightened in on herself. *Breath of life, bones of mine, what is happening here? I've never seen one this bad!*

The village cried as if hurt just by the wind of her approach. All around those diseased sails flew its citizens. Now they were close enough that T'sha could hear their voices—shouting, crying, demanding, trying to give orders. Above it all, she heard the wordless keening of the village's pain. It was dying and it did not know how to save itself. In its fear, it called desperately for its people.

D'seun snatched the bulky caretaker unit from out of the kite's holder and launched himself into the air. T'sha dipped her muzzle. The caretaker might be able to speak to the village where a person could not.

"Engineer K'taan," T'sha bawled into her headset as she launched herself into the air. "Where are you?"

"Approaching from leeward. We have you in sight."

"Get a catchskin under the village. We can't let the rot fall into the canopy!"

"Yes, Ambassador!"

Flies clustered everywhere, the eternal flies that should have been clustered around the clouds. The insects scattered in angry swarms around her wings. The smell was unbearable. T'sha closed her muzzle tightly and tried not to think of what was filtering in through her skin.

Bubbling gray fungus turned the nearest sails slick. Even as she watched, great patches melted and sagged. Speckled liquid ran down what was left of the clean white skin. Something unseen whimpered.

"Gaith! Gaith!" T'sha called through her headset. "Answer me! Are you there?"

No answer. None at all.

D'seun flew straight into the thickest crowd and started forming them up into an orderly flight chain. As soon as the formation was spotted, people started flocking toward it, leaving fewer to flap in panic around the dying village.

T'sha ordered her headset onto a general-call frequency. "This is T'sha So Br'ei Taith Kan Ca'aed, ambassador for Ca'aed, to anyone who can hear me. I need Speaker T'gai Doth Kan Gaith at the center of leeward."

She got no answer. It was possible there was nothing healthy enough left to hear the call.

Ten yards below the city, K'taan directed a group of four researchers to stretch out the transluscent, life-tight catchsheet. It wasn't big enough. Two other researchers rushed in, carrying an additional sheet. They sealed the sheets together and spread them again. That was just enough if the wind did not take too much. They needed to get a quarantine blanket around the village as soon as possible. Why were those not grown generally?

Why is this happening at all?

"Ambassador T'sha."

T'sha wheeled on her wingtip. Behind her floated T'gai. His tattoos branched all the way to the roots of his crest now, but the crest was dimmed by age.

"Speaker T'gai." T'sha touched his forehands. "Good luck to you."

"Good luck to you, T'sha. Ambassador T'sha." His crest ruffled softly.

She tried not to feel the weakness in his words. "Why didn't you report this?" she asked as gently as she could.

"We thought . . . we thought . . ."

We thought we could take care of it. T'sha dipped her muzzle to let him know she understood. No people wanted to believe they could fail their city, or even their village. No one wanted the shame of having to make promises because they were not skilled enough or rich enough to care for their own, so they struggled in their silence until it was too late.

There were always dangers, particularly in the smaller villages such as Gaith, that drifted on their own rather than following in the wake of a larger, older city. Cortices got too closely bred and became unable to cognate as required. Builders and assessors went insane and undid the work they were supposed to enhance. Corals used too many times without enough interior variety bleached in thin winds. Cancers took hold of the village's bones.

But now, infections were spreading around the world. A fungus or a yeast that should have been easy for an engineer to excise would instead burn through a city, breaking down everything it touched, sometimes turning from the city and attacking the people.

Even so, that usually took weeks. This . . . T'sha didn't dare let that thought go any further.

"We'll talk about that later." T'sha turned her mind to the problem. "I'm here with Ambassador D'seun and my survey team. We'll send some of them for kites and other transports. There are several healthy cities traveling this stream. But first you need to assemble your people. We'll need to have you checked out to make sure you are carrying nothing infectious." *We cannot let this spread. We dare not.*

T'gai withered. "We must tend our village. . . ."

T'sha swelled gently, trying to calm him with her authority. It felt strange. He was so much her senior in years. But now, she outranked him, and she must not shrink from that. "It has gone too far for that, Speaker. We need to quarantine Gaith. You must call in all the promises you have owing and divert them to diagnosis and prevention. Your ambassador will need all your help with that when he returns."

Speaker T'gai dipped his muzzle. "Yes, of course, Ambassador. You are right."

"Good." She glanced around. The catchsheet was stabilized and anchored to the village's sail struts. Someone had released a slurry of inch-long cleaners onto the sails. They slithered across the sails' skin, ingesting the bubbling growths until the toxicity became too much and they dropped onto the catchsheet. The skin left behind was almost transparent. Even as T'sha watched, the wind tore through the skin, leaving the sail in tatters. The sail mewled and tried to draw in on itself.

She pulled her gaze away. D'suen had a great line of people gathered in the orderly chain now. That would be where T'gai could help.

"Find your teachers to keep gathering your people together. Bring your engineers and doctors. We must determine what's gotten out and how far it's gone."

"Yes. Yes." The speaker swelled again to the lines and proportions she knew. "Thank you, Ambassador."

T'sha deflated until she was just a little smaller than T'gai. "With you, I am still just T'sha, Speaker T'gai." She returned to her normal size. "Go. We will do what we can."

As she watched T'gai fly away, she tried to enumerate what needed to be done. *We need a quarantine blanket. We need a team to find what cortices are still working. A way to repel these flies. . . .*

Life gone insane. Life taking more than it needed, swinging from balance into chaos. T'sha circled until she was upwind of the stench and the sounds of pain. The canopy was lush underneath them. The wind had good weight and texture. This rot seemed to be interested in animal materials; maybe at least the plants below would be safe.

T'sha tensed her bones. They could assume nothing. She'd have to go down and look. If the rot had gotten down there, they would probably be forced to cut it out. That made for a wasteful, inelegant cure, especially with so much of the canopy dying on its own, but they couldn't risk this getting carried any further.

Who knew what spores were already in the wind? Was this even really a fungus, or was she being fooled by appearances? T'sha shivered. On top of it all, here were a thousand more refugees. Some healthy cities would probably still take them in, but they would also demand hefty promissory obligations against the time Gaith, or a replacement, could be regrown. The children huddling under their parents' bellies would be declared adults before the village was free of its debts.

In an earlier time, some of the adults certainly would have offered to bind themselves into lifetime slavery to individuals who could help their children, but that was a practice that had been out of favor for at least two hundred years. Most teachers said accepting such a promise came very close to actual greed. Looking on this sight, T'sha was grateful.

But what sort of promises would T'gai be able to obtain for his people? They were good engineers, but if too many of them had to be indentured away to serve other cities, they would never be able to resurrect their village. They would become permanently homeless, scrabbling for their right to stay wherever they could find space, maybe permanently deprived of their votes.

"I've sent word of our situation to the High Law Meet." D'seun dropped into T'sha's line of sight.

T'sha shook her wings. "There isn't much to report yet."

"Not much to report!" D'seun bobbed up and down as if the sheer force of his exclamation rocked him. "Gaith is dead and decaying in front of our eyes! We have to spread the word!"

"Until we have a cause, that will do nothing but raise a panic." T'sha stopped. "Which is the idea, isn't it?" she murmured. "If the Law Meet panics, they will approve your candidate world without debate, won't they?"

"How can you even be thinking of debate?" demanded D'seun. "Surely this shows us there is no more time. We must make New Home ours or we will all die!"

A dozen different thoughts, realizations, and responses rippled through T'sha. But all she said was, "You and my engineers have the situation under care. I must return to Ca'aed to make sure the latitude quarantines are coordinated. May I borrow your kite?"

It was not a request he could easily refuse. "I will ask for a promise against this."

"A proportionate one, I'm certain."

T'sha found the required wind and flew back to the place where D'seun's kite waited. She gave it orders with the most urgent modifiers. The kite unfurled its wings without hesitation. Its engines sang as the air forced through them. T'sha flattened herself against the perches, wishing the team had brought a dirigible instead. But no need had been seen, no emergency anticipated. Certainly nothing like this.

The memories of the gray, bubbling growths coating Gaith's sails and the black ashlike substance clinging to its walls flew round and round inside T'sha's mind and she could not banish them.

D'seun had been a little right. This was new and this was deadly. The High Law Meet did have to be told. But told what? Told how? That was the next question.

The kite chattered in command language, sending the message on ahead that they were on an emergency run and traffic should clear the gates. Everything had some task to keep them busy, but not T'sha. All she could do was hang on until they reached the walls of Ca'aed.

The kite kept to the clearest routes. T'sha saw dirigibles and other kites in the distance, but did not ask any to be hailed. Even further away she saw the sails and walls of the Ca'aed's wake-villages. The villages saw her as well, and their voices began to pour through her headset.

"I've heard the message of Gaith. My speakers are on the alert. All precautions are being taken." This was T'aide, a young and confident village, strong in its faith of its people. "Good luck, Ambassador."

"Message received from Gaith. The diagnostics are roused." P'teri, an ancient village that had spread its boundaries so far there was talk of it growing into its own city. P'teri was cautious and content, though, and had so far been unwilling to agree to the expansion. "Good luck, Ambassador."

Terse, protective T'zem came through next. "My people are well. I will keep them so. Look to Ca'aed, Ambassador."

I do. You may be sure that I do.

Ca'aed itself shimmered in the distance now, its breadth dominating the horizon. Kites, dirigibles, and people swarmed around it like flies. No, no, not like flies. Like hunter birds, like shades, or even puffs. Ca'aed would not fall to the flies.

Ca'aed was an ancient city. It's pass-throughs, arches, sails, and gardens had grown huge and richly colored with age. Its highest sails nearly raked the clouds, and its sensor roots dragged in the canopy. Where villages skimmed and bobbed on the winds, Ca'aed sailed ponderous and stately, as if it graciously allowed the winds to carry it along.

T'sha's family had helped the city grow its shells and sails. They had protected it and been protected by it for thirty generations. They had been pollers, speakers, teachers, engineers, and ambassadors. Always, always, they had worked directly with Ca'aed, heard its voice, helped it live.

No, Ca'aed would not fall.

Ca'aed spread like a person fully inflated with their wings flung wide. Its walls were deeply creviced, making a thousand harbors into which to guide its people or their vehicles. It drew people in and exuded them again, as if people were what it breathed. Its lens eyes sparkled silver in the daylight. It watched the people come and go so it could advise them as to their routes and their loads or simply to wish them good luck. Lacy fronds of sensors stretched between the sails, constantly testing the winds, looking for riches to steer into and disease to steer away from. Ca'aed was careful. Ca'aed was well advised. Ca'aed might act quickly but never rashly.

"No wonder you have no husbands yet," her younger sister T'kel had teased her once. "Your love is all for the city."

"That is no bad thing," her birth father had replied. "If someone in the position to make promises does not love the city as well as she loves the people in it, she may grow careless with her promises and perhaps overtax its capacities. This can force growth where growth is not ready or even advisable." He'd been answering T'kel, but his attention had been on T'sha. That had been while she was being debated in the general polls as a speaker, but already her father was trying to convince her to start building a base to become ambassador.

"Welcome home, Ambassador," came Ca'aed's familiar voice from her headset. "Have you answers from Gaith? Is there a name for its illness?"

"We don't know yet." All T'sha's hands clutched the perches uneasily.

"But you are confident it will be found?"

"Not as confident as I was." T'sha deflated just a little. "I have to send the kite back to Gaith. Open your gates for me?"

"Always, T'sha. Give me your kite."

T'sha spoke the words to transfer command and Ca'aed took over, pulling the little kite unerringly into one of its harbors. As the rich brown walls surrounded them, Ca'aed's welcomers fluttered out of their cubbyhole and surrounded T'sha in a swarm of reds and greens. They lighted here and there on her back and wings, tasting the emissions of her pores and flitting away again for Ca'aed to be sure there were no dangerous tastes, that she carried nothing hidden with her from Gaith.

But nothing was found, and the pebbled gates at the end of the harbor, which constantly strained and tested the winds for the beneficial elements as well as for the harmful ones, opened a portal for her to dart through. One of Ca'aed's fronds brushed her as she passed, a touch of reassurance and welcome.

"An old city," her birth father had often said, "becomes as full, rich, and complex as the canopy underneath, and its life becomes as tightly intertwined."

T'sha sometimes thought "tangled" would be a better word. The inside of Ca'aed was decidedly a tangle. Bones braced it, corals defined its spaces, and ligaments bound its elements together. Plants and animals gave its walls color, and its air weight and life.

Between them, Ca'aed was a shell full of shells. Small

dwellings and family compounds were tethered to each other
and to the city, but were not part of its essential substance.

Ca'aed's free citizens flew through its chambers, intent on
their various businesses, or merely enjoying the tastes and tex-
tures of their world. Its indentured worked down in the veins
and chasms of its corals, growing, researching, comparing, because the city could not be wholly aware of the workings of
every symbiont and parasite, any more than a person could be
aware of the workings of every pore.

Music, perfumes, voices, flavors filled the air, vying for attention, pressing against T'sha's skin, filling her up with the
vigor of life. The memory of Gaith made the miasma all the
more precious. The people of Gaith had lost all of this when
they lost their village. But, with care, T'sha might still be able
to help them get it back.

T'sha flew into the tangle of life, angling herself vaguely toward her family's district. "Ca'aed, I need my brother T'deu.
Where is he?"

"Your brother is in the promise trees."

Of course. T'sha beat her wings, turning her flight up toward
the city's sculpted and vented ceiling. The promise trees were in
this finger of the city. She would not have to snag a passing kite.

A solid turquoise and cream carapace encapsulated the
promise trees and kept out not only the winds but all that the
winds might carry. The ligaments that twined around its oval
walls and anchored it to Ca'aed's living bones did not themselves
live. They carried neither information nor nutrition and so could
not be used to tamper with anything within the carapace.

The only entrance to the trees was a long tunnel that was so
narrow that only one person at a time could fly its length. Pink
and gold papillae tasted the air around each entrant, making
sure that he or she was a free citizen of Ca'aed. If the entrant
was a stranger to the city or an indenture, it made sure he or
she had received permission from the city or a speaker to
come. If not, the ends of the tunnel would seal and Ca'aed
would call for the district's speaker.

Entering the trees was like flying straight into the canopy. It
was a jungle of leaves, stems, branches, and trunks, all grown

into one another. They spread from the center of the room to the carapace. They climbed the walls, until patterns of intertwining stems and roots covered the carapace's grainy hide. All the colors of growing life shone there in a delicate riot. It all appeared extremely fragile, but the slightest root was many times stronger than the thickest metal wire T'sha had ever touched. It was as beautiful to T'sha as any temple.

Inside the trees' veins flowed the DNA records of every registered promise of the world of Home. Not all promises were registered. Promises passed every day between friends and family that had no need to be here, but promises between businesses, between cities and villages, between ambassadors and any person or any city needed to be recorded. Their fine tendrils of implication needed to be tracked. In here were promises of marriage, merger, birth, inheritance, indenture, trade, service, and sale.

None of this luxuriant growth was necessary, of course. All of the promise registries could have been contained in a set of cortex boxes, and in a younger city it might have been, but the beauty and elaboration of Ca'aed was one of the aspects of it that T'sha had always loved about her city.

T'deu, T'sha's older brother, hovered near the top of the chamber, away from the other trackers and registrants who dotted the chamber. T'deu was an archiver, trained in the reading and tracking of promises. T'sha wove her way through the maze of stems and branches until the air of her passage brushed against him. Her brother turned on his wingtip and leaned forward, rubbing his muzzle joyfully against hers.

"Ambassador Sister!" he said, softly but happily. She and T'deu shared the same birth mother. His father had entered the marriage because of a political promise, and hers had been promised in to help his family when their city fell into trouble. She and T'deu had been raised together and never lost their friendship, even after they were both declared adults and sent out to make their own lives. "It is good to have you here, no matter what the circumstances."

"Thank you, Archiver Brother." T'sha pulled away just a little. "You heard about Gaith."

He dipped his muzzle. "Ca'aed spread the word to the speakers, and the speakers have not been silent."

T'sha's bones bunched as she winced, but she smoothed them out. "Brother, we need to redirect this wind. It is going to be used to rush us into an untenable situation."

T'deu peered up at her, as if he could see into her mind and touch her thoughts. "If you tell me so," he said, but he did not sound certain.

T'sha accepted his words and dismissed his tone. "I want us to bring Gaith's body here."

Her brother deflated in a long, slow motion. "That's dangerous, T'sha—"

"No, listen, there are advantages here. If we give Gaith's engineers the resources to regenerate and resurrect the city and they give us the knowledge and experience they gain from the task, we will be able to turn around and make our own promises with that information, should this strain of disease spread."

"It will mean bringing in a potential contagion, though," T'deu reminded her. "You'll have to take a vote on that."

"I'll get the votes. Can you design me a promise that will do the job?"

"I can design anything you like." T'deu waved one wing at the maze of stems and branches around them. "I could grow you a tree that would outline ownership of the clouds above us. Implementing it—"

"Is my job," said T'sha, cutting him off. "Make sure you graft P'kan's engineers into its branches. They hold several promises against the city. This will help close those down."

"Of course, Ambassador," T'deu said, deflating with mock servility. "Anything else?"

"Should fresh thoughts sprout, I'll share them with you."

T'deu moved even closer, making sure his words reached only her. "Why are you really doing this, Ambassador Sister? It is not only for the profit of the city, or even for the good of Gaith."

"No," she admitted. For a moment she thought of telling him he did not need to know, but that was not true. To design a truly effective promise, he needed to know the ultimate goal, especially if the promise were complex, as promises dealing with cities ultimately were. Trying to integrate the wrong person could jeopardize the entire balance. "I want to be sure Gaith is studied, and studied immediately. If I leave it free for D'seun to take over, he'll fly the village's bones all around the world and show everyone what horrors we are exposing ourselves to if we don't all flock to New Home immediately."

"He'll still try to use Gaith's illness to overfly you," said T'deu.

T'sha shook her wings. "I won't let him. All D'seun's attention is fixed on a single point. If he will not voluntarily see the whole horizon, he must be made to see."

T'deu dipped his muzzle again. "As my Ambassador Sister says. I'll start growing your promise."

"Thank you, Brother. Good luck." She brushed her muzzle against his briefly and launched herself back toward the entrance.

And now there are only a thousand meetings to arrange. The district speakers must hear all of this of course and be brought around. That could be expensive. I'll have to organize the pollers for a citywide referendum, but their schedule should be light right now, except for the poll D'seun has so thoughtfully called for. T'sha emerged from the tunnel into the filtered light of the city. She turned her flight toward the city center and her family's district where she kept her workspace. "Ca'aed?"

"Yes, Ambassador?" answered the city.

"Ca'aed, I have a case to put to you. It concerns your well-being, so I cannot move without you."

"What is it?"

As T'sha flew, she told Ca'aed her plan to bring Gaith to the city to allow Gaith's own citizens to effect its resurrection in return for sharing their knowledge with Ca'aed's engineers, thus saving the Kan Gaith years of potential indenture for their food and shelter in some other city.

Ca'aed was silent for a moment. "We have the room to bring the Kan Gaith here," it said finally. "Our binding of promises with them is not strong or detailed, but there is some exchange that could be worked out." Again, the city paused. T'sha suspected it was mulling over the conversation T'sha had held with T'deu. "We do need to know what infects Gaith," Ca'aed went on. "Yes, bring it here. I agree. I will start working on precautionary plans so we can implement this action as soon as you have secured the people's votes."

"Thank you, Ca'aed," said T'sha earnestly. "This is not just to further my cause with the High Law Meet. There is good for all concerned here."

"Yes," answered Ca'aed. "I do comprehend the good in this."

Something in the city's voice kept T'sha from asking what else it comprehended.

T'sha's workspace was a small coral bubble in her family's compound. The veins holding her records twined all around its insides, spreading out crooked tendrils of blue and purple. It was not as grand or complex a space as many ambassadors had, but T'sha preferred to work on the wing and conduct her meetings and requests in person.

This time though, that would be impossible. She needed all of her specially trained cortex boxes to organize a meeting of the city's thirty district speakers and coordinate their schedules. Each speaker, in turn, would have to reserve time with their chiefs and the pollers because this was a voting matter. The entire process would take dodec-hours.

T'sha was not even halfway finished when the room told her D'seun waited outside.

"Let him in," she said, reluctantly. She was not quite ready for him yet, but she had no polite way to delay.

D'seun drifted into her workspace. He looked shriveled and settled at once on a perch.

"Good luck, D'seun. Can I offer you some time in the refresher? Surely whatever you have to say can wait an hour or two until you are restored."

"No, it cannot wait." He lifted his muzzle. "I must hear you say that you now understand that we cannot wait to find another world to be New Home. I must hear you say we will work together in this."

Shock swelled T'sha. That really was all he thought about. There was no swaying him, no changing the focus of his mind.

"I understand that we are not always as wise as we think we are," she told him fiercely, leaning forward from her own perch. "I understand that we might not know all the rules of life, and that if we act like we do, we are breeding disaster, for ourselves and for these New People."

"I respect your caution, Ambassador T'sha, but I cannot let it endanger us any further." Righteousness swelled D'seun to his fullest extent. "I will proceed with the poll of your families."

"I know that," replied T'sha calmly. "I'm already arranging time with the speakers and the pollers. You will have your vote."

D'seun cocked his head. His eyes examined her from crest to fingertip, trying to guess what made her so complacent. If he succeeded, he gave no sign. "Thank you for your cooperation then, Ambassador. I will wish you good luck and go prepare for the vote."

"Good luck, Ambassador D'seun." T'sha lifted her hands. D'seun lifted his briefly in return and flew away.

T'sha watched him go. *There are advantages to dealing with someone whose attention has narrowed to a hairsbreadth,* she thought. *He has not yet thought to make a try for Gaith's body.*

"Ambassador?" came Ca'aed's voice suddenly.

"Yes, Ca'aed?"

"I want you to know, I'm going to vote in favor of using D'seun's candidate for New Home."

"What?" T'sha stiffened. "Ca'aed, why?"

"Because I'm afraid, T'sha. I'm afraid that what happened to Gaith will happen to me and to you."

T'sha shriveled in on herself as the city's words washed through her. Ca'aed was afraid. She had never heard the city voice such a thought before. What could she do against that?

"We will protect you, Ca'aed," she murmured. "But who will protect the New People?"

"You will find a way."

T'sha dipped her muzzle. "I will have to."

Chapter Three

"This is your seven a.m. wake-up," said the room's too sweet voice. "This is your seven a.m. wake-up."

Around Veronica, the hotel suite woke up. The lights lifted to full morning brightness. In the sitting room, the coffeemaker began to gurgle and hiss, while a fresh lemon scent wafted out of the air ducts.

Vee, who had been awake for an hour already, looked up, sniffed the combination of coffee and lemon, and wrinkled her nose.

"Should've shut off one of those," she muttered.

She looked back down at the desk screen in front of her with its list of names, degrees, and recent publications. She frowned for a moment and then moved Martha Pruess to the top of the list. She was a research fellow in photonic engineering from the Massachusetts Federated Institute of Technology, and her list of publications took up half the screen.

"Checking out the competition?"

Vee jumped, twisting in her seat. Rosa Cristobal, her friend and business manager, stood right behind her chair. "Jesus, Rosa. Don't sneak up on me. It's too early."

"Sorry." Rosa tucked her hands into the pockets of her thick, terry-cloth robe. "But that is what you're doing?"

"Yeah." Vee sighed and tugged on a lock of her hair. "Rosa, I am not going to get this."

"They invited you," Rosa pointed out, as patiently and as firmly as if this were the first time she'd said it.

"Why?" Vee spread her hands. "They need scientists, engineers. I'm an artist, for God's sake. It's been years since I've set foot in a real lab."

"You've got a Ph.D. in planetary atmospherics and your name is sitting pretty on five different patents."

"Which you will remind them of." Vee dropped her gaze back down to the list. *Actually, maybe Avram Elchohen should be at the top. He's got a few more papers on optoelectric engineering—*

"Which I will remind them of." Rosa reached over Vee's shoulder and touched the Off key. The desk screen blanked. "Get dressed, Vee. The interview's at nine and you do not want to be late."

"Yes, Rosa," said Vee in the tones of a child saying "Yes, Mommy." She got up meekly and headed for her bathroom. "And shut off the lemons, will you?"

"Yes, Vee."

After her shower, Vee dressed in an outfit she'd bought especially for the interview—wide navy-blue slacks and a matching vest with matte buttons over a sky-blue silk blouse. She stepped into the makeup station and selected a minimalist setting. The mirror glowed gently as it scanned her face and sent color instructions to the waldos, which responded by laying on just a hint of bronze to highlight her cheekbones and jawline, and a touch of deep wine to her lips.

"Close your eyes please," said the same too sweet voice that had given the wake-up call. Vee did and felt a quick puff of powder. She opened her eyes. Now her lids had a hint of burgundy coloring and a discreet sheen of gold dust glimmered on her cheeks, the very latest in conservo-chic.

"Routine complete," said the station.

Vee studied herself in the mirror for a minute. It was a good face, with high cheekbones, strong nose, soft chin. Her brows were so pale as to be almost nonexistent. The rest of her was what she called "Nordic swizzle-stick fashion," very long, very white, and very thin. "Handy for hiding behind flagpoles," she liked to joke.

Vee wound her mane of silver-blond hair into a tidy coil and pinned it in place. She selected a scarf that matched her blouse and fastened it so it covered her head but fluttered freely down over her shoulders. She nodded at her reflection, pleased. The effect was businesslike but not stuffy. It said that here was a person to be taken seriously.

Vee had been stunned when she saw the v-mail message from the Colonial Affairs Committee. She had sat in front of her living room view screen for ten full minutes, playing and replaying the recording.

"Hello, Dr. Hatch. I'm Edmund Waicek of the United Nations Colonial Affairs Committee Special Work Group on Venus."

Good breath-control exercise there, Vee remembered thinking, facetiously. Edmund Waicek was a tall man with red-brown skin and black eyes. A round, beaded cap covered his thick copper hair. His age was indeterminate and his clothing immaculate.

"As I am sure you are aware, there has been a remarkable discovery made on the world of Venus. We have found what appears to be the remains of an alien base or facility of some kind. Because of the vastly important nature of this development, the C.A.C. has decided to assemble a team of specialists to examine and evaluate the discovery." He leaned forward and flashed a smile full of carefully calculated sincerity. "We have reviewed your academic record and subsequent accomplishments, and we would like to invite you to participate in the interview process to see if you can take your place on this historic mission." His expression grew solemn. "We will need your answer by Tuesday the eighteenth at nine a.m., your local time. Thank you for your attention to this matter. I look forward to meeting you."

The Discovery on Venus. Of course Vee had heard of it. It was a solid indication that there had once been alien life inside the solar system, an idea that had been given up on years before Vee had even been born. When she was feeling cynical, she would tell herself it was nothing more than three holes in the ground. Except it was. It was three holes in the ground dug by nothing human, and they had left behind what everyone was certain was a laser, or maybe it was a laser component of a larger machine.

It was that laser they wanted her to go up and take a look

at. Well, they wanted someone to go up and take a look at it, and her name, somehow, had made the short list.

Veronica Hatch, science popularizer, temperamental artiste, and noted personality. The U.N. was setting all that aside and going back to the part of her that was Dr. Hatch, the part that had patents and papers and could do actual work.

"Vee?" came Rosa's voice.

Vee realized she hadn't moved. She was just standing there, staring at the reflection of a serious, competent stranger, and clenching her fists.

"Coming." Vee smoothed out her veil and turned away from the mirror.

Rosa was in the sitting room, drinking what was probably her second cup of coffee. How she could suck that stuff down on an empty stomach Vee had never known. Rosa had selected a tunic and skirt suit in shades of forest green with emerald trim and a pale, silver scarf to cover her black hair. She looked Vee up and down and gave a small nod of approval as Vee twirled on her toes to show herself off.

"Very nice." Rosa drained her mug. "Do you want to order in, or go out for breakfast?"

"Would you mind if we dropped by the Coral Sea? I promised Nikki."

Rosa made a face. "That place is overdone."

"Hey." Vee drew herself up indignantly. "I helped design the effects on that place, thank you very much."

"And you overdid it." Rosa stood up. "In your usual stylish, trend-setting way." She grabbed her briefcase off the couch. "Let's hit the deck, shall we?"

Vee and Rosa took a glide-walk up through the layers of the Ashecroft Hotel to the main pedestrian deck and the clean, clear, Pacific day. U.N. City had been built during the first decade of what some people still called the Takeover. The Takeover happened halfway through the 2100s, when the United Nations went from being a pack of squabbling diplomats to a genuine world-governing body. Because national feeling still ran very high back then, it was decided that the seat of world government would not be given to any one country. It would float around the world on the oceans. The mobility created some trouble with time zones, but that was deemed a minor problem compared to the endless bickering caused by the debate over where to put the capital of the world.

The city itself was huge. Toward its center, you couldn't even tell you were on the ocean. Ashecroft was in the fashionable edge district however, and the first thing Vee saw when they emerged was sunlight sparkling cheerfully on the broad, blue Pacific. In the distance she could just make out three of the cordon ships that sailed in a ring around the city, serving as escort and border guard.

On the main deck, U.N. City was wide awake and in full swing. Crowds of people swarmed between the buildings and the parks. Their skins were every color, from snow white to midnight black. They wore all styles and colors of clothing and every possible level of body enhancement, both organic and mechanical. Some drifted between the boutiques, studying the holo-displays that took the place of windows. Some strolled along the city's sculpted rail looking out at the calm, sapphire ocean, maybe hoping to see dolphins or, better yet, whales. Some just hurried from glide-walk mouth to glide-walk mouth, catching a few precious moments of sunlight between meetings and appointments down in the heart of the city.

How many of them are hustling to something related to the Venus Discovery? Vee felt a twinge of guilt at being happy for U.N. City's restrictive public assembly policies. You could barely move in Chicago without tripping over another "citizens meeting" or "public discussion" about Venus's underground chambers and their contents and what, if anything, should be done about them.

The Coral Sea Cafe was a few blocks from the railing, nestled in the corner between one of the observation towers and the Council of Tourism Welcome Center. The mirrored door scanned them both, found them admissible, and slid itself open. Vee stepped into the undersea-scaped interior with its wavery, water-scattered light, which she had fine-tuned for them. Schools of tropical fish swam lazily across the walls. The chairs and tables mimicked rounded stones or coral outcroppings.

"Just too-too," murmured Rosa. Vee slapped her shoulder.

A woman almost as tall and thin as Vee emerged from the office door, probably alerted to their arrival by the door. She looked like she was in her mid-twenties, but Vee knew she was using body-mod to keep middle age firmly at bay. Not even forty, Nikki had already waved her rights to children and signed up for long-life.

Nothing like knowing what you want.

A circle of blue glass shone in the middle of Nikki's forehead, probably concealing a personal scanner and database to let her know just who she was dealing with.

"Vee!" Nikki cried happily.

"Nikki!" Vee exclaimed, embracing the woman with the expected level of fervor. "Love the third eye. You look great."

"And you look"—Nikki pulled back just a little—"subdued."

"Ah." Vee held up one, long finger. "Someone's actually vetting me for a science job today."

Nikki's smile grew conspiratorial. "This is about the Venus thing, isn't it? I heard your name on the lists."

"Well surely, nothing important can happen without my name on it," announced Vee regally.

"Surely, dear, surely," said Nikki, grasping Vee's hand.

Rosa coughed.

"Oh, right. Nikki, breakfast? Clock's ticking."

"Of course, dear." Nikki ushered them to a corner booth shaped like a supposedly cosy undersea grotto. "I'll have your waiter over three seconds ago."

"There's a relativity problem there, Nikki," said Vee as she slid into her seat.

"What?" Nikki's face went politely blank.

"Science joke. Never mind." Vee smiled sunnily. "Have to get back into practice."

"Of course. Good luck, Vee." Nikki squeezed her shoulder and breezed away.

Rosa was looking at her. "What?" asked Vee.

Rosa picked up her napkin and made a great show of smoothing it across her lap. "It just never ceases to amaze me how fast you drop into the artiste persona."

"Hey." Vee stabbed the table with one finger. "That persona has kept us both living very comfortably. I wouldn't complain."

"Never," said Rosa flatly. "Just commenting." She called up the menu from the tabletop display and began examining it.

The cafe was tony enough to have real humans as servers, but, fortunately, not so over-the-top as to put them in any form of swimwear. Rosa and Vee ordered coffee, white tea, rolls, and fruit cups from a young man in the ultratraditional server's black-and-white uniform.

When he left, Rosa jacked her briefcase into the table and unfolded the view screen.

"How're we doing today?" Vee asked. If Rosa heard her, she gave no sign. She just skimmed the display and shuffled the icons.

"Your money's good," Rosa said at last. "The family trusts are percolating along nicely, and I think we're going to be able to put Kitty through college without a problem."

"Same as yesterday."

"Same as yesterday," agreed Rosa. "Want to see the latest on the Discovery?"

Vee shrugged, trying to be casual about it. "Might as well see what I'm getting into." Inside, her stomach began to flutter and she wondered where breakfast was. Food might help settle her down, except all of a sudden she wasn't hungry.

Rosa lit the back of the screen so Vee could follow along and called up her favorite news service.

The lead stories all came under the heading of *The Discovery on Venus,* as they had for the past month. Today was a pretty light news day. Only three new stories had been added since Vee checked it last night. Rosa touched the title *Venus Colonists Say No Help Needed* and the *Silent* option. The main menu vanished, and the text and video story unfolded in front of them.

Sources at Venera Base, home to the incredible discovery of what may be signs of alien life on Venus [long-range, color-enhanced picture of the spherical settlement with its airfoil tail floating through billowing clouds], are saying that the governing board strongly resents the formation of the new United Nations subcommittee on Venus. The governing board insists that the Venerans already in residence have sufficient expertise to deal with this most unexpected find.

While Dr. Helen Failia, founder of the base and head of Venera's Board of Directors [video clip of a short, gray-haired woman with a severe face giving a lecture to a group of what looked like college students], still refuses comment, sources close to the board say that petitions have been filed to render the Discovery [dissolve to the now familiar glowing hatchway] proprietary to the funding universities and therefore outside the realm of government probes or restrictions.

Dr. Bennet Godwin [jump cut to a split picture with a still shot of an iron-gray-haired man with permanent windburn in one half, and a hardsuited figure standing on a yellowish-red cliff in the other half], also on Venera's board, had this comment [the man's picture flickered to life].

"We welcome all serious research into any aspect of the world of Venus. That's what Venera Base is here for. What we cannot welcome, or tolerate, is interference by nonscientists in what is a *scientific* inquiry [the face froze]."

Dr. Godwin later issued the following clarification of his statement [the face flickered to life again, but now much more rigid and controlled]. "When I said nonscientists, obviously I meant unauthorized or inexpert personnel. This discovery is of massive importance to all humanity, and its investigation must be conducted in the open with all available assistance and resources."

"Who got you to add that disclaimer?" murmured Rosa, picking up her newly arrived cup of coffee and sipping it appreciatively. Vee swallowed some of the peach-flavored tea and poked at a strawberry in her fruit cup. The scent of fresh fruit and baked goods was failing to bring back her appetite in a rather spectacular fashion.

She read on.

When asked what he thought about Dr. Godwin's comment, Edmund Waicek [dissolve to the same man who had

sent Vee her interview invitation], spokesman for the newly
formed U.N. Work Group on Venus, said only, "We are glad
that Dr. Godwin and the rest of the members of Venera Base
realize how important openness and cooperation are at this
historic time. This discovery affects the whole of humanity.
Humanity's elected representatives need to assist in its un-
covering and understanding."

"Mmmph." Rosa buttered a croissant and bit into it. Vee drank
a little more tea, trying to get her stomach to open up enough
that she'd actually be able to get some food down. The only
thing that little piece made clear was that there was animosity
between Venera Base and the U.N. That did not bode well, and
Venera was probably going to live to regret it. It also meant she
was walking into a hornets' nest, which made it even less likely
that a controversial candidate would get the job.

"Eat, Vee," ordered Rosa. "You're not doing either of us any
favors if you go in there on edge."

Vee obediently munched on strawberries, kiwis, mango, and
pineapple. But she couldn't make herself face the rolls. Instead,
she watched Rosa's screen. The other two stories were public-
reaction sensation videos. One showed a public meeting in
good old free-speech Chicago. The other was an interview
with a pair of bald, neutered, Universal Age synthesists explaining how this was the first step toward the human worlds
being accepted into the Greater Galactic Consciousness. There
were, of course, links to the thousands of papers, discussions,
and wonder-sites that had mushroomed since the Discovery
was announced.

There had been aliens on Venus, and Earth was alive with all
the wonder that the idea brought. At first, a lot of people had
been worried that there would be riots and panics, but, so far,
no one had seen fit to go twentieth over the news.

Something on Rosa chimed. "Time to go," she said, shutting
down her briefcase. She picked up a danish and put it into
Vee's hand. "Eat."

Vee gnawed the pastry without tasting it while Rosa authorized an account deduction on the table's screen. As they left,

the fishes on the wall called, "Good luck, Vee," causing the other patrons to whisper and stare.

Vee made a mental note to tell Nikki never to do that again without permission and followed Rosa out the door.

Their appointment was in the J. K. McManus administration complex, which lay deep in the heart of U.N. City. It took Vee and Rosa twenty minutes, four glide-walks, and three ID scans before they reached the central atrium of the gleaming crystal-and-steel administration mall. Philodendrons, morning glories, and passion flowers twined around glass-encased fiber-optic bundles that stretched from floor to ceiling. Diplomats, admin- istrators, lobbyists, and small herds of courier drones flowed in and out of transparent doors. They jammed the elevators and escalators running between the complex's eight floors. The muted roar of their voices substituted for the rush of wind and waves on the deck.

Vee and Rosa presented themselves to a live human security team and were asked to write down their names and leave a thumbprint on an impression film registry. In return, they were presented with audio badges and directed to Room 3425. The badges would tell them if they took a wrong turn.

Rosa clipped the badge to her briefcase strap and stepped onto the nearest escalator. Vee followed obediently, brushing restlessly at her tunic and smoothing down her veil.

They want me here. They want me here. I've done good, solid work and it's on record. I can do this. They believe I can do this, or they wouldn't have invited me in.

Room 3425 was a conference room. Rosa presented her badge to the room door, which scanned it, and her, before slid- ing open. On the other side waited an oval table big enough for a dozen people. An e-window showed a view of a tropical park on the sun-drenched deck with parti-colored parrots preening themselves in lush green trees.

The room had three occupants. Edmund Waicek sat at the conference table looking like he'd just stepped out of the story clip Vee viewed at breakfast. Next to him sat a tiny Asian woman in a pale-gold suit-dress. Her face was heavily lined, and her opaque red veil lay over pure-white hair. Behind them stood a slender, dark man who could have been from any of a hundred cities in the Middle East or North Africa. He wore a loose, white robe and a long orange-and-red-striped vest. A plain black cap covered his neatly trimmed hair. He turned from his contemplation of the parrots as the door opened and gave Vee a look that managed to be both amused and critical.

Mr. Waicek was on his feet and crossing the room toward Vee before Vee had a chance to step over the threshold.

"Dr. Hatch, thank you for coming." He shook Vee's hand with a nicely judged amount of firmness. "I'm Edmund Waicek."

"Pleased to meet you, Mr. Waicek," said Vee, extricating her hand.

"Call me Edmund," he said, as Vee guessed he would.

"Edmund," she repeated. "This is Rosa Cristobal."

"Delighted to meet you Ms. Cristobal. Allow me to introduce you both to Ms. Yan Su. She is the Venus work group's resource coordinator."

"Pleased to meet you both." Ms. Yan's voice was light and slightly hesitant, giving the impression that English was not her first language. Underneath that, though, lay a feeling of strength and the awareness of it. "You will forgive me if I ask your field of specialty, Ms. Cristobal. The nature of your relationship with Dr. Hatch is not exactly clear."

Rosa gave a brief laugh. "No, it is not, even to me, some days. Primarily, I am Dr. Hatch's manager. I coordinate her projects and her contracts. Demand for her skills is very high, as I'm sure you know, but you would be amazed at the number of people who try to pay less than those skills are worth."

"And this is Mr. Sadiq Hourani, whose province is security," interjected Edmund smoothly.

Weird way of putting it. Mr. Hourani gave them a small bow. Vee noticed that his eyebrows were still raised and his expression was still amused.

Rosa laid her briefcase on the conference table and sat next to Ms. Yan. "First of all, let me say that we are extremely excited to be considered for this project." She jacked her case into the table, which lit up the clear-blue data displays in front of each of the participants.

"As we are to have you here," beamed Edmund. "We have reviewed Dr. Hatch's credentials in both the engineering and information fields and found them very impressive. Very impressive indeed."

"Thank you." Vee inclined her head modestly.

Edmund's smile grew fatherly. Vee kept her face still. "Our questions here will be of a more personal nature," he went on.

"What? Rosa didn't get you my gene screens?" Vee's flippancy was reflexive, and she regretted it even before Rosa's toe prodded her shin.

Ms. Yan laughed dryly. "No. Health issues, if there are any, will be addressed later. These are more questions of political outlook, approach, and general attitude toward—"

"Political outlook?" interrupted Vee.

"Yes," said Ms. Yan. "I wish this mission were purely a question of research and exploration, but it is not."

A spark of suspicion lit up inside Vee. She tried to squash it but was only partially successful. She'd grown up in the remnants of the old United States. Her grandfather had talked almost daily about the Disarmament, when U.N. troops went house to house confiscating guns and arresting the owners who would not peacefully hand them over, and worse. Personally, Vee thought her grandfather was nuts for romanticizing the freedom to shoot your neighbors, but his distrust and distaste for the "yewners" had taken root in some deep places, and she hadn't managed to shake it yet.

"Of course," Rosa was saying smoothly. "An effective team is more than just a collection of skills. Personalities have to mesh smoothly, and there must be a unified outlook."

"Exactly." Edmund's chest swelled, and Vee knew they were in for a speech.

Apparently, Ms. Yan knew it too because she quickly asked, "Have you ever been to Venera before, Dr. Hatch?"

"Once, about eight years ago." Vee did not miss the dirty look Edmund shot Ms. Yan, but she suppressed her smile of amusement. "As part of my Planets project." Vee's initial fame and the basis of her fortune was made by her creation of the first experiential holoscenic. It was a tour of the solar system, set to the music of Holst's *The Planets*. She had taken people inside the clouds of Venus, the oceans of liquid ice on Europa, the storms of Jupiter, and the revolt in Bradbury, Mars, for the movement "Mars, Bringer of War."

It suddenly hit Vee what they must be leading up to.

"I have always particularly liked the Veneran segment of *The Planets*," said Ms. Yan. "Most people see Venus as hellish. You made it beautiful."

"Thank you." Tension tightened Vee's back. *When are they going to say it? When are they going to say it?*

"Your section on the Bradbury Rebellion was rather less beautiful," said Edmund.

Vee caught Rosa's "be careful" glance and ignored it. "I strove for accuracy," she said, aware her voice had gone tart. "And comprehension." The "Bringer of War" segment showed the people being marched into the patched-up ships which were launched without regard to their safety, but it also showed the crowds rallying around Theodore Fuller and his cause, the shining faces, the great hopes of the dream of freedom before that dream had tarnished and twisted.

Edmund's expression fell into a kind of hard neutrality. "Yes, some of your images were quite . . . sympathetic." He glanced at a secondary display on the table in front of him. Vee wished she were close enough to read the items listed there. "What are your feelings about the separatist movements here on Earth?"

This is it? Vee looked incredulously from one face to the other. Both Edmund and Ms. Yan were perfectly serious. Even Mr. Hourani, who had not uttered one word since the beginning of the meeting, had lost his little amused smile. *They want to judge my fitness based on how I feel about separatists?*

Rosa's warning prod against her ankle grew urgent. Vee dismissed it and heaved herself to her feet.

"You want to know how I feel about Bradbury? I was seven years old when that mess happened. I didn't have an opinion, just a few vague feelings. *The Planets* show was for money and to show off what you could do with my new holography tricks." She planted both hands on the table and leaned toward the yewners. "You want a political yes-sir, pick one of your own. You want an Earth Über Alles, find a Bradbury survivor. You want somebody who can take a look at your Discovery and just maybe come up with something useful to say about it, then you want me. But I will not"—she slammed her hand against the table—"sit here and be interrogated because I may have had a thought or two."

She turned on her heel and stalked out of the room.

The corridors passed by in a blur. She slapped her audio badge down on the counter at the security station without breaking stride. She saw nothing clearly until she found herself up on the deck in the blazing sunlight, staring out across the blue-gray waters and clenching her hands around the warm metal railing.

Well, Vee, you crashed that one pretty good, didn't you? She bowed her head until it rested on the backs of her hands. *What the hell were you doing? Did you really think they were looking for the dilettante?*

Vee was not going to whine about her fate. She had made her choices for money, yes, but also for love. She was good at her art. She understood light and the machines that manipulated it. She could shape light like a potter shaping clay. She knew how to blend it and soften it to create any color and nuance the human eye could detect. She knew how it controlled shadows and reflections. She knew how it scattered and bounced and played mischievous tricks on the senses. She knew nine-and-ninety ways it could be used to transmit messages. The lab had become mind-bogglingly boring right about the time the money from her patents and the resulting holoscenics had really started to come in. She'd taken off for the artistic life, along with the ability to buy her college debts away from her parents' bank and keep her brothers and sisters from ever having to go into debt for themselves.

But sometimes she felt she'd missed the chance to do something real, the chance to explore as well as create, to question the nature of the universe in ways art couldn't reach by itself, to say something that would last, even if it was so obscure only ten other people understood it.

An accomplishment her family back in its naturalist, statist town wouldn't have to feel ambivalent about.

"You know," said Rosa's voice beside her, "there's this old saying that goes 'Be careful what you pretend to be; you may become it.'"

Vee lifted her head, blinking back tears of pain as the light assaulted her eyes. "How fast did they throw you out of there?"

"They didn't, actually." Rosa leaned her elbows against the railing. The salt breeze caught her silver scarf and sent it fluttering across her face. She pushed it away. "I spread some fertilizer about sensitive geniuses, which they seemed willing to sit still for. They, or at least Ms. Yan and Mr. Hourani, seemed impressed by your strong political neutrality." The wind plastered her scarf against her cheek again, and she brushed it back impatiently. "I'm less sure about Mr. Waicek, but I do believe he's leaning in our direction."

Hope, slow and warm, filled Vee's mind. "You're kidding."

"I have one question." Rosa rubbed her hands together and studied them. "Do you really want to do this?" She lifted her gaze to Vee's face. "They were giving you purity in there. This is going to be a political situation. You've seen the news. Everybody's got a position. Everybody wants referendums. You're going to be quizzed and dissected and watched, and you're going to have to put up with it. Quietly. No more scenes like that one." She jerked her chin back toward the glide-walk mouth. "So, I'm asking you, Vee, as your friend and your manager, do you really, honestly, want to be a part of this mission?"

Vee stared out across the blue water under the brilliant sky. Nothing on Venus was blue. It was all orange and gold and blazing red. Yet someone had been there, had set up their base there, and then left. Where had they gone? Who were they? Why had they come in the first place? They might have left the answer behind them. It might be in that laserlike device.

Do I really want to be a part of finding that answer?

"Yes," she said, to sea and sky, and Rosa. "Oh yes. I want this."

Out of the corner of her eye, she saw Rosa nod. "Okay, then. I think you'll get it."

Vee's smile spread across her face. "If I do nothing else real in my life, at least I'll get to do this," she said softly.

For a moment, she thought she heard Rosa mutter, "Whatever *this* is," but then she decided that she didn't.

The image of a spring meadow high in the Colorado Rockies surrounded Yan Su as she sat behind her desk. She paid no attention to it. Instead, she focused on the wall screen, which she had set to record her message to Helen Failia on Venera Base.

"Hello, Helen. I just saw the latest commentary from out your way. Now, you know I don't interfere." Pause for Helen to insert whatever comment she had on that score. "But you've got to sit on Ben Godwin for the duration. I've done my best with the investigative team makeup. They are as close to what you asked for as I could manage. But this will not, I repeat, will not, hold up to certain types of scrutiny. Assure Dr. Godwin that if he lets the spinners do their job and is patient, this will all blow over and your people can get back to work.

"I'm doing my part down here, and we're making progress. You will all get what you want, but you've got to keep quiet." She paused again, tapping her fingernails against the glass of iced tea sitting on her desk. "I know this isn't easy, Helen, but believe me, it's the only way. You also need to keep your security chief on the alert. Every single cracker on three planets is going to be trying to get into Venera's systems, trying to get 'the real story.'" She made quotation marks with her fingertips. "The rumors in-stream are bad enough without that." She sighed softly. "Take care of yourself Helen. You've inherited quite a situation."

A quick keystroke faded the recording out and shunted the message into the queue for the next com burst out to Venus. Helen would receive the message in an hour or two.

Su finished her iced tea and rattled the ice cubes a couple of times as she stared at the sunlight on the distant snowy peaks. God, how long until she'd see the real thing again? She felt certain there would be nothing in her life but Venera and its Discovery at least until the "investigative team" came home, and maybe not even then. A lot would depend on how well Helen was able to handle her people and her sudden fame.

Su remembered the first time Helen Failia sailed into her office. Forty years ago, no, forty-five years ago, and she still remembered.

It had been a long day of in-stream meetings and screen-work. A headache was just beginning to press against her temples. None of this had left Su in the best of moods.

"Thank you for agreeing to see me, Ms. Yan." Helen Failia was not yet forty then. She wore her chestnut hair bundled up under a scarf of dusky-rose silk. Her handshake was firm, her smile genuine, and her movements calm and confident. Despite that, Su got the strong impression of restless energy brimming just below the surface of this woman.

"Now, what can I do for you, Dr. Failia?" Su asked as she handed Helen the cup of black coffee she'd requested. The woman was a very traditional American on that score.

"I'm building a research colony on Venus," said Helen, taking the seat Su waved her toward. "I want to know what governmental permissions I need."

Just like that. Not "I'm exploring the possibilities of . . ." or "I'm part of a consortium considering building . . ."

"You're building on Venus?" Su raised both eyebrows. "With what?"

She hadn't been able to get another word out for thirty minutes. Helen had brought scroll after scroll of blueprints, encyclopedic budget projections, and lists of potential donors. Everything was planned out, down to which construction facilities could supply which frame sections for the huge, floating city she had designed.

When Dr. Failia finally subsided, Su was ready to admit, privately, she was impressed. In an ideal world, Dr. Failia's proposal would be quite feasible. Unfortunately, Su had already been on the C.A.C. long enough to know this was not an ideal world.

Perhaps a gentle hint in that direction. "Wouldn't it be more practical, Dr. Failia, to start with a temporary facility funded by perhaps one or two universities?"

"No," said Helen at once. Su raised her eyebrows again, and

Helen actually looked abashed. "I'm sorry, but no. Venus is a vast, complex world. It's active in many of the basic ways that Earth is active. It has an atmosphere, weather, and volcanic activity." Dr. Failia's eyes shone. At that, Su remembered where she'd heard Dr. Failia's name before. Helen Failia had been a member of the Icarus Expedition that had gone out, what was it? Two? No, three years ago. She was now one of the four people who had actually walked on the Venusian surface.

It also looked as though she had fallen in love down there.

"In a temporary facility," Dr. Failia was saying, "a few researchers could study a few aspects of the planet for a few months at a time. But in a real facility, such as Venera"—she tapped the screen roll—"people could specialize. Careers could be dedicated to the study of Earth's sister without requiring people to remove themselves from their families. The work could be made practical and comfortable for years at a time. We would not be limited to snapshots; we could take in the entire panorama."

Earth's sister. It is love. Su shook her head. "And the industrial applications? Are there any commercial possibilities?"

Helen didn't even blink. "In all probability, industrial and commercial applications would be limited. Mining or other exploitive surface operations would remain prohibitively expensive due to the harsh conditions."

All right, at least you're willing to admit that much, Dr. Failia. Su folded her hands on the desk and mustered her "serious diplomat" tones. "You do realize that the colonies which have paid off their debts and become going concerns all have some kind of export or manufacturing base?"

"Until now, yes."

Su found herself having to suppress a laugh. The question hadn't even ruffled the surface of Dr. Failia's confidence. "So you are hoping the research value will offset the economic liabilities?"

"Research and publicity." Helen thumbed through the screen rolls on the desk, pulled out the one labeled "University Funding" and presented it for Su's inspection. "Research departments in both universities and private industry are fueled by their papers as well as their patents. From a publications stand-point, Venus is more than ready to be exploited."

Su nodded as she skimmed the numbers again. It was all true and reasonable, as far as it went. But the fact was that the pure-research colonies had never worked. The small republics, and even the big universities, were unable to keep them funded. The United Nations was unwilling. Nobody said it out loud, of course, but the established wisdom was that the plan-ets should be saved for industry, and now for the long-life re-treats that the lobbyists were proposing as a way for those who had children but wanted extended life spans to have it all. They could live in specialized colonies with continued gene-level medical treatment without straining the balance and re-sources of Mother Earth.

Su found herself extremely ambivalent about that idea. But this one . . . Su liked the vision of this gigantic bubble of a town, sort of a U.N. City in the Venusian sky. She liked Helen's enthusiastic and detailed descriptions of not an outpost but a real community, as self-supporting as any off-world colony could be, given over to exploration and research. True, this vi-sion ignored most of the political realities and historical exam-ples, but that did not lessen its attractiveness. Su did not get much chance to dream anymore, and she found herself enjoy-ing the opportunity.

Still, no politician could afford to dream for too long. *It'll be shot down by the rest of the C.A.C. if it gets in their line of sight,* she reminded herself with a sigh. They did not like approving doomed projects. It made for snide comments in-stream and low scores on the opinion polls.

But maybe, maybe there was a way around that.

"I will be honest with you, Dr. Failia," said Su. "Without the money in account, this is not going through."

To her credit, Helen Failia did not say "But . . ."

Su leaned forward, making sure the other woman met her gaze. "However, if you can get at least some of the start-up money, I think its chances are very good. Very good."

As Su watched, light sparked behind Dr. Failia's dark eyes.

"Well, thank you for your time, Ms. Yan." She stood up and held her hand out. "I'll see you when I have my money."

Su also rose. "I look forward to it."

They shook hands. Helen gathered up her screen rolls and left without a backward glance. Su sat back down behind her desk and watched the door swish shut. Her headache, she noticed, had vanished.

"Desk. Sort recording of completed meeting and extract proposal details for the construction of Venera Base," she said thoughtfully. "Assume acquisition of adequate funding. List applicable regulatory and legislative requirements that must be met for construction of the proposed base." She paused. "Also extract voting records of C.A.C. members and project probable votes should proposal come to committee as offered in this meeting."

Helen, after all, was not the only one who had work to do if Venera was to . . . well . . . fly.

It had taken five years, but the money had been found; the base had been built, and for forty years after that, Helen kept it running. She scraped, scrounged, begged, borrowed, and worked the stream with a skill Su had seen only in the very best politicians. She had help of course. Sometimes, Su felt that while Helen had raised Venera, Su herself had raised Helen. She'd taught the older woman the finer points of publicity and spin doctoring. She'd steered her toward the more sympathetic funds and trusts. After the Bradbury Rebellion, Su had helped Helen make sure that all their money came from Earth so there could be no tangible connection between Venera and any suspect persons, who, at that point, included everyone who did not live on Mother Earth.

Helen had never married, never had children. Venera and its prosperity had been her entire life.

And she had almost lost it. Su tried to imagine what that felt like and failed. Her own life had been tied to so many different things—her husband, her son, political ambitions, and the colonies. Not just Venera, but Small Step and Giant Leap, Bradbury, Burroughs, Dawn, the L5 archipelagoes, all of them. They deserved their chance to flourish. Mother Earth needed her children, but like any flesh-and-blood parent, she needed to treat them as people, not possessions.

However, since Bradbury, with its deaths and exiles and threats, and since the long-life colonies had become a credit-filled reality, it had not been easy to convince anybody else in power of this.

For the moment, Venera at least was going to be all right. Su studied the donations list displayed on her desktop. If even half these promises were fulfilled, Venera was not going to even have to think about money for another five years.

Which is all to the good, Su rubbed her temples. *There is nothing bad about this. If we want any colony in the public eye, it's Venera.*

She shook herself. This was not anything she had time for. The Secretaries-General had called a meeting for the afternoon, and Su had to get her candidate files in order. Despite what she'd told Helen, there was still the very real possibility that Edmund might withdraw his backing from one or two of her people, and she might have to make her case to the Sec-Gens without any help at all. Secretary Haight was very much committed to the status quo, but Kent and Sun had a little more leeway in their thinking and saw the political opportunities inherent in loosening the grip on the planets a little. She would have to play to them if she wanted to keep the U.N. from just walking in and taking over the Discovery, and she wanted that very much.

The door chimed and Su looked at the view port. It cleared to reveal Sadiq Hourani and Su ordered it open. He walked in and Su waved him to a chair. Sadiq was on the very short list of people whom she would always see.

Su sat back and regarded him for a moment. "Tell me you have good news."

"I have good news," said Sadiq promptly.

"Really? Or are you just saying that?" Sadiq had been assigned to the C.A.C. security and intelligence work group ten years ago. In that time, Su had learned to trust him, despite the fact that he kept more hidden than she would ever learn about. It had not been easy, but it had been worth it.

Sadiq returned a small smile. "Really. We've negotiated an

end to that potential media standoff in Bombay. They're to have some unmonitored access time to the investigative team and some of the Veneran scientists so they can ask questions without, and I quote, governmental interference, end quote."

Su raised both her eyebrows. "And you capitulated with all humbleness?"

"That I did."

"And you went in there knowing what they really wanted?"

"That I did," repeated Sadiq. "It's my job, you know."

The news of the Discovery had been received with calm just about everywhere. There were a few hardcase places—Bombay, Dublin, Old L.A.—where tempests threatened to start up in the stream. The stream was the systemwide communications network that had evolved out of all the old nets and webs that had spanned the globe since the twentieth century. It was possible for discontent in-stream to spill out into the real world. Part of Sadiq's job was to make sure it never did.

"So." Su leaned back and folded her hands in her lap. "Do you know what the Secretaries-General really want to see us about?"

Sadiq shrugged. "To hear about Bombay, for a start, and the other hot spots. They should have reviewed our Comprehensive Coping Strategy by now. They also, of course, need to give their blessing to the investigative team roster so the full committee won't be able to bicker too much."

"Have you ascertained whether Edmund's going to behave?" Su had known from the beginning that Edmund was going to be difficult. Since he had been appointed to the C.A.C., he had been one of the loudest anticolonial voices they had, and that was saying a great deal. His initial idea had been to send out a team that would investigate Venera at least as thoroughly as it would investigate the Discovery.

"I believe he will." Sadiq studied his neat hands for a moment. "You know, Su, you are going to have to speak to him again, sooner or later."

"Yes, I know." After Dr. Hatch and Ms. Cristobal had left, Edmund had started in on one of his canned speeches about the "absolute necessity of choosing members who will not be blinded by propaganda or sentimentality and will be willing to examine *every* aspect of the Discovery." Su, suddenly unable to stand it another minute, had stood up and said, "You don't want an investigation; you want an inquisition," and stalked out.

The memory made her sigh again. "That is no way for a grown bureaucrat to behave. Especially now," she added.

"Especially now," echoed Sadiq. "Especially on one of your pet projects."

Su eyed him carefully to see if there was anything hidden under that statement, but Sadiq's face remained placid. "Yes," she admitted. "This one's mine and I can't hide from it." She was about to add a question about Edmund Waicek, positive that Sadiq had spoken with him before he walked into her office, but Sadiq had stiffened and his eyes darted back and forth. Su closed her mouth. Sadiq wore a phone spot, so he could be reached at any time. This could be anything from a request for authorization on an expense report to notification of an outbreak of public violence.

When Sadiq had focused on her again, Su asked, "Anything wrong?"

"We seem to have a demonstration on the deck." Sadiq stood. "Peaceful but illegal. Care to come?"

"Not really." Su waved him away. "I'll see you at the Sec-Gens this afternoon."

"Until then." Sadiq left her there. The door swished shut behind him. Su sat still for a moment, then swiveled her chair toward her working wall. "Window function," she ordered, "show me political activity identified on main deck."

A patch of Colorado sky cleared away, replaced by the image of one of the observation towers. Normally, the side of the three story building was a blank, forbidding gun-metal gray. Today, however, someone had managed to hang a gigantic sheet screen from the side and light up a scene of Venus and Earth orbiting around each other in a display that was as pretty as it was inaccurate. A crowd had gathered at the foot of the tower to watch the show. In front of the casual observers, a set of feeders with briefcases and camera bands had already jacked into the deck and were rapidly dropping the entire experience into the stream.

Venus and Earth faded, replaced by a man of moderate coloring and moderate age, wearing a suit so conservative he might have bought it in the previous century.

"And what are we doing with this wonder, this Discovery?" He swept one hand out. Venus appeared, neatly balanced in his palm. "We are using it as a focus of fear. We are using it to tighten the chains already on the wrists of our brothers and sisters in the colonies. Millions of people whose only crime is not living on Mother Earth." He closed his fist around the Venus globe. The low moan it gave was gratuitous, Su thought, but it did make its point. "We must, every one of us, ask what is our government so afraid of? Aging men and women who failed in their dream?" The starry background blurred and shifted until the speaker stood in a bare red-ceramic cell filled with people whose eyes were dark and haunted. "The guilty have been punished and punished again. Must we punish their children now?"

Before the speaker could answer his own question, the screen went black. A groan rose from the assembled crowd. Three people in coveralls of U.N. blue appeared on the observation tower's roof and started rolling up the screen. Still grumbling, the crowd began to disperse. Show's over.

"Window function off."

The screen melted back into the meadow scene around her.

Su considered. That wasn't much as demonstrations went, but it would give her an opening to talk with Edmund. Su rubbed her forehead. Her mind had been shying away from the memory of how she'd left the morning's interview. What had happened? What had snapped? There was no excuse, none, especially now, as she'd said to Sadiq. If she didn't find a way to clean up after herself, it would be . . . bad.

"Desk. Contact Edmund Waicek." *Compose yourself, Su. Don't let the boy get to you. There is too much going on for that.* "Put display on main screen."

The whole wall cleared until Su saw Edmund's clean, blank-walled office. Edmund himself was hunched over his desk screen. He did not look up.

"I'm rather busy, Su. We do have a meeting this afternoon."

"Yes, I am aware of that." *Calm, calm, calm.* "Were you

aware that we've just had a separatist demonstration on the main deck?"

Edmund's head jerked up. "What?"

Su waved her hands in a gesture both dismissing and soothing. "It was small. Sadiq's people have already handled it." She lowered her hands. "But it did draw a crowd. Here. People were listening. The speaker was making sense to them."

Edmund's face went cold. Su held up her hand again before he could even open his mouth. "It does matter. This is U.N. City, and our people were listening to the idea that perhaps the restrictions on the colonies have gone too far." She spread her hands. "There is more than one kind of bias we need to avoid here, Edmund. If it appears that we are sending up a team that has an anticolonial agenda, we run the risk that their conclusions will be discounted by popular opinion. We have both been around the world far too many times to pretend that doesn't matter."

She watched Edmund's expression waver as that thought sank in. "We cannot be seen to encourage irresponsible rhetoric," he said, resorting to some rhetoric of his own.

Good. He's running short on arguments. "Of course not. We must be seen to be aiming for a strict neutrality. That is where people like Veronica Hatch can benefit us. People appreciate that she put a human face on a terrible tragedy. On both sides of the tragedy."

Edmund did not like that idea. She could tell that much by the stony set of his jaw, but he was at least thinking about it. "If we're taking her and the other one"—he glanced at his desk—"Peachman, I want security on the team."

"My thinking exactly," lied Su. "Sadiq can pick the best available, and we can submit their names to the Sec-Gen along with the others."

"All right," said Edmund. "You've got your team, Su. But it had better not overstep its bounds."

"It won't, Edmund. I'll see you this afternoon."

Edmund nodded and broke the connection. Su collapsed back into her chair. *That was a near thing.* If Edmund had been just a little more angry, it would not have worked. But it did, and that was all she needed to care about at this moment.

Still, there was one more call she should make.

"Desk. Contact Yan Quai."

This time, the sky was replaced by a static scene of a white railed veranda overlooking a misty cityscape.

"I'm sorry," said a gender-neutral voice. "Yan Quai is unavailable—"

"Quai, it's your mother."

The voice hesitated. Then, the veranda cleared away and revealed Quai's apartment, which hadn't been cleaned up in a while. Clothes and towels were draped over the arms of chairs. Screen rolls lay heaped on every flat surface, held in place by empty cups and glasses full of something that might have once been either beer or apple juice.

In the middle of it all sat Quai at his battered desk. Su automatically looked him over. He hadn't shaved. His hair was now black and blond, and the holo-tat on the right side of his throat was a winking blue eye this week.

In short, her son looked just fine.

"Hello, Mother," he said cheerfully. "Slow day in the corridors of power?"

"Not particularly." Her lips twitched, trying not to smile. "As you've said, saving the worlds is a full-time job."

Quai's own smile was tight and knowing and made him look frighteningly like his father. "Especially when you have to kiss up to the C.A.C. to do it."

Su let that pass. "We've just had a little demo on the decks here, Quai."

"Really?" His face and voice brightened considerably. "Who managed it?"

"I don't know. I thought you might."

Quai shook his head, and Su believed him. If he had known, he would have just evaded the question. They did not agree, she and her son. He felt she did not go far enough in her politics, and she felt that by attempting to undermine the system, he was worsening the condition of those he was supposed to be fighting for. Despite that, they had a tacit agreement that each would avoid lying to the other, if at all possible.

"Well, just in case anyone in your acquaintance gets ideas—"

"Us?" Quai laid a hand on his breast. "We operate strictly within the law wherever we are, Mom; you know that."

"I don't for sure know any different," responded Su blandly. "But just in case, you might pass along the word that the C.A.C. is very edgy right now and that that edginess is getting communicated up the legislature. The more unrest there is right at this moment, the bigger the potential backlash."

They looked at each other, each of them replaying conversations from both the distant and the not-so-distant past in their heads.

"All right, Mom." Quai nodded. "Not that anybody I deal with would arrange illegal public demos in U.N. City or anywhere else, but I'll see if I can leak the generalities of this conversation where they'll do some good."

"That's all I ask." Su bowed her head briefly in a gesture of thanks.

A flicker of worry crossed Quai's face. "Take care of yourself out there, Mom. Okay? I'd hate to see you lose your footing."

Su smiled. "I will take care. I love you, my son."

"Love you, Mom. Good-bye."

Su said good-bye and shut down the screen. She shook her head and sighed. Quai was good people. How had that happened? Abandoned by a nervous father, left with an obsessive mother, he still managed to make his own way. He went overboard, it was true, but not as badly as some, and at least he really believed in what he did.

So do you, she reminded herself. *At least, you'd better, or all your work's going to fall apart and Helen's going to be left out there on her own.*

That thought stiffened Su's shoulders. No, she would not permit that. She bent over her desk screen and laid her hands on the command board. Time to get back to work.

CHAPTER FOUR

T'sha's kite furled its bright-blue wings as it approached the High Law Meet. Unlike other cities, the High Law Meet's ligaments ran all the way down to the crust, tethering the complex in place. The symbolism was plain. All the winds, all the world, met here.

"Good luck, Ambassador T'sha," the Law Meet hailed her through her headset. "You are much anticipated."

"Is it a pleased anticipation or otherwise?" asked T'sha wryly as the Law Meet took over her kite guidance, bringing it smoothly toward the empty mooring clamps.

"That is not for me to know or tell," said the Meet primly. Amusement swelled through T'sha.

T'sha had always found the Meet beautiful. Its shell walls were delicately curved, and their colors blended from a pure white to rich purple. Portraits and stories had been painted all across their surfaces in both hot and cold paints. When the Law Meet was in dayside, the hot paints glowed red. On nightside, the cold paints made dark etchings against the shining walls. The coral struts were whorled and carved so that the winds sang as they blew past. More shell and dyed stiff skins funneled and gentled the winds through the corridors between the chambers. The interior chambers themselves were bubbles of still air where anyone could move freely without being guided or prodded by the world outside.

T'sha sometimes wondered if this was a good idea.

As ever, the High Law Meet was alive with swarms of people. The air around it tasted heavy with life and constant move-

ment. T'sha counted nine separate villages floating past the
Meet with their sails furled so the citizens who flew beside
their homes could keep up easily. All the noise, all the activity
of daily life blew past with them.

Below, the canopy was being tended by the Meet's own conservators. It was symbolically important, said many senior ambassadors, that the canopy around the High Law Meet remain
vital, solid, and productive. But as T'sha watched, a quartet of
reapers from one of the villages, identifiable by the straining
nets they carried between them, as well as by the zigzagging
tattoos on their wings, descended to the canopy. A conservator
flew at them, sending them all winging away, back to their village with empty nets, no food, seeds, or clippings to enhance
their diet, their gardens, or their engineers' inventories.

T'sha felt her bones loosen with weariness. *It must be kept
productive. Certainly. But if not for our families, then for what?*

T'sha inflated, trying to let her mood roll off her skin. There
was important work to be done, and she had to be tightly focused. Her kite dropped its tethers toward the Law Meet's mooring clamps. T'sha leaned back on her posthands so she could
collect her belongings: an offering for the temple, the congratulatory banner for Ambassador Pr'sef's latest wedding, and the
bulging satchel of promissory agreements which she had negotiated in return for the votes she needed. She had promised
away a great deal of work from her city and her families for this
vote. She had to keep telling herself that they all gave freely and
that she was doing this for the entirety of the people, not just for
herself. This was necessary. It was not greed.

The clamps took hold of the tethers and reeled the kite in to
a resting height. T'sha launched herself into the wind, her
parcels dangling from three of her hands.

A temple surmounted the High Law Meet. It was a maze of
ligaments and colored skins, covered in a complex blanket of
life. In the corners and catches, puffs, birds, flies, algae bubbles, smoke growers, and a hundred other plants and animals
collected. Funguses and danglers grew from the walls and fed
the creatures who lived there, until the winds that blew them
in blew them away again.

As she let those winds carry her toward the temple's center, T'sha tried to relax and immerse herself in the messages of life present in every plant, every insect and bird. She had only marginal success. There was too much waiting on the vote in the Meet below to allow her to give in to her meditations.

The temple's center was ablaze with tapestries, each illustrating a history, parable, or lesson. Congregants were supposed to let the random winds blow them toward a tapestry and consider its moral. This time, however, T'sha steered herself toward a small tapestry that fluttered alone in a deep curve of the wall. It was ancient, woven entirely from colored fibers taken from the canopy. It depicted a lone male, his hands bony, his skin sagging, and his muzzle open in muttered speech. His rose and violet crest draped flat against his back as if he lacked the strength to raise it. All around him stretched the crust, naked to the sky.

As T'sha drank in the tapestry's details, a teacher drifted to her side. "Tell me this story," he said.

The words spread the warmth of familiarity through T'sha. Her youth had seemed dominated by those words. Her birth mother, Pa'and, had brought T'sha teacher after teacher, each more taxing than the last. Whether the lesson was maths, sciences, history, or even the geographies of the wind currents, they all seemed to start their quizzing by saying "Tell me this story."

"Ca'doth was the first of the Teacher-Kings," began T'sha, keeping her attention fixed on the tapestry, as was proper. "Contemplate the object and its lesson. This is the way to learn." Which of the parade of teachers had first told her that? "He led twenty cities in the Equatorial Calms. But he wanted to harvest eight canopy islands that were also claimed by D'anai, who was Teacher-King for the Southern Roughs. A feud began. Each king made great promises to their neighbors to join their cause. Arguments and debates lasted years. Ca'doth, who was the greatest speaker ever known, persuaded the winds and the clouds and even the birds to help him." T'sha's imagination showed her Ca'doth, strong and healthy, spreading his wings to the listening clouds.

"What he wanted most was that the living highlands should

stop feeding his enemies," she went on, falling into the rhythm of her recitation. The teacher hovered close beside her, encouraging her with his silence. "But no matter how long he flew around the highlands, they made no response to his great speeches." The smallest of the monocellulars originated in the living highlands, which expelled them into the air to be the seeds for all other life in the world.

"At last, he realized he would have to fly inside the highland to make it hear him. He dived straight down the throat of the living highland, beating his wings against winds of solid lava. He passed through a chamber where the walls were pale skin, a chamber of white bone, a chamber of silver plasma, and a chamber tangled with muscle and nerve. In each he heard a riddle to which he did not know the answer." For a moment, she thought the teacher would ask her the riddles, but he did not, and she kept going. "Finally, Ca'doth came to a chamber where the air around him shimmered golden with the pure essence of life, and he knew he floated within the soul of the living highland.

"'Why do you feed my enemies?' he cried. 'They steal what I need to live. I have promised away all my present that I may gain a future for my children, and yet you feed those who would destroy them. Why?'

"The soul of the highland answered him, 'Life cannot choose who it helps. If your enemy came to me first, should I starve you instead?'

"But Ca'doth did not listen. He argued and pleaded and threatened, until the highland said 'Very well, I will not feed your enemy.'

"Pleased, Ca'doth passed through the chambers, and there he heard the answers to all the riddles but could not tell which answer fitted which riddle. He emerged into the clear and returned to tell his family the highland would no longer feed their rivals.

"But when he reached his birth city, the city and all within were dead, starved.

"The highland would not feed the rivals, but the highland would no longer feed Ca'doth's people either. Ca'doth turned from his rule and his other cities and drifted on the winds for the rest of his life, trying to fit the answers to the riddles."

The teacher dipped his muzzle approvingly. "And what is the meaning of this story?"

"All life is linked," answered T'sha promptly. "If that is forgotten, all life will die." *Even the flies,* she sighed inwardly. *Even the fungus. Even I and D'seun.*

T'sha deflated before the teacher and flew respectfully underneath him. She slipped around the side of the temple to the gifting nets and deposited her offering—a pouch of seeds and epiphytes that her own family had recently spread in the canopy. They were having great success in healing a breech in the growth. Hopefully, the temple's conservators could make use of them as well.

As she sealed the gifting net up and turned, she found herself muzzle-to-muzzle with Z'eth, one of the most senior ambassadors to the Meet. T'sha pulled back reflexively, fanning her wings to get some distance.

"Good luck, Ambassador T'sha," said Z'eth, laughing a little at how startled her junior colleague was. Z'eth was big and round. Even when she had contracted herself, she was a presence that filled rooms and demanded attention. She had only three tattoos on her pale skin—her family's formal name, the rolling winds, indicating she was a student of life, and the ambassador's flock of birds on her muzzle. Despite her sparse personal decoration, there was something extravagant about Z'eth. Perhaps that was only because there was no promise so rare or exotic she would not make it if it benefited her city. T'sha could not blame her for that. The city K'est had sickened when T'sha was still a child, and Z'eth's whole existence had become dedicated to keeping her city alive.

"Good luck, Ambassador Z'eth," said T'sha. "I was on my way to your offices from here."

"No doubt to speak of things it is not appropriate to discuss in temple." Z'eth dipped her muzzle. "Shall we leave so we may converse freely?"

"Thank you, Ambassador."

Z'eth and T'sha let themselves be blown through the temple corridors and out into the open air.

As soon as they were a decent distance from the temple's walls, T'sha said, "I have the promissory for you regarding the imprinting service for the cortices grown in your facilities."

"Excellent." Z'eth tilted her wings and deflated so she descended smoothly alongside the High Law Meet. It was a delicate path, as the winds between the walls were strong and unpredictable. T'sha followed but had to flap clumsily to keep herself from being brushed against the painted-shell wall.

"I have not envied you these past hours, Ambassador." Z'eth whistled sympathetically. "It is hard during your first term, especially if your first term is a historic one." One of the arched corridor mouths opened behind them, but Z'eth wheeled around, dipping under the corridor instead of entering it. T'sha followed her into the shallow, irregular tunnel underneath the real corridor, a little surprised.

Z'eth drifted close, her wings spread wide. Her words brushed across T'sha's muzzle. "You needn't worry about the vote. Your quiet promises and the work Ca'aed has done with Gaith have been most impressive. I have spoken where I can. Between us all we have turned the flow. You'll have your appointment."

T'sha nearly deflated with relief. At the same time she was conscious of Z'eth's steady gaze on her. Despite the promises she had already made, she still owed the senior ambassador, and it was a debt that would need to be paid before long.

T'sha resolved not to worry about that now. "Thank you again, Ambassador Z'eth."

"You are welcome. I will see you in the voting chamber." Z'eth lifted herself to the corridor mouth and disappeared inside.

T'sha floated where she was for a moment, remaining in place more because she was in a calm than from actual effort.

They had towed Gaith's corpse encased in its quarantine blanket into Ca'aed's wake. The rotting had so deformed it that it looked less like a city than an engineer's experiment gone hideously wrong. Its people worked on it diligently, sampling and analyzing and salvaging, but it would have taken a thicker skin than T'sha's not to feel the despair in them. It had taken Gaith a handful of hours to die. Who knew which village, which city, might be next?

And here was T'sha, doing her best to keep them all from what looked like the nearest safe course. She had quizzed the team supervisors from the other candidate worlds extensively. The seeds had not taken hold on any other of the ten worlds. Only Number Seven could readily support life.

But life might already have a claim on Number Seven. In spite of all, T'sha could not let that fact blow past. She had to see for herself that D'seun's team was not ignoring a legitimate claim on the part of the New People. Now, according to Z'eth, she was going to get her chance.

Is this right, what I do? Life of my mother and life of my father, it has to be, because it is too late for me to do otherwise.

She shut her doubts off behind calculations about how many promises she could deliver before she was called to hear the vote. She lifted herself to the corridor mouth and joined the swarm of ambassadors and assistants propelling themselves deep into the Meet.

In the end, she was able to deliver four of the eight notes, staying long enough to give and accept polite thanks with each ambassador and discuss general pleasantries and the work being done on Gaith. She had to use her headset to leave message for the rest. The Law Meet was calling them all to hear the results of the latest poll.

When T'sha arrived, the spherical voting chamber already brimmed with her colleagues. There were no perches left. She would have to float in the stillness and try to keep from bumping rudely into anyone else.

"Good luck, T'sha," murmured tiny, tight Ambassador Br've as she drifted above him.

"Good luck," added Ambassador T'fron, whose bird tattoos were still fresh on his skin.

Their wishes warmed her, but not as much as the security of Z'eth's promise.

T'sha found a clear spot in which to hover near the ceiling. Because the High Law Meet was currently on the dayside, the family trees, which were written in hot paints, glowed brightly against the white and purple walls. Each showed the connections and the promises of connection between the First Thousand. T'sha scanned the trees for her family's names and found them, unchanging and immutable. She was their daughter. Her ancestors had birthed cities. She would save them, but not at the cost of their people's souls.

She looked down between the crests and tattooed wings and spotted D'seun's distinctive and overmarked back. He was practically touching the polling box. T'sha wondered whom he had made promises to and if he had anyone as powerful as Z'eth sponsoring his cause. If he'd managed to bring in H'tair or Sh'vaid on his side, the vote might not be as set as Z'eth believed. The mood of the meeting tightened rapidly around her. The announcement would come soon. Her bones shifted. Soon. Soon.

The polling box had been grown in the image of a person without wings or eyes. Its neural net ran straight into the floor of the voting chamber and was watched over by the High Law Meet itself. It would not be moved, and it looked with favor on no one. It was solid and impartial.

The box lifted its muzzle and spoke in a voice that rippled strongly through the chamber.

"The poll has been taken, recognized, and counted. Does any ambassador wish to register doubt as to the validity of the count contained in this box?"

No one spoke. T'sha tried to breathe evenly and hold her bones still.

"No doubt has been registered," said the box. "A poll has been taken of the ambassadors to the High Law Meet on the following questions. First, should candidate world Seven be designated New Home? If this is decided positively, the second question is, should the current investigative team whose names are listed in the record continue under the leadership of Ambassador D'seun Te'eff Kan K'edch D'ai Gathad to establish the life base necessary for the growth of a canopy and the establishment of life ways for the People, with such expansion and promises as this project shall require?"

T'sha's wings rippled. Her skin felt alert, open to every sensation from the brush of her own crest to the gentle waft of a whisper on the other side of the chamber.

"Is there any ambassador within the touch of these words who has not been polled on these questions?" asked the box. Silence, waiting, and tension strained her bones as if they were mooring ligaments in a high wind.

"No ambassador indicates not having been polled," said the box. "Then, the consensus of the High Law Meet is as follows. On the first question, the consensus is yes, candidate world Seven is New Home."

The rumble and ripple of hundreds of voices filled the chamber. T'sha remained still and silent. That was never the real question. The vote had to be yes. D'seun was right about that much. His peremptory poll of Ca'aed had confirmed that all the families agreed with the choice.

"On the second question," the box went on, "the consensus is that Ambassador D'seun Te'eff Kan K'edch D'ai Gathad shall continue as the leader of the investigative team, that the current team will continue in the task of creating a life base with such expansions as are required for that task, provided that one of those expansions shall be the addition of Ambassador T'sha So Br'ei Taith Kan Ca'aed for the purpose of observing and studying the life currently named the New People. She shall ensure that these New People have no legitimate claim to New Home world that might counteract the validity of the consensus on the first question."

There it was. She could now go to New Home herself and make sure the New People had no legitimate claim on the world. T'sha's relief was so complete, she almost didn't feel the congratulations erupting around her. When she was able to focus outward, she found herself in a storm of good-luck wishes and a hundred questions. She answered all she could, as fast as she could, while mentally cataloging the messages and calls she'd have to make as soon as the chamber opened again.

It might have been a moment or a lifetime later when D'seun rose to meet her.

"An interesting addendum, Ambassador T'sha," he said flatly

and coolly. "You have been working toward this for some time, I take it."

T'sha met D'seun's gaze and spoke her words straight to him. "Surely, you could not have been unaware of what I was doing. I was hardly secretive."

D'seun's bones contracted under his tattoos, and T'sha felt a swirl of exasperation. She shrank herself a little to match him. "D'seun, there is no reason for us to be enemies on this. We both want the same thing. We both want to make New Home a reality. If that is to happen, we cannot discount the New People."

"We cannot let their presence override everything we must do, either." He thrust his muzzle forward. "You question and delay, you counter and debate everything! Every time we try to warn people what happened to Gaith, there you are, assuring us all that it isn't so very bad, that we must just wait until its disease is understood, that we have the resources to understand." His words tumbled harshly over her. "There is no more time. There is no way to understand. We must leave."

T'sha deliberately deflated and sank, resisting the urge to fly right under him to make her point. "I am only one voice, D'seun. All the rest of the Senior Committee for New Home are your supporters. There will be very little I can do."

D'seun dropped himself so he could look into her eyes. "Do not flutter helplessness at me, T'sha. What 'little' you can do, you will do."

"Is there some promise you would give my families to have me do otherwise, D'seun?" asked T'sha bluntly. "How much will you give for me to disregard our new neighbors? Is there enough to make that right?"

D'seun did not answer.

"No, there is not," said T'sha. "We are together in this, D'seun, until the task is over."

"Until the task is over," D'seun said softly. "Until then."

D'seun rose from the world portal into the candidate world, now New Home. Its clean winds brushed the transfer's disorientation off him. A quick turn about showed him P'tesk and

T'oth waiting on the downwind side of the portal's ring. D'seun flew quickly toward them.

"Good luck, Ambassador D'seun." P'tesk raised his hands. "Is there news?"

D'seun touched his engineers' hands. "Engineer P'tesk, Engineer T'oth. There is news, but not all of it is good. Let us return to the test base, and then I can tell our people all at once."

As often as he had done it, it was strange to D'seun to fly over the naked crust without even a scrap of canopy to cover it. He could barely taste the life base they had seeded the winds with. He imagined sometimes that this was not a newly emerging world, but a prophecy as to what Home might become—lifeless stone and ash sculpted by sterile winds.

So it will be if T'sha has her way.

Their base was little more than a few shells tethered together with half a dozen infant cortex boxes to nurture the necessary functions. Not comfortable or companionable, but it served its function, as they all did.

"Team Seven," D'seun called through his headset, "this is Ambassador D'seun. We are gathering in the analysis chamber. I have word of the latest vote from the High Law Meet."

Like the rest of the base, the analysis chamber was strictly functional. The undecorated walls showed the shell's natural pearl and purple colors. Separate caretaker units, all holding their specialized cortex boxes, had been grown into the shell. That and a few perches were all there was to the room.

D'seun, T'oth, and P'tesk arrived to find T'stad and Kr'ath already waiting for them. They all wished each other luck as the others filtered in. D'seun's gaze swept the assembly—his assembly, his team who had worked so hard to prove the worth of their world. He laid claim to them all, and if that was greedy of him, so be it. After so much work and so many promises, he had earned the right to be a little greedy.

"Where is Engineer Br'sei?" D'seun asked.

The others glanced around the chamber, as if just now noticing Br'sei was gone.

"Engineer Br'sei?" he asked his headset.

After a brief pause, Engineer Br'sei's voice came back. "I'm at Living Highland 45, Ambassador. I'll listen in over the headset. I have to check the stability of the base seeding here. I think we may be running into some trouble from the high salt content of these lavas."

"Then listen closely." D'seun raised his voice to speak to the entire assembly. "The ambassadors to the High Law Meet have voted. This world, our world, is declared New Home!"

All around him, voices trilled high, fluting notes of jubilation. D'seun let them enjoy. They had all worked so hard. Thousands of dodec-hours of observation and analysis. Millions of adjustments in proportion and organization on the most basic levels. Sometimes it felt as though each molecule had been hand reared. But they had made their promise to the whole of the People, and they had kept it. Life could be made to thrive here in these alien winds.

"That is not all the news, however," D'seun said, cutting through their celebration. He waited until the last echoes of their chaotic song died away. "Something new has happened on Home."

All their attention was on him, and he told them about Gaith. For the first time there was no danger of interference from T'sha, and he could tell what had really happened. An entire village had died an indescribable death in such pain as life should never know. It had happened in a few hours. A life the villagers thought they knew, a life they had grown and cherished for thousands of years, had gone insane. Insane as it was, it would turn on other life until nothing was left but a mantle of death surrounding the entire world.

When he was finished, not one of them remained their normal size. They all huddled close to their perches and close to each other, small and tight, as if they could draw their skin in far enough to shut his words out.

"I know the dangers of haste," he said at last. "I was taught, as you all were, that haste is equal to greed as a bringer of death. But this time, to be cautious is to die. This new rot will not wait for us to make our careful plans."

Soft whistles of agreement filled the room. D'seun let himself swell, just a tiny bit. "There are those who do not understand this, however. There are those among the ambassadors who insist that we wait. For what? I ask. Until our cities all fall? No, they reply. Until we are sure of the New People."

Silence. The New People. No one liked the mention of them. The New People might be poison, and everyone here felt that in every pore.

Time to remove that poison. "We are all concerned about the New People. We have watched them as closely as we are able. You have labored with great care to understand their transmissions to each other and their commands to their tools. You have spoken to me in a straightforward fashion, as dedicated engineers should, about the fragility of life and the resources of community and the claim of life upon its own home. But I must ask you other questions now."

D'seun focused his attention completely on P'tesk. "P'tesk, have we found any new life here? Any life we did not ourselves spread?"

"No, Ambassador," said P'tesk. "Except for our life base, the winds are clean. The living highlands do not really measure up to that name—none of the ones we've observed anyway."

"T'vosh." D'seun switched his focus to the youngest engineer. "Have we seen signs of mining or sifting for the hard elements?"

"No, Ambassador," T'vosh answered quickly. "And among the transmissions, we have heard no plans for such."

"No plans that we understand."

The last was spoken by Tr'es. D'seun did not let himself swell in frustration. It was a good point. Besides, Tr'es's birth city was Ca'aed, as was T'sha's. She would have to be handled carefully in the time to come.

"None that we understand, yes." D'seun dipped his muzzle. "Our understanding is far from perfect. Our ability to separate image and message and tool command is not complete, although we have made great strides. The New People may be making plans for legitimate use of this world." His gaze swept the assembly. "But they have not done it yet. When has a mere plan, an unfulfilled intent, ever been grounds to withhold a resource?" He let them think about that for a minute. "Most importantly"— he spread his wings wide—"nothing has prevented them from detecting the life base. Nothing has prevented them from finding us. They have made no move to challenge our claims or to contact us as one family contacts another when there is a dispute over resources." *Let those words sink through their pores; let their minds turn that over.* "There is nothing, nothing, in the laws of life and balance which prevents us from moving forward and laying legitimate claim to this empty, pure world."

Whistles of agreement, notes of encouragement bathed D'seun. This would work. He had them convinced. "Despite this, for reasons of her own, the ambassador of Ca'aed"—he glanced at Tr'es—"is doing all she can to delay the transformation of this world, and she is citing the presence of the New People as her reason."

Tr'es was not intimidated, not yet. "How could she do otherwise?" Tr'es asked. "They are here. Ambassador T'sha is both cautious and pious."

"Ambassador T'sha has acquired the body of Gaith Village for the people of Ca'aed," replied D'seun. "She has indentured all Gaith's engineers to the resurrection of the village. She hopes to exact many promises for herself and her city, even while the new rot spreads on the winds."

Silence, deep and shocked, filled the chamber, broken only by the slight rustling as the engineers inflated and deflated uneasily.

"Surely there is a misunderstanding," stammered Tr'es. "This cannot be the stated goal."

"It is not the stated goal," said D'seun softly. "But I fear it is the true goal. I grieve with you and your city, Engineer Tr'es, but power has turned many a soul sour. This is why the teachers warn us so stringently against greed. Through greed we turn the very needs of life against each other."

Tr'es covered her eyes with her wing in confusion and denial. D'seun said nothing, just let the silence settle in ever more deeply. At last, Tr'es lifted her muzzle. "What are we to do?"

D'seun felt satisfaction form deep in his bones. "Ambassador T'sha is coming here herself to inspect the claims of the New People. We must make sure she is given no reason to doubt that this world is free for us to use." He focused his attention on each of his engineers in turn. "She must have no opportunity to question what we do here." He pulled his muzzle back and drew in his wings. "I will make no move without your agreement. You are not indentured, and I do not lead without consensus. We will take a poll now. Vote as your soul's understanding moves you. Let me hear from those in agreement."

One by one, his engineers whistled their assent. Even Tr'es whistled agreement, low but strong.

"I thank you," said D'seun softly. "Soon, all your families will have cause to thank you as well. We can move forward with our work now, without doubt or hindrance. Enjoy, my friends. Soon promises will be made in your names and on the backs of your skills."

More wordless songs of delight and triumph rang out. D'seun swelled to his fullest extent to take in every note and nuance. It was then he realized that his headset had remained silent. Br'sei had not added his vote.

Sudden suspicion flowed into him. "To work, to work, my colleagues, my friends. We do not have time to waste!"

His happy words sent them all scattering to their tasks. Not one of them commented as he flew out into the clear air to claim a kite. He too had work to do, and they were all aware of it.

Right now, his work was to find Engineer Br'sei.

Br'sei glided around the side of the living highland. His bones tightened nervously, barely allowing him the lift he needed to fly, even down here in the thick air near the crust.

You are being ridiculous. He forced himself to relax and gained a little height. *You have grown things that are a thousand times more terrifying than these New People.*

But nothing stranger.

In truth, he was here only because Ambassador D'seun demurred every single time Br'sei suggested they place close surveillance on the New People. D'seun worried about being seen, about the New People raising a peremptory challenge to their presence if they were seen. The ambassador seemed completely disinterested in the New People's explorations of the crust. Even now, when their activities had increased so markedly.

If the New People had a legitimate claim on this world, it could be disastrous, but it must be known. Br'sei listened to D'seun's stirring words through his headset and heard the enthusiastic agreement of his colleagues. Grim silence settled within him. D'seun spoke, D'seun inspired, but D'seun did not know. Br'sei, on the other hand, had to know.

So Br'sei flitted around the highland, weaving in and out of its stony ripples to spy on the New People and see what could be seen.

Below him, Br'sei saw the flat, wing-shaped carriers that the New People used to take themselves from place to place. They had smooth hides and glistening windows and were unbelievably clumsy. However, they seemed to serve their purpose well enough. Grace may have been sacrificed for durability.

No New People walked the surface between the transports. Perhaps they were dormant now. Br'sei dipped a little closer, equal parts of fear and excitement swelling his body.

Then, he saw movement on the ground. Two lumps of what he had first taken for crust moved toward the transports. From their shadow rose what looked like one of the People's own constructors.

Br'sei backwinged, holding his position and watching. The constructor and its accompanying tools glided between the transports as if sniffing at their sides, seeking what? He spoke to his headset, but it could pick up nothing from them, no exchange, no projection, nothing but silence.

At last, the tools retreated to a deep crevice in the highland wall. Br'sei dived after them, bunching himself up tightly to fit between the stone walls where they hid.

The tools made no move as he came within their perceptual range. Now he could see that the one was indeed a constructor. It had the umbrella, the deeply grooved cortex and the manipulator arms. The other two had only eyes and locomotors. Overseers? Recorders maybe?

"What is your purpose?" asked Br'sei in the most common command language.

No reply. Br'sei repeated the question in four of the other command languages he knew, also with no result.

Frustration tightened Br'sei's bones. "Who made your purpose? Engineer D'han? Engineer T'oth?" Neither name elicited any reaction. The tools stayed as they were, unmoving, unresponsive. Br'sei's crest ruffled. A tool should at least respond to its user's name. "Engineer P'tesk? Engineer—"

"Ambassador D'seun."

Startled, Br'sei's wings flapped on their own, lifting him and turning him. Ambassador D'seun flew over a ridge in the highland's wall and deflated until he was level with Br'sei and the tools.

"Good luck, Br'sei," said D'seun amiably. He spoke to the tools in a command language that Br'sei couldn't even recognize the roots of. The constructor touched the ambassador's headset. Br'sei realized with a start that he must be using a chemical link, something Br'sei hadn't seen in years.

"I would ask you what you're doing here, Br'sei," said the ambassador, "especially as this is Highland 76, not 45. But I imagine you feel you have the right to ask me that question first."

"I don't wish to presume, Ambassador." Br'sei sank diffidently. "But yes, I do wish to ask that question."

The constructor drifted away from Ambassador D'seun, who spoke another few words of his convoluted command language. The constructor headed back to the crevices of the highland with the two overseers crawling after it.

D'seun watched them go until the tools could no longer be told apart from the crust. "At the moment, the tools are monitoring the patterned radio wave transmissions between the New People and their transports, as well as their transports and their base." He swelled, just a little. "We need to refine our translation techniques. It still takes even our most adept engineers four or five dodec-hours to achieve what we think is an approximate translation of any given message."

Br'sei stared at the ambassador, framed there by the living highland. "It is difficult to accomplish such a work from a distance." He fought to keep his voice mild. "But you have said repeatedly that you do not want any tools within a mile of the New People, wherever they are."

Ambassador D'seun deflated slowly, as if he were too tired

to keep his size and shape anymore. "I have wrestled with a great dilemma since we originally dropped the wind seeds onto this world, Br'sei. Now, you have the dubious honor of sharing it with me." He turned to face Br'sei. "But perhaps we should speak somewhere more comfortable?"

"If you wish, Ambassador." *Patience,* he told himself as his bones twitched. *The only way you're going to get your answers is by waiting him out.*

Br'sei had been helping to design the seeds for the candidate worlds when he first met D'seun. Br'sei was young for an adult, having been fully declared in his eightieth year.

Back then, there were still debates raging over what the nature of the seeding should be. Should it be a wide variety of organisms, both useful and strictly supportive, to make sure the candidate world would accept a range of life? Or should it be a single organism so that when it did begin to spread, there would be fewer interactions to calculate when the overlaying began?

Br'sei had been of the opinion that broad-seeding was the correct method, and his experiment house was working with two dozen different microcosms to show the differences in effect between broad-seeding and mono-seeding.

Then D'seun had flown up to the door without sending advance notice and asked for a tour and an appointment with Br'sei. Because D'seun was a speaker then, he got both.

The experiment house was an old, wise workplace with heavy screens and thick filters to keep its interior air absolutely sterile. Its cortices were complex and well grown, each able to monitor its crystalline microcosms for hours without supervision or correction, leaving the engineers free to work on projection and innovation.

Br'sei led D'seun from cosmos to cosmos, showing him the hardiness of the broad-seeding in the miniature ecosystems as opposed to the flimsy strains of mono-seeded cultures.

"The broad-seeding provides its own support system, you see, Speaker," said Br'sei as they paused to study yet another microcosm. The sphere's lensing sides allowed them to see through to the microscopic organisms thriving in the simulated cloud.

"Yes." D'seun pointed his muzzle at Br'sei. "But that is not truly the point, is it?"

Br'sei remembered how his crest had spread at those words. "Forgive me, Speaker, but that is the entire point."

"Forgive me, Engineer, but it is not," D'seun replied. "The point of the initial seeding is not to establish life, but merely to establish that life is a possibility. First we establish that life can exist on a world; then we survey that world carefully, understanding it thoroughly in its pure, prelife state. Then, and only then, can we start laying out the basis for a new canopy, one we design and supervise in its entirety." He turned his gaze back to the microcosm, deflating a little as he did. "We have acted too often without understanding. We must not do that with our new world. I fear we will have only one chance to make this plan of ours work."

Br'sei had felt himself swelling at that point, ready to argue, but the speaker's words flew ahead of his. "What I see here convinces me that you and yours have a tremendous understanding of how life can be built and layered. Your life-base designs are strong and rich." D'seun whistled, pleased. "I would like to talk to you about providing members for the initial teams, as well as engineers and designers for when New Home is found."

The implication that brushed against Br'sei was that this discussion would take place only if Br'sei agreed to the idea of a mono-seeding. The speaker did make several excellent points, and the idea of Br'sei and his own team working on the foundations of New Home was a powerful lure.

"I think I could be convinced, Speaker," Br'sei admitted, fanning his wings gently to keep himself close to D'seun. "Let me bring some of my engineers, and let us discuss this. Some new microcosms may need to be designed."

"Thank you, Engineer Br'sei," said D'seun, and the words sank deeply into Br'sei's skin. "Bring your people. Let us think about what we may do together."

In the end, with Br'sei's help, D'seun had triumphed. As a result, Br'sei and his team, which he picked out with D'seun's help, were given the most promising world to seed with a mono-culture of their own design.

It had worked and here they were, with D'seun as ambassador and Br'sei as collaborator.

Br'sei's wings faltered slightly as that thought filtered through him.

"I have been thinking, Engineer Br'sei." D'seun banked into an updraft. The warm air from the highland with its delicate taste of life lifted him high. "We say 'Life spreads life' all the time, but we do not ever hold still long enough to think what that should really mean."

"Should mean?" Br'sei's crest ruffled and spread flat, helping him keep an even path in the turbulent wind from the highlands. Pockets of heat and cold bumped against him, making him have to work to keep his position steady relative to the ambassador. If he was not careful, he would be trapped by the same eloquent arguments D'seun had used on the youngsters. "Not 'does mean'?"

"On Home, I would have said 'does mean.'" The updraft spilled D'seun into the cooler air and he drifted down again until he was level with Br'sei. "But here we are dealing with new possibilities. Here we can say 'should mean.'"

Br'sei deflated just a little. The ambassador's words were like a storm wind. They could sweep you along to an unknown destination before you even realized you were in a current too strong for you to fight.

"And have you decided what 'Life spreads life' should mean, Ambassador?"

"Not yet." D'seun cupped his wings and hovered in place in a relative calm. "But I am wondering if it involves surrounding yourself with things that do not live."

"What?" The single word burst out of Br'sei before he could even think about what he said.

D'seun dipped his muzzle. "Their transports, their base, they do not live. They are metal and ceramic without any living component I can find, and I have looked carefully."

"But that's . . ." Br'sei searched for a strong enough word and found nothing. He gathered his thoughts again. "They are other.

Their life is different from ours," he said, trying to give his words weight, but all the time he was thinking, *Their home does not live? How can it care for them? How can they care for it?*

D'seun glided close to him. "The question is, are they life we can live with?"

Br'sei deflated reflexively as the last sentence touched his muzzle. "Do you think they are insane, Ambassador?" Insanity was the gravest accusation that could be made against another being, worse than greed, worse than jealousy. Insanity meant they would ravage the life around them and that they would have to be stopped before they could damage the larger balance.

D'seun's bones bunched tightly and he sank. "I don't know, Engineer. I do know they frighten me."

"Then why—"

D'seun's teeth clacked but his amusement was grim. "Then why did I fight so hard for this world? Because this is the world where our life can exist, Br'sei. The only one we have ever found where it can."

Their home does not live. Br'sei rolled his eyes upward, as if he thought to see the New People's base floating overhead, drawn by the thought. The New People had not been his study or concern. His time had been spent with the highlands, the clouds, and the wind seeds. Even so, someone in the team should have told him about this.

Unless an ambassador told them not to. . . . But that was too much even for Br'sei, and he did not struggle when his thoughts swerved back to the New People. *Do they isolate themselves from life, or do they just need to isolate their kind of life? How can we know?*

"I have worked hard to keep this knowledge quiet, Engineer Br'sei," said D'seun, as if he read Br'sei's thoughts. "There are those who would take the facts of how the New People live and create a panic to spread across all the winds of Home. Ambassador T'sha, to begin with."

Br'sei shook himself. "Do you have so little faith in your colleagues, Ambassador?" he asked, being deliberately blunt.

"No." D'seun swelled. "I have so much experience with them. T'sha is rich. She hands out promises as if they were

guesting gifts. She does not want this world for New Home because of the New People. I have managed to block her so far,
but what if she were able to cry insanity?" A single beat of his
wings brought him towering over Br'sei. "Would any of the
People be willing to run from insanity toward insanity?" Now
their muzzles touched and the ambassador's words sank deep
into Br'sei's skin. "How long does Home have left for us,
Br'sei? Twenty years? Forty? How long will it take before a new
world can support us in all our billions?"

"At least fifty years," admitted Br'sei.

"So, we have no time to waste in panic and argument."

"But—"

"But if the New People are insane, they must be treated as
such." D'seun let himself drift away. "If they are not, they must
be treated as such. Right now, we know only three things—
that they have no legitimate claim on this world, that we cannot decide on their sanity until we understand them better, and
that we cannot waste time looking for yet another candidate
world."

Br'sei's bones bunched together. He would have plummeted
had not the warm plumes from the highland cradled him. "I am
not so sure, Ambassador."

D'seun dipped his muzzle. "Of course not. These are not
small thoughts. This must all be digested and studied from all
angles. But tell me this: you do truly agree that action without
knowledge will lead to disaster?"

"It can," admitted Br'sei.

"And you do agree that we have no time to waste in the creation of New Home?"

Br'sei dipped his muzzle. "I have seen the cities rotting too,
Ambassador. I heard your tale of Gaith. I am aware our time is
short."

"Good." D'seun flew over him, letting his hands graze
against Br'sei's crest. "Then give me this much. Do not panic
Ambassador T'sha when she comes. Do not tell her how much
we know." He turned on a wingtip. "And help me understand
the New People. With knowledge, your doubts and mine will
all be resolved. We will not be fumbling and flapping in our

helplessness, as we must on Home, where the diseases and their progeny have flown too far ahead for us to ever understand, let alone overtake. Here, we must always know how to proceed."

We must always know how to proceed. Br'sei let D'seun's words echo inside him. He wanted to believe that was possible, but sometimes he doubted it. What he did know, however, was that D'seun had convinced himself of the rightness of his words, and a mere engineer would not change Ambassador D'seun's mind.

Ambassador T'sha, however, might be able to, and if she couldn't change D'seun's mind, she might be able to sway the Law Meet, which even D'seun could not ignore.

But Br'sei would have to steer a careful path. If D'seun did not think Br'sei was convinced, the ambassador would find a way to have him removed from the team. That was very much D'seun's way.

"I shall work with you, Ambassador." Br'sei inflated himself until his size was equal with D'seun's. "Together we will see what we can find."

I do not, however, promise you will like what I will do with what we find.

It was not until they had returned to the base and dispersed to their separate tasks that Br'sei realized D'seun had never answered one question about the tools near the New People.

Chapter Five

A fresh United Nations flag dominated the rear wall of the passenger clearing area. Its sky blue background made a stark contrast to the soft, shifting reds and golds that the walls had been set for. Ben was glad to see, however, that Helen had drawn the line at welcoming banners.

Ben stood beside Helen and Michael. The assorted Veneran department heads ranged past them in a ragged line. Beyond the hatch, they could hear the soft whirs and bumps of the docking corridor extending and clamping itself to the newly arrived shuttle.

"Here they come," announced Tori from the control booth.

"The intercom better be off in the corridor," muttered Helen.

"Tori knows what she's doing," Michael assured her, somewhat absently.

Ben said nothing. He was too busy dealing with his own emotions. Anger, irrational and completely out of proportion, seethed inside him. He feared that if he had to open his mouth, it would all come spilling out in an unstoppable red flood.

God, I knew it was going to be bad, but I didn't expect it to be this bad.

The last time he'd seen the U.N. come into a colony, he'd been in a holding cell, watching lines of neatly dressed judges and bureaucrats arrive with their armed escorts. There seemed to be hundreds of them, all there to deal with the "criminals" who had "broken the rule of law in Bradbury." He remembered the fear he'd felt, wondering what would happen to them all now, and the deep shame at that fear.

None of the people standing next to him now knew about that cell or that he had ever lived on Bradbury at all. He'd managed to disconnect his records from that past and that person. But he could not disconnect his memories, even if there were times he wanted to.

Like now.

The hatch cranked itself open. Ben's stomach clenched itself involuntarily. *Get over it! They're just tourists. They're going to be rumpled and gravity dizzy and slightly stupid, like any other crowd of Earthlings.*

Edmund Waicek, the man Ben considered to be the most dangerous member of the C.A.C., had cheerfully sent Venera's governing board a list of their invaders. Ben had to admit, Helen had worked her end quite well. It could have been a lot worse.

The first two down the ramp Ben recognized as Robert Stykos and Terry Wray, the media faces. Their job was to create the in-stream "news" presentations on the U.N. investigation of the Discovery. Both had been restructured to look exactly average, only more beautiful. They might have been brother and sister, with their coffee-and-cream skin, big brown eyes, and shoulder-length black hair (hers pinned under a bronze scarf, his pulled back into a ponytail under a red beaded cap). But where Stykos was tall and broad, Wray was petite, almost elfin. Both wore glittering camera bands on their foreheads and command bracelets on their wrists.

"Mr. Stykos, Ms. Wray." Helen, in full public relations mode, stepped forward and shook their hands. "Welcome to Venera Base. I'm Dr. Helen Failia. Allow me to introduce my associate, Dr. Bennet Godwin, who is our head of personnel and chief volcanologist. . . ."

So it began. Stykos and Wray both looked long and hard at him, making sure their cameras got a good image of him smiling and shaking their soft hands. Lindi Manzur, the architect, beamed up at him as if she'd never met anyone more fascinating, except maybe Troy Peachman (was that a real name?), the comparative culturalist (whatever that was), at whom she kept glancing fondly as he followed her down the line, shaking everybody's hands with a kind of firm enthusiasm that came with practice.

What have you two been doing for the past week and a half? he wondered snidely.

After them came Julia Lott, the archeologist, a sturdy fireplug of a woman with a square face and tired eyes. She was followed by Isaac Walters who looked so uncomfortable that Ben had to wonder if he'd ever left Mother Earth before.

Out of the corner of his eye, Ben saw Grace Meyer smile broadly and step forward from the line.

Oh, right, this is the biologist, he thought as he passed Walters down to Michael.

Next, a tall, pale woman in artistic black and white swept up the line. Veronica Hatch, here to look at the laser and pronounce judgment. In contrast to Walters, she seemed ready to parachute down to the ground and start digging in.

There was a pause then, just long enough for Ben's anger to start simmering again. There were only two people left to come.

Angela Cleary and Philip Bowerman emerged together from the docking corridor. She had sandy skin and sandy hair, which she wore short under her white scarf. He was darker, with wavy hair and tropical skin and eyes that took in the entire room at a glance. Both of them were tall, broad in the shoulders and narrow at the waist, people whose bulk came not from body-mod, but from work. They both wore the blue tunics with white collars that were the uniform of U.N. security assessors on official duty.

Ben's blood ran hot, then cold. It must have showed in his face. He knew Michael was looking at him, but he couldn't help it. He'd sat for hours in little windowless rooms with uniforms like these, being recorded and interrogated until he couldn't think straight, couldn't remember if he'd implicated his friends or not, couldn't decide whether his own lies still made sense. All he could do was feel his burning eyes, raw throat, and aching bladder.

What if they know me? What if they were there? The thought rose unbidden from the back of his brain.

"Pleased to meet you, Dr. Godwin," Cleary was saying. Ben focused on her, a little startled, but she just smiled politely.

Ben stuck his hand out and shook hers. It was strong and slightly calloused. He made himself look into her amber-colored eyes. He saw no hint of recognition there, and relief, as irrational and unlooked for as his anger and his fear, almost robbed him of his balance.

"Pleased to meet you, Ms. Cleary," he answered in as steady a voice as he could manage. *Too young,* he thought to himself. *Security has limits on how rejuvenated you can be, and they're both way too young to have been at Bradbury.*

That realization allowed him to greet Bowerman with something approaching equanimity.

Then, it was over. The yewners mingled with the department heads, making polite small talk about their voyage and the base. Helen flitted between the conversational groups, reminding everyone of the reception scheduled for that evening. Grace Meyer walked Isaac Walters a little way off from the general crowd and talked to him in low, urgent tones. Michael took charge of Cleary and Bowerman and was telling them about the provisions he'd made to get them access to base records regarding the Discovery. Stykos and Wray stood back and photographed it all.

Then, in groups of twos and threes, the yewners and their chaperones began to make their way to the elevator bundles. The crowd thinned, and Ben found he could breathe again.

The sound of footsteps echoing through the docking corridor turned Ben around again. Another person emerged. This one wore a tan tunic and trousers with blue ID patches, the standard uniform for crews on distance ships. It took Ben a moment to recognize him.

"Hello, Dr. Godwin."

Joshua Kenyon, one of Venera's atmospheric researchers, held out his hand. Well, no, he wasn't exactly Venera's. He'd never made the commitment to live on the base. He just came up every now and again to do his work on Rayleigh scattering in the upper atmosphere and then went back down to Mother

Earth to analyze and publish what he'd found. Because of that, Ben found himself unable to really like the man.

Kenyon was also not scheduled to be back for at least another six months.

"Hello, Dr. Kenyon." Ben shook his hand. "This is unexpected, especially in uniform."

Kenyon blushed a little. "I know. They weren't even going to let me back up. Special flight for U.N. VIPs only. But I knew a couple of guys on the crew, and they kind of smuggled me in." He gestured at his uniform. "Not to spec, I know, but when I heard about the Discovery, I couldn't help myself. I'm really hoping Dr. Failia will let me get a look at that laser."

Of course. Kenyon used lasers constantly in his work. Ben's dislike for the man did not change the fact that Kenyon was probably one of the best optical engineers Venera had access to. Of course he wanted a look at the laser. He'd be just the person to pull the machine apart and see what it was made of and what it was for.

Ben shook his head regretfully. "I'm sorry. Helen's put a ban on any Venerans, or anyone else, going down there until the yewners . . . the U.N. team has finished up. Doesn't want anybody to get in their way or to challenge whatever theories they come up with by presenting a whole bunch of facts. She says there'll be plenty of time for that later."

Kenyon's face fell one muscle at a time. "I may just ask her anyway," he said at last. "Do you think getting on my knees and begging would help any?"

Ben did not laugh. "She's got her hands full, Dr. Kenyon. I think it'd be better if you just waited until the investigative team's finished."

Kenyon's eyes searched Ben's face, and Ben saw in them the knowledge of his, Ben's, personal dislike. That was all right; he'd never supposed it to be a secret.

At last, Kenyon blew out a sigh. "Okay, if that's the way it is, that's the way it is. I'll wait." He paused. "Or did you rent out my room while I was gone?"

"No, your quarters are still right where you left them." Venera kept a set of apartments for people like Kenyon who came and went on regular schedules. Ben stepped aside. "Sorry you went through all this for nothing."

The thought *no you're not,* flickered across Kenyon's face, but he quickly smoothed it out. "Thanks," he said as he strode past Ben, heading for the elevators.

Alone, Ben let his shoulders sag. The U.N. flag fluttered in the breeze from the ventilator shafts, and Ben found his hands itching to go over and rip it down.

Pull it together. You have more important things to worry about.

Ben focused his eyes on the corridor and marched past the flag, almost as if it wasn't there.

The door to the Surveyors' lab opened as soon as it identified Bennet Godwin, just as all the doors on Venera did. That fact could still amaze him. There had been a point when he assumed he'd never be trusted again.

And I may be about to blow all of it. He shoved the thought aside. This was not some petty academic political battle. This one was for the real world.

Except for Derek Cusmanos and several dozen neatly arrayed survey drones, the cavernous room was empty. All the personnel who'd been assigned to Derek were off either in the scarabs or in their own offices, poring over years of satellite data, looking for more alien bases. The mammoth wall screens showed a series of seemingly random still shots—the mushroomlike dome of a pancake volcano, the ripples of one of the lava deltas, the ragged, concentric rings of a collapsed crater.

Derek himself crouched in front of one of his drones. This was one of the surface surveyors, which looked like miniature scarabs with eyes and arms. Derek had it turned over on its side so he could get at the hatch in its belly. Whatever he saw there was so absorbing that he did not look up as Ben started across the floor.

"Derek?"

Derek grunted and held up one finger. Ben stopped where he was, folding his hands behind his back and getting ready to wait. Derek, like most of the mechanical engineers Ben knew, had the tendency to get completely absorbed in his work. Ben studied the rows of drones with their spindly arms, picks and containers for taking samples, lasers for measuring, cameras for every kind of photography. Derek knew them all. Had built half of them. Had come very close to losing his job because no one felt the need to fund a human mapmaker when drones and computers could do that just fine. The drones themselves could, of course, be cared for by the same staff that took care of the scarabs.

Derek finished his repairs or adjustments, closed the hatch, and heaved the drone upright onto its treads. Only then did he stand up and really acknowledge Ben's presence.

"Afternoon, Dr. Godwin." Derek plucked a sterile towel out of the box and started wiping his hands with it. "What can I do for you?"

"Afternoon." Derek had been one of Ben's students when he was still teaching. Ben had long ago given up trying to get the younger man to use his first name. "Have you got the new pictures of Ozza Mons?"

"Fresh in." Derek tossed the towel down the recycling shaft and plunked himself behind the sprawling, semicircular desk that was in his main workstation. The desk woke up, and he typed in a quick command sequence. The wall image of the lava delta disappeared, replaced by the ragged, ashen gray throat of an old, massive volcano. "Looks pretty dead."

"May just be dormant." Ben studied the picture, but the familiar sense of excitement failed to rise in him. "We'll have to go down and look at it."

"If you can get a scarab for anything but ogling the Discovery." Derek shook his head at his keyboard. "It's amazing, you know? I mean, I knew, once we found it, that the Terrans wouldn't think there was anything else worthwhile up here, but I thought the Board . . ." He stopped.

Ben held up his hand. "Now that the tourists are here, everybody's supposed to go back to their normal duties. Dr. Failia wants to give your visitors plenty of room to play."

Derek made a sour face. Ben returned a smile and changed the subject. "Have you found anything that looks like another outpost?"

Derek shook his head. "They've given me the entire geology

department, and we've got every surveyor, from the satellites to the minirovers, set on fine-tooth comb, but there's nothing."

"Think we will find anything?"

Derek started but recovered quickly. "How would I know?"

Ben shrugged. "You found the first one. I thought you might recognize . . . traces."

Derek didn't look at him. His gaze wandered over the silent ranks of surveyors with their waldos, cameras, and caterpillar treads. They were heavy, blocky, reinforced things, completely unlike the delicate machines Ben had worked with on Mars. "The drones found the first one, Dr. Godwin, not me. But there are no traces of anything around it. It's just sitting there, a random occurrence." He paused and finally returned his gaze to Ben. "Or have your people found something new?"

Ben barked out a laugh. "You have all my people. You're going to hear anything long before I do." Then, he paused, as if considering a new thought. "Although . . . well, you've got a trained eye. Can I get you to take a look at one of the new batches of images your team passed me?"

"Sure." Derek poised his hands over the command board.

"It's file number AT-3642."

Derek entered the number and brought up the picture on the wall screen. It was a black-and-white still shot, taken from one of their ancient satellites. It showed a gray raised ring with a dark center and long pale ridges radiating from the sides. Derek studied it for a moment.

Ben leaned one hand against the back of Derek's chair and peered at the image, as if trying to see it in greater detail.

"Looks like a tick," Derek said. A tick was a type of volcano found only on Venus. It got its name because from above it looked like a gigantic, round-bodied insect with its crooked legs sticking out at irregular angles.

"Yeah, it does," said Ben, watching Derek carefully. "Except it's never been mapped."

"Oh? Well, that describes a lot of the planet." Venus had three times the land area of Earth. Detailed mapping was the work of multiple lifetimes. "Do you want me to put it on the list for close study?"

"No, no." Ben shook his head. *Especially since it does seem you've never seen it before.* "You've got your hands full. Just see about routing me a couple of close-ups during the next flyover, okay?"

"Okay." Derek made a note on one of his flat screens. "Was there anything else?"

"Not really." Ben straightened up. "Will I see you at the reception?"

"Maybe." Derek turned his attention back to his command board. The lava delta reappeared on the wall, this time with the white lines of a measuring grid laid over it. "When I'm done here."

"You should consider putting in an appearance," Ben suggested with a small smile. "I think Grandma Helen is counting noses. If she isn't, she'll be reviewing the tapes later."

Derek glanced up. "Thanks, Dr. Godwin. I'll show myself."

"Good choice." He patted the boy on the shoulder and showed himself out.

Ben walked down the broad corridor to the elevator bays and, as was his habit, took the sweeping staircase instead. Space was Venera's one true luxury, and Ben had to admit he reveled in it. The stairs were wide, and the ceilings were high. There was room for people coming up, going down, and just standing around talking or leaning against the outer railing. The elevator shafts made mini-atriums, so he could look the whole, long, dizzy way down and up again and hear the sounds of purposeful life drifting to him from each of the twenty-four decks. Ten thousand people living and working peacefully together. It could be paradise if it were allowed to be.

Ben turned off at the landing for the administration level, getting ready to head for his office. But he stopped in midstride and glanced at the clock on the wall. Quarter of five, with the reception at six. No one would think anything of it if he didn't stay at his desk until the required hour.

And what Ben really wanted to do could not be done in the office.

So he returned to the stairs and walked down three levels to the residential section. The apartments took up most of the two levels above the farm and one level below. Everyone had a full suite of rooms: bed, bath, study, living, and kitchen. Even the visitors. With the soaring ceilings, full-spectrum lights, and generous use of e-windows and greenery, you could almost forget you were in a colony.

In his own rooms, Ben always kept one of his screens set to show the clouds outside. He did not want to forget.

Other than that, Ben's apartment was pretty much as he had moved into it. Someone looking for evidence of the owner's personality would have had to work hard. After a while, they might have picked out the shiny chunk of obsidian on the end table by the couch, the brightly polished garnet on the half-wall that divided the kitchen from the living room, and the piles of open screen rolls on the desk, coffee table, and couch. From this they could have concluded that the owner liked rocks and was dedicated to his work.

As his door shut behind him, Ben crossed to the sofa. He picked up a pile of screen rolls to clear space for himself and sat down. His briefcase rested on the coffee table. He didn't jack it in; he just woke it and called up a privately encrypted file that waited for both the password and the scan of his fingertips from the command board.

The file opened for him and displayed a picture identical to Derek's AT-3642.

It did look like a tick. It had the circular center and the ridges radiating out like crooked legs. In black and white and two dimensions, those ridges appeared to be level with the ground—until you had spent a day looking at everything you had as if they were alien artifacts because you couldn't help yourself, until you enlarged it and refined it and squinted at it for hours.

Then you saw it was not level with the ground, that the ring was, in fact, sitting well above ground level, and that the "ridges" might be supports of some kind.

He couldn't be sure, of course. The only way to be sure would be to fly one of Derek's prize camera drones in there, shine a laser over the thing, and make a holograph of it. But close study of anything on Venera involved other people—assistants and their supervisors, Derek as the drone keeper;

Helen, who had to know what was going on at all times. Ben did not want anyone, *anyone*, else involved in this yet. Anyone on Venera anyway.

What Ben knew currently was that this object was approximately 1.3 kilometers across and that it had been there somewhere between 40 and 170 years. The *Magellan* probe sent up in the 1990s hadn't seen it, but the *Francis Drake* had, and the *Francis Drake* went up just as the first plates of Venera were being bolted together.

So never mind where the Discovery with its three little holes in the ground came from. Where did this . . . *thing* come from?

But no one was looking at it, except him. Derek's complete nonrecognition had told him that. If someone else had been checking out this spot or this object, Derek would have confirmed it. Everyone else was looking in the ground for more holes. No one had looked up.

Ben's first thought had been to rush to Helen with this, but he'd hesitated. He told himself that it was just because he wanted to be sure. He didn't want to speak before he had the facts.

But that wasn't it, and even as he was rationalizing his actions at three in the morning, he knew that.

Ben slumped backward and ran his hand over his scalp, scrubbing the gray bristles that were all that was left of his hair. Male-pattern baldness he'd never bothered to get corrected. He hated med-trips when they were necessary, never mind the idea of getting stuck in one of the capsules for cosmetic touch-ups.

He'd had a full head of chestnut hair at Bradbury. He'd been so young. Ben chuckled to himself. *God, when did twenty-seven get to be young?*

He'd taken his own sweet time getting through college. Some of his friends joked he was in on the "eternity program." Ben replied he was just looking for something to get excited about. Comparative planetology, with its possibilities for exploration and discovery, had come close to filling the bill.

Then he went to Bradbury for his post-doc work and he found the real thing.

Theodore Fuller was just picking up steam when Ben arrived. No one on Earth took him seriously, but in the colony itself, that was another story. The stream was full of his words and of people talking about them.

Ben had arrived at Arestech, Inc., to set up shop in their lab and run their surveyors with every intention of ignoring Fuller's message. But he couldn't help hearing. To his surprise, Fuller didn't talk about the good old days of the nation states, like most people who had grief with the U.N. did. He didn't talk about the past at all. Instead he talked with enthusiasm and delight about the present—how modern technology had finally made possible a truly free flow of information, information available to each and every human being no matter who they were, no matter where they were. Information made it possible for everyone to control their own lives completely in a way that had never been possible before. It could bring them into contact with whomever and whatever they needed. They could pick and choose what their lives held. There was no more need for middlemen or for central government.

After all, what did governments do? Provide security? There were no more nations to wage war on each other. Personal security could be provided by electronics or a private company, depending on the needs and desires of the individual. The government regulated commerce? Why? The market, like nature, could take care of itself and had for a long time now. When was the last real economic collapse? Late twenty-first century, wasn't it? Before the stream was truly established.

How about rule of law? Employment for lawyers and bureaucrats mostly. A person who felt unjustly treated could seek satisfaction in courts run on the same principles as any other business. The ones in which the arbitration and settlement procedures were seen as just and fair would have the most subscribers and work with the greatest number of private security companies. Those who didn't like the justice of one system could subscribe to another which they read about and evaluated in-stream.

The central government did not need to exist. It was an idea from previous centuries. It was like the great North American weed called kudzu. It had invaded so long ago no one remembered where it came from. They just knew it was there, and they spent a lot of time, effort, and money dealing with it because no one knew how to get rid of it. No, because no one was ready to do what was necessary to get rid of it.

Well, the good news was that dealing with the U.N. was a lot easier than dealing with kudzu. All you had to do to get rid of government was say no. Simple. Direct. Say no, show the bureaucrats the nearest ship out, and get on with your life. Your life, your money, your future. Yours. No one to say who could and could not build on the planets, no endless rounds of licensing for ships and shipping, no one to hedge or ban scientific research that frightened them, no one to ever again supervise bloodbaths like the U.S. Disarmament.

Ben had had no blaze-of-light revelation. He'd started reading because he almost couldn't help himself. Fuller and Fuller's ideas were all anybody talked about. He had to find out for himself whether they would work or not.

The answer shocked and scared him. It could work. The free flow of information was the key, just as Fuller said. The U.N. had been, in some ways, a necessary stage to eliminate the barriers imposed by nation states and national currency. But now that it had nothing external to fight against, it had turned around, like all powerful governments had throughout history, and started to feed on its own, and people put up with it because they couldn't see any way past it.

Bradbury and its people could show them. Bradbury could push the U.N. out the door and thrive. When they did, the rest of the worlds would see that it could be done, and done safely and quickly. It would start with Mars, out on the frontier, but it would spread all the way back down to Mother Earth herself.

It should have worked, but they moved too fast. Fuller got bad advice, or maybe he just got overconfident, but they overestimated the number of their followers in Bradbury. Too many people just stood around and did nothing. Too many other people actively tried to undermine the revolution and were judged dangerous to the implementation of the new system. Transporting all the dissenters back to Earth turned out to be a bigger problem than had been anticipated. During the process of transportation, someone got sloppy and didn't run safety checks on all the ships that carried the dissenters away.

Then there were the ones who misunderstood what was happening and decided to take charge in their own way before the security systems could be established. Revenge had overwhelmed the fragile court corporations.

None of that changed the basic principles. Fuller's ideas still held. But twenty years had passed and no one else had found the time or the place to put them into practice.

Until now.

Ben stared at the clouds displayed on his view screen. They billowed and boiled, filling the world outside. Even after so long, they could still be awe inspiring.

When he'd first stood inside the Discovery, his thoughts had tumbled over each other, almost too fast for him to follow. Awe, fear, wonder, humility, and then, slowly, almost shamefully, came the idea that he might be able to use this great thing that had happened. This might be the catalyst for the shift in thinking that would be needed to finish what Ted Fuller had started.

The more he thought, the more he saw and uncovered on his own, the more certain he became. This was it. It just had to be managed, that was all. Not suppressed, not lied about, just managed. Everything could be made to work out for the best for all the worlds, including Venus, if they just moved carefully.

Well? He tapped his fingers restlessly against his thigh. *If you're going to do it, do it. If not, put your file away and go get dressed up for the yewners.*

Ben leaned forward and jacked the case into the table. He set up a quick search code, attached his best encryption to it, and dropped it into the queue for the next com burst to Earth. Then he got up to shave and change for the reception.

One of the features of the stream that few people bothered to take notice of was that if you constructed your packet correctly, you did not actually have to store your information anywhere. So many different, completely untended machines were constantly receiving and rerouting data that it was possible to keep a packet bouncing between them. Ben had several packets that had been flying from relay to relay for twenty years now. He'd lost three to badly timed hardware upgrades that he'd failed to get wind of, but other than that, his most secret information bounced happily around the solar system, untraceable, not only because of its encryptions, but because it seldom landed anywhere long enough for any one machine to make a complete record of its contents.

The disadvantage of this was that it took awhile to find the packet, once you did go looking for it.

Ben returned to his case, clean shaven and dressed in tunic and trousers of a suitably conservative blue-gray. A matching cap with black beading covered his head. He checked the screen display.

Success.

His searcher had recovered the packet in one of the repeater relays between Earth and the Moon and had rerouted it back to Venus. Ben accessed his four-tier decryption key and added the password.

The packet opened to display the face of an aging man with dark hair, pale skin, a suggestion of a beard, and mud-brown eyes under heavy brows. His name was Paul Mabrey. He had assorted degrees from assorted universities. He worked as a risk assessor for various small companies, spending his time traveling from colony to colony, mostly on Mars, looking at new market niches and good suppliers. He took med-trips and vacations back on Mother Earth regularly but not excessively. He had been in Bradbury during the rebellion, and while it was felt that he had some sympathies toward Fuller's faction, surveillance on him had been turned off over fifteen years ago because he never did anything remotely suspicious.

He was, in fact, the man Ben used to be.

Once upon a time, Ben, then called Paul Mabrey, had been dismissed by the yewners who had taken over Bradbury as being of little consequence. They did, however, post automatic surveillance over him, as they did every rebel, just in case. For three years, Paul behaved himself meekly, like a good defeated puppy. He watched his friends jailed, watched Fuller hauled back to Earth for trial and incarceration. He watched the yewners take up posts on every street corner and randomly search the passersby. He watched the taxes go up and the licenses go down and travel get restricted. He sat in his apartment at night and hated himself because there was nothing he could do, not now, not ever again, because the yewners would never really take their eyes off him. The free flow of information that Fuller had touted as the route to the future would make it impossible for him to hide.

He had one thing left to him. The yewners had not quite uncovered the extent of what Paul had done for Fuller. He'd specialized in helping make clip-outs—in-stream ghosts of people who wound up on various payrolls and mailing lists and who, eventually, wound up with various levels of access and permission to various segments of the communications networks. When the uprising came, those clip-outs gave the software corruption teams that Paul was a part of a handle on the U.N. networks, which he used to shut them down.

Minor stuff, really, a low-level hacker trick.

But what he labored over at night, almost every night, was not. It was researched and tested, a little bit here, a little bit there. It was years of learning under Fuller's best, a few minor bribes, a couple of slow, painful system break-ins, and a whole lot of patience.

Then, Paul received notice that his surveillance period was up and he was declared rehabilitated. Good luck to you, Mr. Mabrey.

Paul, grimly satisfied, had closed the letter and gone in-stream to request permission politely to travel to Giant Leap on business. The yewner bureaucrat on the other end was in a benevolent mood that day and let him go.

Two weeks later, Paul Mabrey left for Luna. He arrived at Giant Leap and stayed for three months, working on various consulting jobs and contracts. Then—according to all available records, anyway—Paul Mabrey went home.

That same day, a man named Bennet Godwin, who had—according to all available records—arrived in Giant Leap on Luna from the Republic of Manhattan space port, got a job as a geologist for Dorson Mines, Inc.

No one knew how many clip-outs floated around the stream.

Usually they were used by people wishing to perpetrate some kind of fraud. They were vague constructs, tied to a few vital records and easily torn apart or scared away by semideter-mined scrutiny.

A very few were like Paul, who sat in-stream and stared at Ben out of eyes that could have been his own. Paul had been nurtured and cared for. He had aged as Ben had aged. He had subscriptions to the major news services and joined in-stream discussions on various items of interest. He had credit accounts, and he used them. He drew pay from companies he consulted for. He vacationed, theatered, and kept apartments in Giant Leap and Burroughs. He even had personal contact codes, which a simulation would answer and alert Ben when they were used.

Now, it was time for Paul to come back to life. Paul was going to get hold of some very interesting information and pass it along to a few old associates. Paul still had a few tricks up his sleeve to keep the yewners from noticing he'd revived some acquaintances that were still, after all those years, under surveillance and travel restrictions.

Paul still had a chance to prove he was not useless.

Ben, heedless of the time, hunched over his briefcase and started typing.

"... with mutual cooperation and free exchange of ideas we will together unravel this, the greatest of human mysteries."

Vee applauded politely, along with the rest of the gathering. Dr. Failia smiled and stepped out from behind the podium, shifting immediately from solemn speech-giver to smiling greeter-of-friends-and-strangers. Vee found herself grinning. The speeches had been well delivered and short, the food was good, and the view . . . the view was stunning.

Vee hadn't stood in Venera's observation hall for eight years. She had forgotten the impact of being surrounded by the huge, constantly shifting landscapes of gray, white, and gold created by the clouds. Observation Hall was ringed, from the white floor to domed ceiling, with a seamless window of industrial quartz, so it was possible to stand and stare until you felt as if you were alone and exposed in the midst of that boiling alien mist.

Not that that's going to happen tonight. Vee felt her mouth quirk up. *The place is way too full.*

A couple of hundred Venerans plus the investigative team circulated around tables loaded with appropriate predinner snacks and beverages. Stykos and Wray, camera bands firmly in place, flanked the tall dark woman who Vee vaguely remembered was head of meteorology. Lindi Manzur stood in front of the window, a little too close to Troy Peachman, who was gesturing grandly as he expounded about something. Vee smiled softly and turned away from their private moment.

Everyone in the gathering had made an effort to show some gold or silk. Vee herself had been torn between wanting to put on a good show for the cameras and not wanting to break the conservative veneer she'd been carefully cultivating during the entire week-and-a-half flight up here.

In the end, she'd selected a green-and-gold paneled skirt, with a green jacket trimmed with gold piping and an abbreviated gold turban with a green veil falling down behind to cover her unbound hair. It looked good enough to make the story cut, but not so outrageous as to offend academic sensibility.

Apparently, however, she was not circulating enough. Out of the corner of her eye, Vee saw Dr. Failia making a beeline for her.

"Good evening, Dr. Hatch. Thank you for coming."

Vee shook her hand. "I'm sorry I'm late, Dr. Failia. I'd forgotten just how big Venera is."

"After a week on a ship, it can take some getting used to, yes." Dr. Failia nodded sympathetically. "Tell me, did you have a chance to review the visuals we've taken of the Discovery?"

"Yes, in between learning how not to get squashed and burned when we go down." Vee smiled to let Dr. Failia know she was kidding.

Dr. Failia laughed once, politely. "And did you form any initial plans as to how to proceed?"

"Yes. The first thing we need is a spectrographic analysis, to find out what kind of laser we're dealing with." Vee warmed as she talked, excited about the possibilities her research might open. "Then, I think . . ." Vee's gaze strayed over Dr. Failia's shoulder. Michael Lum, the security chief, waited two steps behind her.

Dr. Failia followed her gaze. "Excuse me, Dr. Hatch," she said hastily. "Please, help yourself to the buffet."

Dr. Failia crossed quickly to Lum, who murmured something in her ear. They both looked up at the entranceway, just as Bennet Godwin walked through. Failia frowned and strode over to the latecomer.

Uh-oh, Vee turned away and skirted the conversational knots as she made her way to the food tables. *Somebody's getting demerits for tardiness.*

The buffet was a good spread, with the Western traditional cheese and crackers, but also with couscous, falafel, and various flat breads, triangles of toast with what looked like mushroom paté, miniature empeñadas, and some blue pastry things that Vee, with all her experience of artsy receptions, couldn't put a name to. Glasses of wine flanked bowls of ginger and fruit punches, as well as silver samovars of tea and coffee.

Vee was debating over what to sample next, when she felt someone walking up to her side.

"Excuse me. Are you Dr. Veronica Hatch?"

Vee turned to face a sparsely built man with ruddy skin and tawny eyes. He was only a few centimeters taller than she was. He wore a blue baseball cap over his thick brown hair instead of a more fashionable brimless cap or half-turban. It made a pleasantly rebellious contrast to his formal gold-and-black tunic and trousers. Vee decided she liked him.

"That's what they tell me," Vee answered cheerfully and extended her hand. "Hi."

"Hi." He shook her hand with a good grip, which was also pleasant. Most people got a look at her long, thin hand and adjusted their greeting touch to something overly delicate. "I'm Joshua Kenyon. Josh."

Ah. His name rang memory chimes inside Vee and brought up the titles of several recently surveyed publications. "Vee. I've read you."

He did not, to his credit, look at all surprised. Dr. Kenyon had about a gigabyte of published work on tracking particle flow and interaction in the Venusian atmosphere using real-time laser holography techniques. Vee's job, before she got her first patent and turned to experiential holograms, was "time-resolved sequential holographic particle imaging velocimetry," which was the official way of saying she took four-dimensional images of particles in dense plasmas. Most people didn't know she'd done serious lab work. Some refused to believe it.

"Are you going to be leading the research on the laser?" Vee asked, as she picked up one of the blue pastries. "And do you know what these are?"

"That's crab rangoon, dyed blue to preserve some of the mystery of life," said Josh promptly. "And the research on the laser is actually what I wanted to talk to you about."

"Oh?" Vee arched her eyebrows. "Shall we get out of traffic?"

"Good idea."

Vee paused to collect a small plate of blue things and followed Josh over to one of the little round tables covered with a white cloth that always seemed to spring up like mushrooms at these gatherings.

Vee sat and pushed the pastries toward Josh, who shook his head. Vee took one and nibbled the edge. Yep, crab.

A flash of orange in the clouds caught her eyes. A delicate flurry of sparks spiraled up through the mist, tiny petals of brightness scattered through the impenetrable fog.

"Star trails." Vee smiled at the beauty of the small event. "We must be going over one of the volcanoes."

Josh checked the position readout set in the floor. "Yeah, Xochiquetzal Mons. It went active, I guess twenty years ago now."

"They're beautiful." As Vee watched, the clouds swallowed the sparks whole, but a fresh trail swept along the wind as if these new sparks wanted to follow their friends.

Josh nodded in thoughtful agreement. "Make me nervous, though."

"Why?" Vee cocked her head at him.

A look of frank surprise crossed his face, followed by a sudden realization. "You didn't get down to the surface last time you were here, did you?"

"No need." Vee shook her head and nibbled another pastry. "I was just here for the clouds."

Josh took off his cap and smoothed his hair down before replacing it. His face said he was considering some internal question. Then, apparently, he got his answer.

"Well," he said, "you met Michael Lum, right?"

Vee nodded. In fact, she could see him through the crowd, pacing alongside Philip Bowerman talking about whatever spooks and spies talked about. Vee found herself wondering where Angela Cleary had gotten to. She did not seem to be in evidence anywhere.

"Michael's a good guy," Josh went on. "He's a v-baby. Born here. His parents were almost the first people on the station when Helen opened it up. His father, Kyle Lum, was a climatologist, and he was out doing some surveys of the lower cloud layer when the scarab ran into a star trail." He stared out at the sparks as they danced away into the clouds. "Sheered off one of the wing struts, dropped the entire scarab. They got their parachute out, fortunately, but they slammed into the side of one of the mountains. The rescue team dropped after them, within minutes, but when they got there"—Josh shook his head—"the hull had ruptured. There was nothing left."

Vee glanced back at the fading sparks. A shiver ran up her spine. "I think I'm glad I didn't know that when I was photographing them."

Josh laughed a little. "Sorry. Not the best subject of conversation, especially with a newcomer."

Vee waved his words away. "Don't worry about me. So"—she brushed a few crumbs from her skirt—"what about the laser?"

Josh took off his cap again and smoothed his hair down once more. "It's not actually about the laser," he said. "It's about getting a look at it."

"How so?"

He blew out a sigh that puffed his cheeks, put his cap back on, and looked down at his fingertips as if to see his words written there. Vee waited.

"I work on Venera on a regular basis. I do my stints here for about nine months at a time and then go home and do the lecture and paper routine. I was on Earth when the news about the Discovery dropped into the stream. When I heard about the laser, I didn't even think about it. I just got myself onto the next ship back. I assumed . . ." He shook his head and started again. "I assumed, since I was known and had a longtime affiliation with Venera, that I'd be able to get on the short list for a look at the thing, maybe even a chance to help in the analysis." He lifted his gaze. "But, no, that's not the way this is going to play. The laser is your territory for now, they're telling me. After that, maybe we'll see, but in the meantime, it's just you."

"I see," said Vee, and she really thought she did. "And you think I can get you a piece of this?"

"I don't know," he admitted. "But it seemed worth a shot."

"Why the rush?" she asked breezily. "It'll be there after I'm done with it."

The look he gave her indicated his estimation of her mental acuity had just taken a header. Vee grinned. "Got it. You want to see what the aliens left too."

"Don't get me wrong, I love my work." He tugged on his cap's brim. "I always wanted to be out in space, but there are days when I'm very aware that I'm really just a glorified weatherman." His eyes grew distant. "This is the stuff we've forgotten to dream about."

Vee felt her grin widen. *Joshua Kenyon, you're a romantic! I thought they'd put the last of your kind into zoos.* "I don't see how there could be any problem with it. It's not as if . . ." She cut herself off but glanced around the room. There was Troy, glad-handing yet another patient Veneran with Lindi trailing behind him. There was Julia at the buffet, being photographed by Terry, and there was Robert, staring straight at her while Isaac seemed to be occupied in keeping as many bodies between him and that window as possible.

"As if?" asked Josh.

One corner of Vee's mouth turned up. "As if they've overloaded us with skilled workers. And I include myself in that." She slumped backwards and stared at her plate with its blue bits of pastry. "I swear, I don't know what they were thinking when they picked this bunch."

Josh looked at her carefully. "You really want to know?"

Vee thought about it for a minute. "Yes," she said.

Josh sighed, lifted his cap, smoothed his hair down, and replaced it. "Because you're harmless."

"What?" Vee straightened up slowly, uncertain that she'd really heard those words.

"I talked to some of the other atmosphere people about the U.N. team. I was wondering the same thing. Turns out that Grandma Helen pulled a whole set of strings to make sure whoever the U.N. sent up wouldn't be able to do much in the way of actual investigation. She wanted all the glory, and all the publications and the money, to go to Venerans."

Vee's face flushed. Anger gathered in the back of her mind. The real work to the Venerans. That she understood. But there was plenty to go around. There had to be. Wanted to get a team that couldn't do much . . . brought her up here not because they respected her skills, but because they suspected she lacked them. Just another pretty popularizer. Just another stupid face.

Vee's jaw clamped down so hard her teeth started to ache. She stood.

"Vee . . ." began Josh. "I'm sorry. I shouldn't have—"

"Don't worry about it," she said without looking at him. Her gaze swept the room until it fastened on Helen Failia, who didn't think she knew enough. Who didn't think she could do this job and had her handpicked because of that.

Vee strode across the room, barely seeing where she was going.

Slow down, Vee. Slow down! This is not going to do anyone any good, especially you. She stopped in her tracks. Her chest had tightened, and she was breathing way too hard. *Stop and think what you're doing. You throw a fit now, and you'll just be proving their point.*

In the back of her mind she heard Rosa's voice: "Be careful what you pretend to be."

Vee turned away from Failia, hoping the woman hadn't noticed her angry approach and abrupt change of plan. Evidently not. No one came up to her as she found an empty table and sat. The cameras were occupied; so were the other U.N. investigators, with each other and the cameras and with the whole wide cloudscape, and not one of them knew why they were here.

I'm gonna kill her. Vee bowed her head into one hand. *I'm gonna kill myself. What was I thinking? I actually believed—*

"Dr. Hatch?"

Vee looked up. Terry Wray stood over her.

"If this little tableau turns up in-stream—"

"It's off, it's off," Terry reassured her, lifting her hair out of the way so Vee could see the band was well and truly dark. "But are you okay?"

Vee pushed her veil back over her shoulders. "Not right now, but I will be."

"Okay, good." Terry smiled. "You're one of my star attractions. I'd hate it if you stomped off or anything."

"Oh no," replied Vee sweetly. "They're not getting rid of me that easily." A thought struck her. "Terry, can I use you shamelessly for a minute?"

A whole variety of expressions crossed Terry's face from amused curiosity to interested calculation. "As long as we stay in public, sure."

Vee squeezed her hand. "Turn that thing back on, and when I start talking to Helen Failia, come up and start paying attention, okay?"

Terry looked down her snub nose at Vee. "Okay, but I get an extra interview for this."

"Done."

Vee rose, pasted her best sunny, vapid smile on her face, and slipped over to where Helen Failia stood talking with Philip. Vee waited for a pause in the conversation and then strode forward, timing her attack.

One, two, three, she pauses for breath and . . .

"Dr. Failia, good, you're still here."

Helen turned toward Vee, all solicitous. "What can I do for you, Dr. Hatch?"

"Well"—Vee folded her hands in front of her—"I hadn't realized Dr. Kenyon was going to be on base. I thought he was still on his Earthside swing."

Helen's expression went slightly rigid as she held back some impolite emotion. "Ah, you know Dr. Kenyon?"

"By reputation. I've read his work." She glanced across at Josh and let her smile grow even happier. "I'm so glad he'll be with us. I don't mind telling you." Vee leaned forward confidentially. As she did, she saw Terry coming into range on the very edge of Helen's field of view. "I'm excited about this opportunity, but my lab work was all done a long time ago. Without someone who's in better practice, I'm afraid I might make a mess of things." She laughed lightly. Dr. Failia looked gratifyingly disconcerted.

"I'm sorry." Vee pulled back and blinked rapidly a few times. "He *is* coming down with us, isn't he? His help would be utterly invaluable to me." *Come on, there's the camera, you see it. You aren't going to admit you're sending down a half-assed team, are you?*

Helen Failia didn't even hesitate. "If you feel Dr. Kenyon can be of assistance, of course he will be included in the investigative roster." Only a slight darkness in Helen's clear eyes told Vee that she did not think this was an excellent idea.

"Marvelous." Vee beamed. "Thank you so much." For good measure, she shook Dr. Failia's hand before she turned away and strode out the door.

"That was pretty shameless," murmured Terry behind her.

"You should see me when I'm trying." Vee turned, and her smile was feral. "Thanks. Contact me when you're ready for that interview."

"Never fear." Terry's face grew thoughtful. "You should be careful about getting to like this too much, Dr. Hatch."

"You know, I've got a friend back home who says the same thing." Vee felt her face soften. "You're probably both right too."

Terry gave her one more thoughtful look. *Sizing me up,* thought Vee. *For what?* "I've got to get back," was all Terry said. "See you tomorrow."

"Bye."

Vee let her go and started walking down the corridor, suddenly both tired and frustrated. *Hope this doesn't get you in any kind of trouble, Josh, but I was not, I was not, going to let her get away with this. You and I.* She paused before the elevator. *We're going to make something of this, and Dr. Failia can just sit back and watch us.*

Kevin Cusmanos hated accounting. Especially late at night after an evening spent smiling and chatting with a glass of wine in his hand when what he really wanted was a beer. He hated staring at the rows of figures in their little boxes and checking them on a split screen against the individual logs where everyone was supposed to enter all their individual orders and purchases but never did.

However, it came with the job. So he sat in his office with coffee steaming in a plastic mug, ancient Afro-Country playing over the speakers, and a burgeoning dislike of Shelby Kray, one of the new guys who could not seem to get the hang of keeping track of his money.

The door, which Kevin never locked, swished open. Kevin glanced up briefly and saw Derek framed in the threshold.

"Hey," said Derek, a little tentatively. He still had his party clothes on—black slacks, red tunic, and cap.

Now's not a great time, little brother, thought Kevin, but all he said was, "Hey."

Derek wandered in and dropped down on the stiff sofa Kevin kept for visitors. Most offices had chairs, but Kevin insisted that it was traditional for a mechanic to have a rundown sofa, so a sofa he would have.

"So, when they dropping you down?" asked Derek.

Kevin eyed him, trying to see what he had really come in for. "Couple of days. Gotta get at least some training into the tourists first."

Derek tapped the back of the sofa, sort of in time with the music. "They're going to be sending Josh Kenyon down with you. Did you know that?"

"Yes." Derek still wouldn't look at him. "Ben let me know at the end of the reception. Said it was Dr. Hatch's idea." *Come on, Derek, say it, whatever it is. It's just you and me here.*

But Derek just changed the subject again. "And you're taking Adrian with you?"

Kevin sighed and looked back down at his screen. "Yeah, Adrian will be with me in Scarab Five. Charlotte and Bailey are taking down Fourteen." The problem, he decided was that Shelby wasn't used to the idea of human backup for computer records. He'd come from a fully automated and fully profit-making environment.

Just have to take him aside and teach him the importance of counting those beans. . . .

"I don't envy you, Kevin."

"I don't envy me either," muttered Kevin before he realized Derek was not talking about correcting Shelby's accounting behaviors.

"You expecting problems?" Derek was working hard to make the question sound like idle curiosity, and he was failing miserably.

At least now I know what you wanted to talk about. Kevin leaned back with a sigh. "Actually, Derek, I am, and you should be too."

Derek shook his head and dropped his gaze, smiling a little. It was an old gesture, a little-boy gesture Derek had picked up when trying to put one over on teachers, and principals, and pretty girls. "Well, we'll just all have to do our best, won't we?" he said brightly. When he looked up again, all he saw was Kevin's blank expression.

"I guess so," Kevin ran one finger along the edge of the desk. "Dr. Meyer talk to you lately?"

Derek nodded, relaxed. "Yeah. She doesn't mind the pause. She's got lots of new data to correlate, she says, especially with the biologist they sent up."

Kevin met his brother's eyes. He saw all the uneasy trust in them, all the shaky confidence that everything was still going to be okay because not only was one of the big shots in on this, his big brother was too. A thousand things jumped into Kevin's mind all at once, all of them needing to be said. Hell, begging to be said.

Derek slapped his hands down on his thighs and got to his feet.

"Derek . . ." started Kevin.

"What?"

And if I say anything, then what? He won't stop. I'll just scare him, and if he's scared, he'll give it all away. It's not just Michael we're dealing with now. We've got the U.N. here. "Never mind."

Derek shrugged. "Okay, then. I won't."

"Okay."

Derek walked back out into the main hangar. The door swished shut behind him. Kevin rested his elbows on his desk and stared at the screen. The rows of dollar figures and time signatures made no sense. They were just numbers, tidy sets of numbers that didn't mean anything at all.

What had ever convinced him that they did?

"We were ready to make the recording, Ms. Cleary," called Phil through the open door.

"Thank you, Mr. Bowerman," Angela shouted back. "I'll be right there."

Philip and Angela had requested adjoining suites on the grounds that they'd have to be doing a lot of screen work together and they didn't want to have to monopolize a conference room. Angela wasn't entirely sure Dr. Failia believed them, but she wasn't sure she cared either.

Angela pulled out a chair from under Phil's dining table and swiveled it to face the wall screen. She sat down and flattened her screen roll on her lap. As she did, Phil pressed the Record key and started talking to the wall screen.

"Good evening, Mr. Hourani. This is preliminary report you asked for. We've had several conversations with Michael Lum, the chief of security here. He's cooperative, if not terribly enthusiastic. We've established a monitoring approach on com traffic to and from Mars that everybody can live with. . . ."

"We're monitoring transmission levels, just for the past six months as opposed to the previous couple of years, seeing if we get any jumps," put in Angela.

"We've also checked dips into known stream hot spots," Philip went on, ticking off a point on the screen roll he had spread out on his lap. "There's a few Venerans who like to talk separatist politics, but they're all in the shallows, nothing going on down in the depths." He glanced at Angela. *Your turn,* he mouthed.

Angela found her next point on her own roll. "Bennet Godwin was late to the U.N. reception tonight, but we got in a face-to-face. My impression is that he seems more sour than serious. If he's doing anything other than being sympathetic to the Bradburyans and being annoyed at U.N. interference with his schedule pad, he's doing a tremendous job of hiding it."

"In short, sir," said Philip, "so far so good. There seems to be nothing going on here but science and general good clean living." He reached for the Send key, but Angela frowned, and he hesitated.

"The only thing is . . ." She started and then stopped. Could be nothing, probably was nothing, but if it wasn't . . ." *Say it Angela.* "The tension around here is thicker than the cloud cover. During the reception, I felt as if I was in a shark pool, and the sharks were all waiting for the first hint of blood."

The corner of Philip's mouth quirked up. "You ever dealt with a research facility that's short on funding before?"

Angela shook her head. "But this one isn't anymore."

"True, but if you've been living in fear for a while, it can take time to bleed away."

Angela shrugged. "I offer it for what it's worth." She paused. "Mr. Hourani, you should also know that I will be the one going down to take a look at the Discovery with the rest of the investigative team. Phil required me to engage in an obscure North American combat ritual known as scissors-paper-stone to determine which of us would take the plunge, and I lost."

Phil's smile was all benevolence. "And on that note . . ." Philip touched the Send button, and the record light faded out in time with the glow of the screen.

Angela dropped the screen roll on the couch and yawned hugely. "Want something caffeinated?" asked Philip.

She shook her head. "I was on coffee all through dinner; any more and you'll be peeling me off the ceiling."

"Scotch then? The base distillery's surprisingly good."

She waved him away. "Want the boss to catch me with a glass in my hand? We're on the clock until he takes us off it."

"Relax, Angie, he can't see you from Earth."

"He'd smell it on the ether." Philip opened his mouth, and she held up her hand. Philip shrugged and let it go, picking up his notes instead. They each settled down to their own work and their own thoughts until the screen chimed again and lit up with an incoming message.

Mr. Hourani's head and shoulders appeared on the screen. The wall behind him was completely blank, so he was probably in his own office rather than one of the conference rooms.

"Good evening, Mr. Bowerman, Ms. Cleary," said Mr. Hourani. They'd both given him permission to use their first names, but Angela had never heard him do it. "Thank you for your initial report. Your compromise on the Venus-Mars communication monitoring is excellent. I doubt we'll see anything there, but if we do, it would be best if the Venerans see it too. We are conducting this one in the full blaze of media jurisprudence. You in particular are being watched. If we make an accusation we must be very, very certain of our facts or we will be vilified from one end of the stream to the other." He gave them a small, ironic smile. "I know. Someone is going to do that anyway, but I'd prefer it if they were wrong and we were right." Mr. Hourani turned over a sheet in front of him. "Now, as to Ms. Cleary being the one to actually visit the Discovery, all I have to say is, given Mr. Bowerman's fondness for ancient combat rituals, I would have expected you to be ready for this eventuality." He flashed a look full of his best mock severity. "I can only hope you will do better next time." His face softened instantly back into his normal, neutral expression. "Continue with your good work. I will be very interested in what you uncover." The connection faded to black.

"Excellent job, Ms. Cleary," said Phil.

"Excellent job, Mr. Bowerman," replied Angela. They shook hands vigorously. Angela rolled her screen back up and stood. "I've got training tomorrow morning. You want to get together afterwards and do an initial rundown on the Mars monitoring?"

"Sounds good." Phil stretched his arms up over his head and let them swing back down. "Tough going on the EVA stuff?"

Now it was Angela's turn to shrug. "Getting in and out of the suits is a pain, but other than that . . ." She shrugged again. "Actually, I'm kind of looking forward to this. It's not a chance that comes around every day."

"You're right there. I just"—Phil waved his hands as if looking to catch hold of the right words—"cannot get excited about going down into that hellhole."

Angela chuckled and slapped him gently on the shoulder. "Wimp. You go through space just fine."

"Ah"—Phil held up one finger—"but if the ship springs a leak in space, chances are you'll have time to do something. One of those scarabs springs a leak, and you're going to pop like a balloon."

"Actually, I'll flatten and vaporize." She smiled at him. "They showed us a video. See you at breakfast?"

"You bet."

In her own room, Angela laid her screen roll on the desk. She stared at it for a moment, trying to understand what was bothering her. So far, the assignment had been a walk in the park. Everybody, everything, was as they were supposed to be, with just enough little variations and surprises to assure her that she was seeing them all accurately. The underlying tension could easily exist because Venera Base was a colony, a unique colony in a unique situation to be sure, but a colony all the same; and colonists did not generally like yewners, with good reason.

From the outside, Venera looked simple, but when you got inside, you saw it was anything but. It was called a research base, so everyone saw the scientists and the engineers and seldom got beyond that. But the majority of the ten thousand people on the base were not scientists. They were maintenance staff, shopkeepers, teachers, administrators, farmers, skilled and unskilled workers, children, and what Angie called "support spouses," people who kept the house and raised the children and did the business of living so the other spouse could take care of the other kinds of business. As on any isolated base, people were largely defined by what work they did. Your work determined who you socialized with, where you lived, how you were treated in the social hierarchy—and there was definitely a hierarchy, with the scientists at the top. She hadn't quite defined the bottom yet. It was somewhere between the butchers and the farmers.

Not that there were bad neighborhoods here or anything like that. Grandma Helen would never have permitted it. Everything was clean, everyone was looked after one way or another. Everyone had some kind of community to keep them going—villages within the village.

All of which helped explain one of the other things Angie had found. Some people had spent their life savings and a whole lot of time trying to get here. It was far more peaceful than Mars and, unlike the Moon, was uncontrolled by corporate interests. It was also far friendlier than Earth. There were people who saw this as paradise, and Grandma Helen as Mother Creation.

All day Angela had talked to people: on the mall, on the education level, in the food-processing plants, and all day she had heard the same thing. "Grandma Helen, she's a great woman." "Grandma Helen, she keeps this place going." "Grandma Helen knows what she's doing." It was amazing. It was a little frightening.

But still, there was something. Snippets. Near misses. Hesitations. She shook her head. She'd tell Phil about it at breakfast tomorrow. One of the things she liked about her partner and her boss was that they paid attention to unformed concerns. Maybe together Phil and she could dig out whatever her subconscious was trying to tell her.

Angela smiled. One thing was for sure. If Venera Base had secrets, it would not be keeping them for very much longer.

Chapter Six

"My fellow Ca'aed continues to enjoy its health?"

The sad envy in the city's question shivered through T'sha and made her shift her weight on the kite's perches. Disease and too many sterile winds had crippled the city of K'est. Pity surged through T'sha as her kite carried her through the city's body. The supporting bones shone white around her, as bleached as the corals. The only colors seemed to be the painted shells, with their sayings and teachings written in beautiful calligraphy overlaying graduated shades of rose and lavender.

"Ca'aed has been fortunate," T'sha replied to the city through her headset. "I have brought Ambassador Z'eth a new cloning of skin cells that have worked well for us."

"Ah," sighed K'est, "I look forward to receiving them."

Although long illness had given K'est a slight tendency toward self-pity, the city was not yet dying. Far from it. Everywhere, T'sha passed people alive with purpose. They tended and studied. They sampled and directed. In several places, she saw clusters of constructors and their attendants grafting living tendons onto dead bones and transplanting coral buds that glowed pink and orange with vibrant life. Although the winds swirling outside the city were thin, inside its sphere they were thick with life and nutrition. It was almost as if the engineers had turned the entire city into a refresher chamber. T'sha felt her skin expand to take in the richness flowing all around her.

All of this life was the result of Ambassador Z'eth's tireless efforts. Another ambassador would have given up long ago and indentured her people to other cities for the best terms she could get. Perhaps she would have gone so far as to try to grow a village from what little still lived of her city.

Z'eth, however, soared over her tragedies. It was known that K'est had suggested that her people disband and allow her to die, but Z'eth would not hear of it. Instead, she had bargained and bartered for her city's needs with a zeal that left the most senior of the High Law Meet in awe. Her city, her people, were not rich and might not ever be again, but they were alive, and if they were not strong, they were still proud.

T'sha had to admit Z'eth's call for a private meeting made her nervous. Z'eth could wring promises from the clouds and the canopy, and T'sha was beholden to her on several levels. What did Z'eth want from T'sha? Or, even more important, what did she want from Ca'aed?

Z'eth's embassy lay beneath the city's central temple. The embassy was a chamber of shell and bone twined with ligaments and synaptic lace to connect it directly to the major sensory nodes of the city. What the city felt was transmitted to the embassy without the city even having to speak. Z'eth could tell by the tone and texture of her embassy walls how her city fared.

T'sha gave her kite to one of the embassy's few healthy mooring clamps and presented herself to the portal. It recognized her image and essence and opened for her.

"I have told the ambassador you are here," said K'est. "She is in the debating chamber."

"Thank you." T'sha slipped cautiously forward.

The embassy was crowded. So many people rested on the perches and floated in the air that T'sha could barely find room to glide through the corridors. T'sha glimpsed tattoos as she wove her way between them. Some were engineers and teachers, which she had expected, but most were archivists and trackers.

Of course, not even the city could keep track of all Z'eth's promises. If there is enough of the city to work complex issues . . . T'sha winced at her own thoughts. K'est lived. It would grow strong again. Z'eth was dedicated and would see it happen.

T'sha laughed softly at herself. Old superstitions. Send a bad thought out on the wind, and it would land where it began. A pessimistic thought about K'est's health could affect Ca'aed's.

At last, T'sha made her awkward way to the embassy's debating chamber. The room filled with the scent and taste of people. Words crowded the air and bumped against T'sha's wings. In the center of it all hung Z'eth, her posthands clutching a synaptic bundle as she listened to an engineer, a teacher, and an archivist. For a moment, T'sha thought she might be taking the pulse of her city as it listened to the same discussion and weighed the words.

T'sha waited politely in the threshold. Eventually, Z'eth disengaged herself from her advisers and glided a winding but still dignified path to the door.

"Good luck, Ambassador T'sha." Z'eth raised her forehands. "I'm sorry you find such a crush here. We've had a heavy day. K'est is suffering from a vascular cancer in the upper eastern districts. As you can imagine, we must work quickly."

The news shook T'sha's bones. "Good luck, Ambassador," she said hurriedly, even as she touched Z'eth's hands. "Please, allow me to return some other time. You have too much to do here without—"

Z'eth fanned her words away. "You leave for New Home in two dodec-hours, do you not?"

"Yes," admitted T'sha, "but—"

"Then my words must touch you now." Z'eth lifted her muzzle, as if tasting the air to find a quiet space. "Let us go to the refresher. It is not the place for polite conversation, but—"

"Gladly, Ambassador," T'sha dipped her muzzle.

"Then follow me, if there is room," Z'eth added ruefully.

They made their way through the corridor, sometimes flying, sometimes picking their way from perch to perch, but at last the refresher opened for them. T'sha allowed the thick air to surround her. The circulation pushed her gently from point to point, allowing her own toxins to disperse while her skin took in what nutrients the room had to offer. The walls sprouted fresh fruits and other dainties, but T'sha did not sample any, even though nervousness had emptied her stomachs.

Z'eth let the room float her for a while. It seemed to T'sha her skin was drinking deeply of quiet as well as nutrition. As T'sha watched, Z'eth swelled, opening her pores and relaxing her bones.

The moment, however, did not last. Z'eth returned to her normal size, angling her wings and spreading her crest to hold herself still against the room's circulating breezes.

"I have been following up the records of your votes, Ambassador," she said as T'sha brought herself to a proper distance for conversation. "You have been lavish with Ca'aed's promises."

T'sha resolved not to drop her gaze or twiddle her postfingers. "Now is not a good time to narrow our chances of success on the candidate world." She could not yet bring herself to call it New Home. D'seun's words still echoed through the High Law Meet. His friends were many, and they had promises they could call in at a moment's notice. Without constant countering, there was still the danger that a vote might be taken to ignore the New People altogether and simply start full-scale conversion of the candidate world into New Home.

"Ambassador T'sha," sighed Z'eth, "as one who has represented her city for a long time, let me warn you—if Ca'aed got sick now, you would have nothing to save it with."

T'sha lost her balance for a moment and drifted away. Z'eth's words touched her secret fear. She had not even voiced the worry to Ca'aed itself, although she suspected Ca'aed knew. "Ca'aed is strong and has the wisdom of years."

"The past did not help Gaith. We are flying into the nightside, Ambassador T'sha, and we may not come out." Z'eth dipped her muzzle. "Especially if we do not have New Home."

"Ambassador." T'sha hesitated. "Did I have your vote only because of my promises?"

Z'eth swelled. "No." The word was strong against T'sha's skin. "I believe you are correct. We must understand the New People. We must know they have no claim on the candidate world. If a feud began, we could be divided if there were . . . questions about our right to do as we do. We cannot be divided."

T'sha felt as if all the air had rushed away from her wings and that she must fall. "A feud with the New People? How can it even be contemplated?"

"If we both want the same thing, and we both have justifiable claims, how can it not be contemplated?" returned Z'eth. "Ambassador, I know that your mother favored teachers from the temples for your education, but you are not that naïve. We have a severe problem. We need New Home. We have New Home underneath us. We must be ready to secure it. We cannot question that."

Even if the New People truly have a legitimate claim? Ambassador, what are you asking of me? In the next moment T'sha knew, and the realization tightened her skin and bones. Z'eth wanted T'sha to go in and study the situation, as mandated by the vote in the High Law Meet. Then, no matter what she found, Z'eth wanted T'sha to say that the New People had no legitimate claim to the candidate world.

"Ambassador Z'eth . . . I cannot promise to give you the answers you want."

"I know that." Z'eth drifted even closer. The taste and touch of her words flooded T'sha's senses. "I am not asking you to say anything you do not see. I am asking you to understand how serious this matter is. How deeply we need this done. I am asking you to imagine scars on Ca'aed's hearts and the ancient walls crumbling to dust on the wind because the life has been bleached out of them. I am asking you to imagine your city in pain." She paused. "I am asking you to imagine what I have been through with K'est."

Shame and confusion shriveled T'sha. Already Ca'aed was afraid, a fact that never left her, even though her city had never spoken to her of it but that once. What if . . . ?

"I have never underestimated the dangers," said T'sha, uncertain whether she was trying to reassure Z'eth or herself.

"I think you have, Ambassador," said Z'eth, cutting her off. "I am sorry, but I believe what I say to be the truth. You are young, you are rich, and you have all the Teachings behind you. I have only my crippled city and my people promised down to their grandchildren."

T'sha clamped her muzzle shut. If she tried to speak now, she would only spurt and sputter like a nervous child. Even so, she could not believe what filled the air between them. Ambassador Z'eth wanted her to discover that the New People had no legitimate claim to the candidate world so that if those New People wished to begin a feud over the world, the People themselves would not even consider that the New People's cause might be legitimate.

Z'eth asked for this without facts, without sight or taste or any other concrete knowledge.

She asked T'sha to tell this heinous lie because she, Z'eth, feared for her city.

No, no, that's not all, T'sha tried to banish the thought. *There is more to it than that. She fears for her city's people, for all of us.*

But even if Z'eth only feared for her city, surely that was fear enough. T'sha tried to imagine Ca'aed as ill as K'est. What would she do? What would she not do?

And she owed Z'eth heavily for her support. Without her, T'sha would not be going to the candidate world at all.

But what was the point of T'sha going to question D'seun's work if she took the answers with her?

T'sha tensed her bones. "I will remember the touch of your words," she said. "I feel them keenly. They will not fall away from me in the winds of the candidate world."

"Thank you, Ambassador," said Z'eth gravely. "That is all the promise I ask."

Thank you, Ambassador, for that is all the promise I can give. "Is there anything else we must discuss? As you said, I must leave soon, and I still have so much to settle with Ca'aed and its caretakers."

Z'eth dipped her muzzle. "Care for your city, Ambassador. May it stay strong for your return."

They wished each other luck and parted, Z'eth to find her advisers, and T'sha to find her kite.

What T'sha could not find again was her calm. As her kite flew her home, T'sha turned Z'eth's words over and over again, searching for comfort, or at least a kinder interpretation in them.

A feud with the New People. It was not something she had even considered. If the New People had any kind of claim on the candidate world, surely, the People themselves would simply leave. Life served life. Life spread life. Sane and balanced life did not spend itself in useless contest. It found its own niche and filled it to the fullest. The People were sane and balanced and would not feud with the New People.

But what if the New People feud with us?

All of T'sha's bones contracted abruptly at the thought. *No.* She shook herself. *It could not happen. There are things which must be true for all sane life. If they have no claim, they cannot contest our claim. There would be no reason for them to. Z'eth is a great ambassador, but perhaps she has been fighting too long for the life of her city.*

Not that she is growing insane, T'sha added to herself hastily. *But perhaps her focus has narrowed.*

That was a good enough thought that T'sha could pretend to be content with it. But even so, Z'eth's words about a sudden illness touching Ca'aed left a nagging fear. Almost instinctively, T'sha ordered her headset to call Ca'aed.

"Good luck, Ambassador," came the city's voice. "How went your meeting with Ambassador Z'eth?"

T'sha deflated. "I will tell you, Ca'aed. I don't know which upset me more, Z'eth or her city."

Ca'aed murmured sympathetically. "Visiting the sick can be distressing."

A silence stretched out between them, while T'sha worked up the courage to ask the question that would not leave her alone. "Ca'aed?"

"Yes, T'sha?"

T'sha deflated even further, as if the weight of her thoughts pressed down on her. "You said . . . you said you were afraid that you would suffer, as Gaith suffered—"

"I am afraid, T'sha. I cannot help it."

"But I may find that the New People have a legitimate claim on the candidate world. What then?"

Ca'aed was silent for a long moment. When it did speak, the words came slowly, as if the city had to drag them out one at a time. "If they live in the world, if they spread life and help life, and still their life and ours cannot live together sanely, I believe we must then find another world."

Love welled up out of T'sha's soul. She did not question her city's words. If the words were not completely true, she did not want to know. She wanted only to believe. While she had Ca'aed with her, she could do anything and needed no other ally.

As Ca'aed's sphere came into view, their talk turned to the provisions made for T'sha's absence. Together they reviewed the promises of authority and caretaking and agreed to their wording. Ca'aed reported it was getting on well with Ta'teth, the newly selected deputy ambassador, but that Ta'teth's sudden elevation still made him nervous.

T'sha couldn't blame him. She knew what it was to sit cloistered in a waiting room while all the Kan Ca'aed considered your skills, your family, the promises you had made and accepted, and told the pollers who went from compound to compound whether they believed you were worthy of their trust. And this was before the question was even officially put to Ca'aed itself.

"He will calm down soon, I believe," said Ca'aed. "Wait. Ah. Your parents speak to me and ask me to remind you that you agreed to stop by your home and talk about marriage promises."

"Do they?" T'sha clacked her teeth hard, once.

"You should have your own household."

Indignation swelled T'sha back up to her normal size. "Are those your words or theirs?"

"Both."

I am surrounded. "You are my city, not my marriage broker."

"You are my citizen as well as my ambassador. I speak for your welfare. Does your own body not speak to you of children?"

"Frequently." *This is a lovely conversation to be having right now. It is not a distraction I need.*

"Well then?"

"All right, all right." T'sha rattled her wings. "Take me there. Public affairs must wait for affairs of the home and egg, it would seem."

"Sometimes, T'sha." A rare flash of humor brightened Ca'aed's voice. "Sometimes."

Ca'aed spoke to T'sha's kite and took control, guiding it between the swarm of traffic—kite, wing, and dirigible that always buzzed about Ca'aed and its wake villages. T'sha's birth family lived near the top of the city. When she was young, she and her siblings had played chase, darting in and out of the light portals that made up their personal ceiling.

The family Br'ei had encouraged a garden around the tendons that tied their private chambers to the main body of the city. Anemones in all the colors of life puffed out eggs and pollen that sparkled brightly in the approaching twilight. T'sha paused in front of the main door, intending to take time to organize her thoughts, but she misjudged her distance. The door caught a taste of her and opened.

Her birth parents waited for her in the center of the greeting room—pale Mother Pa'and who seemed to fill any room with her presence even when she was contracted down to the size of a child, and brightly shining Father Ta'ved, who had an aura of calm around him that could work on T'sha better than ten hours in a refresher. The interlocking rings of their marriage tattoos still appeared as dark and strong against their skin as they had when T'sha was a child.

Father Ta'ved's city had fallen to a slow rot, one of the first. Mother Pa'and's family could not bear the idea of their friends all falling into an ordinary term of indenture, so they arranged for Ta'ved to enter into a childbearing marriage with their oldest daughter. After two children, Ta'ved and Pa'and decided they both liked the arrangement. Ta'ved liked not having the pressures of his own house to worry over, and Pa'and found him an excellent father and friend. So, they renewed the promise. Pa'and even gave Ta'ved the option of bringing other spouses into the household, but he had never used it.

"Good luck, Mother Pa'and, Father Ta'ved." T'sha rubbed her

parents' muzzles. She noticed, gratefully, that they had decided to leave her little sisters T'kel and Pa'daid out of this family conversation. T'deu had probably absented himself.

"Now." T'sha backed just far enough away so she could see their eyes. "Let me see if I can guess how this will go. Mother Pa'and, you will wish me the best of luck on my new mission." Mother dipped her muzzle in acknowledgment. Father clacked his teeth, just a little. "And you, Father Ta'ved, will mention that this is likely to be the work of a lifetime. Mother, you will agree with him and say how hard it is to do the work of a lifetime with no family to support you, to have to promise constantly and barter for everything that you need instead of being surrounded by those who are dedicated to helping you because their future and contentment are tied to yours." T'sha swelled, spreading her wings to encompass the whole room. "Father will agree profoundly, and I, so moved by your arguments, will fly instantly to the marriage broker, pick myself out three husbands and a wife, and not leave for the candidate world until my entire load of eggs is thoroughly fertilized." She subsided.

"Am I right?"

Mother clacked her teeth loud and hard, shaking with her amusement. "You could have gone straight to the marriage broker, Daughter T'sha, and saved your breath to choose your spouses."

T'sha deflated to her normal size. "Mother, Father." She thrust her muzzle toward them, pleading. "I promise, when my business on the candidate world is done, I will graft myself onto the marriage broker until I have found someone to be madly in love with, someone to sire my children, and someone to keep my home. Will that satisfy you?"

"Deeply," said Mother Pa'and. "You will never be in a better position to make those promises than you are now."

T'sha's crest ruffled. "And if we're done predicting my imminent political death?"

"Daughter T'sha." Father Ta'ved sank just a little. "You know that is not what we're doing here."

"I know, Father Ta'ved, I know." T'sha brushed her muzzle against his. "But I have been given so much, both in responsibility and authority, that to spend time seeking after a household of my own before I've done my duty by the People and my city . . . It feels greedy."

Father Ta'ved swelled proudly. "Such a feeling does you great credit, Daughter T'sha. But children for your family and your city is not a greedy wish."

T'sha clacked her teeth, both in mirth and utter exasperation. "Enough! Mother, Father, you have my promises and I have an important appointment. Can we wish each other luck with full souls and leave all this for when I return?"

Mother Pa'and rubbed T'sha's muzzle with her own. "Of course, Daughter. Good luck in all you do."

"Stand by your feelings, Daughter," Father Ta'ved murmured as he caressed her. "They are sound and alive."

"Thank you, and good luck to you both." T'sha drifted away toward the portal. "And if, when I return, you have word of someone from a good family who is interested in perhaps two years of mutual promise to help us both learn how to set up a house and work within a marriage, I will not be sorry to hear of them."

Her parents' approval all but radiated off her back as T'sha flew out the door.

The remainder of her time passed quietly. She met with her newly selected deputy and found him much as Ca'aed described. The district speakers were content with his credentials and competence. He would do well as soon as he had something to do. She checked in with the indentures working on Gaith and found all there going smoothly, if slowly, and the quarantines being rigorously maintained.

Back at home, she played with her sisters and chatted about innocuous things with her brother and his father, pretending nothing much was happening in any of their lives.

Finally, she soaked herself long and thoroughly in the refresher, eating until her stomach groaned and her headset reminded her it was time to leave for the World Portals.

T'sha loaded herself and her tiny caretaker bundle aboard her kite. It felt her weight and let Ca'aed guide it out into the open air.

"Good luck, Ambassador," said Ca'aed as its portal closed. "I will miss you."

Sorrow deflated T'sha, although she struggled against it. In the past few hours, she had been able to forget about Z'eth's words and about D'seun's formidable support. Now, it all flooded back. "I'll be back soon, Ca'aed, with only good news."

"I believe you, T'sha," said her city. "I believe in you."

T'sha let those last words warm her all the way to the World Portals.

The portals themselves were not alive. Too much metal was required in their construction to allow them life and awareness such as the cities possessed. Instead, the great cagelike complex was maintained by a veneer of life—scuttling, twiglike constructors, flat stately securitors, and busy recorders that were all eye and wing.

T'sha reached the gate and was touched briefly by the welcomers, which identified her and opened the portals. T'sha sent her kite back to Ca'aed and hesitated, looking through at the tools swarming over the lifeless struts and conduits. She shivered. At the best of times, T'sha did not like the World Portals. They made her uneasy, gliding through a huge cage that was insensible to her presence, unable to care who she was or what she needed.

"Ambassador T'sha?" A recorder swooped into her line of sight. "Technician Pe'sen has asked this one to direct you to your portal."

"Proceed."

T'sha followed the recorder along the approved path, staying well away from the engineers, technicians, and their tools. All around her, she heard the low, strange hum of mindless machinery. The air tasted of metal and electricity. Two of T'sha's stomachs turned over, and she wished she had eaten more lightly.

The cage opened before her, and T'sha saw the seventh portal stretching out parallel with the canopy. It was a ragged starburst, like a huge silver neuron. T'sha picked Pe'sen out from among his colleagues circling the big, blocky monitor station.

"Technician Pe'sen." T'sha flew past the recorder and touched her friend's hands. "Good luck. I promise my passage will not damage any of your children." Pe'sen would go on at length about the difficulty of growing and training cortices that could adequately translate the condition of a nonliving entity.

"That's what you say now." He shook his head mournfully. "But I know you ambassadors. If it can't vote, you don't care for it."

T'sha whistled with mock despair. "I repent, I repent. I have learned better." Pe'sen clacked his teeth at her. "Are you ready for me, my friend?"

"Always, Ambassador." Pe'sen glided back diffidently, leaving her path clear. "If you'll enter the ring, we will send you to New Home."

T'sha tried to keep her posthands from clutching her bundle, even as she tried to keep her bones relaxed. She was partially successful. She flew across the vast, open expanse of the ring until she reached the center. She hovered there, waiting, while Pe'sen and his colleagues worked their magic.

T'sha didn't understand how the World Portals worked. Pe'sen's patient explanations of the function of waves and particles, actions at a distance, and the flux-fold model of nonliving spaces brushed past her skin and left no impression. In the end, all she really knew was that Pe'sen understood it and had made it work flawlessly hundreds of times.

Then why am I ready to bolt from fear?

Through her headset, she heard Pe'sen give the activation command. The ring sang, a high, keening note. The metalic-electric taste of the air grew overwhelming. The air below her rippled with pure white light. T'sha clutched her bundle and drew tightly in on herself. The air around her bent, brightened, and pulled her down. . . . And then she was not falling down into brightness but rising up from darkness. Clear air supported her wings, and T'sha could breathe again and look around herself.

All she saw was desert. The candidate world was gold and gray in its twilight. The wind felt firm and familiar under her wings. It was strong with the scent of acid, gritty with dust, and dense with the swirling clouds and smoke from the living mountains. For all that, the wind was sterile. She could smell no life anywhere.

The sterility, though, was not distressing, as it was on Home. Here, the wind felt clean. They could do anything here, plant anything, breed anything, spread all the life they needed. New Home, new life, new hope. Her bones quivered with an excitement that was the last thing she expected to feel.

"Amazing, isn't it?" D'seun flew from his perch on the edge of the ring and hovered next to her.

"Yes," she answered, all animosity lost in wonder. T'sha tilted her wings to rise higher. Below all the winds spread a naked crust laced with cracks and ravines and double-walled ring valleys. Twilight dulled its colors underneath her. But ahead, she could see the deepening darkness of the nightside, and there, the crust glowed more brightly than she had ever seen on Home. "It truly is amazing."

She banked back to D'seun. He was speaking to the mooring cortex next to the clamp that held the portal's kite. He turned his muzzle toward her. "I am getting a signal from the base. They are not far and are moving slower than windspeed. Shall we go on our own wings?"

"I'd like that." T'sha felt herself swell at the prospect of traveling through the fresh winds.

"Let us, then." D'seun launched himself onto the wind, sailing toward the nightside with its blackened air and brightly shining crust. The twilight they flew through turned the wind a smoky gray.

"When I first came here, I never thought to find anything without life beautiful," said D'seun. T'sha started at the brush of his words. "I keep dreaming that because this world in itself is so beautiful, so balanced, the life we spread will be the same."

A fine sentiment, one T'sha could easily agree with. The wonder of the place seeped through her skin and settled into her bones, carried by the willing wind. But she could not afford to let the feelings sink so deep that she stopped thinking. That was something D'seun might be counting on.

"The balance will depend on us," she said.

D'seun said nothing in reply. They coasted together in silence. T'sha tried not to believe that D'seun was plotting strategies in his own mind, but she did not have much success.

"There is our home." D'seun pointed his muzzle over his right wing. T'sha followed the angle of his flight.

The base drifted steadily through the thickening twilight, heading toward the darkness. They were almost fully into night now. The swirling clouds glowed orange and gold with reflected light, their wrinkles and grooves turning into black patches of shadow.

"Base One," D'seun spoke into his headset, "this is Ambassador D'seun, approaching with Ambassador T'sha."

"We are open for you both, Ambassadors" came a vaguely familiar voice. "Approach as you are ready."

They were now close enough that T'sha could see between the sails. The outside of the base's shells bristled with antennae and sensors. Their roots and ligaments created a net around ten or twelve bubble chambers that reflected the crust's light even more intensely than the clouds. T'sha had stayed in similar outposts on many of her engineering journeys when she was part of the teams trying to repair the canopy.

A windward door stood open for them. T'sha and D'seun let themselves be swept inside. The door snapped promptly shut, cutting off the wind and allowing them plenty of time to slow and bank into the main work chamber.

The company inside that room also felt familiar. Researchers and engineer clung to their perches or draped across boxes of supplies and tools, watching their instruments, inscribing their reports, or talking earnestly. She had worked with such people for most of her life, before she had decided to make her opinions public.

One engineer, a dark-gold male with a deep-purple crest, climbed from perch to perch until he stood beside them.

"Welcome back, Ambassador D'seun," he said, and T'sha realized his was the familiar voice she'd heard on her headset. She scanned his tattoos quickly. "Welcome, Ambassador T'sha," he said. "I don't suppose—"

"Actually, I do, Engineer Br'sei." T'sha touched his fore-hands. "We worked together on the D'siash survey."

Br'sei whistled agreement. "And I'm glad to be working with you again. Let me introduce you to the rest of our team. . . ." He hesitated, his gaze sliding sideways to D'seun. "If that is acceptable, Ambassador."

"As you see fit, Engineer." D'seun settled onto a pair of perches, letting his wings furl and his body deflate.

But from Br'sei's hesitation, T'sha knew that this was not always D'seun's sentiment.

She said nothing about it. She followed in Br'sei's wake as he introduced her to the ten other members of the Seventh Team. She greeted those she knew by name and skimmed their reports. Wind acidity, speed, current direction, how the world was layered, the location of the living mountains and how frequently they erupted. Maps of seeding plans. Diagrams for new bases, equipment lists, and promises. All the concerns of a preliminary research base, but the scale was staggering.

To spread life to a whole world. To turn this desert into a vibrant garden and watch the People take possession, raise that life, and use it to spread their own life, all their lives, even further. A myriad of ideas sang inside her, swelling her up as surely as an indrawn breath.

In that moment, floating there in the still air of the analysis chamber with all the possibilities of this empty world swirling inside her, T'sha had to fight to remember there were other issues here.

"What kind of attention are we currently paying to the New People?"

D'seun looked disappointed, as if he expected the marvel of this new world to overwhelm her strange obsession with the other people. "We have mapped and timed their satellite fly-overs. We arrange not to be where they are looking." A standard tactic. Stealth was important during a race to claim a resource. "If they've seen the portal, they have not made any change in routine to investigate it."

"At the moment, they are spending most of their time on one

area of the crust," Br'sei volunteered. "They seem to have found something of great interest down there."

T'sha cocked her muzzle toward Br'sei. "Something they can use to spread their life?"

"We don't know . . ." said D'seun irritably, "yet."

"They are beginning to spread their machines further out across the crust," Br'sei went on, sending a disapproving ripple across D'seun's wings. "Our speculation is they are looking for more of whatever it is they've found."

T'sha gripped a perch with one of her posthands so she could keep facing Br'sei. "But have you determined whether or not they've started to make legitimate use of any resource?"

Br'sei's gaze slid uneasily over her shoulder toward D'seun. She felt the tension in the air around her and heard the small rustle of skin and bone as the other engineers shrank or swelled nervously. "They aren't mining, if that's what you mean. Unless you've determined there's another legitimate use of the crust."

T'sha's wings rippled. What had passed between Br'sei and D'seun? She felt a kind of urgency flowing from the engineer, but without words she could make no sense of it. "They might be planting. They might be building homes."

"Homes?" repeated D'seun sharply. "Don't be ridiculous. They live in the clouds."

Slowly, T'sha turned to face him where he swelled on his perches. "My point is this," she said deliberately as she pulled herself tight. "We don't know what they're doing. If it is legitimate use, we might have to change our working plan for seeding New Home."

"You could go and ask them, I suppose," said D'seun, his voice full of bland sarcasm.

"I wish that I could," said T'sha smoothly. "But the High Law Meet authorized me only to observe, and I have no doubt you will be all too happy to report me should I overfly my commission."

They eyed each other, swelling and deflating minutely in their uneasiness, very aware that they were arguing in front of subordinates in defiance of good manners and good sense.

T'sha mourned for that one fleeting moment when they were joined in admiration of this new place. It had been a false promise of easier times.

Finally, D'seun settled on one size. Some of the belligerence vented from his body. "I'll be most interested to see your plan for a more thorough observation and study."

Perhaps he just hopes to keep me out of the way, thought T'sha and then she realized that was unworthy. D'seun wanted what she wanted, the birth of New Home. At the moment she was obstructing that.

She swallowed her bitter thought. "I would be willing," she said. "May I make a call for two or three volunteers?" She looked at Br'sei. He dipped his muzzle minutely in answer. He'd be willing to help.

"Certainly," said D'seun. "We will grow a chamber for you."

And perhaps this will give me a way to calm my own fears. Perhaps the New People are doing nothing legitimate. Perhaps we may take this world without taint of greed. I would like that. I would very much like that.

But the memory of the tension surrounding the engineers touched her again. No, the question was not whether something was wrong here, but what that wrong was and how far it had gone.

T'sha deflated and looked longingly at the silent walls. Already, she missed Ca'aed.

Chapter Seven

I am actually doing this. I am going to touch evidence of other life, of another world.

Raw excitement had stretched Josh Kenyon's mouth into a smile that felt like it was going to become permanent. He lay in the swaddling cradle that would serve as his crash-couch for Scarab Five's drop to the Discovery. It would also be his bed for the next two weeks. All around him, he heard soft rustles and mutters as his fellow passengers wriggled in their straps trying to get comfortable. All of them were from the U.N. team—Julia Lott, the archeologist, Terry Wray, the media rep, Troy Peachman, who called himself a "comparative culturalist" and was apparently there to look for any sociological insights and implications, and, of course, Veronica Hatch.

They were all nervous and fussy, very much a bunch of impatient tourists. But that was all right. Seeing the Discovery was worth anything—working his way up as a junior grade maintenance man, begging Vee for a slot on the team, even getting into Grandma Helen's bad books, which he had, quite thoroughly.

The morning after the reception, Dr. Failia had called him into the Throne Room, a place he'd been to only a couple of times before. While he'd stood awkwardly in front of her desk, she'd reviewed something on its screen that seemed to absorb her whole attention. At last, he realized she wasn't going to invite him to sit down. So he sat without invitation and got ready to wait.

She kept him there in silence for another good five minutes before she finally looked up to acknowledge his presence.

"Thank you for coming, Josh," she said, with only the barest hint of politeness in her voice. "I wanted to inform you personally that Dr. Veronica Hatch of the U.N. investigative team has requested your presence to help her examine the Discovery's laser." Dr. Failia's voice was calm but tinged with something unpleasant—suspicion, maybe, or disapproval. Josh sat there with a stiff smile on his face, torn between elation and feeling like a guilty child.

"Since you'll have far more experience with EVA's than any other member of that team, I'm counting on you to take the position of team leader, to show the others around the Discovery and make sure they do minimum damage to the site."

"But, Dr. Failia . . ." Josh spread his hands. Despite the cold look she gave him, Josh forced himself to continue. "Kevin Cusmanos has a thousand times more experience than I do. Shouldn't he be going out with the team?"

"That was the initial plan." Dr. Failia's eyes grew hard. "But we want as few people down there as possible. Every new bootprint runs the risk of damaging something priceless. Since you're going, you get to baby-sit and Kevin gets to do what he is specifically trained for—supervising the scarab and the essential mechanical support system for the team.

Josh swallowed. "Yes, of course."

"Thank you, Josh," she said without warmth. "I appreciate your help."

Did she know I talked Vee into this? Or was she just peeved that one of the yewners monkeyed with her plan? Josh shook his head at the ceiling. He had no way of knowing. The whole interview had left him confused. The times he had talked with Dr. Failia before, she had been businesslike but friendly, quick with a small joke or useful observation. He'd never seen her so forbidding.

It doesn't matter. You're here. You can worry about the rest of your life later.

The low ceiling over him held a view screen that was controlled from down in the pilot's seat. Right now, it showed an image of the hangar seen through the scarab's main window and surmounted by the back of Adrian Makepeace's head and shoulders.

"Please make sure the status lights over your couches are all on the green," Adrian was saying. "We have no flight insurance. Anybody who doesn't have a green, just holler, and we'll make sure there's nothing else to holler about. Any non-greens?"

"Going once, going twice . . ." added Kevin Cusmanos.

Josh reflexively checked the four indicator lights at the bottom of his screen. All of them shone bright green, indicating he was properly strapped in.

"They're enjoying themselves, aren't they?" murmured Julia from the couch next to Vee's.

"I don't think they get many tourists out here," said Vee. Josh heard her squirm and couldn't blame her. The couches took getting used to. He also decided not to correct their impressions of what the pilots thought of them. He'd spoken out loud that once to Vee at the reception, and she still got an angry gleam in her eye when she had to talk to Grandma Helen.

"Not many tourists?" muttered Julia. "Not too many people interested in a dive into Hell? Imagine."

Josh rolled his eyes up to try to get a glimpse of the women. He could see Veronica's feet, and Julia's. He could also see part of Julia's hand, which clutched the side of her couch so hard the fabric bunched up in her grip.

"Are you going to be all right?" asked Vee.

"Eventually, yes," Julia sighed. Josh watched her deliberately relax her hand. "This is just like being at the top of the thrill vid, you know? I hate this part."

"It gets easier," volunteered Josh. "Wait until you've done a dozen or so."

Josh spoke with more confidence than he felt. Most of his work had to do with atmospheric particle scattering, which could be done from the comforts of Venera Base and its optics lab. He could count his trips down to the surface on the fingers of one hand.

"A dozen or so," murmured Julia. "There's something to look forward to."

"It's the adventure of a lifetime," intoned Troy Peachman from his couch on Josh's right. "You should be alive to every facet of the experience."

"Alive is what I'm hoping for."

"We could record you," suggested Terry Wray helpfully. She had the couch to Julia's left. "That way you could work on your reactions each drop until you've got the keeper. Something suitably calm, yet awestruck."

"Next time," answered Julia. "I want a run-through first."

"Always a good idea," said Terry. "I can't tell you how many disasters I've had to shoot that missed all the dramatic impact just because the victims wouldn't take a minute to get their responses right."

"Well then," came Adrian's voice through the intercom, reminding them all that the speakers were open on both ends. "Let's see if we can get it right."

"Wing deployed and green at twenty percent inflation. Drop conditions green. Scarab status is go," said Kevin.

"Ready when you are, Control."

"Ready, Scarab Five," said yet another voice, this one from the hangar control. "Opening doors."

"See you on the up-trip," said Kevin.

Josh thought he heard Troy breathe something about "falling into history" but hoped he was wrong.

The view screen's feed switched down to a camera in the scarab's belly. The desk rolled past underneath them, fast and faster, until it shot away, leaving a swirl of impenetrable gray cloud.

The scarab fell. As always, Josh's stomach lurched and his body strained against the straps. His heart flipped over, a purely reflexive reaction. There was nothing he could do about it but lie there, keep his eyes on the screen, and concentrate on controlling his breathing.

On our way. They won't call us back now. We're really going to do this! The smile on his face stretched even wider.

Layers of cloud pressed against the camera. Adrian's voice, again for the sake of the tourists, droned through the intercom.

"Wing position optimized," said Adrian calmly. "Everybody okay up there? Just relax and let the couch take care of you. We're at forty-eight kilometers and looking good."

All at once, the clouds parted. Below them spread the surface of Venus, as red and wrinkled as anything Mars had to offer. It was getting closer at a rate that made Josh's heart flip over again.

"Inflating wing," rumbled Kevin. "Wing inflation at fifty percent."

Outside, the ground's approach slowed to a more leisurely pace. Features began to resolve themselves. Some wrinkles became riverbeds cut by ancient lava. Others became delicate ripples in the ground, like furrows plowed by a drunken farmer. The colors on the ground divided into rust red, burnt orange, and sulfur yellow with streamers of coal black drifting through them.

"Beautiful," breathed Troy, and this time Josh had to agree with him.

"Fifteen kilometers from touchdown and everything green and go," said Adrian. "You're not getting the most interesting landscape, but it's tough to make a good landing anywhere interesting."

"Julia, have you opened your eyes yet?" asked Veronica.

"No," Julia said, her voice pitched only slightly higher than normal. "I'll wait until we get to the ground."

"Suit yourself." Vee shrugged in her straps. "The colors are amazing."

"I'll bet."

"Three kilometers," said Adrian. "If you squint to the upper right of your screens, you'll see beacon A-34, which means we're right on target."

Beneath them, the largest furrows spread apart. Smaller furrows following the same drunken path appeared between them. The whole plain became a huge, wrinkled, color-splashed bedsheet, bent at the edges, as if viewed through a fish-eye lens. The high-pressure atmosphere played all kinds of interesting tricks with the light.

The patch of ground Josh could see became smaller and darker, until only a few rocks were visible. Then nothing but blackness, followed fast by a crunching noise from below. The scarab came to rest on a small slope, tilted up and to the left.

"And that, ladies and gentlemen, is a perfect landing," said Kevin. "You are now free to come out and see the world through the big window."

Julia was already fumbling with her buckles. Vee obviously took a second to read the directions beside her screen, because she was on her feet and heading out into the main cabin before Julia was even sitting up. Josh waited behind to make sure Julia, Troy, and Terry had successfully extricated themselves and then followed Veronica out.

Outside the front window, the rumpled landscape stretched as far as he could see. The horizon, such as it was, was lost in a dim blur that might have been dust or mountains or simply the thick atmosphere distorting the light. They were a fair way into the long Venusian day. The dim sunlight that filtered through the clouds showed a ground that reminded Josh of the Painted Desert; red, brown, orange all mixed together along with great stretches of black, rippled stone left over from old lava flows. Here and there, an outcropping of halite or obsidian glinted dully in the ashen light.

Josh watched the investigative team crowd around the pilot seats, craning their necks to see out the window. Then he saw the muscles in Kevin's jaw tighten.

"We've got a drive ahead of us," Josh said, trying to sound polite, if not cheerful. "We can use the time to get into suits. That way there'll be less of a delay when we reach the Discovery."

And less time Kevin has to deal with you guys crammed into the cockpit.

As if to confirm Josh's thought, Kevin glanced up at him and Josh read a silent thank-you in his eyes.

The statement brought universal agreement, and the team of tourists started filing back toward the changing area. Vee gave Josh a knowing look as she passed. Yeah, she would be the one to figure out what he was really trying to do. That was all right as long as she didn't try to counteract it. Kevin gave Adrian the nod, and Adrian unbuckled himself to follow the tourists.

"And here's where the fun really starts," he muttered to Josh as he passed.

You'll forgive me if I agree with the words and not the tone, thought Josh as he followed Adrian down the corridor to the suit lockers. *I can't believe we're almost there.*

The scarab crawled forward along the uneven ground. Its bumping, rocking motion added to the confusion of the suit-up procedure, but eventually Josh and the rest of the team all got safely into their hardsuits. Adrian, with Josh's help, double-checked everyone's equipment and connections and made them run down the displays to make sure those were all functional.

Everything looked green and go. Mechanical failure in the suit—joint failure, pump failure, loss of seal integrity—any of these could mean instant death. If that knowledge added extra tension to the team, Josh couldn't see it. Even Julia, now that she was on the ground, seemed to have calmed down and become wrapped up in the business of checking her equipment, as if this were something she did every day.

Admit it. You can't see beyond your own nose right now, unless it's to look at that hole in the ground, Josh admonished himself. But he couldn't really make himself care. The Discovery waited for them. He had made it. He was going to be inside, soon, very soon.

Finally, the scarab came to a lurching halt.

"We're here!" called back Kevin.

Here. We're here. I'm here.

The U.N. investigators climbed into the airlock. Josh closed the interior hatch and found a place on one of the benches. The pressurization pump's steady chugging filled the air. Next to him, Terry Wray fussed with the camera on her chest. Her normal band rig wouldn't be able to tolerate the conditions out there, so she'd have to make do with the equipment that came with the suit, and from the look on her face, it did not meet her standards. He watched Julia Lott's lips move as she removed something on her private log channel. Next to her, Troy Peachman did the same. It looked like the two of them were holding a whispered conversation. Vee, sitting on the bench between them, flashed Josh one of her mischievous grins.

"Some fun, eh?" Her voice sounded harsher than normal through the intercom. Josh wondered if she might actually be nervous.

"Not yet," he answered. "But trust me, it will be."

Now, Josh could feel the tension winding the whole team tight. The small talk and idle speculation picked up pace, as did the meaningless shifting of weight and all the other little movements restless people make when waiting. There were the usual complaints about trying to use helmet display icons that relied on eye movement and how the water-straw kept bumping up against your chin. Finally, Troy Peachman heaved himself to his feet and started pacing between the inner hatch and the outer.

Veronica watched him for about two minutes before she apparently had enough. "Oh, sit down, Troy, it's not going anywhere."

"How do you know?" he asked with the bluff humor he apparently cultivated. "Aliens put it here. Maybe they're out there taking it away again."

Terry tried folding her arms and found that didn't work. "If they were going to do that, they would have notified me."

"You?" asked Troy, surprised.

"Yeah. I'm a media drone. We're all aliens. Didn't you know that?"

"I had wondered," replied Troy blandly.

A brief collective laugh filtered through the intercoms. Before it died, the light above the outer hatch flashed green, indicating pressurization was complete.

Instantly, everyone was on their feet. Josh worked the locking lever on the outer hatch. With a clank and a thump, the hatch swung inward to reveal the rough, intensely colored world beyond.

"Have a good trip," said Adrian as Josh stepped out. Dust and stone crunched beneath his boot. To the right loomed the cliffs of Beta Regio, with its volcano thrusting up toward the boiling sky and ribbons of lava trailing down its sides. On the edge of his vision, Josh saw Scarab Fourteen creeping down beside a fresh, flowing lava stream, and he wondered how Charlotte Murray and her crew were holding up with their load of tourists.

Then he saw the Discovery's entrance squatting in front of them, and the rest of the world went away. He took three heavy steps forward before he remembered he was supposed to be leading a team out here.

His eyes found the intercom icon and opened the general channel. "Okay, everybody, try to step where I step. The ground is pretty lumpy out there."

They only needed to cross about ten meters to the hatchway. The hardsuits and the uncertain footing made it slow going, but with every step, the hatchway got a little bigger, a little clearer. He could see the handles on the side of the lid, make out the dim reflections on the curve of its gray ceramic sides, see the little scores and pits that had been made by the burning sand brushing past on the lazy wind.

Then he was standing next to it. It was there, under his glove. He couldn't feel anything, but he could see his hand on the lid.

It was a long moment before he realized the others had ringed the hatch and stood waiting for him.

"I'll open the hatchway now." Josh grasped two of the handles, bent his knees, and shoved. The cover swung aside, just as he'd been told it would. Julia clapped her hands in silent applause. Veronica stooped and ran one gloved finger over the handle he'd just used, and grunted. Peachman tromped forward eagerly.

"Hold on," said Terry. "Can we get a shot of the empty shaft?"

"Sure." Josh stepped back and let Terry come forward and point her camera and light down the steep well with its ladder. *Just don't take too long.* He laughed silently. *Get a hold of yourself. Vee was right, it's not going anywhere.*

"Got it," Terry said, sounding satisfied. She stepped back from the hatch and turned toward him.

"Okay," said Josh, trying to keep his voice calm, as if he had already climbed down into the Discovery a hundred times. "I'll go first and show you how it's done."

Josh planted his boots onto the first rung and, moving carefully, started climbing down the well. Darkness engulfed him and his suit's lights clicked on, illuminating the black rock with its charcoal veins. He had to keep himself pressed close to the rungs to prevent his backpack from scraping against the shaft wall. His throat tightened. He'd never been inside Venus before, and he could not escape the feeling that he was being swallowed.

Josh's boot touched level stone and his lights showed him the bubble-shaped room dubbed "Chamber One." He moved back from the ladder.

A shiver ran up his spine. *This place is not ours. This is other. There is someone else out there, and we know nothing about them.* That was too huge and too strange a thought not to merit a moment of sheer wonder.

There wasn't even that much to see here—the base of the ladder, the six holes gaping beside the smooth curving wall. The real prize lay through the narrow tunnel that opened by his right hand. Down there lay Chambers Two and Three and the laser.

"Okay, next," he said into the intercom. "Keep close to the rungs; don't bump your pack if you can help it." They'd all been briefed and run through the simulators, but it wouldn't hurt to remind them.

"Yes, Papa," said Vee. He watched her green form descending carefully, foot searching momentarily for each rung. But she reached the bottom without incident and came to stand beside him.

"Next," Josh said.

"Here we go," answered Julia. While the archeologist worked her way down, Veronica walked over to look at the inner doorway, if a small, rounded entry to a low tunnel could be called a doorway. Josh was torn between watching Vee and keeping an eye on Julia, who, if anything, was moving less steadily than Vee had, and wishing they would all *hurry up*.

"Vee, what are you doing?" asked Josh, to distract himself. She was crouched down and running her fingers over the threshold.

"Exploring the secrets of the universe," she answered. Her voice sounded flat, tight.

Troy descended right after Julia, followed closely by Terry. As soon as Terry was down, she whistled softly and began examining the smooth, rounded walls. Julia bent over the six holes laid out in a straight line at the base of the ladder. Josh was willing to bet she was talking animatedly into her log. Veronica stayed where she was, turning from the inner threshold to the mouth of the entry shaft and back again. Troy just stood in the middle of it all, a look of sheer delight on his face.

"Incredible. It just feels incredible."

Although part of Josh suspected Troy was, yet again, playing for the cameras, part of him nodded in agreement. He'd run through the videos and holographs a hundred times, but that was nothing compared to standing in the middle of the Discovery, feeling the stone surrounding them and wondering, just wondering.

Freed from his initial bout of amazement, Troy started hopping around the chamber like a kid in a candy store. He bent over the six holes with Julia; he ran his hands over the inner threshold with Veronica. He peered eagerly over Wray's shoulders to see whatever it was they were looking at, all the time murmuring, "Incredible, incredible."

"Can we see the rest?" asked Veronica abruptly.

Josh blinked. "Sure." *And I thought it was just me who couldn't wait.*

"One second," said Terry. "I need a shot of all of you with the light from the shaft coming down." She shuffled closer to the ladder. "Say cheese, but keep on doing what you're doing." People bent or walked, stiffly and reluctantly, but Josh supposed that would later be put down to the suits and the pressure. "Okay. All done."

Great. "Okay. The main chamber is through here." Josh gestured down the horizontal tunnel. "Again, I'll go first. It's hands and knees. Go slow and try not to bump your packs."

The inner tunnel was even more constricting than the entry shaft. The smooth, narrow way was completely dark except for the small black-and-gray area illuminated by his suit lights. He crawled forward without feeling anything but the insides of his gloves against his hands and the padding of his suit under his knees. There was no sound except his own breathing.

"It makes a slight rise here in the middle," he told the people behind him, whether they were following or waiting in Chamber One. He couldn't tell. There was no room for him to turn his head to look. His general plate displays told him only that their intercoms were up and running, not where those intercoms were.

The tunnel undulated sharply, forcing Josh flat onto his stomach. He shinnied up to the rounded crest and slid back down again. He hoped none of his tourists would find this too much for their dignity. Probably not. Troy seemed the most likely to make a fuss, and he wouldn't do it while there was a risk of being recorded. If they were nervous about the world around them, they seemed to be burying that feeling under the excitement of exploration.

Another two meters and the tunnel opened up into Chamber Two, the main chamber of the Discovery.

Josh got to his feet and turned around in time to see Veronica emerge from the tunnel. She stood up and moved back from the tunnel's mouth, turning as she did so she could take absolutely everything in.

Chamber Two was a bubble, like Chamber One, but three times as big and twice as high. Michael Lum had joked that this was obviously an alien church, because it was so hole-y. Circular niches a meter around and ten centimeters deep had been carved into the walls. Small shafts perforated the floor, ranging between one and six centimeters in diameter. Robot surveyors sent down those shafts found they interconnected at different levels underground. Maybe they once held a pipe network.

Tiny holes that sank into the walls at regular intervals might have been for staples or brackets of some kind, holding up shelves or wiring or clothes pegs for all they knew. An entire section of floor had been dug away for about a half meter, making a shallow, smooth-walled depression at the eastern curve of the chamber. At the bottom of the depression were still more holes—two ovals of eight holes each were surrounded by numerous minute holes drilled at seemingly random intervals.

Not even the stark evidence of human intervention could dampen Josh's delight at finally standing in the middle of the Discovery. Every last one of the holes now had a cermet tag next to it with a number designation. It had taken almost a week just to get all the holes tagged. The measurements still weren't finished. Hopefully Julia would be able to make a contribution to that effort with the miniature survey drones she carried in her pack.

From the ceiling hung three quartz globes. Inside them, you could see a tangle of filament wires. Big, pressure-tolerant, alien light bulbs. No one had managed to find the power source though, and God, how they'd looked.

A low, round doorway opened across from the tunnel. This one led to another smaller bubble room, almost a closet. Chamber Three. The laser was in there. Josh's curiosity was almost a physical force pushing him toward that other doorway. He kept still with difficulty while, one at a time, the remainder of the team emerged from the tunnel.

Every last one of them looked up and around, just as Veronica had. Josh had a feeling a number of jaws had dropped open. It even took Terry a moment before she started systematically aiming her camera again.

After that, it was a replay of the scene in the antechamber, except nine times more intense. Snatches of competing conversations jammed the radio until everyone remembered about the private channels. Troy and Julia crowded the edge of the pit, pointing and gesturing. Terry tried to record everything at once. Only Veronica didn't move. She stood in the middle of Chamber Two and frowned up at the lights.

In return, Josh frowned at her. He opened a private channel between them. "Vee? We're here to see the laser?"

She focused on him slowly, as if his words reached her from a long way away. "Yes. Right."

"This way." He pointed to the low doorway. His hand almost shook with eagerness. *Let the other tourists fend for themselves for a while. Let's see what the neighbors left for us.*

Josh ducked through the low doorway, for the moment not really caring if Vee followed him. He turned to the right, and there it was.

The laser rig stood next to the far wall of Chamber Three. Whoever hollowed out the chamber had left behind a single wedge of polished rock. It had been planed off at a forty-five-degree angle and tapered up from the floor until it was about level with Josh's waist. A mechanism fastened to its surface and pointed toward a pair of short, narrow holes let in the ashen light from the surface.

Clumsily, Josh sat down. Now the laser rig was about level with his nose. "We're dealing with little green men all right," he said to Vee. "If this was working height for them, they couldn't be much more than a meter tall."

Vee said nothing. She just sat down beside him.

The laser itself was nothing much to look at right off. Its body was a dull-gray half-pipe about a meter long. Two tubes with roughly triangular cross sections projected out of it and pointed toward the holes to the surface, their flared ends almost touching the living rock.

"There's a set of staples down here," said Josh, leaning into the base of the half-pipe and pointing to the thick metal fasteners. "They pull out." He gripped one carefully in his thick glove fingers and pulled as gently as he could. The staple eased out a little ways, then stopped.

"Anybody analyzed the cover?" asked Vee.

"It's a ceramic. They think it's refined from local earths. Maybe shaped by some kind of laser tomography."

Vee just grunted. Josh pulled out the remaining staples. Then he lifted the cover away to reveal an interior that glittered with black glass, crystal, and gold.

And there it all was—the power points tucked into the two long, black glass (maybe) tubes, with what were unmistakably Brewster windows set into either end. The tubes themselves contained . . . what? They didn't know yet. Mirrors of incorruptible gold (probably gold. Looked like gold) stood at either end of the tubes. Golden strips had been laid down in neat patterns along the tube supports. Pairs of thick lenses had been positioned at the end of each tube that was closest to the wall, with the smaller of the pair on the inside (almost definitely a beam expander), and in front of them was a pinplate to focus the light and send it . . . where? He looked at the holes to the surface. To do what?

Much of the answer to that question would depend on what was in those black tubes, which would tell them what kind of laser they were dealing with. The presence of the tube told them it was a gas laser, but what kind of gas laser?

When they knew what kind of laser it was, they could work out what it had been used for. And when they knew what it was for, they would know what these people were doing here, and when they knew what these people were doing here . . . the universe would open up wide.

He wanted to say this to Vee, but he didn't. Something was wrong with her. She seemed closed off, and he couldn't tell why.

Well, you can sort that out later. "Can you get the monochrometer out of my pack?"

"Right." Vee stumped around behind him and he felt the small jostlings as she undid the catches on his pack and pulled out the equipment.

While Vee squatted next to the laser to position the boxy analyzer and pump down the suction cup at its base, Josh pulled their portable floodlight out of her pack and lined it up with the monochrometer on the other side of the tubes. When both devices were switched on, pure white light would shine through the tubes into the monochrometer, which would analyze the absorption patterns and report. Then they'd know what lay inside the opaque glass.

Vee jacked the monochrometer into her suit. "Okay. Go."

Josh pressed the power-on switch and the light flashed on, so suddenly and intensely bright his faceplate dimmed. He imagined a faint humming as its beams passed through the tubes. Another shiver of fear and excitement went through him, brought by the awareness that he was doing something no one else had ever done before. Even Vee's closed expression softened as she read off the monochrometer's conclusions. "Okay, we've got hydrogen in there, a little neon, and"—she paused—"carbon dioxide." She stared at the device. "It's a CO_2 laser, Josh."

"Makes sense, doesn't it?" Josh was aware he was grinning like an idiot. "Not only does CO_2 make for a versatile, powerful laser, but our aliens have been making heavy use of local materials. If there's one thing Venus has and to spare, it's CO_2."

"Right." Vee pulled the monochrometer jack out of her glove's wrist, turned her back, and left.

Josh did not let his jaw drop. Veronica marched through Chamber Two and climbed back into the tunnel toward Chamber One.

"What was that?" came Troy's voice.

I have no effing idea, thought Josh.

"Is there a problem?" Julia stood up from her crouch over the carved-out section of floor.

"No, no." Josh waved them back. Both curious and confused, he crawled back through the tunnel to Chamber One. He got there just in time to see Vee climb the last rungs of the ladder and disappear over the side of the hatchway.

Josh opened their channel. "Vee? Vee? What are you doing?"

No answer. Josh flicked over to the channel for the scarab. "Adrian? This is Josh."

"I hear you, Josh, what's up?"

"How's Dr. Hatch's suit doing?"

"She's green and go here. Something wrong?"

I have no effing idea. Josh stared at the ladder. He did not want to chase after her. If she wanted to be a temperamental artiste, that was her business. The laser was waiting for them both. If she didn't care, fine.

Except that there were so many ways she could get herself killed out there.

Josh carefully closed down all his com channels except the one to the scarab. When he was sure no one could hear him but Adrian, he started swearing softly, and he climbed the ladder back to the surface.

As he emerged from the hatch, he saw Vee crouched about ten meters away, apparently staring at one patch of ground.

"Vee? What the hell are you doing?" Josh demanded as he started stumping toward her.

"More holes." She pointed.

"Yes, I know. We found those. They should be tagged." Two squares of four small holes drilled neatly into the earth on the right side of the hole the laser pointed through.

"Yes." She stood up and started walking back toward him. Josh stopped in his tracks.

"You want to tell me what's going on?"

Apparently, she didn't. She said nothing as she passed him and climbed back down the ladder. Josh choked off another set of curses and returned to the hatch. While he watched, she lumbered down the rungs, walked to the center of the chamber, and laid down on her back, her faceplate pointing up at the ceiling.

Bewilderment warred with exasperation as Josh climbed down the ladder and stood over her. "Are you okay?"

"Fine, thank you." Her voice was bland, almost bored, and her expression matched.

"Are you going to be able to get up all right?"

"I'll call if I can't."

He paused. "You having an artistic snit of some kind?"

"Probably. You're in my way."

"Excuse me." Josh stepped back and wished he could run his hand through his hair. He just watched the still form lying on its back and staring at the ceiling, looking for all the world like an empty suit that had fallen over. *Well, so much for the idea that you'd turn out to be the reasonable one.*

Seeing nothing else to do, Josh crawled back through the tunnel to Chamber Two.

"Is Veronica all right?" asked Troy.

"She's fine," Josh assured them all as he straightened up. "She's decided to pursue an independent investigation."

Those few words satisfied everyone. *Everybody knows how artistes are,* thought Josh as he returned to Chamber Three. *I wonder how much she trades on that?*

He pushed the thought aside. Whatever Veronica wanted to do—as long as it didn't actively involve killing herself, damaging equipment, or wrecking the site—didn't really matter. He could still work. Every part of the laser had to be measured, labeled, gently sampled, and precisely cataloged and videoed. The work and the wonder of it all soon swallowed up thoughts of anything else.

Every so often, movement in Chamber Two caught his eye. Vee went back and forth between the main chamber and the antechamber three separate times. Once, she came into the laser chamber and just sat by the wall for a while. He ignored her. Eventually, she left.

At 14:00, his suit clock chimed. So, he knew, did everyone else's, but he spoke into the intercom anyway. "That's time, folks. We need to head back."

"Another few minutes—" began Troy.

"We've got two weeks," replied Josh. "You don't want to run low on coolant out here, do you?"

That got them. All at once, everyone was ready to go. No doubt Derek had showed them the record of Deborah Pakkala, whose coolant circulation had failed on her, and how she had cooked to death in her suit before she reached the scarab, twenty meters away. Josh eyed the radio icons to flip over to the channel for Scarab Five. "Adrian, Kevin, we're coming in."

"Roger that, Josh," came back Adrian's voice. "We'll be ready for you."

Josh took a quick head count. All present, except for Vee.

"Vee?" called Josh over the public channel. "Time."

"I heard" came her voice, clear, tight, and slightly bored, as it had been for the entire afternoon.

Shaking his head yet again, Josh led the way back through

the tunnel. He shinnied over the rise and stopped. Vee's suit, on its back again, blocked the tunnel.

"Vee," he said, refusing to be surprised or angry. She would not take the wonder of this day from him. He would not let her.

"Right." Using the tunnel walls as traction, she turned herself over onto her stomach and crawled out ahead of him.

Josh led the team up the ladder and across the rough, barren ground to the scarab. The airlock hatch stood open, waiting for them. They took their spots on the benches. Josh shut them inside and signaled Adrian. The outer hatch's light blinked red as the depressurization started.

"So, Dr. Hatch," began Troy conversationally. "Did you find what you were looking for?"

"Not yet." She gave him a sunny, meaningless smile. "But as Josh said, we've got two whole weeks."

"Two weeks," said Julia less enthusiastically. "If it doesn't kill us. I feel like I've been lifting weights for four solid hours."

"It's the pressure," said Troy. "We'll get used to it, I'm sure. Isn't that right, Josh?"

Josh shrugged but then remembered his suit wouldn't show the movement. "Not really, no, but you learn your limits and how to pace yourself."

"Do you think you'll ever get used to the idea you're crawling around inside an alien artifact?" asked Terry.

Josh felt his mouth quirk up. "Is this on or off the record?"

Terry sighed exasperatedly. "Civilians. If the answer's really good, I'll ask to use it."

"My God, an ethical feeder," murmured Josh, and the remark earned him a round of laughter. "The answer is, no, I don't think I'll get used to it, and I don't really want to get used to it. We are in the middle of the most incredible thing that's ever happened and I never want to forget that." He smiled. "Good enough to use?"

"Are you kidding?" said Terry. "The boss willing, I'm going to open with that."

"And what about you, Veronica?" Troy angled himself to face her. "How did you feel inside the Discovery?"

Veronica didn't move. "Oh, I was impressed," she said distantly. "Very impressed. The sheer scale of the undertaking. It's amazing."

The team nodded solemnly.

The depressurization finished, and the green light shone over the inner hatch. Josh worked the hatch and everyone spilled gratefully over into the changing room. Adrian stood ready to help them out of the bulky suits and supplied cold water from the scarab's fridge. Josh glanced down the corridor and saw movement through the main window. Team Fourteen was on the ball and heading down for their turn at the Discovery.

By the time Josh looked up from his water bottle again, Vee had vanished. The rest of the team crowded around the kitchen table, eating sandwiches and drinking water and fruit juice in quantity. They all speculated freely and at top volume about what they'd seen, what it meant, and how they were going to frame their findings for Mother Earth. Vee did not reappear.

Conscience caught up with Josh. He drained the last of his juice and climbed through the side hatch to the sleeping cabin.

Veronica sat cross-legged on her coach with her briefcase open in front of her, typing frantically. Her lips moved as the keys clacked, but he couldn't make out what she was saying to herself.

"Are you all right, Vee?"

She looked up, startled, and for a moment he saw naked anger on her face. She wiped it away. "Fine."

What is it? What is the matter with you? He sat on the edge of the floor. "You really should at least have something to drink."

She reached down next to the couch and pulled out a bottle of water. "I'm fine, really."

"Anything you want to talk about?"

Anger flickered back across her features. "No."

One more try. "You know, this is supposed to be a team effort."

"I'd heard," she replied dryly.

Leave it alone, he told himself. *Let her play her game. This is not your business.* But there was a challenge in her eyes that grated at him. No, not a challenge, an accusation.

Josh picked his way to her couch. "What have you found?" He crouched down next to her.

With three keystrokes, Veronica blanked her screen. "Nothing I'm ready to talk about."

"Listen to me," he whispered fiercely. "You've got an act going, fine. You can play with Peachman's head, and Wray's. But you play with the Discovery, and so help me, I will make such a stink you will be booted all the way back to Mother Earth without benefit of shuttle. This is not a gallery show. This is so far beyond important we can barely understand its implications. I will *not* let you screw around with this."

Vee's angry eyes searched his face. Josh did not let his expression waver or soften. At last, Veronica dropped her gaze. Her fingers moved across the command board and typed out one line of text. She turned the screen toward him. Josh read it and his heart thudded hard in his chest.

It's a fake.

Josh sat back on his heels and met Vee's gaze. "You're out of your mind."

She frowned hard and typed.

Keep it down! We have no idea who's in on this. Go back to dinner. Tell them I overdid it and am taking a nap. Whatever. Get your briefcase out and mail me. I'll spell it out.

She added her contact code at the bottom.

Josh looked at her again. Vee's face and eyes had hardened. Whatever she'd found, or thought she'd found, she was serious about it, and if she was right. . . .

No. She can't be.

Without another word, Josh returned to the kitchen nook.

"Everything all right?" asked Troy.

"Oh yeah," lied Josh, picking up his empty juice cup and carrying it to the sonic cleaner so he wouldn't have to stay at the table and look at anybody. "It's easy to overdo it out there if you're not careful. Vee just needs to lie down and get some extra fluids."

And get her head examined. He shut the cup in the cleaner. *God, if she's doing this for self-aggrandizement, I'll kill her.*

The meal finished, the dishes got cleared, and people spread out as much as the scarab allowed, giving each other the mental space necessary for sane and civil interaction in a confined space. Adrian shuffled back to the changing area, probably to run the post-EVA suit checks and recharge batteries and tanks. Kevin was up front in the pilot's seat, running over something on the main displays. Terry commandeered one corner of the kitchen table and downloaded the day's records into her smart cam. She watched the display, apparently oblivious to anything else. Julia retreated to the couch compartment.

Josh went into the analysis nook, opened one of the overhead compartments, and retrieved his own briefcase. Perched on the nook's one stool, he jacked it into the counter's power supply and accessed his mail.

He typed, *I'm up and open. Connect to this contact,* and sent the message across to the code Veronica had shown him.

He waited, trying not to fidget. He wished he'd thought to make a cup of coffee before he started, but now that he had started, he didn't want to leave the case. Anybody could come down the corridor and read the screen. He wanted all this cleared up, now.

Another line of text spelled itself out across the screen.

Up and open. Now, first question. What's anybody going to do with a CO_2 laser on Venus?

Josh felt his brows knit together. *What?*

What's the atmosphere out there made of? CO_2. What's going to happen if you fire a CO_2 laser into a CO_2 atmosphere? The beam is going to be absorbed almost immediately. What good is that going to be? The setup makes no sense!

Josh took a deep breath, steadying himself. A grand outburst was not going to accomplish anything. *We are obviously not seeing the whole mechanism. That's clear from the pattern of holes on the outside. There was something else here.*

Pause. He lifted his cap up, smoothed down his hair, and replaced it. New text appeared.

Dead convenient, isn't it? Anything that couldn't be cobbled together from local materials is conveniently missing from the scene, like a power source for the laser, like any kind of repeater or reflector that you couldn't make out of salt and stone. And what about the lights?

The lights? typed Josh, genuinely mystified.

The lights! There are three lights in the whole place and they're all in one room. Did somebody just climb down into the dark? Crawl through dark tunnels? Send messages in the dark?

Josh remembered her lying on her back in the antechamber, staring at the ceiling. Now genuine irritation flared. What did she want, a guidebook? They were supposed to be looking for possible answers for these questions. That was why they were all here. *This installation was built by aliens; we can't except to understand their motives.*

No. That's the tautology whoever set this up wants us to start using. Anything that doesn't make sense can be put down to this all being done by aliens. OF COURSE it doesn't make sense to us.

Use Occam's Razor, Josh. What's the simpler explanation? That aliens came, undetected, to Venus and created an outpost, which they left half of in permanent darkness. Then they abandoned it, leaving just enough clues behind to let us know they were there. Or is the simpler truth that somebody set up a mysterious looking fake to gain some fame and fortune?

Or funding. Josh thought involuntarily. *Oh, Christ. Funding.*

His head felt light. The soft, background sounds of movement, random clanking, and soft conversation seemed unbearably loud. He tugged hard on the brim of his cap and looked over to the kitchen, wishing for coffee.

No. This was not happening. She was reading the data wrong.

More text spilled across the screen. *There is nothing in there we don't understand or that we couldn't make, given the proper facilities. Anything we might not understand is missing. It's a SETUP.*

Josh took a deep breath and forced his fingers to type in a reply. His hands had gone cold, he realized. *How come after weeks of camera work, measuring, tagging, and analysis, no one else has reached this conclusion?*

No one else wanted to, she replied.

Josh suppressed a snort. *And you did? Or maybe you just want to get back at Grandma Helen for thinking you're harmless?*

A long pause this time. A blank screen and a strained mental silence. *Is that what you think I'm doing?*

I think it's possible, returned Josh.

Fine. The connection shut down.

Josh sat there, staring at his screen, reading and rereading the words shining on its gray surface.

A fake? Impossible. Ridiculous. The amount of time, money, and material it would take to rig up a fake like this would be incredible. Nobody on Venera would have access to those kinds of resources.

Except maybe Grandma Helen.

Josh's spine stiffened. No. Now that really was crazy. She'd never do anything like this. No one would.

But, damn, hasn't it brought the money rolling in. Right when Venera needed it.

Josh shook his head. Crazy, crazy. The Venerans were scientists. If there was a cardinal sin among scientists, it was the falsification of data. If you got caught, it meant scandal, possible lawsuits, and the complete ruination of a career.

But if you didn't . . . Josh found he did not want to think about it. Anger darkened his mind. Vee'd done it. She'd stolen the day. Now, instead of wonder and excitement, he was filled up with suspicion and fear.

Josh slapped the case lid down. He stowed it away automatically, out of the habit of living and working in confined spaces. Then he shuffled sideways into the kitchen. No one else was there. He heard the sonic shower going. He heard voices from both sides and up front. He thought about coffee, but instead he opened the fridge and rummaged through the scarab's small stock of beer, pulled himself out a bottle, and twisted the top off.

"Everything all right, Josh?"

Josh turned. Adrian stood there, a suit glove in his hand.

"Yes and no." He sat at the table. Adrian put the glove on the table and reached into one of the overhead bins. "What's the matter with that?"

"Microfracture in one of the seals. Nothing big." He pulled down a tool kit and a plastic pack containing the silicon rings that helped seal the gloves to the joints in the suit cuffs.

Josh watched him work for a while; then he looked around carefully and said in a whisper. "Adrian, what do you think of our tourists?"

Adrian shrugged. "They're tourists," he murmured. Adrian had lots of practice at not being overheard. "They're looking for something profound or amazing to send back to Mother Earth. Saw it on Mars all the time. Idiots racing down Olympus Mons in go-carts and writing articles about what a deeply expanding experience it was." He frowned at the flawed seal for a moment. "Terry Wray's pretty cute though."

Josh chuckled. "If you like media bland."

"But it's such a cute kind of bland." Adrian inspected his work. "That'll do. I'm going to check the fit."

Adrian left him there and Josh sat alone listening to the comings and goings of the others. The air smelled of soap, sweat, minerals, and vaguely of sulfur. Josh glanced at the hatch to the couch compartment. What was she doing in there? Who was she telling her theory to? Her manager back on Earth? Julia or Troy, or one of the other team members?

Terry Wray and her camera?

Josh felt the blood rush from his face. If Vee told her ideas to anybody, *anybody,* there would be an outcry like nothing that had been heard yet. The Venerans, all of them, would stand accused of fraud. The U.N. would move in for real, work on the Discovery would be wrenched away, money would dry up, and Venera would fold, and work would stop because there would be no place to do the work from.

Stop it, Josh. What's a little more controversy?

Or are you starting to believe her? Are you starting to agree there's not one thing in the entire Discovery that could defi-

nitely not *have been made by a human with the time and resources?*

Josh swallowed hard. Feeling detached from himself, he got up and walked to the couch compartment and opened the hatch. The lights were down. Julia snored gently in her couch, one arm flung out into the aisle. Josh stepped around her.

Vee still sat up on her couch with her briefcase open on her knees. She glanced up briefly at him and then seemingly dismissed what she saw. Her hands never stopped moving across the command board.

"Don't," whispered Josh. "Don't go public with this."

"Why not?" she asked mildly.

"Because you'll ruin them. The Venerans."

"They deserve to be ruined." Bitterness swallowed all pretense of disinterest.

"All of them?" Josh leaned as close as he could. She had to hear him. He had to make her hear. "Everybody who lives in Venera deserves to be ruined? That's what'll happen."

Vee's hands stilled. "It's a fake, Josh. What do you want me to do? Perpetuate a fraud because the Venerans have been living beyond their means?"

Julia snorted and rolled over. Josh bit his tongue and waited until she subsided. "You don't give a shit about anybody but yourself, do you? You just want to show them all up. Noted artiste uncovers fraud where scientists fail. Click here to read."

Her face had gone perfectly smooth and expressionless. "Of course. What else would it be? It couldn't possibly be I believe what I'm saying or that I might be right."

Josh clamped his jaw shut around what he'd been about to say. Julia rolled again with a rustle of cloth and a sighing of breath. Josh glared at Vee as if he could make her see reason by sheer force of will. She just sat placidly, her face immobile, her eyes unimpressed.

Josh felt his teeth grind together. She'd do it. She'd ruin everything. Everything.

But what if she's right?

"What if I promised to go out now and mail Michael Lum?

Tell him your suspicions, have him double-check to make sure all the funding's on the up and up. Would that satisfy you?"

Vee's gaze searched his face, considering. "It would be a start," she said at last.

Score one. "Would it at least keep you from telling Stykos and Wray about all this?" he pressed.

There was a long pause, and then Vee nodded.

"Okay, then." Josh unbent himself as far as the room allowed.

"Josh?" Vee's whisper stopped him.

"What?"

Her face was lost in shadow, so he could not make out her expression, but he heard the weight of her words. The anger, the flippancy had left, and all that remained was honest feeling—tired and a little worried. "I am not doing this to show anyone up. I am not doing this because I'm angry at Helen Failia. The Discovery has been falsified and whoever did it deserves whatever they get."

"We'll see."

He left her there and returned to the analysis nook, shaken and confused. She couldn't be right. But what if she was? Surely somebody had already investigated everything to make sure all was in order. But what if they hadn't?

His stomach tightened. *It's happening already. The idea's taking hold. Nothing to do but clear it out, one way or the other.*

Josh got his case down from its bin and brought it back to the analysis table, setting it down next to his half-finished beer. He jacked the case in, turned it on, took another swallow of beer, swore to himself, or maybe at himself, and started typing.

Chapter Eight

Michael rubbed the heels of both palms into his eyes. When he lowered them, he blinked hard and read Josh Kenyon's note again.

Dear Michael,

Sorry I can't do a v-mail, but this has got to be kept quiet. I spent the day working with Dr. Hatch, and she spent the day getting convinced that the Discovery is a fake.

I want to laugh at the idea, but I can't. She's making some good points, especially about the fact that there is nothing down here a human couldn't have made, given resources and time. There's also the fact that some facets of this laser we're studying don't make sense.

I know I'm not a Veneran, and I'd never tell you your job, but can you let me know you've checked everything out? The money's good, the logs are good, and so on? If I don't get something to tell Dr. Hatch, she might just go straight to the media drones.

Thanks,

Josh

Michael could picture Josh in the scarab, hunched over his case, swearing as he typed, not wanting to believe, but not being able to dismiss a reasonable premise without checking it out.

A hazard of the scientific mind.

And the security mind.

Had they checked for the possibility of fraud? Of course they had checked. That was the first thing they did after the governing board had come back up from the Discovery while the implications still made them all dizzy. Helen had run the money down. Ben had done the personnel logs. Michael had checked their checking, and everything looked fine. In the meantime, Helen had sent their best people down to the Discovery to start cataloging and looking for any sign of human intervention.

They'd turned up nothing, nothing, and more nothing.

Only then had Helen called the U.N.

So what was Veronica Hatch seeing? What possibility had they left open? Or was she just playing for the cameras? She might be the type. She certainly acted like the type.

It didn't make any difference, though. If this went into the stream, the accusations were going to fly, and everything Venera did regarding the Discovery would be called into question.

Michael stared out at the world beyond his desk. Administration was Venera's brain, even if the Throne Room was its heart. Unlike most of the workspace on the base, administration was not divided up into individual offices and laboratories. Each department had an open work section with desks scattered around it.

The arrangement made this one of the noisiest levels on Venera, second only to the education level. The idea was to keep everybody out in the open, so the left hand always knew what the right hand was doing. It met with limited success, but by now everyone was so used to it, no one really worked to change it.

As always, the place was a hive. A noisy hive of a thousand competing conversations, some with coworkers, some with residents or visitors who had complaints. His people wore no uniform, but they all had a white-and-gold badge pinned to their shirts to identify themselves.

He had forty people working for him right now, counting the U.N.'s contribution of Bowerman and Cleary. Since it was the day shift, about half of the security personnel were at their desks, dealing with complaints or paperwork or helping Venerans fill out forms for passports, marriage licenses, or taxes.

Only a handful of those people knew exactly how close they'd come to losing their home.

Or how close they still are, Michael chewed thoughtfully on his lower lip. *If the validity of the Discovery is called into question, the money flood is going to dry up, and we'll be right back where we started.*

Enough. The accusation had been made. The only question left was what to do about it.

First thing, revisit the evidence. Make sure the investigation was as complete as he thought it was four months ago. Second, check out Dr. Hatch. If she was doing this to call attention to herself, maybe she'd done similar things in the past. It might help to have that to hold up to her, or to anyone else who came calling.

Of course there was somebody on the base who knew all about Dr. Hatch. Michael pictured Philip Bowerman—a big man, serious, but with a sense of humor that ran just below the professional surface. From the beginning Bowerman and Cleary had been polite, circumspect, and very aware that they were unwelcome. Michael, in return, had made sure his people were polite, circumspect, and very aware that Bowerman and Cleary were just doing their job.

Still, the idea of going to the yewners with this made his stomach curdle.

And not because you're worried you might have let something slide past that they'll catch. Oh, no.

Michael straightened up. "Desk. Contact Philip Bowerman." Bowerman was wired for sound, as were most U.N. security people. He and Cleary had given Michael their contact codes within minutes of his meeting them.

"Bowerman," the man's voice came back. "How can I help you, Dr. Lum?"

"I've got one or two questions about the U.N. team to ask you."

"Okay," said Bowerman without hesitation. "I'm in the Mall, but I'll be right up."

"No, that's okay. I'll come down."

Eleven years as head of security had given Michael a refined appreciation of how Venera's rumor mill worked. There would actually be less talk if Michael "ran into" Bowerman at the Mall than if he sat closeted with the man at his desk behind sound dampeners. Lack of talk was something much to be desired right now, especially with Stykos and his camera band roaming the halls.

"Desk," said Michael as he stood. "Display Absence Message 1. Record and store all incoming messages, or if the situation is an emergency, route to my personal phone."

"Will comply," said the desk. Its screen displayed the words AT LUNCH, LEAVE A MESSAGE.

Michael tucked his phone spot into his ear and threaded his way between the desks, heading for the stairs.

Michael walked down past the farms, past the gallery level with its harvester and processing plants, its winery, brewery, bakery, and butchery, past the research level, and past two of the residential levels with their concentric rings of brightly painted doors, and past the educational level where the irrepressible sound of children's voices rang off the walls. Below the educational level waited the Mall.

From the beginning, Venera had been designed to support whole families. Helen had wanted people to be able to make a long-term commitment to their work. The open Mall with its shops, trough gardens, food stalls, and cafelike seating clusters was one of the features that made the base livable for years at a time.

The Mall was about half full. An undercurrent of voices thrummed through the air, along with scents of cooking food, coffee, and fresh greenery. Meteorologists clustered around a table screen, probably getting readings of a storm from the sampling equipment Venera carried in its underbelly. Off-shift techs and engineers played cards, typed letters, ate sandwiches, or sipped coffee. Graduate students took advice and instructions from senior researchers, and senior researchers tossed ideas back and forth between each other. A pod of science feeders held a whispered argument among themselves. If the gestures were anything to go by, it was getting pretty heated. Families, knots of friends, and loners drifted in and out of the shops or stood in line at the food booths. Around the edges of the hall, a couple of maintenancers spritzed the miniature trees and dusted off the grow-lights. A cluster of children played with puzzle bricks at their parents' feet. If anyone's gaze landed on him, they waved or nodded and he returned their greetings reflexively. Michael no longer knew the names of everyone on Venera, but he knew most of the faces, and he couldn't bring himself to think of anyone aboard the base as a stranger.

This was his world. It was not the only one he had ever known, but it was the only one that had ever truly known him.

Spotting Bowerman took only a quick scan of the room. The man stood out in his subdued blue-and-white tunic. Venerans went in for bright colors.

Bowerman had picked a table near the far edge of the Mall under a pair of potted orange trees. He spotted Michael before Michael was halfway across the floor and lifted a hand.

"Please, sit down." Bowerman gestured toward the empty chair as Michael reached him. "Mind if I go ahead?" he nodded at his lunch—soup, fresh bread, a cup of rich *chai,* spiced Indian tea that Margot at Salon Blu imported.

"Please. I'm actually going to meet my wife for lunch right after this."

"You two have kids?" asked Bowerman, breaking apart his small loaf of sourdough bread and spreading it thickly with butter.

"Two boys," said Michael, going with the conversation and not bothering to mention that Bowerman surely knew this from reading Michael's files. "You?"

Bowerman shook his head. "Not yet." He bit into the bread, chewed, and swallowed. "This is good. I didn't expect such good food, or so much space." He gestured with the bread. "I've only been to Small Step on Luna, and on Mars once. I got used to the idea that colonies are cramped."

Michael noticed Bowerman did not say where he'd been on

Mars. "Our one real luxury," he said, repeating the stock phrase.

"So." Bowerman put the bread down and picked up his soup spoon. "How can I help you?"

Good question. Michael hesitated. He'd made up his mind to do this while he was behind his desk, but now that he faced Bowerman, he had trouble putting the words together. He was about to tell the U.N. there might be a problem aboard Venera. Venera was a colony, and the U.N. looked for excuses to make life difficult for colonies. That was a fact. What if Michael was about to give them such an excuse?

Bowerman wasn't looking at him. He concentrated on his soup, making little appreciative slurping noises as he ate. *I could get up and leave. I could invent something small and leave, go tell Helen what's going on, and let her handle it. I could do that.*

"One of the investigative team has raised a question about the validity of the Discovery."

Bowerman paused and set his spoon down. "Oh?" The syllable could have meant anything from "Oh, really?" to "Only one?"

Going to make me say it, aren't you? Okay, I'd do the same if I were you. "We investigated this exact question extensively when the Discovery first came to our attention. I assume you saw the reports?"

Bowerman's gaze turned sharp. Michael had his full attention now. "They looked thorough. Do you think you missed something?"

Michael sighed. He appreciated the lack of judgment in Bowerman's voice. Just one pro talking to another. Anybody could miss something. It happened. "I don't know," he admitted. "But if a fraud accusation is going to be made, that isn't good enough. I have to know."

Bowerman nodded soberly. "How can we help?"

Michael studied his fingertips. The scent of beef and tomatoes reached him from Bowerman's soup and his stomach rumbled. "If this is a fraud, it cost money," he said slowly. "And

Venera was running on a wing, a prayer, and short credit. If somebody did this, they got money from somewhere."

"Or shuffled it from somewhere," said Bowerman quietly.

Michael just nodded.

"Who could do that?"

"Most easily?" Michael didn't look up. He didn't want to see Bowerman's eyes, weighing, calculating, running ahead with different scenarios to see how each of them might fit. "I could. Ben Godwin or Helen Failia. After us, the department heads."

"But Dr. Failia is in charge of base finance, isn't she?"

Michael nodded again. Helen had kept that position for herself. She raised the money, she counted the money, she divvied the money up. It was no small task, but she would not delegate it. Occasionally, Michael suspected Helen did not want to admit she was not entirely in control of this city of ten thousand.

Bowerman was silent for a long time. "All right. I'll call down to Earth and start a trace on the incoming funds for, say, the year before the Discovery's announcement. Will that do?"

Now Michael looked up. Bowerman's face was understanding but not pitying, which he also appreciated. "How quiet can you keep this?"

"I'll do my best," he shrugged. "But I have to tell my boss."

"Who will have to tell the Venus work group?"

Bowerman nodded one more time. "But trust me, they will not want to let this out until they're sure. There've been a lot of speeches made about your Discovery, and nobody's going to want to look like they bought vaporware. We'll sell it as double-checking your facts. Just doing our job." He smiled thinly. "Everybody knows we don't trust your kind."

Michael gave a short laugh. "So they do."

"I'd recommend two other things." Bowerman tapped the table gently with his spoon. "First you let me ask my boss, Sadiq Hourani, to order an audit of Venera's books. If we go over it all, when we find nothing, no one will be able to accuse you of hiding anything. Also, if Angela and I do it, well . . ." He smiled again. "We can be obnoxious. We don't live here and nobody likes us anyway."

"Good idea," admitted Michael. "What's the other thing?"

"Let me get Angela checking around the team down there. See if anything suspicious is going on, let her talk to Hatch, and so on. See what the position is on the ground."

"Also good," Michael paused. "I don't suppose you can let me have what you've got on Dr. Hatch, can you?"

Bowerman's stirred his soup, considering. "I might be able to leave a file unsecured here and there."

"Thanks." Michael's phone spot rang the two-tone reminder chime. Michael tapped it in acknowledgment, gratefully. "I've got to go. I'm meeting my wife."

"Go." Bowerman waved the spoon. "I'll stop by tomorrow. Let you know what the preliminary view is."

"Thanks," said Michael again. "I appreciate it."

Bowerman smiled his acknowledgment and returned his attention to his cooling soup.

Michael didn't hang around. He headed for the nearest stairwell and climbed back up toward the educational level. Jolynn was headmaster for grades one through six and they were going to have lunch in her office. She was having it brought in.

He tried not to think. He tried to blank the conversation he'd just had out of his mind and concentrate on the outside world—the voices, the faces, the sights that he knew as well as any man from Mother Earth knew the rooms of his house or the streets of his city. He'd grown up here with tilt drills, suit drills, and evacuation drills. He'd always known that inside was safe, and outside was poison.

But he'd never believed that the outside could touch him, not really.

He'd been on Earth when his father died. For the first time, he was walking under a sky that rained water, not acid. He was breathing air that didn't come from a processing plant and seeing the stars at night. He was infatuated with Mother Earth.

His mother's v-mail came. Dad had had one of those accidents they warned you about. Venus had used one of her thousand tricks to kill him or take down his scarab. Same thing. There was nothing to bury, nothing to burn. Just a lifetime of memories ringing around his head and Mom asking him to come home.

He went. But he swore not to stay. He went so he could attend the memorial service and help sort out the will and all the other red tape death generates. All his remaining energies he bent toward trying to convince Mom to come back to Earth. She'd been born there, after all, and she was getting old, despite the med trips. Since long-life was not something she wanted for herself, what was keeping her there, in a world that would kill her?

Come down, come back, come home. This home. Our real home, where Michael was going back to and fully intended to stay.

"You do what you have to, Michael," she said. "And grant me the right to do the same."

"This is no place for a human being to live, Mom. Trapped in a bubble like this."

She'd sighed, with that annoying infinite patience she was capable of. "Some trap. The door's open Michael. Go or stay, it's all up to you." She'd taken his hands then. "I love you, Son. If you want to live on Earth, then that's what you should do." She'd meant it too, every word.

So Michael had gone. He'd finished his degree, he'd found work, and within a year, he'd come back to Venus, found work again, met Jolynn, and gotten married.

He'd never questioned what he'd done, but he'd never really understood it either. He'd never been able to point to any one thing and say, "That was it; that was why I left Earth." He'd been lonely, it was true, and the vast global village of Earth with its snarl of republics could be confusing to someone who'd grown up with one set of people his entire life. But neither of those things was entirely the answer.

On days like today, he still wondered. He did not regret, no, never that. His life was too sweet, too rich, for regret, but all the same, he did wonder.

Jolynn's office was at the end of a hall that the older kids called "grass row," presumably because your ass was grass if you got sent there. The door was open just a little, and Michael stepped into the ordered chaos—shelves and racks of screen rolls, text pads, an insulated lunch box, two deactivated animatron cats, and a worse-for-wear rubber ducky left over from a disciplinary action involving some overimaginative first graders. In the middle of it all sat Jolynn with her rich brown-black hair and beautiful amber eyes, smiling her smile that always held her own special brand of terse amusement, and just waiting for him to bend down and kiss her.

"Hello to you too," she said when he pulled back. "Sit and eat. Some of us are on a schedule." She lifted the lid off the lunch box.

About half an hour later, they had lunch reduced to salad containers, sandwich warm-wraps, and a couple of empty ice cream cups scattered on her desk. It wasn't until then that he realized Jolynn was just looking at him.

"What?"

Her eyes sparkled, and he heard her unspoken accusation.

"I am listening," he said indignantly.

Jolynn snorted. "Maybe." She set her spoon down next to one of the toy cats. "Shall I tell you what's wrong?"

Michael leaned back and folded his hands. "Please do." He'd known this was coming. He hadn't wanted to talk during lunch. He'd just wanted to be here with Jolynn in her quiet, cluttered office, away from everything else. He knew she'd notice his silence, but he still hadn't been able to get himself to make more than brief answers to her remarks about her day, their children's upcoming tests, and the intramural soccer tournament.

Jolynn bunched one of the warm-wraps into a ball and stuffed it into her empty ice cream cup. "What's wrong is that Grandma Helen has left you out of the loop and you are not doing anything about it."

How does she know? How does she always know? "I don't know that there's any loop to be left out of."

"Of course you don't. You're not asking."

Michael sighed and tapped his spoon against the edge of the desk. The plastic ticked sharply against the metal. "Jolynn, why did you come back?"

"From where?" She stuck one of the ice cream cups inside the other.

"College. On Earth." He tossed the spoon into one of the empty salad containers. "You went, just like the rest of us. Why'd you come back here?"

"Because I couldn't resist the lure of all this glamour?" She waved both hands at her cluttered, windowless office and smiled. "I don't know. I couldn't get the hang of Earth, I suppose." She paused, and her gaze focused on the wall, but Michael knew she was seeing her own thoughts. "I could have been a school administrator on Earth, anywhere I wanted, but I didn't feel like it would mean anything. My roots were all up here, everybody I really knew, everybody who really knew me, and . . . I guess I was just more comfortable with edges to my world."

"Edges?" Her words nibbled at him, reaching toward meanings inside himself that he had been trying to tease out all morning.

Jolynn nodded. "We're all stuck together up here. Everybody's got a place and something to work toward, and Grandma Helen's at the top of it all. As long as she's there, there's somebody else to make sure the world's all right. It's not all on you." She dropped the ice cream cups into the lunch box. "That's kind of a scary thought. I came back because I want to be looked after."

Michael nodded in agreement. "But it's there, isn't it? I think every v-baby's got it. As long as Grandma Helen's around, everything's going to be okay." He met Jolynn's eyes, her beautiful warm eyes. "So, what do we do if something goes wrong with Grandma Helen?"

"Tell me," she said.

So, he told her about Josh's letter and his talk with Philip and how, on the face of it anyway, Helen herself was the logical first place to look, and how he didn't want to believe that.

Jolynn smiled in sympathy and took his hand. "You said it yourself. Us v-babies, we want Grandma Helen to take care of us. We don't want to think about her not being there or being flawed. It's as bad as the day you find out your own parents are just human beings."

Michael gently squeezed her fingertips. "Yeah, it feels like that. But—"

"But nothing." Jolynn dropped his hand down onto the desk and pushed her chair back. "You go looking where you need to look and you don't come home until you've got the truth."

"I'll tell you what's wrong," Michael pointed at her. "My wife is always telling me what to do, that's what's wrong."

"Divorce lawyer's a com burst away," she returned calmly. "I'm ready whenever you are."

Michael stood up, took her face in both hands, and kissed her gently. "I'll be home for dinner." He started gathering up the lunch litter.

"Good." Jolynn grabbed up the cups and dumped them both down the solids chute. "Chase has sociology homework. That's your bailiwick."

"And while I am educating our youngest"—Michael used one of the spoons to send a few lettuce leaves down the organics chute and then dropped the spoon and the dishes into the solids chute—"what will you be doing?"

"Going to a teacher conference with our oldest. Dean wants Chord in the fast track. I want to hear what Chord thinks." Jolynn looked skeptical.

Chord was eleven, just gearing up for adolescence and all its attendant delights. "He could do it, if he were willing to try."

"And with Chord that's always the question, isn't it?" Jolynn sighed and shook her head. "Well, what will be will be, and all that. I'll see you tonight." She gave him a parting kiss and sat back down. "Now, get out of here. Some of us have work to do."

Michael grinned at her as the door slid shut between them. Now he had it, all the reason he needed to do his job, as hard and unpleasant as it might get. He'd arrested friends before. He'd told hard truths, in public. He did it because he loved his home, his wife, his sons. This was his place and it was a good place, and he would not let anyone change that.

Not even Grandma Helen.

Yan Quai had planned on being early to the performance mosaic at Shake & Jake's, but a customer had called with a last-minute order, and by the time he got out of the stream, got changed, caught the monorail, and paid his admission fee, he was an hour late and the place was jammed.

Shake & Jake's had been a warehouse or factory at some point. Now, it was a series of performance spaces. The cocktail and chat crowd circulated on catwalks, balconies, and platforms, looking down on the dancers and actors below. Each act had its own stage with a seating area bounded by sound-dampening screens so the music and dialogue couldn't get out and the rumble of casual conversation couldn't get in. The air smelled of clashing perfumes and spicy snacks.

Quai leaned over the railing on one of the catwalks, watching a trio of French cirque-tradition performers in sparkling costumes giving an exhibition of slack-wire walking. To their left, a slender couple danced a sensuous and elaborate tango. To the right was the obligatory Shakespearean scene. He couldn't hear, of course, but it looked like Macbeth and the witches. The audience seemed enchanted.

Mari, you always do throw a good party.

"Quai!"

Quai turned toward the sound of his name. Marietta shouldered her way through the crowd.

"Mari!" Quai hugged his friend and hostess. Marietta wore a scarlet sheath dress without any kind of head scarf at all. Her shoes were high-heeled pumps in a matching red, with ribbons that wrapped around her ankles. "What's this? Going historical?"

"Like it?" She twirled. Quai shook his head. Mari grimaced and smoothed the front of the dress down. "Yeah, well, actually, it's uncomfortable as all creation. I can't breathe and my feet are *killing* me. I'm not doing this again." She returned her focus to Quai, and a cheerful expression covered her face again. "So, how's your end of the revolution going?"

Quai laughed. Mari's direct approach to politics, and life in general, was legendary among her friends. "Slowly, slowly. There's a lot of thought drifting around the stream that now is the time to be a still water and run deep and not give the yewners an excuse to come busting in." No need to mention where that thought was coming from, of course.

Mari leaned against the wall to take the weight off at least one of the killer shoes. "Yeah, I've been hearing that, but I don't know. I'd feel a lot better if I knew what we were waiting for."

"Ah." Quai held up one finger. "But we do know. We're waiting for the yewners to be relieved that we didn't kick up a fuss at the height of the Discovery brouhaha and for them to relax. Then it's our turn."

"Mmmm." Mari shifted her weight to the other foot. "I'm not entirely convinced, but I'll take it under advisement. I like to know what the money I raise"—she swept her hand out to encompass the entire performance space—"is going toward."

"Same thing it's always been going toward, Mari," Quai assured her. "Finally returning full citizenship rights for the colonists."

All the colonies had suffered at the result of the Bradbury Rebellion. All colonists had a harder time getting seats on the U.N.-controlled shuttles that flew between Earth and the planets. They found it impossible to obtain licenses for starting manufacturing or shipping businesses. Their privacy was invaded more frequently, their taxes were higher, and not one of them had been allowed to hold an independent election in twenty years. Yes, they all suffered, except maybe the long-lifers in their resorts.

Mari's skeptical look did not entirely fade. She pushed herself away from the wall. "Speaking of colonists," she said, looking away from Quai to scan the room, "there's a feeder here who wants to talk to you."

"You let a feeder in here?" Quai was stunned. One of the other things Mari was famous for was her careful guest list.

"Yes," she answered calmly. "Frezia Cheney. Do you know her?"

Quai thought. He subscribed to eight or nine shallow news services and hung around three or four of the deepwater ones. That made for a lot of names to forget. "I've heard of her," he said finally. "A Lunar, isn't she?"

Mari nodded. "And she's got a reputation for fair and ruthless reporting all across the stream. We could use a few more like her." She touched his arm. "Just give her ten minutes, and I'll pull you out."

"If she wants to talk about my relationship with my mother—" said Quai sternly.

"She won't, Quai, I promise."

Quai set his mouth in a straight line and favored Mari with one of his Grade A sour glares. Mari responded with a pitiful look that made the most of her big, brown eyes. Quai laughed and relented.

"Okay."

Mari opened her mouth, but Quai pointed a finger at her. "Ten minutes, that's it. After that, you come get me. I want to go see the cirque troupe, and I promised Eli we'd do some coordinating."

"I swear." Mari held up her right hand to promise and grabbed Quai's wrist with her left. "Come on."

Quai sighed inwardly and let himself be pulled along.

He had over the years become extremely wary of stream feeders. Only a few had ever actually wanted to talk to him. Mostly they wanted to talk about his mother. If they were pro-U.N., they wanted to know why he chose to damage her life with his outspoken causes. If they were separatists, they wanted to know why he didn't denounce her timid politics more frequently.

This particular feeder sat in a wingback chair in a little parlorlike cluster of seats and tables. As Mari and Quai crossed the dampening field, the muted roar of the party fell away. Frezia Cheney was a fine-boned woman with pale copper skin and coffee-dark eyes. She was conservatively dressed for this party—loose gold trousers and a knee-length white tunic with gold embroidery around the collar and cuffs. A gold beaded cap covered her black hair, which had been pulled into a knot at the nape of her long neck.

"Frezia Cheney," said Mari as the woman stood up. "This is Yan Quai. Quai, this is Frezia Cheney."

"How do you do." Quai shook Ms. Cheney's hand. As he

did, he noticed the clear plastic exoskeleton extending out of the woman's tunic sleeve to cover her hand. Not only was Ms. Cheney a Lunar, she did not spend much time at all on Earth. If she did, her muscles would have been able to manage the gravity without help.

"Thank you for agreeing to see me, Mr. Yan." Ms. Cheney withdrew her hand and sat back down a little hesitantly. The exoskeleton allowed her to move freely, but it could not disguise a Lunar's mental discomfort with full gravity. "I am sorry about having to bring this to a social gathering. Would you prefer I made an appointment to meet you at your office?"

Two points for the appearance of consideration, anyway. "No, this is fine," Quai said, casting a significant look toward Mari. "I understand having a crowded schedule."

Mari patted Quai's shoulder as she left. Quai sat in the second wingback chair, which was turned so he was almost knee-to-knee with Ms. Cheney.

"Something to drink?" asked Ms. Cheney.

"Scotch, thanks," replied Quai, and Ms. Cheney sent the table scooting away with orders for two.

"Now." Quai crossed his legs and pulled out his best businesslike voice. "What can I do for you, Ms. Cheney?"

Ms. Cheney smiled. "Don't worry, Mr. Yan. I have no intention of asking you about your mother."

Not yet, anyway, thought Quai, but he kept his expression bland. "Well, that's refreshing."

Ms. Cheney gave him a knowing look. When he didn't react, she just shook her head. "I'm much more interested in a little company called Biotech 24."

"Biotech 24? And they are?"

"A little stream company that's been giving money to various research projects out in the planets, including to a Dr. Meyer up on Venera Base so she can study what she thinks is microscopic life in the Venusian cloud banks." The table returned, and Ms. Cheney handed Quai a short, stout glass.

"And why would you be interested in them?" Quai sipped his drink. One of the other things Mari did really well was catering. This was the pure stuff. No rapid distilleries for Mari's patrons, no sir.

Ms. Cheney wrapped her fingers around her glass. Quai heard the minute hum as the servos tightened her grip for her. "Because a friend of a friend of ours wants to know if there's separatist money behind it."

"A friend of a friend of ours?" Quai felt his eyebrows rise. "Is there a name involved here?"

Ms. Cheney lifted the glass and cradled it in her augmented hands but did not drink. "Paul Mabrey."

Quai whistled long and low. "Now there's a memory. I thought he'd ceased to exist." Quai had researched the Bradbury inquisitions thoroughly. He looked on it as a necessity. So many people popped their heads back up once every five years or so that you needed to know whether they were the real thing or whether they were on the yewner's fishing teams. His mother's colleague Mr. Hourani was particularly good at getting old revolutionaries to turn on the new separatist movements.

"There was a rumor he was gone." Ms. Cheney's face was guarded. "But he's back, and he wants to help, or at least not do any harm."

"I see." No one had ever accused Paul Mabrey of actually cooperating with the yewners, that Quai had heard. There was, however, a kind of automatic suspicion attached to anyone who got out of Bradbury without having to go to trial. He'd have to check the stream, see if there was any gravitational attraction between Mabrey's name and Hourani's. "Is Mabrey the friend, or the friend of the friend?"

"He's the friend." Ms. Cheney still did not drink. Quai started to wonder why she'd bothered to send for a drink she didn't want. Probably so she'd look companionable.

"And the friend of the friend?"

Ms. Cheney did not miss a beat. "I'm not at liberty to say."

Quai took another swallow of his own drink. She didn't know what she was missing here. "Then I'm not at liberty to speak."

They regarded each other for a long moment, weighing their private considerations and deciding how much they could give or how much they had to hold back.

"If Biotech 24 is working with you, then there's a potential disaster brewing," said Ms. Cheney. "The yewners are ordering an audit of Venera's books. They won't miss this."

That caught Quai off guard. He let the silence stretch out too long before he was able to answer. "And were that to be any kind of a problem, Paul's friend might be in a position to do something about this?"

"Yes."

Which pretty much told Quai who the friend of a friend was. There was only one place where the organized separatists had been able to make any inroads on Venera. The Venerans were so ruthlessly apolitical that it wasn't funny. Sometimes Quai wondered if it was part of the boarding oath. "We the undersigned agree not to have any opinions whatsoever."

Well, well, Ben Godwin has decided to move from sympathizer to player. Dicey time to try it. I wonder what changed his mind?

I wonder what Paul Mabrey has been up to all these years? Maybe it's time to dither.

"Listen, Ms. Cheney," he began. "I'm only loosely jacked in to that end of—"

Ms. Cheney snorted and waved one hand. "If you don't want to tell me, Mr. Yan, just say so. The only person who knows more than you about where the Terran separatist money comes from is our hostess."

Quai smiled, just a little. "I've heard that one too. If it's true, then Heaven help the separatists, because nobody knows what's going on."

Ms. Cheney studied him in silence for a minute. Then she said, "The game's starting up again, Mr. Yan. This may be our last, best chance to break from Earth. The longer the yewners can be put off, the better for us." She set her drink back down on the table, still untasted. "Now is not the time to be invisible. Now is the time to let them know we're here."

"There I do not agree with you." Quai shook his head.

Ms. Cheney shrugged, a move that made her servos buzz angrily. "And there's a lot of us on Luna who disagree with your disagreement. But that's all right. Unless"—she turned her head so she regarded him out of one shining eye—"that's what's keeping you from answering my questions?"

Quai took another sip of scotch and rolled it around in his mouth for a moment, considering the possibilities. He had to agree that having the yewners track down the origins of Biotech 24 would not be a good idea. However, at least as far as he was concerned, and he was the one being asked here, neither Paul Mabrey nor Ben Godwin were good risks. On the other hand, Mari trusted this woman, and Mari's judgment was sound.

Also, it was worth a little payback to know that the Lunars were not willing to sit back and wait.

Of course, Ms. Cheney could not be speaking for all the Lunars, any more than he and Mari worked with all the Terran groups. There were knots and bunches of people who called themselves separatists, or procolonials, or planetary-rights representatives scattered all across four worlds, and in the L5 archipelagoes to boot. Some of them held summits together. Some of them actively hated each other. They had all been born out of the Bradbury Rebellion, but their principles divided them more than they united them.

Sometimes Quai wondered why the yewners considered them any kind of threat.

Still, if he gave Ms. Cheney what she was looking for, she might be able to give him an inroad to the Lunar separatists if he needed it later.

"Yes, there's separatist money in Biotech 24," he said at last. "No, it would not be a good thing if the yewners knew that."

Ms. Cheney nodded. "Thank you."

"You're welcome, Ms. Cheney." Quai set his drink down on the table and stood. "Anything else I can help you with?"

"Not at the moment." She stood also and held out her hand. "But I may want to talk to you in the future."

"And I may want to talk to you." He shook her skeleton-encased hand, barely able to feel the flesh under the plastic cage.

"I look forward to it."

They said good-bye and Quai walked away to find Mari. It wasn't hard. She stood out like a scarlet exclamation point in a crowd of men and women in earth tones and gold. She spotted Quai and extricated herself from the group.

"I see you got yourself out."

"Years of experience." Quai leaned against the railing and looked down on the stages. A cirque performer was juggling now, a brilliant cascade of green glowing spheres. "Mari, did you know what that was going to be about?"

"Of course," she answered simply.

Quai cocked an eye toward her. Her face was free of any suspicion or apology. "And you trust her all right?"

Now Mari frowned. "I wouldn't have sent you in there if I didn't, Quai; you know that."

"I do." Quai rubbed his hands together. "I just . . . I don't know."

Mari touched his shoulder. "What's the matter?"

He looked up at her. Her hand was warm and felt very pleasant where it was. A pretty woman, Mari, a good friend, and a savvy businessperson. They needed more people like her. "You ever wonder if we know what we're doing? If we're the right ones for the job?"

She laughed and patted his back. "Constantly. But we're all there is."

"I guess."

"Come on." She took his arm. "You're not having fun, and that'll be no good when I start pressing for account deductions. Let's go watch the cirque troupe."

"In a second, Mari." Quai straightened up and gently extricated his arm from hers. "Can you get me a secure line? I've got to send out some mail."

"Sure. Hang for a minute." Mari threaded her way expertly through the crowd, heading for the offices in the back.

Quai hung. He watched the performers and the audiences, and the talkers and the drinkers. He wondered how many people here really believed that the colonists deserved better than they were getting and how many of them were just here because Mari knew they had deep pockets and wanted to pretend they were involved in daring underground politics.

How many of them had waived their right to kids in favor of

long-life? How many of them wanted to have both the kids and as much immortality as money could buy and had already re-served a slot in some resort on the Moon or Mars where they could retreat once they reached age 120? That was the deal. You got long life, or kids, or you left Mother Earth behind.

And for the hundred-millionth time Quai told himself his ac-tivism was not about his father's decision to take the waiver and leave him.

Mari came back with a minipad. She slotted it into the bar, hit a couple of command keys, and handed him the stylus. "It's all encrypted under some of my best stuff, so don't send any-thing they'll want to trace. The yewners will think it's me."

"Never." Quai took the stylus and considered the blank screen for a moment.

Finally, he wrote: *Old friends operating under alias in tar-geted area. Working toward mutual goal. With their efforts, we might get there sooner rather than later if we just sit back and let it happen. But maybe keep one eye on the Moon.*

He addressed the message to an alias and sent it out. The contact code he sent the scrambled package to was a group box. Buyers and sellers of all kinds went in there to keep up on gossip, to give leads to friends, that kind of thing. All of it was scrupulously legal, of course, or, at least, all of it was so far unaudited.

Quai sat back and fingered the holotattoo on his neck. He could barely believe things were really happening. Ever since he'd thrown in with the separatists, he'd gotten used to the idea that it was going to be a long, hard slog. Ted Fuller rotted in an isolation cell. Mars was discovering easy economic bene-fits in lining up to serve the mines, the heavy industries, and the long-life resorts.

But now, now, he could see the end. He could almost touch it. Okay, not the end, but the beginning. The new beginning.

He'd never really believed he'd have this kind of help, or that the people they needed so badly would come around.

But he did and they had, and now it was a whole new game.

* * *

"Well, well," murmured Alinda, pushing her heavy braid of hair back over her shoulder. "Don't push the Send key yet, ladies and gentlemen."

Grace looked up from her desk. "What are you mumbling about, Al?"

Alinda's dark eyes sparkled and Grace groaned inwardly. There was nothing Alinda Noon loved more than a good rumor.

That is the biggest problem with v-babies, thought Grace. *They all believe gossip is a social grace.*

The three of them sat along the curving wall of Chemistry Lab Nine, their desks a small island on a sea of cluttered work-benches and metal-sided analyzers.

"Looks like reports of aliens on Venus were a bit premature," Alinda went on.

Grace froze. "What?" she demanded.

"I win the pool." Al called over her shoulder to Marty, who'd frozen his own simulation to listen. "I said the yewners would be crying fraud within a week of getting here."

"What are you talking about?" Grace heaved herself to her feet.

Alinda blinked, startled. "Nothing catastrophic, Grace, really. The yewners are calling for an audit of base books and time logs. Only one reason for it. They think we've been playing games with time and money."

Each word thudded hard against Grace's mind. "But they don't know?"

"Know we've been playing games?" Alinda's brow creased.

"That the Discovery's is a fake!"

"Of course not. Why? Should they?"

Alinda's blank look, Marty's stupid, stunned stare were suddenly more than Grace could stand. "Pay attention, little girl!" she roared. "That Discovery is saving your job and your precious base! If it gets taken away, this whole place is going into cold storage! There is nothing funny here!"

Grace wanted to shake her. She wanted to smack him. Instead, she strode into her private office and slammed the door. She knew outside a whole cloud of whispers was now rising,

most of them containing her name. She had just given the entire lab something to chew over for weeks. She gripped the
back of her chair and squeezed.

*Get it together, get it together. Nothing's happened yet. It's just
an audit. Of course there had to be an audit.*

But it wasn't just an audit; it was another round of questions
and inspections and sideways glances and gossip and more
questions and nobody believing what she'd found.

For just a minute there, it had been going so well. The outside world was actually listening to her. For once, the great
Helen Failia hadn't been able to divert her funding or try to
monopolize her research assistant's time.

On the wall of her office, Grace kept a still shot of an absorber chain. It had been taken by a stasis microscope and
looked like someone had taken forty gray-and-white tennis
balls and stuck them together in a ring that twisted in on itself.
Not in the neat double helix, but more like a bedspring wound
far too tightly and then folded over in the middle and fed back
into itself.

This small tangle had been her life for ten years. She and her
team had isolated this as Venus's mysterious ultraviolet absorber. Snarls of this little molecule created the dark bands that
showed up in the cloud banks. There had been praise and papers and money, and even Helen had been happy.

Which had all been fine, but then Grace had discovered that
the compound was alive.

"Now, I'm not saying it's a yeast or an alga," she tried to tell
them. "But it must be considered on a level with a virus or at
the very least an autocatalytic RNA molecule. It absorbs energy;
it exudes waste chemicals." Ozone and water molecules were
more concentrated in the absorption bands than outside them.
This had been independently measured. "It has an identifiable
internal barrier to increase electrochemical potential. And"—
she'd stab at the table, or the chart, or the nearest person with
her index finger as she got to this part—"it reproduces itself."

There was the snag. The molecules were highly active, always combining and recombining. But Grace couldn't get anyone else to say that this process was definitely reproduction,

and she hadn't yet been able to duplicate its peculiar gyrations in the lab. The consensus of the rest of the worlds was that the intense ultraviolet light hitting the top of the cloud layer broke apart the molecules, which re-formed once they'd dropped far enough down in the clouds to be out of reach of the worst of the UV.

But she hadn't stopped. She had years' worth of observations. She scrabbled for independent confirmation of her results. She fought to bring biologists and chemists to Venera to look at the absorbers, just on the chance that someone else would finally see what she saw.

For the first time in her long life, Grace was certain about what she was doing, and that certainty had almost ruined her.

Grace brushed her bangs from her forehead and stared at the absorber on her wall. She hadn't planned on becoming a long-lifer. She'd planned on taking her 120 allotted years, getting a decent life, getting married, having a kid and passing on, leaving the kid, or the work, or both, behind to say Here Lived Grace Meyer.

But it hadn't worked out that way. She'd gone into chemistry because it could be applied in so many different fields, not because it interested her for its own sake. She'd wandered from job to job. In each one, she found she was a solid middle-of-the-road performer. She was good enough but not brilliant, never brilliant. Always the third or fourth name on the few papers that her work groups published, never quite making the patent disclosures.

Her first marriage had bombed, the second had petered out, the third . . . the third had barely existed. After the third, she realized she'd been wandering from husband to husband the way she'd been wandering from job to job, so she swore off marriage.

It was after that that she'd headed for "the planets," hoping in her vague, wandering way that her life waited for her outside Mother Earth's sheltering arms.

And then you found it, and nobody listened to you. Grace laughed and shook her head. *Too perfect.*

But I made them listen. She smiled at the picture of her little, personal discovery. *Even if just for a little while, I made them listen.*

And if the yewners discovered how she'd managed that particular feat, then it really was over. Everything. Here Lived Grace Meyer, Fraud.

No, she dug her fingers into the chair's fabric until her nails bent against the frame. She'd wiped the trail clean. She'd reviewed all the records and put them back the way they were supposed to be. There was no linkage. Nothing.

Nothing you can think of anyway.

Grace closed her eyes. Now it wasn't just routine logs sitting in the endless streams of screenwork that Venera generated. Now it was individual files being scrutinized by Michael Lum, who'd apprenticed under Gregory Schoma, the man who designed Venera's security. Now it was two yewner cops helping him.

All that skill and brilliance trained against the work of Grace Meyer, who'd never been able to get anyone to believe she might actually be more than just competent.

So what do you do about it? Grace opened her eyes and focused on the image of the absorber, the real discovery, the true evidence of life on Venus. *You go back over everything. You make sure there's nothing you've missed. Come on, Grace, it's basic research. You've been doing this for seventy years. Go in there and see if you can find yourself.*

Grace pulled the chair away from her private desk and sat down, waking the command board with her touch. As she started shuffling her icons, she realized she'd have to do something about Alinda. She and Marty would spread news of Grace's outburst across half the base, with embellishments, if Grace didn't give them something else to think about. She did not need for her name coming to the yewners' attention. Not like this, anyway.

Grace fixed a smile onto her face and walked back out into the main lab and up to Alinda's desk.

"I'm sorry, Al," she said, meaning it. "That was completely uncalled for. I've been sitting on the edge just a little too long."

Alinda, as quick to forgive as she was quick to talk, waved

Grace's words away. "It's okay, Grace. We all want this to be real, and our department's got more reason than most."

Grace nodded. "Just one more attack on the data. Only to be expected." She shrugged. "What would you say to a show of unity? The microbrewery's got a new batch coming out today. We could close up shop early and go try a sample. My treat?"

Al's face lit up. "Sounds great. You in, Marty?" She turned to her fellow researcher.

"The boss's buying beer?" Marty's thin grin split his face. "You bet I'm in."

Grace smiled down on them. Kids. Easily distracted. Michael and the yewners would not be so easy. With them, she'd have to be careful; she'd have to be thorough.

For the first time in her life, she really would have to be brilliant.

Chapter Nine

T'sha found Tr'es in the life research chamber. She hovered silently in the doorway and watched the child work. *No, not child. Stop thinking like that.* Tr'es was small, it was true, almost as small as a male, and her crest shone blue as sapphires, undimmed by age. But she was an adult, picked out by Br'sei shortly after her Declaration. She followed his promises and left Ca'aed's care for Ke'taiat's, to become one of Br'sei's best engineers, or so T'sha understood.

Even so, there was something furtive about Tr'es, or at least there was when she was around other people. Here, though, alone with her maze of microcosms, caretakers, and simulators, she was intent and confident. Reverse engineering, that was Tr'es's specialty. Find something that existed and track it back through all its previous stages. Take it apart until you understood it and put it back together again.

Rather like what I'm trying to do here. T'sha poked her muzzle into the room. The gesture did not catch Tr'es's attention. The engineer just hovered in front of her simulator, talking nonstop in a specialized command language and watching patterns that might have been wind currents on the nightside, or neurochemical diffusion, flow across its surface.

T'sha flew all the way into the room, careful not to touch any of the microcosms or their connecting tubules.

The shadow of her movement crossed the simulator's surface, and Tr'es whirled around, startled.

"Oh, ah, good luck, Ambassador T'sha." She raised her forehands. "I didn't . . . I—"

"You were absorbed in your work." T'sha glided carefully between the tools, both living and nonliving. "I know how it feels."

Reassured, Tr'es inflated slightly. "Is there something I can share with you, Ambassador?"

"I hope so." T'sha finally spotted a pair of rods that she was fairly sure were perches and settled onto them. "I understand it was you who did the initial work on the raw materials D'seun took from the New People." She had listened to the caretaker of the reports for an entire dodec-hour and had practically had to be carried into the refresher, she was so exhausted. Fear had kept her listening. Fear and suspicion, because of what she could not find.

Tr'es dipped her muzzle. "He wanted me to map neural branching and chemical diffusion patterns to see if we could link that and the gross physiology to the transmissions we were receiving and make a start on the language translation."

She seemed about to go on, but T'sha interrupted. "And you have made great progress, I see."

Tr'es shriveled a little, embarrassed. "We have done our best. The New People are complex. They have at least as many command languages as we do, and those patterns are all bound up with their person-to-person speech. Teasing them apart has not been easy."

T'sha whistled her appreciation. "No, it would be extremely difficult. Your good work will make your birth city proud."

At that, Tr'es puffed up fully. "How does Ca'aed?"

"Very well." T'sha whistled more approval at the warmth with which Tr'es spoke of her blood home. "You have been here a long time, haven't you? Perhaps a trip back to Ca'aed is indicated."

Tr'es cocked her head first to one side, then the other. "I'd like that, Ambassador T'sha, if Ambassador D'seun would agree. . . ."

T'sha decided to spare her from having to go on. "We can leave the discussion for later if you think that would be better." This was a rough wind. T'sha had some authority over Tr'es, as ambassador from her birth home, but if Tr'es's loyalties weren't all promised to D'seun, she was the only one on the team, except possibly for Br'sei. Br'sei, however, was older, much more complicated, and much better at hiding what he really knew, so T'sha had decided to tackle Tr'es first.

Tr'es had swelled even further. She was almost her normal size now. "Yes, that might be best."

"Then that's what we'll do." T'sha stretched her wings. The child . . . Tr'es was as relaxed as she was going to get. Now was the time to ask the real question. "Tr'es, how did the New People's raw material come into our possession?"

"I was not there," said Tr'es, just a little too quickly. "Ambassador D'seun said there was an accident and all that remained of the New People who suffered was raw material, which he collected for study." She shifted her size uneasily. "For me to study," she added like an admission.

T'sha dipped her muzzle. "That study sounds as though it was arduous," she said, carefully keeping the touch of judgment from her words. "How did you deal with the extreme cold?"

"Carefully," said Tr'es, with a flash of engineer's humor. T'sha clacked her teeth. "At first we used only nonliving tools. Then, working from the New People's material, we were able to grow some specialized microcosms that were able to keep their liquid transfer media intact and yet perform useful work."

Again, T'sha whistled, this time genuinely impressed. Tr'es was no child when it came to skill. To not only propagate an alien life but to make a useful tool of it with only a few years of study, that was a feat indeed.

Unfortunately, it did not change the reason T'sha had come. "They are delicate things, the New People," she said. "Ambassador D'seun must have moved very quickly."

Tr'es hesitated, but then dipped her muzzle. "That is my understanding," she said softly.

T'sha thrust her muzzle closer. "Did no new people arrive to claim the raw materials of their own?"

"They may have, later, but"—Tr'es rattled her wings uneasily—"raw materials are raw materials. They belong to whoever claims them first."

"True." T'sha dipped her muzzle. "We are fortunate Ambassador D'seun was so alert. The translations would be going much more slowly if you had not had anything to work with."

Tr'es's relaxation vanished. She pulled herself inward, minutely, just a couple of bones at a time, as if she were hoping T'sha wouldn't notice. "I believe he was waiting for such an occurrence."

"Waiting?" T'sha pushed closer.

Tr'es's skin trembled as she deflated. "I have work to do, Ambassador. Is there anything else I can share with you?"

T'sha let go of her perches and glided forward until the tip of her muzzle just brushed Tr'es's bright-blue crest. "How quickly did D'seun move to obtain the raw materials, Tr'es?"

Tr'es jerked away and turned to face her simulator again. She spoke a few words in a command language T'sha didn't know, and the diaphanous patterns were replaced by a more familiar wind grid.

"Tr'es," said T'sha, although the engineer was no longer looking at her. "What has D'seun made you do?"

"He made me do nothing," said Tr'es without taking her gaze off the simulator. "I have made promises."

T'sha moved up next to her until they hovered wingtip to wingtip. T'sha did not overfly her, not yet. Tr'es still might talk without overt intimidation. "This is not about promises. I was sent here by the High Law Meet, just like you were. We're here to do what's right for the People."

"That's what I'm trying to do," Tr'es said miserably, huddling in on herself.

"Tr'es."

T'sha turned her head, her muzzle still open to speak. Br'sei glided through the doorway.

"D'tak needs some help in the surveying chamber," he said, brushing a forehand against Tr'es's wing. "There's an unpredicted mutation in the preparers we seeded in Highland 98. We need to find out where it came from."

"Yes, Engineer Br'sei." Tr'es swelled instantly with relief. She flew away without giving T'sha a second glance.

Br'sei faced T'sha, saying nothing, waiting for her. It was a remarkably discomforting tactic.

"Excellent timing, Engineer," remarked T'sha at last.

"Forgive me, Ambassador T'sha." Br'sei sank a little with a humility T'sha was certain he did not feel. "But if you're going to make trouble for someone, it really should be for someone who can handle that trouble."

"I am making trouble?" T'sha pulled her muzzle back. "I thought I was doing my job."

"That is what everyone here thinks." Br'sei's wings fluttered, bobbing him dangerously close to some of the carefully aligned microcosms. "Unfortunately, everyone has conflicting ideas as to what that job is."

"I see." T'sha dropped until she was level with him. "And what do you think *your* job is?"

"I was brought here to establish a life base on this world, one that could form the foundation for a canopy, for our lives," said Br'sei without flinching or hesitation. "I've done that."

T'sha moved in closer. She wanted to breathe him, taste him thoroughly. She wanted there to be no chance of misunderstanding even one word. "There is more in you," she said.

"Yes."

Closer. Make him aware of you. Let him be unable to escape the touch and taste of you. "Is it some promise to D'seun that keeps you from telling me?"

"In truth, no, it's . . ." He inflated suddenly. "Ambassador, T'sha, have you seen the New People yet?"

The question caught T'sha off guard and she backed away. "In truth, I haven't. I have been busy going over reports and trying to understand—"

"What Ambassador D'seun has been doing with his team." Br'sei finished her words and pointed his muzzle toward the doorway. "The New People's home is near. Will you come with me to see it?"

Eagerness and caution both tugged at T'sha. "Can we do so in safety?"

"If we keep our distance, we can, but we will need a dirigible." Br'sei spoke a few command words into his headset. "It will meet us at the mooring point." He glided out the door. T'sha rattled her wings to the empty air and followed.

They reached the fat, white dirigible without encountering D'seun. T'sha felt a bit like a child breaking curfew. It occurred to her to wonder if Br'sei had made sure D'seun was away before he came to her. Br'sei was cautious enough to think of such a thing.

The dirigible opened its doors and waited for them to fly aboard.

T'sha settled herself on one pair of perches while Br'sei spoke in the dirigible's command language. The dirigible gave its confirmation, closed its doors, and began to rise.

They flew straight up into the shifting clouds, far up past the temperate zones to where the air was cold and thin and the gases themselves began to freeze into liquids. T'sha stroked one of the dirigible's tendons in sympathy. It had been bred for harsh conditions, but this could not be comfortable.

Br'sei said nothing during the flight. T'sha let the silence float between them. He was making decisions, that much was obvious. She needed to give him room. He was not some overawed child who needed to be alternately coaxed along and reminded of his responsibilities. Br'sei had been declared adult before T'sha had even been born. Whole cities owed their lives to his work, and if he was successful here, the whole world would too. D'seun would take the credit for it, as ambassador. But T'sha at least would know who had grown the life, who had really spread it.

And I will make sure that others do too, she vowed silently. *You have my promise.*

"There," said Br'sei suddenly.

T'sha let go of her perches and floated up beside him. Through the dirigible's eyes she saw a sphere of silver with its wings and tail spread wide to catch the winds. Thick tendons connected an elaborate exoskeleton to dull-gray skin.

"It's a city!" T'sha clacked her teeth delightedly. "Clearly, that is a city. Why did no one say!"

"It's not alive."

T'sha turned one eye toward him. "What?"

"It's not alive," he repeated slowly and forcefully, allowing each word to sink into her skin. "None of their cities are. They're metal."

T'sha pulled in on herself, almost unwilling to understand. "Ca'aed has metallic extensions, Engineer. That doesn't mean—"

"I don't mean metallic extensions, Ambassador." Br'sei swelled and spread his wings. His hands all grabbed a perch to keep him from bumping into the ceiling. "I mean metal. The shell, the tendons, the bones. That was built, not grown. It is not alive. None of their cities are."

"That's . . ." T'sha stopped, searching for words.

"Morbid? Disgusting? Frightening?" suggested Br'sei, clenching and unclenching his posthands in his agitation. "I have thought all of these things."

T'sha struggled. To live encased in metal, to not even try to emerge. How must that be? "I would not be able to tolerate it," she said slowly. "I would go insane. But I have a friend, Technician Pe'sen, who would be fascinated by this."

Br'sei clacked his teeth once, sharply. "Technicians always are a bit morbid, aren't they? To give yourself over to the science of the never-living, I suppose you must be." He whistled. "I have thought we might need one or two technicians on this team before we are done." He gazed at the distant silver sphere again, clenching his hands around his perches. "But, I ask myself, as a good engineer must, because their environment would make me insane, does it follow that they must be insane? There are many creatures in the canopy who eat what would poison a person."

T'sha remained silent, feeling the pattern of his words with care. Where did these questions come from? Were they wholly his own, or had someone said something to him to lift the questions up? Someone who might be Ambassador D'seun?

"Have you found an answer to this question yet?" asked T'sha carefully.

"No." He faced the graceful, lifeless sphere that held all there was of the New People on this world. "I have seen what there is to see of them, and of us, and my thoughts have swung back and forth until I'm no longer sure what wind blows them." He deflated. "I was hoping that your thoughts would be steadier than mine."

"Engineer Br'sei." T'sha glided to his perch and settled there, her wings touching his, her crest brushing his back. "What has D'seun told your team?"

Br'sei did not look fully at her, but neither did he deflate. He just spread his crest, as if seeking his balance in a difficult wind. "That you are greedy and dangerous. That you are rich and young and do not see beyond your own ambitions. That we must not say what we know of the New People because too many in the High Law Meet would be frightened and advocate finding another world so as not to be too near this potential insanity. That the People are dying and if we do not succeed with this world, we are all of us dead." Br'sei cocked his head. "He was most convincing too."

"Yes," murmured T'sha even as anger swelled her body. "I imagine he was. Even Tr'es believed him." *Stop, stop. Now is not the time. Swallow it, save it, breathe it out later. Lose control and you'll kill what you're growing with Br'sei.*

Her patience though was raw and withered. Her worries, her suspicions swam around inside her body, threatening her internal vision. She could not trust her subtlety now. She was too rocked by what Br'sei had said. She needed to ask her questions right now. There was no alternative.

"Engineer Br'sei." She let go of the perch and swelled herself out as far as her skin allowed. "Was there life in the New Person when Tr'es took it apart?"

"No," he said, simply and immediately.

"Was there life in the New Person when you took it apart?" She spread wings and crest to their fullest extent, towering, dominating with her size as she could not with her years. "Or was it D'seun's doing?"

"You have promised me nothing that could make me answer that question," said Br'sei coldly. She opened her mouth, but he thrust his muzzle forward. "And before you try, you should review how deeply I and mine are promised to D'seun. He brought us here. He ensured futures for us and our children and all our families—not just free futures, either, but glorious ones. The least of us will head our own households with our pick of spouses. I cannot set all that aside for nothing." The touch of his words was as weak as the words themselves were strong. He was pleading with her, she realized, almost sick with what he could not say, could not do.

One bone at a time, T'sha made herself subside. "I see you are torn. I understand it. I will find what I can do to make this as easy as possible for you."

"He is not insane, Ambassador," murmured Br'sei, as if he were trying out an uncertain idea.

T'sha stiffened against the engineer's words. "If he killed a New Person for their raw materials, he is."

"I don't know that's what he did," said Br'sei, more to the city beyond them than to T'sha herself. "It could be nothing but my fear talking."

"Maybe, Engineer." T'sha was not eager to allow that possibility, but she had to. She had nothing tangible to wrap her hands around. She had nothing but holes—holes in the records, holes in Br'sei's knowledge. Holes were not proof. Holes were suspicion only. "But you must allow that Ambassador D'seun is flying high and that the air around him is very, very thin."

Br'sei clacked his teeth bitterly. "Is that not how we all fly right now?"

T'sha dipped her muzzle. "You are right, Engineer. I wish you weren't."

"So do I, Ambassador," said Br'sei, deflating until he was only the size of a child. "Life of my mother, so do I."

Helen stood as Grace Meyer entered her office. "Thanks for coming, Grace." She pulled a cup of steaming black coffee from the wall dispenser and handed it across to the chemist.

"Thanks." Grace inhaled the aroma appreciatively. Helen had called for fresh coffee specifically for this interview. Grace looked tired, but alert as ever. Grace Meyer pushed herself harder than anyone on Venera, with the possible exception of Helen herself.

But then again, Grace felt she had more to prove, and more to gain, than anyone.

So, how far would that take her?

"Has Isaac Walters pronounced an opinion on your absorbers yet?" asked Helen, drawing a cup for herself.

"We're designing some new experiments," said Grace noncommittally as she sat in one of the guest chairs and crossed her legs. "I'm in contact with him." Walters was down at the Discovery with the rest of the U.N. team.

"Now," Grace said as Helen sat back down behind her desk, "any particular reason why I'm the one being summoned to court?"

Helen sighed. "It's not just you, Grace. The yewners have us all on the carpet. They've called for an audit, so the books have to be opened." She did not say why, but it was hard. She wanted to yell, was it you? Did you put us in this position? Did you tell the yewners that our salvation is a fraud?

Grace's face softened a little. "I suppose that's only to be expected. After all, the eyes of the world are upon us," she intoned. "How's that going, by the way?" she asked in a more normal voice.

Helen shrugged and sat behind her desk, setting her coffee cup down in front of her. "As U.N. publicity, it seems to be a big success. I've been getting congratulatory bursts from our Mr. Waicek telling me what a marvelous job we're doing keeping his people fed and watered." She curled her hands loosely around her cup, feeling the warmth seep into her palms. "I think the C.A.C. folks do not want us to get above ourselves. Because we're a chartered colony, they have a right to look at our books. If they wanted to make real trouble, an easy route would be to say we're not using all our new resources efficiently and that we need to be regulated." Helen sipped her coffee and returned it to the circle of her hands. "So this means we get an audit, and this means that the people with the biggest budget increases are going to get special attention." Helen smiled wanly. "This means you."

"This means me." Grace studied Helen for a minute. Searching her face for what? Helen could not guess. Helen returned the woman's gaze, although it did not take much looking to see Grace's native stubbornness settling in. Helen braced herself for a fight.

In the next moment, however, Grace's expression eased, almost as if she'd learned what she wanted to know. "Okay, Helen. I'll play. What do you need?"

"I need to go over your expenses with you." Helen lit up her desk screen. "If you can jack into your records and follow along, help me fill in the blank spots. I'd appreciate it."

Grace took another swallow of coffee and set her cup down on the edge of Helen's desk. "Well, I won't enjoy it, but let's do it." She worked the secondary command board to open her private logs. "Where do you want to start?"

The next hour felt almost like a ritual. Helen laid out the expense reports for the time immediately up to the Discovery on her desk screen and went down the line, questioning each point of income and each corresponding point of outflow. Grace answered solemnly, pausing to check her private records when her memory faltered. Helen made notes. They both drank their coffee, refilling the cups whenever they emptied.

"Last thing," said Helen finally. The look on Grace's face was one of disbelief. "Really." Grace grunted and made a "come on" gesture. Helen gave her a sour half-smile. "Just the new supporter. Biotech 24."

"Oh, them." Grace ruffled her strawberry-blond bangs. "They're venture capitalists of the old school. Very twentieth. Bet on the underdog kind of thing. I made a pitch that alien RNA might prove to be highly useful, and they dug into their pockets. Not as far as I would have liked, though." She smiled thoughtfully at her coffee. "Although, I haven't been back since the Discovery. We've been too busy."

"Haven't exactly needed to, have you?" Helen looked at her spreadsheets. "People have been waving money in your face."

"It's a nice change," admitted Grace. "For all of us."

"And you've been keeping your people busy spending it." Helen touched a key and a new set of records appeared on her desk screen. "They've been logging in a lot of scarab time as well."

"Oh, yes. I've got Kevin Cusmanos yammering at me for

being too hard on his babies and his pilots." She saw Helen's look and raised her free hand. "Okay, I admit it. I've been pushing. But I've got no idea how long the largesse is going to last. I finally have the chance to make my case and be taken seriously. I wanted to move on it."

Helen nodded. She understood that feeling all too well. "I've just got to keep on top of what's good for Venera, Grace. Our whole colony's on the line here."

Grace shook her head. "You've been listening to Bennet too long, Helen. C.A.C.'s not going to take it away from us for a set of proto-proteins and a hole in the ground. The yewners have got better things to do."

"Let's hope so," said Helen fervently. She blanked her desk. "It all looks good, Grace. Thanks for your patience."

"Not a problem." Grace stood up and pitched the remains of her coffee and the cup into the appropriate chutes. "I take it I'm dismissed."

"Until the next press call." Helen gave her a small smile, and Grace returned it. Helen touched a key to open the door for her.

Grace walked out but paused in the threshold and turned around. "By the way, Helen, it wasn't me."

Helen frowned. "It wasn't you, what?"

"Who's been talking to the yewners." Grace's smile was sly, like someone who knew they'd made a stellar move in a difficult game. "If I were you, I'd bring the subject up with Michael Lum."

Then she did leave. The door shut, and Helen sat there, paralyzed.

Michael? Michael talked to the U.N. without talking to her? Ridiculous. Michael wouldn't even think . . .

No, Michael would think. It was the one thing Michael could be absolutely counted on to do. It was one of the reasons she and Ben had picked him for the board when the slot opened up.

But without talking to her?

Listen to me, will you. Sitting in my throne room wondering who's just stabbed me in the back. A little wind-up Ceaser. Helen's head sank slowly to her hands. *Has it really come to that?*

She'd seen it coming, the money crisis that lay at the root of every question she'd had to ask during the whole long, aching day. More than a year ago, she'd seen the trends and had known a storm was brewing. She'd told no one on Venera.

That was probably a mistake. But she hadn't wanted anyone to worry. She hadn't wanted to disturb anyone's work.

To be honest, she hadn't wanted anyone to leave.

Instead, during her yearly stump trip to Mother Earth, she'd made a side visit to U.N. City and went to see Yan Su.

They'd been in a windchime park. The salty ocean breeze blew through the miniature trees and rang bells representing every republic, from mellow brass Tibetan bells to weirdly tuned Monterey pipes. They sat on one of the autoform benches, ignoring the security cameras that trained themselves automatically on Su as a member of The Government.

The sun was pleasantly hot on the back of Helen's neck as she told Su what was happening—the shrinking pure-research budgets, never huge to begin with, the waning enthusiasm for corporate charity, the inability of the hundreds of tiny republics to support major research grants for their people.

"I hate to say this." She'd smiled tiredly at her friend. "But if nothing changes, we're going to be asking for a government handout next year."

The wind caught a lock of Su's white hair and whipped it across her forehead. Su brushed it back under her scarf. Most people who went in for body-mod had themselves made artificially younger. Su, on the other hand, had herself aged. She looked about seventy-five, but Helen knew she was only a little over sixty. It had to do with respect and camouflage, Su said. A number of her influential colleagues came from backgrounds that respected age. The ones who didn't, underestimated her. Both attitudes could be extremely useful.

"What kind of handout were you thinking of, Helen?"

Just a couple of old women sitting on a bench and discussing the future of ten thousand people. Helen shrugged. "I can show you our budgets. We're going to need between a third and a half of our operating expenses for, say, five years. By then the slump should be over and we should be able to tap into our normal sources."

"You want a loan?"

"I want a grant, but I probably can't have one. So, yes, I'll take a loan."

Su sat there for a long moment. Helen watched her face carefully. She looked tired, and, despite the fact that Helen knew most of the lines and pouches were artificial, she really did look old. Something inside Helen stirred uneasily. The last time she'd seen Su look like this was right after her husband had left. Correction, after her husband had cleaned out their bank account to have himself made back into a thirty-something and run away with a professional wife and blamed Su for it.

He'd married someone who was supposed to have a future, he said, not someone who was going to be stuck in the same dead-end bureaucratic appointment for the rest of their lives, nursemaiding miners and importers when there was important work to be done. Oh, and incidentally, I've decided I want to get genetic rejuvenation past the 120 years everyone's guaranteed, so I've signed over my reproduction rights. The boy's all yours.

Helen couldn't even imagine what that had been like. Su, born and raised in U.N. City, had gone the expected route. She had a career of government service, a family of her own, and a host of people and causes to fill her life to the brim. How did she focus? How did she choose what was important? Helen knew it was how most people lived, but sometimes she wondered how anyone managed when they'd given their heart to more than one thing.

"Helen," Su broke in on her thoughts. "I don't think the money's going to be there."

Helen smiled. "I think we've had this conversation before."

"We have, several times." Su leaned her shoulder against the bench's back. The wind blew her bronze scarf over her shoulder. "But this time its different."

"How?"

Su turned her gaze to the chimes swinging in the breeze. Their random music filled the park but did nothing to lift the chill settling over Helen's heart. "Call it a narrowing of horizons, Helen. Call it a selfishness born of the fact that we can now live three hundred years all on our own and we worry less about leaving something behind that will truly last."

"Can I call it a bunch of cheapskate bureaucrats?" asked Helen lightly.

"You can, if it makes you feel better." Su's smile quickly faded. "But you know as well as I do that since Bradbury—"

"No." Helen pushed herself upright. "No, you do not get to blame this on Bradbury. Bradbury was twenty years ago. Bradbury has nothing to do with the way things are now."

"I wish that were true. For your sake, I truly do. But it's not only generals who are always refighting the last war. Bureaucrats do it, too."

No. No. You are not saying this. I refuse to accept this. "And do those bureaucrats really want ten thousand refugees on their doorstep?"

Su spread her hands helplessly. "The C.A.C. doesn't see you as refugees, Helen. They see you as misfits. You all have citizenship in your parents' republics. They have to take you, and then you're their problem, not the U.N.'s."

All around them wind rang the bells, sending their music out into a world that didn't care about the work of her life or the futures of her people. "You can't expect me to be content with this. I can't just let Venera die."

"I expect them to find you stone-cold dead with your fingers wrapped around a support girder," said Su, perfectly seriously. "They'll have to cut you out of there."

Helen's mouth twitched as if she didn't quite have the energy to smile. "The money's there someplace," she said, because it was so much easier than even contemplating the alternative. "We just have to find it. You're not going to just hang me out to dry, are you?"

"Never, Helen."

Helen had been right about something, anyway. The money had been out there. All it had taken was the Discovery to prime the pump. For a moment, everything looked like it was going to be all right. But now, now . . . everything might be about to change again if the U.N. decided the new rumors were true, if they decided she wasn't handling this right, if Michael said the wrong thing.

Helen stepped up to her window and stared out across the farms. Drones, humans, and ducks made their way between the lush plant life, each with their own mission of the moment. Each with something immediate to do. She was the only one standing still on the whole farming level.

She felt alone. Deeply and profoundly alone, as if she'd lost the feeling for the world around her, the world she'd built from the first dollar and the first strut. She stood in the middle of it, and yet it was somewhere else. Somewhere she wasn't sure she knew how to get to.

Don't be an idiot. She shook herself and returned to her desk. *You have too much work to do to get depressive. First, you have to decide what you're going to do about Michael.*

She knew what she wanted to do. She wanted to call him in right now and demand to know what he thought he was doing, find out how he could betray Venera, betray her, like this. How could he not know what this could lead to? How could he not realize what the U.N. would do with whatever he told them?

The sudden memory of Grace's eyes stopped her. That little smile, that knowledge of possessing a winning move.

Grace had known what this news would do to her. Grace had wanted this. She had wanted to turn Helen against Michael, to send her running off after a traitor, off after someone who was just doing his job but wounding her ego. . . .

Grace had been sure it would work, and it almost had.

Helen realized her hands were shaking. *Oh God, am I that far gone?*

She got up, went into her little private lavatory, pulled a cup of water from the sink, and drank it in three swallows. Then she met her own gaze in the mirror for a long moment.

Am I that far gone?

Almost, Helen. Almost, but not quite.

It was a good face, a strong face, a well-meaning face that

had worked so hard and had almost lost its way. God, had come so close. . . .

Helen removed her scarf and pulled all the pins out of her hair. The mane tumbled down over her shoulders, a waterfall of white and gray. With long, competent fingers she twisted it into a fresh knot and one by one, slid the pins back to their places. She laid the scarf back and pinned that firmly down, too.

"Desk," she said as she returned to her work area. "Locate Michael Lum."

After a pause, Michael's voice came back through the intercom. "I'm here Helen."

"Where's here?"

"Admin. Security. My desk, specifically. Do you want me to come up there?"

"No. I'll come down. Do me a favor though. Find Ben and your friend Bowerman. We need to talk."

"I'm on it, Helen."

"Desk. Close connection."

I will deal with this. We will all get through this, and if this isn't the permanent solution I dreamed it would be, then I'd better find that out now, hadn't I?

Helen strode out the door.

"Hi," said Angela Cleary as the hatch swung back. "Can I borrow a cup of sugar?"

Vee chuckled from her seat in the kitchen nook. It was strange seeing someone emerge from the airlock without a suit on. But the two scarabs had backed up against each other in a clunky but effective docking procedure that preceded what Terry called the "gab and grill." It happened at dinner every other day and allowed the passengers to circulate and talk about their work face-to-face. It also allowed the crews to sit with their friends and talk about the passengers, Vee was certain.

Angela was the first one over, but she was followed quickly by Lindi Manzur, who hugged her Troy happily and fell into talking with him about a theory of universal curiosity as a mainstay of sentient life that they'd been cooking up together. It might even be a good theory. Pity it wasn't going to come to anything. Isaac and Julia made a beeline for the fridge and the mango juice, which they both seemed to live off. Josh grabbed Bailey Heathe, the copilot for Scarab Fourteen, briefly by the hand as Bailey brushed past to the pilot's compartment to catch up with Kevin and Adrian.

Angela moved out of the way of the new arrivals and came to stand over the kitchen table. Vee saluted her with a plastic cup of tea.

"Dr. Hatch," said Angela, her voice low and formal. "I was hoping we could talk. There's some incidents in your background check that I wanted to go over. . . ."

Vee pulled on an expression of surprise. "Yeah, sure." She downed the last of her tea in one lukewarm gulp and stood up. "I think the couch compartment's empty."

It was. Vee touched the lock on the door. Now anyone who wanted to come in would at least have to knock.

"You don't think anybody believed that, do you?" For the past week they had been doing most of their talking via e-mail or the occasional comments on gab-and-grill nights. But now that the investigation was in full swing upstairs as well as down here, Angela was becoming visibly less patient with sporadic communication.

"People have a tendency to believe the Blues are after them personally." Angela shrugged. "So they're not all that surprised to hear we're after somebody else." She picked her way unerringly to Vee's couch and perched on the edge. "Show me what you've got?"

"Just simulations so far." Vee snatched up a pair of used socks off her couch and stuffed them into the storage bin overhead. Then she sat down cross-legged with her case open on her lap and switched on the back screen so Angela could see what was displayed. "But they're based on reality. I found all the drones you're going to see in Venera's current inventory."

Vee had been expanding her image library every day since she'd gotten to Venera, so the simulations actually hadn't taken all that long to put together, once she'd tracked down what she thought of as the component parts.

The screen showed a three-dimensional rendering of the little cup of a valley outside. A fat, multitreaded drone rolled down the lava corridor. It's main features—a tank and a hose.

"Experimental emergency drone," Vee told Angela. "Number ED-445. The idea was it'd be able to carry coolant down to a scarab in trouble. But it could do this too."

The drone extended its hose and planted it against the ground, as if it was nuzzling the stone. In the next second, a huge white cloud rose up around the nozzle and the hose started sinking into the rock, like a drill into cement.

"What's it spraying?" asked Angela.

"Water," Vee told her, and just nodded at the look of skepticism that appeared on Angela's face a moment later. "I checked with Josh on this. He ran a lab-level simulation. The rock outside has no water in it, which makes it stronger than normal terran rock, which is how you can get these massive continents thrusting out of the crust. But, power-spray that rock with water, and it weakens. Add in the fact that the water reacts with the sulfuric acid in the atmosphere, turning the air around the stone into a corrosive, then the rock crumbles." The hose on the screen had already buried itself eight or nine centimeters into the ground. "They could have hollowed out the whole thing with one or two of these. And they do have one or two." She entered another command, and the image skipped forward. "The metal in the ladder rungs and the laser is your basic iron. You could either bring it down from the base, or you could sort it out of the waste rock from the digging."

This section of the simulation showed a "scoop-and-chute" drone next to a pile of dust and rubble. Its shovel-tipped waldo shoved into the pile and came up with a sample of dirt. The sample ran through the chemically sensitive filters in the drone's body, and everything except what was needed got shaken out of its belly.

"What about the delicate work?" asked Angela, without taking her gaze off the screen. "Shaping the ceramics? Making the lenses in the lasers?"

"A lot of that could be done with lasers," said Vee. She skipped the simulation ahead to a neat row of three separate measurement drones, each of which had its array of small

lasers and waldos, so delicate they looked more like insect pincers than human hands. "Take your pick. These are just the
three most likely."

Angela folded her arms and hung her head down. "You
know, there are days I hate my job."

Vee shut the simulation off. "It's a fraud." *Why are you, of all
people, missing the point here?* "I don't care what was about to
happen to their precious base; they don't get to perpetrate a
fraud."

Angela just shook her head. "So you're enjoying this?"

Vee threw up her hands. "Why does everybody think I'm
doing this to get my ya-yas?"

"Because I saw the playback of you at the Dublin gallery
opening when you called the arts minister a bribe-taking na-
tionalist pig, in front of every major news service in the
stream," replied Angela evenly.

"Oh." Vee cocked her head from side to side. "That was
probably not my best day for P.R." She'd frequently wished she
really had been drunk, which was the cover story Rosa worked
so hard to put out for months afterward. "My only excuse is I
was right then too."

"Yes," Angela admitted. "But you have this tendency to be
right in public, loudly. It's not reassuring."

A powerful image of Rosa leaning against the rail in U.N.
City flashed in front of Vee's mind. "Be careful what you pretend to be," Vee muttered.

Angela nodded. "You hear that one a lot in my business."
She slapped her hands down on her thighs. "I'm going to need
a copy of your drone file so Philip can confirm the inventory."
She straightened up. "And I need you to be ready to testify to
the truth of your findings and that you created this without
help or interference."

"Of course." A few more commands and Vee shot a copy of
the simulations out to Angela's contact code. "It's got to be
Derek Cusmanos then, doesn't it? He's the one who has access
to all the drones."

"That would be the logical conclusion based on what you've
seen so far," said Angela.

Vee glanced at her and knew she was not going to get any more of an answer than that. They were investigating her accusations inside Venera, but Angela had wanted Vee to remain independent of any kind of suggestion. "If we can show we arrived at this from separate angles," Angela had said, "it'll be even more convincing when we have to go public with it."

"Well, glad I could help," said Vee.

"I'm sure." Angela headed out the door, leaving Vee sitting alone with her simulated evidence.

Vee had tried to understand. She tried to imagine what it was to have your life shut down, to have to move to a strange new world with such things in it as Earth at its craziest could surround you with. She felt sad, she felt sorry, she wished there was something she could do, but they did not get to lie about this. They did *not* get to lie about life on another world. The hope of finding that human beings weren't alone was such an old, precarious hope. To one day discover that there was somebody else out there who asked the same questions and dreamed the same dreams. Every time she thought about somebody playing on that venerable dream . . . again, *again,* rage shot through her veins.

This was supposed to be real. This was supposed to be her one real thing, to make up for the tantrums and the farces and the pretty veneer she had made out of her life.

And what did they do this for? For money, again, like the worst of the Universal Age frauds. Was it really all that different? Was she the only one here who didn't see that it wasn't different at all?

Except, maybe it was. This one was built for love and worry, not just greed. This was done to fill, not to drain. Maybe it was different. But that just made it sad, in addition to making it wrong.

Vee sighed, closed her case, and stowed it. She looked at the hatchway and decided she didn't want to face the rest of the team. She'd munch on some leftovers later. Her stomach was all in knots. Instead she curled up in the couch, hugging her knees. In the silence, she mourned the loss of a dream, again.

Chapter Ten

"Pressure good, opening airlock."

Adrian brought his hand down on the key that opened the inner hatch. The clank of the portal opening was followed fast by the thumping of multiple pairs of stiff, heavy boots and the clunking of armored limbs as they accidentally bumped into walls and other people in a confined space.

"Another day, another dollar," said Kevin, rubbing the back of his neck.

"So they tell me." Adrian got to his feet and arched his back in a prolonged stretch. The team had gotten good enough at managing their suits that he no longer had to hover around them each time they returned. The snapping of catches and various, wordless, relieved noises drifted up the central corridor. He knew how they felt. He was really looking forward to the end of this run. Terry Wray in particular was becoming a bigger pain in the ass all the time, despite her good looks. For the past week she'd been running back and forth, asking them both for the story of how the base was found over and over, until finally Kevin said to her, "Ms. Wray, you're sounding less like a media face and more like a lawyer all the time."

"What an interesting choice of words, Mr. Cusmanos," she had replied mildly.

After that, Kevin's normal good humor had started to fade, and Adrian had found himself engaging in the unhealthy and unproductive hobby of marking time until the run was over.

The radio beeped. "This is Venera Base calling Scarab Five and Scarab Fourteen," said a woman's voice. Adrian blinked at the speaker grill. That wasn't Tori at flight control. That was Grandma Helen.

Kevin touched the Reply key. "This is Scarab Five. Receiving you, Venera Base."

"This is a recall notice. Five and Fourteen, you are to return to base immediately."

"What? Why?" The questions were out before Adrian remembered whom he was talking to.

"You'll hear all about it when you get back up here." Dr. Failia sounded grim. "Get your people back and get in the air." A soft popping underscored her voice.

Adrian looked at his boss. Kevin sat there, a coffee cup held in both hands. His fingers tightened convulsively, denting and redenting the plastic, making the popping noise. Kevin stared at the radio, but Adrian felt positive he didn't see it.

"We're on our way up, Dr. Failia," said Adrian, not taking his attention off Kevin.

"Good. Venera Base out."

Kevin still just stood there, crushing the cup and letting it go again. Adrian's confusion quickly bled away into cold concern.

"What's going on?" asked Adrian softly.

Kevin shook himself and tossed the cup into the garbage. "We'll find out when we get back up, won't we?" He looked at the floor, the chair, the window, but not at Adrian. "You'd better tell the passengers." Kevin settled himself back in the pilot's chair.

That was no answer, but what could Adrian do? "Right, okay."

As he sidled and shuffled his way down the scarab's narrow central corridor, he realized that the sounds of a team getting out of their suits had silenced. He was not surprised to see them, all in their various stages of unsuiting, standing still and staring at him.

Adrian sighed. "I take it you all heard that? We need you in your couches, please, so we can get in the air."

"Can we get any kind of information here?" asked Peachman.

"There's nothing I can tell you." Adrian spread his hands.

"I'm sure there'll be a full briefing when we're back on base. If you'll just fasten yourselves in, please."

"Surely, there must be something—" began Peachman, half to Adrian, half to his teammates, looking for their support.

"I'm sorry," said Adrian. He was. He didn't know what was going on either, and he wanted to. Probably more than any of them did. Recalls did not happen unless something bad did.

Hatch's expression caught his eye. She was looking at him, speculatively, as if she were trying to guess what was going on inside his head. Kenyon, on the other hand, was watching Hatch as if he were worried about what she'd do next.

But she didn't do anything except bend over and start snapping the catches on her boots. Wray bent over next to her and murmured something Adrian couldn't hear. He heard the reply, though.

"I'm sure you'll get to interview everybody soon enough. Now, shouldn't we do what we're told?" Dr. Hatch gave one of her brainless smiles and started stripping out of the stiff, white, undersuit that covered her everyday clothes.

Tourists. Adrian left them to it and headed back to the pilot's compartment. For a moment, he didn't see Kevin, because Kevin was almost doubled over in his chair, with his elbows on his knees, his head in his hands, and his fingers twined through his thick hair.

"Kevin?"

Kevin straightened up instantly at the sound of his name, but he couldn't wipe the pallor from his face.

"What is it?" Adrian sank into his own chair. "What's happened?"

Kevin shook his head. "I don't know any more than you do." He swiveled his chair around to face the primary controls. "Let's get the preflights done, okay?"

Adrian didn't move. "Look, if we're headed back into trouble, I want to know."

Kevin poked at a few keys, getting readiness displays up on the screens. "You're not headed into anything."

"But you are?"

"Did I say I was?" Kevin scowled at the control panel. "Quit pushing, Adrian. Just do your job."

"You helped, didn't you?"

They both jumped. Hatch stood in the entranceway, her face serious, her eyes probing.

"Dr. Hatch, please, get into your couch," said Kevin. "We're under a recall and we've got to leave now."

"But you did help?" she said.

Kevin reared out of his chair. "What the hell do you care? You and your tourist friends were right, and you showed us all up. Fine. Take the headline and be happy. But if you want to gloat, do it on Mother Earth with your art buddies. This is my ship. For the next five hours I'm still in charge and I'm telling you to get in that cabin and out of my way!"

She didn't move. She stayed right where she was, as if she meant to stare Kevin down.

"I am sorry," she said finally. Then, she turned away and climbed through the door into the starboard couch bay.

Kevin sat back down, shaking.

"What was she talking about?" demanded Adrian.

"Don't start," said Kevin.

"Come on, Kevin—"

"No!" he roared. Adrian reeled back. He'd heard Kevin yell before, at incompetence, at carelessness, but not like this, not this empty, lost rage.

"I'm sorry," Kevin whispered. He cleared his throat. "I'm sorry. Let's get out of here, okay?"

"Yeah, sure." agreed Adrian.

They ran through the preflights mechanically, with no comments or bantering. Adrian kept his eyes on his instruments. He didn't want to look at his boss. He didn't want to see what was eating the other man. Something sure was. Something huge.

Finally, Kevin turned the radio on Venera Base. "Venera Base, this is Scarab Five."

"We have you, Scarab Five," came back Tori's voice. "Conditions are go for your launch."

"Good to hear, Venera." Kevin's response was flat, automatic. "That lightning cleared up?"

"Clear as crystal," answered Tori. "For Venus anyway."

"Thank you, Venera." He switched the radio over to the next channel. "Scarab Fourteen, this is Scarab Five. Are you go for launch?"

"Ready whenever you are, Scarab Five," Charlotte Murray, Scarab Fourteen's pilot, told them. "You got any idea what this is about?"

For a moment, Adrian thought Kevin was going to be sick. "None, Charlotte. Listen, we're good to go here too. How about you follow us up?"

"Okay by me," said Charlotte. "Let's do the drill. Scarab Five, are you go?"

"We are go, Scarab Fourteen." Kevin gave Adrian the nod.

"Engaging wing." Adrian thumbed the button on the wheel stem that raised the wing. The roof camera showed the rack lift and spread, stretching the skin wide. The indicator light shone green and Adrian slid the inflation control up to Full. The wing inflated slowly. Scarab Five shifted uneasily until it finally lost contact with the ground and began its gentle rise toward the clouds.

Kevin pulled the wheel forward with one hand and pressed in the two keys that engaged the flight engines with the other. The flight engines were tiny things, mostly for guidance and stabilization. The wing provided the lift in the dense atmosphere, and once they reached them, the 360-kilometer-an-hour winds in the cloud layers provided the speed.

Kevin eased the wheel forward to angle the wing for a little extra lift. He probably wanted to get as far away from the volcano wall as possible, as soon as possible. Beta Regio never failed to make Adrian nervous. Too many outcroppings, too many weird corners.

Today, though, it didn't bother him half as much as the dead, gray look on Kevin's face. He was not here. His hands were flying the scarab without his head. This was not good.

"Flying a little sluggish, do you think?" asked Adrian to try to draw him out.

Kevin nodded. "A little. Might be some grit in the works. How do the diagnostics look?"

Adrian's gaze swept the instrument panels and screens. "Everything's green and go."

"All right, let me get a little more clearance from the wall. We've got that big shelf coming up." He pushed the wheel down and away, dropping them, swinging them wide, without waiting, without looking.

Without seeing Scarab Fourteen on the monitor.

"Pull back!" shouted Adrian.

The radio crackled to life "Scarab Five, get—"

WHANG!

The whole scarab shuddered and swung wildly to the right. Stunned, Kevin gripped the wheel and pulled back, trying for height.

"What happened?" cried Adrian. A sick creaking sounded through the roof. "We got a critical failure in the wing joints!" Adrian glanced down at the roof camera. The cage around the right wingtip was crumpled in. The scarab lurched and leaned right.

"It was an accident!" Kevin hauled the wheel left. That worked, sort of. The scarab stabilized for a moment but then slowly slewed right and down.

"Okay," said Adrian under his breath. "We're going back down." He hit the radio key. "Scarab Fourteen, Scarab Fourteen, are you there? Come in, Charlotte . . ."

Nothing. No answer. Adrian punched the keys for the sweep cameras in the scarab's belly to scan the ground. All he saw was the broken landscape, crisscrossed by the tracks of old lava flows and the glowing rivulets of fresh ones.

"They're not answering," he said sharply. Kevin didn't seem to notice. Kevin pulled the wheel back and left. The scarab started a shallow dive, dipping a little to the left as it curved gently around.

He heard screams, shouted questions, more creaks and strains. Too much noise, too many possibilities. Oh, Holy God, too many ways to die.

"Deploy chutes," ordered Kevin.

Adrian slapped the key and saw the red message glowing next to it. "We don't have the chute! The hatch is nonresponsive."

Too many ways to die. If one of those creaks was the hull. If they landed too hard on their belly and a rock bit through, if the joints and seals that were moaning all around them gave way. . . .

Something overhead groaned. Then, something snapped.

The right half of the scarab dropped, dragging everything with it. The world rattled and clattered and clanked. Voices swore. Somebody screamed again. The straps bit into Adrian's shoulders.

Oh, Holy God and Mother Creation, I don't want to die!

With a hiss, the outside airbags deployed. The scarab banged against the side of the mountain, bounced back, rattling them all like dice in a tin can, and headed down.

"No response!" shouted Kevin, wrestling with the wheel.

Adrian grabbed the copilot wheel and threw all his weight behind it. It didn't budge. "Nothing!" No steering, no way to get away from the rocks, the sharp rocks that could cut right through them, let in the poison and the pressure. . . .

A bang, and Adrian's body bounced hard against the straps. He bit his own lip to keep from screaming. The scarab's rear quarter hit the volcano wall with a sickening crunch and settled slowly on a drunken angle, head down, right rear corner sticking up.

Adrian didn't try to move. He just sat still, listened to his heart hammer, and watched the thousand red lights shine on the panels.

But it was quiet again, and he was alive.

"Everyone okay?" called Adrian, half to the intercom, half to the air.

Answers tumbled over themselves, but it sounded like the team in the couches had weathered it all right. Better than Scarab Five itself had, that was for sure.

Better than Kevin, who sat blinking at his controls.

"Kevin? Boss?"

"It was an accident. It was an accident," he whispered hoarsely. "I didn't. Oh, God." He stared out the window.

Adrian followed his gaze. In the distance, maybe a couple of hundred meters, it was hard to tell, Scarab Fourteen snuggled against the side of a rough foothill, as if it were attempting to crawl inside the rock. Its treads were crushed. Its hull wasn't the right shape anymore.

"It was an accident," murmured Kevin.

"Shut up!" shouted Adrian. "Just . . . shut up! I don't care what it was!" He didn't. He was scared; he wanted to run, but there was nowhere to go.

Okay. Okay. You know what to do. Do it.

The radio still showed up green. He hit the key for Scarab Fourteen again. "Scarab Fourteen! Scarab Fourteen! Come in, Charlotte. Talk to me!"

Still nothing but silence.

"Send the mayday to Venera," Adrian ordered his boss. "Tell them Scarab Fourteen isn't answering. I'll put together a comprehensive on the damage." *If we've still got hull integrity, we'll be all right. Hull integrity, all the pumps, most of the air tanks. . . .* He cast a quick glance out the window, trying not to see the battered hulk of Scarab Fourteen. The black and gray land outside was a mass of sharp ridges and steep descents, as if someone had slashed through the ground with a razor. Scarab Five had come to rest against one of the sharp-backed ridges. Orange glow oozed in the distance, filling the crevices below them. Lava.

But that's over there. Not here. Adrian dropped his gaze to his hands. *Keep it together. You know what to do. This is why you're here.*

Kevin had pulled himself far enough back into the present to work the radio. "Venera Base, this is Scarab Five. Mayday, mayday. I repeat, Venera Base, this is Scarab Five. Mayday. Mayday. We are down. Scarab Fourteen is down and not responding."

Adrian tuned him out and concentrated on the instruments. Most of the electronics seemed to be functioning. The computer gave him no errors as he requested a comprehensive list of the damages.

Adrian scanned the report. Bad, bad, bad. The rear axle had collapsed. Two panels on the exterior wall had buckled in to the point they were pressing on the interior insulation and had cut through a whole set of coolant pipes on the way. Ice tank one had been completely crushed. So had air processor three.

Okay. First thing, get back and see what's to do about those buckled panels. They break through and we're very, very screwed.

"We have you, Scarab Five." Tori's familiar, infinitely welcome voice sounded from the radio. "Your position is fixed. Rescue team being readied for drop now. What is your status?"

Kevin turned to Adrian. The helplessness on his face made Adrian want to hit him.

"Not good, but not dead," said Adrian toward the speaker. "Crew unhurt. Lost mobility, lost one ice tank, lost one air processor, and have sustained partial loss of one cooling pump. All remaining pumps, scrubbers, and tanks look green. Possible danger of hull compromise. I'm going to check it out now."

Adrian unsnapped his catches and got to his feet. As he did, a new trembling grind vibrated through the scarab's floor. The world shifted backward. Adrian pinwheeled his arms for balance. He stared involuntarily out the window. As he toppled backwards, his eyes told his brain that the scarab hadn't moved, the ground outside had.

The floor hit his back, knocking all the wind out of him. Something hard caught his head, and stars burst in front of his eyes in sync with the pain.

"Holy God! gasped Kevin. "Oh Christ!"

Adrian tried to lift his head, but the world spun. The floor vibrated again. The scarab slid backward. The front end came down with a crash that rattled his teeth and sent fresh flashes of pain through his head.

"Scarab Five, what's going on? Talk to me, Adrian!"

"There's something alive," rasped Kevin. "Venera Base, cancel drop. I repeat, cancel drop. There's something alive out there, and it's coming toward us."

What? Adrian pulled himself to his knees. *I did not hear that.*

"We've found the goddamned aliens," grated Kevin.

Adrian planted one hand on the counter and pushed. He reached his feet and looked out the front window. At first he saw nothing but black rock hunched up between the streams of lava. Then, two of the islands moved. They slid out of the lava stream and over the steady ground. From behind them rose a translucent jellyfish half the size of the scarab, its tentacles tipped with pincers.

The world spun and Adrian toppled back to the floor. Consciousness started to slip away. To his shame, he let it go.

Br'sei flew into the main chamber with the speed born of agitation. T'sha shifted on her own perch, turning away from the recorder and its reports that she was still reviewing to get herself up to speed on New Home and its New People.

D'han and P'tesk lurched sideways as Br'sei blew past. He managed to snag a perch in time to keep from crashing into the wall.

"What's happened?" asked T'sha.

"I . . . there's . . ." Br'sei's muzzle bobbed as he looked around the chamber. "Where is Ambassador D'seun?"

"He's surveying the wind currents." T'sha raised her forehand and beckoned to Br'sei. "What's happened? Talk to me."

"I . . ." Br'sei's teeth clacked. Was he nervous? T'sha's bones bunched in annoyance at his hesitation. D'seun had them all too well trained. Even Br'sei, for all the doubts he expressed to her. She was an interloper. Only approved information was to be shared with her.

I am also an ambassador to the High Law Meet. "Tell me what's happened, Engineer," she ordered.

Br'sei shrank a little in resignation, but maybe also in relief. "There's been an accident."

T'sha's arms stiffened, lifting her off her perch. "Who? How many are hurt?"

"No, none of ours," said Br'sei. "It's the New People."

The words jolted straight through T'sha. "What?"

Br'sei dipped his muzzle. "The overseers watching the New People report that two of their transports have crashed near Living Highland 76. They believe them to be damaged."

There are overseers assigned to the New People? This isn't in the reports. T'sha went very still. "Are their own kind responding?"

"Not yet," said Br'sei.

"P'tesk, D'han, come with me." T'sha spread her wings. "Br'sei, you will sweep the base. Bring everyone we have. Get the dirigibles flying and bring the emergency spares. We need whatever we've got to work in cold and low pressure."

"What? Why?" D'han fluttered. "Ambassador—"

T'sha was already flying toward the door. "We have to help."

"But their own kind will surely respond." P'tesk held out both forehands, pleading.

T'sha hooked a forehand onto the threshold and turned to face him. "We cannot leave them there. The research D'seun has so kindly gathered indicates they cannot be exposed to air." *The research, based on raw materials he collected, which may not have been raw at the time.*

"But if we—" began P'tesk.

"If we what?" demanded T'sha, swelling. "If we go they will find out we're here. Surely. What if we let them die? We are that desperate for our secrecy? We are that uncertain about our claim to this world that we should fail to help life?"

"No," said Br'sei softly, more to P'tesk and D'han than to her. "We are not." He inflated himself. "We have several constructors designed to deal with the New People if necessary. I'll bring them."

Br'sei vanished into the corridor. T'sha winged after him, all but exploding into the open air. She pushed all thought, all suspicion of what had happened here before out of her mind. That was for later. For now, the New People needed her.

"Scarab Five, Scarab Five." The radio called from the main cabin. "Respond. Adrian? Kevin? Come on, answer me!"

"Shit," exclaimed Josh, and Vee heard him start popping the buckles on his safety straps. She started doing the same.

"Maybe you should—" began Julia.

"No." Vee shoved the straps aside and made her way up the steeply tilted floor after Josh.

Adrian lay on the floor in the main aisle, dazed. Kevin crouched beside him, little better.

"What happened?" asked Vee, dropping to her knees next to them.

Kevin swallowed hard. "It was an—"

Josh just shoved his way past them to the radio.

"Scarab Five, Scarab Five!" came a frantic voice out of the speaker.

Josh slapped the Reply key. "We're here, Venera. This is Josh Kenyon."

"What happened? Kevin said he saw the aliens?"

What? Vee froze.

"I'm not seeing anything except Scarab Fourteen," said Josh. "They look hurt. Have you been able to raise them?"

"No. We've got the rescue on standby. If they leave now, they'll make it in three hours."

Josh's lips moved in silent calculation, or maybe prayer. "Drop them down. Now."

"Have you got anybody who can get across to Fourteen and check out their situation?" asked the voice from Venera.

Josh looked at the red lights glowing on the control panels, then back at Adrian and Kevin on the floor.

"We're damaged and have to do control," he said reluctantly. "There's no trained personnel to respond."

Vee stood. Now she could see out the window, and she saw Scarab Fourteen's crippled body alone on the ragged plain, far too near a lava stream. "How much training does it take to shove someone in a suit and get them over here? How much does it take to look around?"

"You'll need to get in." Adrian struggled to sit up. "I can get you in."

"You saw—" began Kevin.

"I saw null." Adrian grabbed a cabinet handle and hauled himself to his feet. "I saw null," he repeated. "We need to get over to Fourteen. We need to stabilize Five." He glowered down at Kevin.

Pride resurfaced in Kevin's eyes. "Don't tell me my job."

"Somebody has to!" Adrian steadied himself against the wall. Fury shook him. "You're not doing it!"

Kevin shut his mouth and pulled back. He took a long,

shaky breath, leaning a hand against the counter. "You're right. Take Josh and Dr. Hatch and two of the others over to Fourteen. Give them any help you can. I'll stabilize us so we can hold out until the rescue drops." He glanced out the window at the still landscape. "If you saw null, I saw null."

"I'll go get your volunteers." Vee hurried back into the cabin.

Her colleagues were as she left them, strapped in and arguing.

"What is going on out there?" demanded Troy.

"We're in trouble, but we're talking," Vee told him. "Fourteen is in trouble and not talking. Terry, Troy, they need us to go over and help. We need to get into suits. Julia," softer, lower, "Kevin's kind of shaky. He's going to need a pair of hands. Wait until we're on our way to Fourteen; then come out and see what you can do."

"When were you elected?" snorted Troy.

"When I was the one who got myself out of this cabin," shot back Vee. "There's lives on the line, Peachman. You want to leave Lindi Manzur to fry?" It was emotional blackmail and she knew it, but it worked. He shut up. "Come on."

Troy and Terry reached the changing compartment shortly after she did. Josh and Adrian were already there. They suited each other up in silence. Vee went through the motions, trying not to think about the broken hulk of a scarab she'd seen. She didn't want to think about how thin its walls were, how they were all deep down inside a poisonous, pressurized crucible that was just waiting for them to screw up so it could burn them all to ashes.

The airlock's inner door closed and the pump started up, but instead of the normal, steady chug-chug-chug, it wheezed, snarled and sputtered, skipped beats and raced ahead as if to catch up.

God, we might not even be able to get out of here, thought Vee. She felt her self-control slipping a little. Which was unusual. She tried to be objective and examine her feelings, but that didn't work. She eyed her helmet icons until she got Josh's channel.

"Do you think they might still be all right?" she asked.

"Same as us," said Josh. "If their hull holds and they have at least one of the pumps and a cooler tank, they can hang on."

She licked her lips and asked the next question. "If there is a hull breach, how long do they have?"

"They don't."

"I didn't think so."

Vee rested her helmet against the wall and listened to the asthmatic pump. She let herself wish long and hard that she hadn't volunteered for this, just to get that feeling out of the way. Then she prayed long and hard that the hull on Scarab Five would hold tight, because if it didn't, she'd just killed Julia by letting her be the one to stay behind. That feeling went away more slowly, even after she assured herself that Kevin would make Julia get into a hardsuit as soon as he thought of it, or that Julia, who was not stupid, just easily stressed, would think of it on her own.

Finally, the outer hatch rolled open, giving Vee a chance to move away from her thoughts. She climbed out, right behind Adrian.

The world outside was like a petrified ocean, with its waves and currents frozen into black stone. Through the ridges, glowing ribbons of lava crept down well-worn paths. She imagined it smelled hot, almost spicy, the kind of smell you could taste.

"They'd get into suits, wouldn't they?" asked Terry on the general channel, echoing Vee's thoughts from the airlock.

"If they could get to them, yeah," said Adrian. "The scarabs have bulkheads that seal if there's a hull breach, just like a ship."

Vee tried to clamp down on her imagination. Now was not the time to paint pictures of the future. Now was the time to slog forward, watch her footing and play it straight. Don't look up. Be like a kid. If you don't look at the scarab, it won't change. It won't get any worse because while you're not looking at it, it isn't there. Slog up the ridges, pick your way down the side, watch the ash piles that have collected in the hollows, notice how the charcoal veins look like the veins in the Discovery walls. Don't look up.

"No!"

Adrian stumbled forward, trying for a loping run but only

sliding and wobbling as he fought the ragged ground and the pressure. Ahead of him, the scarab's side buckled sharply inward, as if it had been punched by an invisible fist. A thread-thin, black crack appeared.

Vee's throat closed up tight.

"Veronica," said Josh, tentatively.

"What?" Vee tore her gaze off Adrian's stumbling form. Josh pointed ahead and to the right. Vee followed the line of his arm, until she saw the edge of the ragged wall the volcano made.

Something white floated next to it. Something shaped like an inverted teardrop or a hot-air balloon.

Vee froze in her tracks, tilted on the side of a stone wave. The balloon flew in an absolutely straight line. Vee saw a glint of silver on its swelling sides, like lenses, maybe.

"That's not from Venera, is it?" asked Vee quietly.

"No," answered Josh.

It was getting closer. Terry had seen it now. She also came to an abrupt halt with Troy right beside her.

"Adrian!" called Josh. Adrian stopped, teetered, and almost fell, but he righted himself, and he saw it too.

The thing flew like the wind. Silver scales covered its white skin. Bundles of red-brown cables held an enclosed gondola to the balloon. At first, Vee thought it was heading for them, but it wasn't.

It was heading for Scarab Fourteen.

The balloon stopped, suddenly, as if it had hit a wall. From the bottom a flurry of . . . things emerged. They sparkled gold in the ashen light. Wings spread out from their oval torsos. Legs (arms?) hung under their bellies.

One carried a fold of cloth, one an egg, one a box, another a blob of gray jelly. They were followed by three others with empty hands. They all flew over Scarab Fourteen. The first of them dropped the cloth. The three with empty hands grasped the cloth and pulled it over the scarab, as if they were fitting a sheet to a bed. The cloth was transparent, but the dim light reflected off an oily sheen on the edges where they held it.

The creatures holding the cloth dropped to the ground. The

cloth made a tent over the scarab. The one with the egg cracked it open. A gout of milky liquid poured over the cloth. It sluiced down the sides, becoming transparent as it did so. The creatures let go; the tent stayed where it was.

The creature with the box shriveled and drew in its wings. It sank until it hovered just above ground level. Now Vee saw a complex series of markings, or maybe wires, running across its body. It pressed the box against the tent and its muzzle moved. Vee tried to set her suit controls to pick up outside sound, but she couldn't get her gaze to stay steady enough to activate the commands.

The one with the jelly blob joined the one by the box. It set its blob down. The blob had an eye and silver lines running through its body.

The blob moved.

It crawled into the box and emerged inside the tent. It lifted up into the air and became a jellyfish with tentacles hanging down, tipped with, what? Claws? Tools? It drifted unerringly toward Scarab Fourteen and slipped into the jagged, black crack in the hull.

Vee wanted to speak but had no words adequate to the task. This was unreal. Surreal. She was frightened, bemused, unbelieving. She wanted to laugh her head off. Her heart fluttered high in her throat and she could hear her blood singing in her ears.

One of the creatures (aliens? There are no aliens. The base is a fake. How can they be aliens?) was looking at her. It had two huge silver eyes, encased, she realized, behind something hard and clear, like a natural lens. But those were unmistakably eyes. She could distinguish the iris, pupil, and white. Huge eyes. Underneath its eyes, it had a wedge-shaped beak, like a bird's beak, or maybe a dolphin's.

It was beautiful. It was incomprehensible. It was looking right at her and she could tell nothing, nothing about what it saw.

Then, she realized it didn't see her at all. It saw a suit, with a smooth plate where its face should be. Maybe it was just wondering what was in there.

Voices were babbling. Voices she knew, but there were too

many of them and she couldn't make out what they were saying. She didn't even really want to try.

The creatures ferried more blobs out of their balloon. They put them up to the box to become jellyfish and enter the space under the tent and eventually the scarab. The creatures themselves flew all around the tent, angels, butterflies, prehistoric monsters glittering gold on a cloudy day. Except for the one that looked straight at her.

Was it trying to divine something? Send a telepathic message? Judge her for salt content? What? What did aliens do?

"Veronica, we've got to go, now!" It was Josh. He had his hand on her arm and he was trying to pull her away. But she wasn't responding. She should respond. He was right. They needed to go, now, didn't they? Did they?

The side of the scarab tore like paper.

"No!" screamed Adrian like it was the only word he had left.

Two jellyfish floated out of the hole in the scarab's side. Their tentacles wrapped around something roughly oblong that shimmered.

It was Angela Cleary. Angela, who'd been helping Vee prove the Discovery was nothing but a fraud. Whom Vee had spent a whole week aboard the shuttle trying to get to know and failing without really realizing it. She'd respected that in a weird kind of way. Angela, who gave nothing away by accident. Angela, who had a sardonic grin and sharp eyes.

"Can't be. She'd be pulp. Less than pulp." murmured Josh. He wasn't pulling on Vee anymore.

Angela wasn't pulp. Something crystalline covered her, like the stuff that made the tent over the scarab or enclosed the alien's silver eyes. The creatures flying over the tent cracked another egg. More milky liquid sluiced over the tent sides. The tent tore and fell away like cobwebs.

The jellyfish turned away from the creatures and began flying toward the team from Scarab Five.

"Get away, get away, get away," chanted Terry, like a mantra. Out of the side of her faceplate, Vee saw someone stumble backward and turn to slog away.

The jellyfish kept coming with Angela, encased in glass, supported between them. They drifted forward until they were about two meters away. Then, very gently, they sank down and laid Angela on the ground. Their tentacles released her and they rose, drifting back toward the scarab.

"Holy God and Mother Creation, what've they done?" Josh moved forward. Vee looked up at the alien, her alien, who hadn't moved. Then, slowly, as if she had to remember how, Vee walked up beside Josh and looked down at the glass coffin.

Angela lay inside, whole, and perfect. Her eyes were closed and her arms lay straight along her sides.

"I think she's breathing," said Josh softly.

Vee bent closer. Yes. You could see it. Barely. Angela's chest didn't so much rise and fall as flutter like Vee's heart. But she was alive under there.

Alive and without a suit on Venus, and there sure as hell weren't air tanks on that glass case. Vee's mind fastened on these details and jolted her body into action.

"Help me!" She grabbed Angela's feet.

Josh grabbed Angela's shoulders. They heaved Angela up as if they were lifting a log and staggered back toward Scarab Five. Fighting pressure and the awkwardness of the suit, Vee could glance up only once. The jellyfish reemerged from Scarab Fourteen, carrying another glass-encased figure in their tentacles.

"Peachman, get back here! I need help!" shouted Terry.

"I'm there. I'm there." Troy waddled more than walked over the ridges. His suit was scored. Had he fallen in his hurry to get away from the aliens? "I'm sorry. Christ in the green, I'm sorry."

Maybe we should have brought Julia after all.

"Kevin, are you watching this?" came Josh's voice over the intercom. "Get that door open!"

"Done!" shouted Kevin. "God, god, is she really alive?"

"I think so." Josh's voice was breathy with hope and uncertainty.

I hope so, thought Vee, *because it means they saved her. It means they're . . . what? Friendly? Doesn't cover it. Human?*

Obviously her brain could take only so much of this.

The airlock door was open. They laid Angela on the floor.

"Take her up!" ordered Josh.

"Can't," came back Kevin's reply. "The pump is almost dead. We can't risk running it more than once. You're going to have to get them all in here. Get moving!"

Vee stared at Josh. "This is going to sound dumb," she said, her voice too high and tight. "Will she be all right alone?"

"I hope so," said Josh. Obviously, that was the phrase of the day.

Vee slogged back toward Scarab Fourteen, wishing desperately that she could run. All she could manage was a fast walk. Sweat poured down her face. Her face plate blinked yellow warnings at her to drink and take a salt tablet. She ignored them.

Terry and Troy were hoisting Lindi Manzur off the ground when Vee and Josh reached them. The jellyfish were arriving with another woman in a pilot's coverall. Must be Charlotte. Charlotte . . . what was her last name?

Why is this bugging me now?

Adrian, all on his own, hoisted Charlotte into his arms and staggered across the broken landscape.

It was ridiculous. It was macabre. But they did it three more times, hefting colleagues and strangers like bricks and laying them neatly down on the airlock floor, trying to make efficient use of space but trying not to think too much because it would slow them down.

They headed back one more time. The jellyfish had another form in their tentacles. But this one was shaped wrong. It was all curves. It didn't have enough straight lines for a human body. The jellies stopped about three meters away this time. When Vee registered what she saw, she had to choke back her bile while part of her mind said, "Ah, that's why they call it 'pulped.'"

The jellies did not put this one down. They carried it back past the gold creatures and vanished into the bottom of the balloon.

"Who was that? Why'd they do that?" asked Terry. "Sorry, sorry, I know you don't know . . . I—"

"It's okay," said Vee. "Really."

There were no more, what? Deliveries? The aliens flew back into their balloon, except the one still one. Vee wondered what it was waiting for. It stared at her with its huge eyes, as if memorizing every detail of Vee's form, as Vee was memorizing its, with the sharply angled wings and the thick, but amazingly flexible neck, the broad body, the crimson and ivory mane that streamed down its neck and the dark lines on golden skin.

Vee took a step forward, holding her hand out. The other's wings twitched minutely, its body swelled, and it drifted forward.

Vee's breath caught in her throat.

A second creature, this one more heavily lined, or wired, came up next to the first one. They hovered close together, their beaks, maybe they were really more like muzzles, almost touching. Then, together they turned and flew back into the gondola under the silver and white balloon.

The moment was gone so abruptly that Vee was a little surprised to find she herself was still there.

And Angela still has no air tank. Vee cursed herself for standing and staring. She turned and lumbered back across the ragged plain.

Last time, last time. You can do this. She held tightly to the thought. Her plate warnings were now more orange than yellow. Her muscles felt stretched out and limp. Sweat trickled down her face, pooling for a moment in her collar before the cloth wicked it away. Her back itched. Her hands had swollen until her gloves felt too tight.

"You all right?" asked Josh.

"Barely," she admitted. "But I'll made it."

From here she could see Scarab Five's open airlock and the glass-encased bodies lying on the floor.

If they can make it, I sure as hell can. She glanced back to make sure the others were keeping up. They limped and stumbled their way back, just as she did. The aliens had vanished.

We'll all make it because we have to back each other's stories up.

They bundled back into the airlock, trying to cram onto the benches. Except Adrian. He squatted down next to Charlotte and laid a hand on her wrist, as if his gloved fingers could feel her pulse through that alien crystal.

"Shut it down, Kevin, depressurize," said Josh as he dogged the hatch. He was panting hard, and Vee saw the rivers of sweat running down his face.

"Doing it now." Kevin's voice had relaxed, weirdly enough, and he sounded more like the pilot who had shepherded them all down than the terrified man she'd last seen on the corridor floor.

The pump began struggling to take them back to human conditions. Relief surged through Vee. She slumped against the inside of her hardsuit. Angela Cleary lay right at her feet, like a corpse that had been dipped in plastic. Vee closed her eyes. Angela was breathing under there. They all were. No one was dead yet. Except that person the aliens took away.

Why did they take the dead one away?

"It's a fake, huh?" Josh's voice interrupted her thoughts and she was grateful, even when she interpreted his tone. "If the Discovery is a fake, what the hell were those? Holographs?"

"You thought the Discovery was a fake?" said Troy. "When we've just seen the builders—"

"The Discovery is a fake," snapped Vee. She started shaking. A thousand different emotions churned inside her and she couldn't put a name to any of them. "Those creatures did not build the Discovery. Did those things look like they could fit through the tunnel? Those were birds, not moles."

"So there are two sets of aliens?" said Troy, sounding dazed.

"Yes," said Vee. "Us and them."

Adrian hadn't moved from his crouch next to Charlotte. He ran his gloves over the solid, crystal casing. Vee had no doubt he was thinking, *How are we going to get them out of there?* Vee sure was.

A sound like a shot split the air. Vee jerked backward. A crack swept down Charlotte's case. It branched out, sending a network of fractures all along the crystal. Another shot, and another and another. The cases shattered.

Well, that answers that.

"Charlotte!" Adrian brushed away flakes of crystal that turned to dust as soon as he touched them. Vee, then Josh, fell clumsily to their knees, following his example. Vee brushed off Angela's face, trying to get the stuff clear before she inhaled it.

Angela gasped, then choked. Her body convulsed under Vee's hand and her face contorted horribly.

"Shit! Kevin! Kill the pump!" cried Adrian. "They're getting the bends! Kill the pump!"

"No! They can't live under this pressure!" Vee yelled. The gauge wasn't even up to three atmospheres. That much pressure was not something an unsheltered body could tolerate. They were going to be crushed. Right in here. Right in front of them.

"The bends will kill them!" shot back Adrian. He was right. If they were brought up too fast, the gases in their blood would turn into bubbles in their veins, and those bubbles would float into their hearts.

But if they remained under this intense pressure, they'd simply be squeezed to death by the air.

No-win situation, thought Vee, almost hysterically.

"Keep us down, Kevin!" shouted Adrian. "Where's the rescue drop?"

"An hour away, tops," came the answer.

"Make sure they know we're under pressure."

They were all on their knees now, trying to hold the contorting bodies down, trying to speak soothing words that could not possibly be heard. The rescued team might as well have been naked to the heat and the pressure. Vee could see Angela's neck muscles swell. A thin ribbon of blood ran from her ear. Vee tried to hold Angela as she curled in on herself, but Vee couldn't tell whether the gesture was helping or hurting. Vee couldn't hear her, couldn't feel her. Angela was outside her. Vee couldn't check Angela's breathing or her pulse. Vee's thick, gloved fingers couldn't even hold Angela's hand.

"Charlotte, Charlotte," murmured Adrian. "I'm so sorry. Just hang on, please hang on."

Please hang on. I'm sorry. The first-aid kit was on the other side of the airlock. Who'd put a first-aid kit in here? No one would be in here when the door was closed without a suit on. That was nuts.

Nuts as it was, these people had no suits. There was no way

to reach them. Angela was beginning to shake. Tears ran from her closed eyes.

Let her be unconscious. Let her not know this is happening to her.

Seconds crawled by. Vee's gaze kept darting from her face-plate clock to Angela. Seconds, minutes, passing. Angela going from tremors, to jerks, to convulsions that kicked and battered Isaac Walters, who lay beside her, as well as Vee's hardsuit. She faded back to jerks and then to tremors, leaving Vee drowning in fear that the next thing to happen would be that Angela's muscles would go completely limp and her dead eyes would roll open.

But it didn't happen. It should have. It should have happened moments after their casings cracked. It should have happened when their scarab crashed, but it didn't. Angela, Isaac, Lindi, Charlotte, Dave the mission specialist, Chen the geologist, Arva the meteorologist, all held on for one more second, and one more, and one more after that.

After an eternity of one more second, Kevin's voice echoed inside Vee's helmet.

"Scarabs Eight and Ten are on the ground! They're on their way. What's your pressure and temp back there? Exactly."

"We're at the three point three atmospheres and fifty-two degrees Celsius," answered Adrian. "Tell them to step on it!"

More waiting. *Hang on Angela, oh, please, hang on.*

Angela was barely even twitching now. Her fingers curled and opened slightly, almost as if they were being blown by a wind. Not much to indicate life. Not nearly enough. Vee laid her hand on Angela's chest and tried to feel its rise and fall. Nothing. Nothing at all.

No. Please. You can't die. You can't die! Help's on the way!

The scarab shuddered. Vee's gaze jerked automatically to the door.

"We've got a docking seal with Scarab Eight," said Kevin. "Just another second, they'll have the door open."

Vee's heart hammered hard. Angela's hand went still.

"No, no, no." She grasped the woman's forearm. "Come on! One more second! One more!"

The outer door hissed open and they faced an identical air-lock and a pair of strangers in hardsuits surrounded by stretcher capsules.

"Mother Creation," whispered one, even as he swung a capsule forward and lifted its lid.

They got Charlotte in, strapped her down, closed the lid, swung the capsule into the airlock, where another person waited to read her vital signs and give the capsule orders for treatment and maintenance. They swung down another capsule, this one for Lindi. Another for Dave.

Angela still wasn't moving.

"They're here, help's here," breathed Vee. She felt tears running down her cheeks. She barely knew this woman who was dying under her hand and Vee couldn't even feel it and help was inches away and she couldn't beg them to hurry because everyone else was as bad or worse and they were already moving as fast as they possible could.

A capsule shut. Another swung into place.

"Okay, Dr. Hatch. We got her."

The med techs lifted Angela away and slotted her into the stretcher capsule, strapped her down, slapped the monitor patches on her, and closed the lid. The capsule's screens lit up instantly.

"Is she alive?" she croaked.

"Oh yeah," said the med tech. "Mother Creation alone knows how, but they're all still with us."

Vee fell backwards and sideways and found herself leaning against Josh. He laid an arm around her shoulder. She couldn't feel it, but she knew it was there.

Thank God, she thought, for the lives in the stretchers and the life next to her now. *Thank God.*

Chapter Eleven

The mooring hook took the ligaments the dirigible let down for it. As soon as the gondola opened its door, T'sha gathered up the cortex boxes they'd used to cope with the New People's shelter and flew straight for the base's main portal. She wanted to get into D'seun's way before he could take his anger out on any of the engineers.

As she had guessed, D'seun was there in the main analysis chamber, quivering with rage. T'sha glided past him into the chamber, making him turn away from the door and its view of the corridor beyond.

"I've heard what you did," he said.

"I am not surprised." She set each of the cortex boxes into their caretaker unit, which would determine whether they needed soothing, debriefing, or reprogramming.

"Why would you do such a thing?" demanded D'seun. "Why would you come into contact with them? It is not in your commission!"

T'sha wrapped her posthands around a perch and settled down to face him. She had to remain calm now. His anger was justified. She had completely ignored the presence of another ambassador while taking an action that could affect all the People. She had deliberately overflown her commission, and there was no going back.

"They were dying, D'seun," she said softly. "What should I have done?"

D'seun swelled. T'sha held her own bones in tight control.

She could not rise to this. Not now. "We had our mandate. We were not yet ready to greet them properly."

"This was not a greeting. This was an emergency." It had been too. Even knowing as much about them as she did, T'sha had been stunned when the cortices reported on the frigid temperatures the New People maintained for themselves and how deeply sheltered they were from the press of the air around them. Their own kind only limped to their aid. They showed all the soul of family members, surely, but they would have been far too late. There would not even have been raw materials to recover, so much would have boiled away.

"You may have jeopardized everything," D'seun shouted. "How can we show we have proper claim to New Home at this stage? They could legitimately call question to what we are doing."

T'sha clacked her teeth. "*I* could legitimately question what we're doing." Her body tried to swell, but she held herself rigid. "D'seun, you are making assumptions for which you have no evidence. We have no idea how they see us. We haven't asked them. We may not even have a way to ask them." There had been the one who'd stood so still under her stare. What was going on in that one's mind? What was passing between it and the others? Had they known the People were there to help? Had it feared they would take the raw materials of their companions' bodies before they were ready to be used?

D'seun leaned as far forward as he could without releasing his perch. He swelled up so huge he looked as if he was about to burst. "You did this deliberately. You did not get your way in the High Law Meet and so you are forcing the issue."

Despite all her self-control, T'sha's wings beat the air in simple frustration. "Did I cause the New People's equipment to fail? Did I make sure you were away from the base when it did?"

D'seun towered over her, rude and showy with his tattoos and his dyed crest, and did not answer. Not one of the other team members had come into the chamber, T'sha noted. Intelligent.

"I will take this back to the Law Meet," said D'seun, deflating only slightly.

T'sha dipped her muzzle. "I've already done so, D'seun. I sent D'han back through the portal with my complete report of the events."

"Your interpretation of events," said D'seun. "I'm sure, once I've spoken to them the engineers will have their own stories to tell."

That was enough, more than enough. T'sha inflated, swift and sudden. She spread her wings out until she was all D'seun could see.

"If I find you've intimidated even the lowest engineer on this team, I will take you before the Law Meet and I will bring up the question of your sanity!"

D'seun shriveled. "You wouldn't."

She cupped her wings to surround him. "Feel my words, Ambassador; feel my life. You know I have cause."

D'seun was so small and tight he would have sunk like a stone had he not been sitting on a perch. It was then T'sha knew. She had not been certain until that moment, but now she was. D'seun had not taken raw materials from the New People. He had taken a life.

Realization rocked T'sha back on her perch.

"I will not forget this," D'seun said.

"You should not." T'sha let go of her perch and flew into the corridor. She was aware of the Seventh Team strung out along the corridor like lanterns around a nightside room. She did not speak to them. Instead, she took herself straight into the refresher and ordered the door to close tightly behind her.

The air in the refresher was rich, thick, and heavy. T'sha took it in gratefully, relaxing her skin, drawing the life-giving air in through her loosened muzzle and feeling her internal poisons release from her pores. It was so hard to feel full here, in this beautiful, empty world. Back home she needed to refresh perhaps once every dodec-hour. Here, every four or five hours that passed left her drained. She relaxed skin, muscle, and bone in the room's gentle breeze and let herself drift.

She'd done it. Oh, she had done it. She'd spent so much effort controlling her body, she'd obviously forgotten to control her mind. Did she really mean she'd call D'seun's sanity into question?

She did. Her skin rippled with small fear. She'd do it. This was too huge. It meant too much. If D'seun would have her sacrifice the New People needlessly, if he had taken one of their lives, he might really be insane. The sane spread life, served it, nurtured it, and in return were served and spread and nurtured by life. The insane were greedy. They killed. They stunted and confined and hoarded life. The sane and the insane could not live together.

T'sha remembered when her family had met on a question of insanity. She'd only just been declared adult, able to fly with the others and add her voice to the consensus. T'thran, a second cousin to her birth family, had deliberately destroyed an entire square mile of canopy. He offered no reason, however closely questioned. He had only wanted to do this thing. It was bad, he said. It was rotted, and the rot would spread.

But there was no evidence. No one else in the entire latitude had witnessed this corruption. Not even Ca'aed could say it had existed. The family asked; they asked everyone they could reach. The wind blew them from day through night and back into day again while they turned the question over. But in the end, every voice polled had called him insane.

Insane. Nothing left to contribute to life but his own raw material. So that raw material had been taken and used to help recreate what had been destroyed.

As would D'seun's be, if she did this and the Law Meet found she was right.

The problem was, of course, that D'seun could make his own case against her. He had already convinced the Seventh Team she was greedy and careless. What if he or some ally took that to a court or the Fitness Review Committee in the High Law Meet? There existed the very real possibility that she would be removed from her special position here, and then who would speak for the New People? D'seun would not, his bullied team would not, and back in the High Law Meet, Ambassador Z'eth most certainly would not.

T'sha floated between disasters and did not know which way to dodge. She only knew that as long as the New People were alive and sane they could not be dismissed, could not be flown over without regard to their needs and their claims. That was right. That was the first Right and the final Right and it would not change, no matter how closely D'seun argued his case and no matter what Z'eth had asked her to do.

"I cannot choose which life to serve," she murmured, calling back the words the living highland spoke to Ca'doth.

T'sha floated, blown by the room's gentle, random breeze, taking in its nutrition and its calm. She had made her move. All that she could do now was wait and see how D'seun would respond.

The Veneran doctors agreed Vee could sleep in her own room if she wore the monitor belt and patches under her shirt and swore to drink two liters of water before she went to bed.

So there she stood in her spacious, comfortable living room, with its autoform furniture and its walls set to a static pattern of mountains and clouds based on Japanese watercolors, and the purple rag rug on the soft-tile floor, completely at a loss about what to do. Angela, Lindi, Isaac, and the Venerans were all going to live, thanks to the intervention of the aliens. She drew a large glass of water from the tap at the sink in the kitchenette and drank some absently. What were they doing down there now? What were they doing there at all? Who were they? Why had they decided to help?

For the first time since coming to Venera, Vee felt trapped. There was a whole new world out there now, and she couldn't reach it.

Nothing you can do about it now, unless you want to put the act back on and try to bully Failia and company to let you back down there.

Vee sat in the desk chair. No. That was not going to get her anywhere. But she couldn't just sit here. She had to *do* something.

Almost idly, she flipped open her briefcase and accessed her drawing programs. She unclipped the stylus from her holder and opened the gallery. Maybe she could draw the scene from the accident, just to pass the time. She could begin with clips from the gallery. She had the backdrops she'd used for her simulations to show Angela, but they were strictly second rate. Might do for a base to build on. Needed color though, and a different scale.

Her mind's eye brought the rescue scene back to the fore, and her hands started to move.

This wasn't a real holograph; this was a computer-generated simulation. She'd have to unpack her holotank and film to make the real thing, but she could make a sketch for eventual transfer to real 3-D. She could show the dim shadows and black rock with the startling threads of lava creeping down the mountainsides. She could show the scarab, bent and crippled in a wilderness of stone.

And she could show the aliens. The gold wings that shimmered and sparkled in the dim light and thick air. The silver eyes. Those eyes, how could she render those eyes? How could she show the intelligence she had felt under the surface as this creature, no, this *person* from another world looked into her own eyes?

Vee zoomed in on the winged form and concentrated solely on it, the eyes, the lines along its skin, the curve of its torso and wings. She worked fast, trying to freeze the memory before it faded. The cameras from the suits and the scarab had surely captured the images, but how long would it be before she had access to them? This was her memory. This was her moment made real in light and code. This is what she'd show the world, all the worlds, so they would understand what had happened.

Water, promises, and time forgotten, Vee drew the first portrait of Earth's neighbors.

Her door chimed, jerking Vee back into the present, where she became aware of a stiff back and ankles, a cramped hand, and a raging thirst.

"Door. Open," called Vee, half-annoyed, half-grateful. She gulped half the water remaining in her glass.

Josh stood in the threshold.

"Hi," he said. "You okay?"

"Oh yeah, fine." She blanked her case screen. It wasn't done yet. Not ready for anyone else to see. "Got caught up in a project. What's going on?"

"Dr. Failia wants us all in the conference room to debrief about . . . what happened. I said I'd come get you."

"Thanks." Vee unbent her protesting back and legs. She got to her feet and drained her water glass. "You didn't have to do this."

Josh's face shifted into an expression she hadn't seen before. It was gentle, yet awkward. "I wanted to make sure you were okay. Things got rough down there, and you were looking at Angela like . . ." He searched for words. "Like she was the only thing holding you together."

"Thanks," said Vee again, and she meant it. "It was bad for a bit. No question. We owe the aliens. Whatever they are, we owe them."

"Yes, we do." Josh shook his head. "Ever since you told me the base was a fake, I'd been gearing up for a huge disappointment. But then . . ." His words trailed off. "I don't know what to think now."

"Me either," she admitted. "Yet. Let's go get debriefed." She crossed to the door and stopped. Something else needed to be said. Something she hadn't needed to say for a long time. She turned back toward Josh. "Thank you for taking me seriously down there. For letting me help."

"That was the real you," Josh said. "I was glad you were there."

"Yeah, well," said Vee, unable to form a better response and kicking herself for it. "Let's see how glad the board is."

Vee and Josh walked to Conference Room One through a Venera Base that seemed abnormally tense. Vee was sure the rumor mill had been incredibly active all day, but from the sidelong glances people were giving them, she was also sure that Dr. Failia and the governing board hadn't yet deigned to release any official information. If it had been Vee, she'd have been going crazy.

They were the last to arrive. The board clustered together at one end of the oval table. The passengers and crew of Scarab

Five ranged around the rest of it. All the U.N. team who were not in the hospital were there. Terry sat next to her partner. Robert Stykos. Julia sat between Troy and Adrian, who was next to a shell-shocked Philip Bowerman. Vee picked the free chair beside Philip. Josh sat next to her. Vee felt absurdly pleased.

Helen Failia got to her feet. She looked determined, as if she was not going to let even this situation get the best of her.

But Philip did not give her the chance to speak. "Before we say anything else here"—Philip looked haggard. No surprise. His partner was lying in the infirmary with tubes in her arms and synaptic stimulators in her ears while all five medical doctors tried to work out how many nerve grafts she was going to need—"I want to know why our outgoing communications are being blocked."

Our what? Vee straightened up. Now she could see why both Terry and Robert appeared particularly grim.

Helen gave a short sigh, as if this were a minor inconvenience. "Venera's governing board has decided that, for the time being, all outgoing communication which contains references to this latest development will be held for transmission at a later time."

"You cannot do this," said Robert through clenched teeth. "You have no right to restrict free communication."

"Venera Base reserves the right to refuse transmission of data which might include proprietary or unpublished information based on work that does not belong to the person requesting the transmission." Dr. Failia said it like she'd memorized it. She probably had. It was probably part of the colony's charter or some similar document.

Philip shook his head. "That is not an acceptable decision, Dr. Failia."

"It is most definitely not acceptable," said Terry. "This is the real thing. We need to get this out as soon as possible."

"No," said Helen flatly. "That was what was done with the Discovery. Now we know that was a fraud. Who knows what this latest phenomenon is?"

"I do," said Troy, his voice husky with awe. Vee had heard

that tone plenty of times down in the Discovery, but this was different somehow. Down there, she'd been quite sure it was all for show, a way to impress Lindi with his depth and give Terry good sound bits. Now though, she got the sudden impression they were hearing what he really felt. "They were saviors. Merciful saviors. They took gentle care of the crew of Scarab Fourteen—"

"They kept Heathe's body," cut in Dr. Godwin. "What'd they do that for? Merciful saviors? Maybe just morbidly curious?"

"We can't know," said Michael Lum. "Not yet. From what we saw we can't even know if we can communicate with them."

"Yes, we can." Vee blurted out the words before she even realized she had spoken.

"What?" said Dr. Failia sharply. Everyone turned to face Vee.

"We can communicate with them," said Vee, slowly this time, letting the ideas bubbling up inside her mind coalesce, giving herself a chance to see them clearly. "They can see." Yes, there it was. The foundation. They could build from there. "One of them was watching me the whole time. Their eyes were made up like a human eye, or near as, which means it's probable they can see in wavelengths we use and resolve images very close to the way we do."

"And assuming you're right?" said Dr. Godwin.

Vee felt herself smile. Ideas flowed through her. This could work. They could do this. "If they can see, we can communicate with them. I don't know if they could hear a radio broadcast, but they might be able to read a letter."

"You want to teach them their ABC's? How?" Dr. Failia's voice was suspicious but not dismissive. Good. Excellent.

"Holographs," Vee told them.

"Don't be ridiculous," said Dr. Godwin. "It'd take years to get a holograph setup that would work."

Vee's smile spread. She loved surprises. She loved the impossible, and this was the most impossible set of circumstances she'd ever been in. "It'll take a week. The hard part's already done."

"What is the hard part?" asked Dr. Failia.

Vee leaned forward. "The hard part would have been getting

a working laser in place, but we've already got one. Whoever built the Discovery took care of that for us. There is a laser down there that Josh says will work under Venusian conditions as soon as we jack it into a power source."

"And you think you can talk to them?" Dr. Lum sounded half-afraid, half-hopeful.

"Maybe." Her gaze turned inward while her mind lined up the things they'd need. "We build a holotank outside the Discovery where they can see it. Line it up with the laser. Wire the laser so it can be controlled from inside one of the scarabs. It's got a double beam, so it can record and project once we get the tank in place. I've brought some of my rapid-replay film with me, so if we can set up some kind of cold-box for the tank to work in, we won't have a problem there—"

"Wait a minute." Philip got to his feet. "Figuring out the mechanics, this is good; we'll need that, but this is not something we can do alone up here. This is not your decision. We need to contact the C.A.C. immediately and let them inform the Secretaries-General what has happened."

"What do you want us to do, Mr. Bowerman?" asked Dr. Godwin. "Let the aliens sit and twiddle their thumbs for weeks until the S.G.s decide which end's up?"

"That's not my decision." Philip planted one hand on the tabletop. "And it's not yours."

"Yes, it is ours," said Dr. Godwin. "This is our home, not yours."

Philip's face tightened. "This involves all of humanity, not just Venus."

"We owe it to all of humanity to give them an accurate picture," said Dr. Lum quietly. "If it is proven the Discovery is a fraud, then we already screwed up once, and look what we started. We can't risk doing that again."

"I appreciate your scientific rigor—"

"It's not science, it's survival," said Dr. Lum. "We are not talking about a few holes in the ground anymore. We are talking about living beings with who knows what capabilities and who knows what reasons for being here. Before we panic the entire range of humanity, we have to know what they can and cannot do and why they're doing it." Dr. Lum let his gaze sweep the entire gathering. "If we don't have some answers when people ask 'what do they want,' we're going to have an upheaval like nothing we've seen since the twentieth century."

"One week," said Dr. Failia. "Dr. Hatch said she can make contact within a week. We will then at least see how they react to our attempts to talk. We can take that to the U.N. It will be better than nothing."

Philip shook his head. "It's unacceptable. This is not your decision."

"Unfortunately, it is," said Dr. Failia. "We're here and so are they. We have to decide what to do about that. Here it is."

Philip said nothing. Vee didn't miss the struggle on his face, though. He was going to try to contact his superiors again as soon as he left the meeting. The board certainly knew it. Despite his determination, however, he was also obviously aware he was a long, long way from any kind of backup.

"Dr. Hatch." Dr. Failia turned to Vee. "I need an honest assessment. Do you believe you can initiate some kind of contact with . . . our neighbors in one week?"

"Yes," said Vee without hesitation. "I'll need Dr. Kenyon's help, but we can do it."

"Please proceed after the meeting then," said Dr. Failia. Vee nodded.

"And for those of us who don't agree with the one week holding period?" asked Robert coolly.

"All outgoing communications are being monitored," said Dr. Lum. "Nothing will be released without authorization."

"I see," said Philip. He looked at Godwin. "It's nice to see separatist principles being applied evenly as always. The U.N. tries to regulate your communication, you howl at the unfairness of it all. But you regulating the U.N.'s, that's just fine."

"You are not the U.N.," said Dr. Godwin softly, but his satisfaction with the statement was unmistakable.

"I am a U.N. employee, just like every other Terran member at this table. What you are doing is not legal and not acceptable." Philip stood and walked out the door.

"You'll excuse us as well," Terry also got up and left, followed by Robert.

As the door swished shut, Dr. Lum woke up the tabletop screen in front of him and touched a few command keys. Vee itched to know what they were, but there was no way to ask.

Dr. Failia sighed as if resigning herself to something unpleasant and focused on her remaining audience.

"Josh, if you could tell us what you know about the accident and what happened afterwards, please."

Josh glanced around the table and then at the door. "For the record, I don't agree at all with censoring communication. That said"—he sighed and folded his arms—"this is what I saw."

They each talked in turn. Four versions of the same experience made a collage that mostly resolved into a single story. By the end of it, Vee had heard the experience repeated so many times it began to feel a little dreamlike. But all she had to do was think about the bodies on the airlock floor and it hit her all over again—the waiting, the fear, the cries of pain. Oh yeah, it was real.

And nothing would ever be the same again. Vee pictured the person hovering in front of her on golden wings and felt herself start to smile again.

She would find a way to talk to the ones with golden wings.

Then the universe would open up wide.

The door closed behind the U.N. investigative team as they left the meeting, cutting off both Veronica Hatch's rapid-fire suggestions to Josh Kenyon and Troy Peachman's continued awed murmurings to whoever would listen.

"Well that's done," said Helen, smoothing her scarf down. "I do hope our new neighbors appreciate what we're going through for them."

Ben smiled faintly at her attempted joke, but Michael's face remained serious.

"There's one more thing," he said quietly.

There was no question as to what he meant. Helen wished there could be. She sighed. "Your people have them?"

"Yes."

"Are you going to ask the yewners to be there for the questioning?" asked Ben in as mild a voice as he owned.

That would be your first priority, Ben, wouldn't it? "No." Helen shook her head. "I would prefer we handle this ourselves for as long as we can." She'd gone down with Michael to arrest Derek. She remembered the hurt on his face, the bewildered betrayal, as if he didn't understand what all the *fuss* was about.

"But you're still going to send them back to Mother Earth for trial?" Ben's face was flushed, but his eyes were cold.

"What else are we supposed to do? No"—Helen held up her hand—"I don't want to hear it. We are sending them back to Earth, eventually." She rested her fingertips briefly on the table. *I do not want to do this. Please understand, Ben, even with all they are about to bring down on us, I do not want to do this.*

She straightened up. "I don't want them paraded through the halls. We'll go down."

"You don't have to do this, Helen," Michael told her as he stood at her side. "I can bring you a report."

He'd said the same thing during the arrest. He was a good boy, Michael. His attempts to shelter her were well meaning. This was even a fairly decent out. No one would question it or think that there was another way to do this.

No one but Helen herself. "No. We all let this happen and we're all going to be made to pay for it, one way or another. Look at this as the first installment."

Remember the others, Helen told herself as she led the board out into the corridor and toward the elevator bundle. *Remember what is real. Our neighbors have saved more than a scarab crew, simply by being there. They have saved us from the worst this fraud accusation could bring.*

It was a strange thought to be having at this moment, but it kept her going as they descended to the administration level and walked in single file into the back of Michael's security area. Murmured conversations started up as they passed, and Helen imagined the waves of whispering spreading out like ripples in a pool. Whispering about how the entire governing board marched in to see the Cusmanos brothers and endless speculations about what they talked about, spreading and merging to join with the speculation about what really happened to the scarab crews.

She'd have to make an announcement soon. But first they had to try to find out who else needed to be held. Michael was certain the Cusmanoses had not acted alone, and Helen trusted him.

Venera's brig was the only cramped place on the base. Little cells, little questioning rooms, all decked with big cameras, it was exactly the opposite of the free spaces. Not torturous, no, but disquieting, especially for long-term residents.

The brig had actually been an afterthought. Helen, for all her careful planning, had not envisioned the need for such a place in her original design. But scientists and academics were human, with their share of the human fallibilities, and house arrest did not suffice for everyone.

Two of Michael's security team brought the brothers into the interrogation room, where the governing board waited for them. Derek, troubled but defiant, and Kevin, hollow-eyed and tired, sat at the end of the table as far from the board as they could get. Derek slumped his shoulders and looked anywhere in the room except at the faces of his accusers. Kevin sat up straight but bowed his head, studying the smooth, wired plastic surface of the table.

Anger grabbed hold of Helen, but she'd been ready for it. What she was less prepared for was the sorrow. Kevin and Derek's parents had been old-fashioned Christians, and she'd been to both their sons' baptisms. She'd written Kevin the recommendation that got him into M.F.I.T., and she'd been there when Ben told Derek he'd won the competitive exams that turned him into the one-man survey department.

Beth and Rick Cusmanos had both retired and moved back to Mother Earth. Helen remembered her own mixed feelings at the bon voyage party. But the sons had both stayed. Stayed to do this to Venera.

Belatedly, she realized Beth and Rick did not yet know what their sons had done, and sorrow struck her again.

"I have your statements in your files." Michael lit up one of the table screens, all business. Whatever he felt watching the men who were his friends, he kept hidden. He just shuffled the icons until he had access to their fact files. "Is there anything you want to add at this time?"

Derek's eyes slid sideways to look at Kevin. Kevin did not look up. "Can you cut us a deal?" asked Derek, a little belligerently, a little hopefully.

Michael's gaze flickered from Derek to Kevin. "I can make sure the court knows you cooperated fully."

"But you can't deal?" pressed Derek.

Helen felt her jaw clench. *How can you talk like this? Don't you realize what you almost did? If there hadn't been something real out there, you would have killed Venera!*

Michael shook his head. "I'm not an officer of the courts, no, but I am recognized as a police officer. It gives me some weight."

Derek snorted, and Kevin glowered at him. "No," Derek said. "It's not enough. The shit's too deep to be shoveled out with a good report card."

"Derek." Ben leaned forward. "Don't do this to yourselves. Don't do this to your friends. You've been caught. It's all over. There's no one to protect anymore."

Derek said nothing.

Helen swallowed her anger. She stood and walked around the edge of the table. "Kevin?" she said, standing next to him.

Kevin sat silently. Helen let the silence stretch. Then, she said. "You're a good man, Kevin Cusmanos. You have done so much good work for us." She meant it, every word. A thousand memories flashed through her head of Kevin, in and out of the scarabs, his attention to detail, his care and diligence in training his people and caring for his equipment. "You're just trying to help your brother, I'm sure of that." More memories—the two of them in the playground, Derek always tearing along behind his older, bulkier brother. Kevin at Derek's promotion ceremony, his chest puffed all the way out. Derek looked so . . . lost really when Kevin boarded the ship for Earth and his degrees, and Kevin shaking him by the shoulder and telling him to cheer up.

Helen laid her hand on Kevin's shoulder. "I'm telling you, it doesn't have to be this bad. We might not even have to send you down there if we can show we know all of what happened."

Slowly, sadly, Kevin shook his head. "There is no way the yewners are going to let you hang on to us. Too many people are going to look stupid as soon as word gets out. There's nothing you can do, Helen."

Regret deep and profound poured through her. That was it then. She touched his shoulder. "There's nothing you'll let me do."

"You're probably right," he said to the tabletop.

"Kevin."

Kevin finally looked up, right into her eyes. Over his shoulder, she saw Derek's face go white. *He's going to tell us.* Hope leaped up inside her. *He's not going to let us down.*

But the moment passed, and Kevin's gaze dropped back to the tabletop. "I can't," he whispered. "I'm sorry."

"So am I, Kevin." She squeezed his shoulder and turned away. "For both of you."

Phil stepped into Angela's cubicle in the infirmary. She was still unconscious. Her face was mottled red and white. The muffling headphones the doctors had strapped over her damaged ears plastered her short hair against her burned scalp. Tubes and patches covered her pale arms lying on top of the rough monitor blanket.

"You're looking good, Ms. Cleary." He sat in the stiff chair beside her bed. Why was there no hospital in existence that had comfortable visitor's chairs? She really did look better. When they'd first let him in to see her, every limb was swollen with bruises and blisters. Her face was a single massive, doughy contusion. He'd seen worse but not on his partner.

They told him she'd been awake briefly, but now what she needed was sleep. She needed to sleep away the pain and the fear and the utter strangeness of what had happened to her. The Veneran doctors were minimalists who did not approve of speed-healing techniques. They repaired the blood vessels and nerves, alleviated the adenoma, and treated the worst of the burns. Other than that, they were leaving her body to take care of itself.

"Well, you've been saying you needed a vacation anyway," said Phil, looking more at the floor than at Angela. She'd been nearly dead when they brought her back. He'd thought it was all over. He'd thought she was gone. He'd been terrified. They'd worked together since he'd joined the U.N. security team. In some ways he was closer to her than to his own wife.

But she wasn't dead. She'd been saved. By strangers. Aliens. It was almost too much. Phil found he didn't really want to think about it. It was a lot easier to concentrate on what was going on inside Venera's walls.

"I haven't written the report for the boss yet," he went on. "The Venerans are screening outgoing transmissions. Somehow I don't think our encrypted stuff is going to get through. I'm going to start looking for holes." He rested his elbows on his knees. "But I don't think I'm going to find any. The guy is very good." He glanced at her. The blanket rose and fell with her rhythmic breathing.

She's getting better. She's going to stay alive. "I wonder how long it's going to take Stykos and Wray to file free-speech lawsuits." He sucked on his cheek thoughtfully. "Actually, the Venerans will probably offer them exclusive coverage of the aliens if they keep their mouths shut until the Venerans are ready."

He rubbed his palms together, feeling skin against skin, feeling how they were slightly damp. Then his thoughts froze the motion.

"How'd he filter out the communications so fast?" Phil straightened up.

You just said he was good. His imagination supplied Angela's words.

"Nobody's that good. He couldn't just shut down everything; it'd look funny. Someone on Mother Earth would notice." He touched Angie's hand. It was warm and dry under the tubes. "A good broad-spectrum communication filter is not something you pluck out of the stream. He must have had them in place." He turned toward her, eyes shining, despite the fact that nothing had changed with her. "I think Michael Lum's been less than straight with us about how wired this base is. That means there might be info we could strain out."

Might be. Maybe. If he was right. But that also meant the not so still waters of Venera ran deeper than he'd believed.

If Michael Lum hadn't told them how much info he had access to, who else hadn't he told?

On the other hand, Michael was the one who'd come to him about the possible fraud involving the Discovery, which made him less likely to be involved in perpetrating that fraud.

"What a mess," Phil muttered through his teeth. He turned his eyes to Angela's blanket and its steady rise and fall. "We're going to have to do some scenario planning here. It's pretty clear the original Discovery was a fake. They've got the guys who actually built it. But I think Michael's right. There were other people involved in planning the scam. We need to find them." He leaned back again, a restless, meaningless movement. "And hope for the moment he's not one of them, although I don't know. . . . Fake base and real aliens." Phil shook his head. "I am not buying the coincidence here. Someone is building up to something, and I can't see what yet." He frowned, both at his thoughts and at the realization that it was so much easier to think of aliens if they were part of a conspiracy or a cover-up of some kind. That felt strange and a little sad.

Angela stirred, a meaningless, restless movement of her own. "Wake up soon, Angie," he said softly. "I need you on the beach with me when the wave hits."

The idiots, thought Su as she surveyed the broken chunks of metal and ceramic tumbling gently through the void. *They couldn't wait. They couldn't hold back.*

She floated upright in the shuttle's observation compartment, one hand hanging on to a wall handle to keep herself still and oriented. The port window currently showed the small debris field. Here and there she could see the bright-yellow suits of the Trans-Lunar Patrol workers, gathering the debris, strapping it into bundles to be hauled into the shuttles and out of the shipping lanes. Small drones spread out in sweep patterns, vacuuming up the dust and marble-sized debris that could pinhole anything that flew through it.

Twelve hours ago, all that debris had been a shipyard engaged in labor negotiations with a union that had outspoken separatist sentiments. The yard was a space station, and the property of a wholly owned Terran corporation, which got it around the "no ship building" rules that applied to the colonies.

It also meant that the colonists cared a lot less about keeping the place in good shape.

The bombs had scattered the yards and the ships across kilometers of heavily traveled space. The Trans-Lunars and the insurance people were still calculating the damage. At least five ships had been hit by debris. The majority of traffic between Earth and Luna was grounded until they could get the wreckage cleared up. It would take days and cost millions.

They just couldn't wait.

"The Union has made a strong statement condemning the bombing," said Glenn Kucera, the U.N.'s Lunar representative, and the person Su kept thinking of as her "host" for this little trip. "They're saying it's radical elements within the organization and that the union is committed to peaceful reform."

"Yes, I heard that," said Su. She couldn't look away. The world outside was all sharp edges against the blackness. Everything was too clean, too clear. It all fell, fell endlessly, silver, white, and black. "How many people died in there?"

"Fourteen," said Kucera. "It went off between shifts."

"And is anyone is custody?" Her mouth moved and questions came out, but Su felt as though someone else were asking them. She was just watching the tumbling debris and cursing the ones who couldn't wait just a few days, maybe a few weeks longer.

"Not yet. We're still following some leads, and of course Mr. Hourani is here to help." Kucera licked his lips. "Su, we've got to diffuse this. Waicek—"

Su nodded. "Edmund was down in U.N. City now, having

himself a little field day, pointing out what unrest, what independent thought in the colonies led to.

"And he's got backup." Su ground her teeth against the curses that wanted to spill out of her. They'd worked so hard to keep things calm, to keep everything going through the transition period. She'd done absolutely everything she could do. Why did it feel like she had never worked hard enough?

Why couldn't you just wait?

Well, while she was up here, she would take some of the wind out of Edmund Waicek's sails. That was all ready to set in motion. She just needed to get through this first.

It took all of Su's strength to turn away from the window and face her host. Even then, out of the corner of her eye, she could still see bits of black and silver tumbling in the darkness.

"I'll meet with the Union reps," she said. "Find somebody to arrest, Glenn. Get this under wraps quickly." Actually, with Sadiq Hourani himself looking into the situation, Su did not give the perpetrators of this violent idiocy long odds.

"I want it under wraps too, believe me." Although Glenn had been born on Earth, he looked like the classic Lunar—tall, spindly, hair cropped short under his cap. He'd gone pretty native up here, but he hid it so he could keep his post. It was a balancing act that Su understood well and did not envy.

Su touched his arm. "We'll pull it out, Glenn. We always have."

He smiled crookedly. "One damn crisis after another, isn't it?" He gazed out the window. "I just wish they weren't coming closer together."

"So do I, Glenn."

They shared a tired, tight smile with each other. Glenn let go of his strap and pushed easily off the wall with just enough force to take him to the threshold of the passenger bay. "So, can I drop you somewhere?"

"Back to Selene, thank you," said Su, primly. "I've got an appointment."

"Will do." Glenn paused. "Thanks for coming up for this one, Su. I know you've got enough going on with Venera."

"I'm not abandoning anybody, Glenn. We're all in this together." Almost involuntarily her gaze shifted back to the spinning debris. *At least, we should be.*

The landing back in the Selene port was perfectly routine. Su emerged with her retinue and Glenn and then sent them all about their business. She really did have an appointment, but this was not a meeting that needed an audience.

Assisted by the weighted undersuit she wore, Su walked to Selene's public caverns. Su visited Luna frequently, but she'd never gotten the hang of light gravity, so she dressed like a tourist to keep from hurting herself or from damaging property by inadvertently flinging things across the room.

She found the cafe where the meeting was to take place in the vine-hung public cavern that served as a small park. She took a seat at one of its gilt-wire tables but did not order anything. Outwardly she was calm, but inside, her stomach churned from the memory of the devastation. Her mind kept running through all the areas where damage control would be needed, and the list was expanding alarmingly.

It was ten minutes later when Frezia Cheney finally emerged from the northeast tunnel. Living on the Moon gave one grace, Su decided, as she watched the feeder walk toward her. Especially in those who were born here, there was an unhurried elegance in their small movements. Maybe it was because things around them fell so slowly that there was no imperative to rush when you reached for something. You could grab hold of whatever you wanted and not even gravity would snatch it away from you.

Su stood up politely as the feeder reached her table. "Thank you for agreeing to meet me, Ms. Cheney."

"I should be thanking you, Ms. Yan." She beamed the smile of those comfortable with cameras and publicity. "Normally there's a three-month waiting list to get to speak to anyone in the U.N."

"Yes," agreed Su as they both sat down. "We are kept on short leashes."

"They've let yours out far enough to reach Luna."

Su smiled deprecatingly. "Ah, that took a little doing. I was officially here doing some labor negotiations . . ." She broke off. "But then, you would know that already."

"I would." Ms. Cheney nodded once. "In fact, I've written about it."

"Of course." Su frequently scanned the stream for her own name. It was partly vanity, but mostly it was to keep an eye on how she was perceived. The bad opinion of her colleagues was one thing, but public opinion turned against her could be the end of her.

Su set that thought aside. "And how was my son when you spoke to him?"

Ms. Cheney's smile was both curious and sly. "He told you about me?"

"Was it supposed to be confidential?" returned Su.

"Oh, no." She waved her hand, dismissing any such suggestion. "But I wasn't aware that you two spoke much."

Now it was Su's turn to smile slyly. "We keep that quiet. It's not good for either of our reputations."

"I suppose not. To answer your question, I'm happy to tell you he was quite well." She paused and her eyes slid up and sideways. Su had the distinct feeling some implant had just been activated. Probably a recorder. "Now, may I ask what you wanted to see me about?" asked Ms. Cheney.

Su folded her hands on the table and smoothed her thoughts out. Time to get to work. "Actually, I also came to Luna about a stream piece."

The feeder tipped her head in polite curiosity. "One I've written, or one you'd like me to write?"

I see, Ms. Cheney, that you've had experience with politicians. "One I'd like you to write. If you're willing to accommodate me, I am in a position to offer you access to the blast site and some of the U.N. personnel involved in the investigation." *And aren't I going to have the time convincing Sadiq to go along with it.*

Ms. Cheney's eyes gleamed for a moment, but experience and suspicion doused the light. "A great deal would depend on what you want me to write."

"Naturally." Su inclined her head. "You know Edmund Waicek?"

Ms. Cheney's eyes slid sideways again. Su was certain the feeder was looking Edmund up, fetching the pertinent details from some internally stored database to be displayed on a contact lens or spoken softly into her ear. "Not personally, but I know his political opinions better than I'd care to."

"You know that his parents died in the Bradbury Rebellion?" Su asked, positive Ms. Cheney had the information available.

One more slide of Ms. Cheney's eyes. *Look that up. Don't make any statement of fact unless you're sure.* "That's been gone over several times. He's made speeches about it."

I have lost more than can ever be recovered, and I am only one of many. Su remembered the speech very well. He'd done it with tears in his eyes. They might even have been real.

"But did you know that they were Fullerists?" asked Su.

"What?" Ms. Cheney jerked out of her internal communion with her data implants. It was just as well. She would not find this little fact in the shallows of the stream. Edmund had made sure of that.

Su nodded slowly. "The senior Waiceks were friends and supporters of Ted Fuller. They sent their son into politics to be a friendly voice for the colonies. Then the rebellion happened, and one of Fuller's . . . less reliable associates feared they'd expose his embezzlements and bundled them off on an unreliable ship with one of the last loads of U.N. sympathizers."

Neither of them spoke for a long time. They sat there with their own thoughts, letting the world flow around them. Su couldn't guess at Ms. Cheney's imaginings. Her own were lost in the thought of the little tin-can ships that were Fuller's real crime. All those ships, pulled from the repair yards when there weren't enough sound vessels in port to exile the dissenters, or suspected dissenters. Ships with poor reactor shielding, ships with spent fuel tanks, ships with hulls already weak or pinholed, just waiting to be cut to ribbons by the random stones that flew between Earth and Mars.

No matter what his apologists said about evil counselors, it was those ships—those dead human beings—not his wish for freedom, that doomed Ted Fuller's cause and all that might have come of it.

"I'm not sure that's exactly the sort of story I'd be willing to publish," said Ms. Cheney after a while.

"I see." Of course. The woman was a separatist. She would not be willing to cast any additional aspersions on the great Theodore Fuller. "Can I ask you to consider the implications that Edmund Waicek covered up his parents' political leanings? It is one of the great media truths that it's not the crime, it's the cover-up, that makes news."

Ms. Cheney pursed her mouth and nodded. "True. True. There may be something there." Su could practically read her thoughts. For the mainstream, political cover-up. For the separatists, the loudest voice against colonial rights is the son of Fullerists. Yes, there was certainly something there.

"Why are you telling me this, Mrs. Yan?"

Su was ready for that one. "I deplore hypocrisy."

"Surely that's not the whole reason."

"Surely it is."

Ms. Cheney leaned back and nodded, an indication that she was prepared to be content with that for the moment. "I believe I can put together something that will return Edmund Waicek's background to public conversation."

"Very good." Su stood, signaling the end of the conversation. "You'll be contacted tomorrow about covering the blast site. Word will be left that you are—" Her phone spot's chime cut off the rest of her words.

"Transmission from Ben Godwin to Yan Quai," said the voice in her ear. "Private recording and decryption process go."

Mother Creation, so soon? "I'm sorry," Su forced her attention back to the reporter. "I've just received a message I must attend to."

"About the Discovery?" asked Ms. Cheney, getting smoothly to her feet. "Or about more separatist activity?"

"I have no comment about it at this time," said Su reflexively. "I'm sorry."

"So am I, Ms. Yan." She smiled. "Thank you for your time."

"Thank you for yours," returned Su.

Su left the feeder there. She had to get away from the cameras and their attendant ears. Her room at the embassy was as private as Sadiq could make it, so she headed there.

The room felt uncomfortably tiny to Su, but for Lunar quarters, it was quite luxurious. There was room for all the essentials—bed, desk, table, three chairs, without any of them having to be foldaways. The bathroom had a separate door and was hers alone.

Luna made some of its money off the tourist industry, but most of it off mining and industry, and the mining and industrial concerns were not interested in taking up room with living quarters.

When Su first had Sadiq Hourani tap Quai's private mailboxes for her, she'd told herself it was a precaution. Quai dealt with some fringe characters and might find himself up to his neck before he knew it. He was just a boy.

But that was a comfortable fiction and she knew it. She'd asked for the tap because she wanted to know what was happening with the separatists. She wanted to keep an eye on them all so she could try to temper their activities, steer them away from the most damaging courses.

She wanted to control them.

The tap was a betrayal of her son's trust. One day he'd find out, and she would pay. Even now, when they were on the same side, he would not forgive this intrusion into his privacy.

Even that stark realization, though, did not make her turn off the tap.

Su had already unplugged the desk and jacked her own case into the wall socket. She sat down in the desk chair and opened the screen. After a few typed commands and three passwords of increasing length, the decrypted stolen transmission printed out for her.

Su felt her eyes widen as she read. Her hands slipped from the command board and toppled into her lap.

Aliens. Aliens on Venus. Not some hole in the ground this time. Not overblown speculation and chancy photographs. Not even microscopic RNA particles. No. These were living beings with minds and wills of their own, and they had saved a scarab's crew.

Su's throat tightened. Implications, wondrous and terrible, poured through her mind too fast for her to take note of them all.

And here was Ben Godwin telling it all to her son, laying out how it could be used by the separatists for their cause. As predicted. But it was one thing to predict and another to see it happening. Some part of her had believed, had hoped, this day would not come even as she had laid down all her strategies for when it did.

One command at a time, Su wiped out the file. It would not do for anyone else to see this.

No, it would not do at all.

Chapter Twelve

T'sha floated in the research chamber of the New Home base, murmuring her worries to her personal cortex box and wishing painfully it was Ca'aed she spoke to. She and D'seun were now in the order of debate for the High Law Meet. A few of T'sha's friends had quietly passed the word that they found it hard to support what she had done, considering that the consensus had been quite clear about the fact that she was to observe and report on the New People, not contact them, and that the New People's own kind were already responding by the time T'sha had reached the accident site. One of those friends was Ambassador Z'eth.

T'sha cupped the soft box in her forehands, stroking its skin, inhaling the calm scents it gave off and murmuring in its recording language.

"I have no pictures to show them. I could subpoena the raw materials Tr'es is examining, I suppose, but how else am I going to show how fragile the New People are? How brave they are being here? Their needs must be very great for them to come to a place that is so hazardous to them." The box mistook her tone of bewildered wonder for distress and plumped itself up soothingly under her restless fingers, letting its gentle cooings drift across her fingertips. "Of my worst assertions, I still have no proof. I—"

"Ambassador T'sha?" Br'sei hovered in the threshold. "You wanted to speak with me, Ambassador?"

"Yes, I did." She spoke the Off command to her box and tucked it back into the caretaker's folds.

Br'sei drifted into the room. He looked alert but calm, with his purple crest only partly raised and his bones relaxed under his skin. T'sha found herself surveying his tattoos afresh. Br'sei was not just a senior engineer, he was a master engineer. He was also a freed indenture and a survivor of D'dant village, where a yeast had turned their home's bones to a froth that had broken in the wind.

"How are the researches on the New People's raw materials going?" T'sha asked.

Br'sei shook his wings noncommittally. "Tr'es is practically flying in circles in her excitement. She swears she's making new discoveries by the minute."

"Which you will confirm, I trust?" T'sha's own crest lifted, just a little.

"The review will be rigorous," Br'sei said blandly. "Was there anything else?"

T'sha glanced toward the door. She could hear no one in the corridor, but that could change momentarily.

"Will you come with me, Br'sei?" she asked. "I need your help deciphering a few new sightings."

Br'sei hovered where he was, watching her steadily for a long moment. Then he whistled his assent.

T'sha took her camera eye out of the caretaker. Its tentacles wrapped comfortably around her right posthand. She led Br'sei out of the chamber and into the open air beyond the base's sails. Several of the team saw them, but that didn't matter. They would also see the camera and assume T'sha needed some help for a survey, just as she'd said.

"You know that Ambassador D'seun and I will be leaving soon to address the High Law Meet," remarked T'sha as the winds carried them away from the base. She spoke a little command language to the camera. It focused its eyes to record the passage of the crust under her. Every bit of data helped.

"I know," said Br'sei. "There is a great deal of speculation around the base as to which of you will be coming back."

"Which would you prefer, Engineer Br'sei?" It was an unfair question, but she needed to know which way his priorities flew.

Br'sei inflated himself, rising just a little higher. "Truthfully, Ambassador?"

T'sha dipped her muzzle.

Br'sei did not look at her. He watched the wind in front of them. They were fully on the dayside now. The wind was clear and smelled only faintly of ash and acid. "Truthfully, I wish you both would go back to your cities and leave us alone to do our work. If the New People don't like what we're doing, they can protest, and we can sort it all out with them." Only then did he cock his head toward her. "But I'm not likely to find this wish returning to me, am I?"

"No," said T'sha, deflating. "I'm sorry."

"I believe that you are." An air pocket dropped them both down. Br'sei recovered smoothly and sailed on. "I believe that you would leave this all alone if you could. I believe that you are like me. You want to do your work and go your way knowing your family is safe, now and forever." He wheeled in front of her so that T'sha had to pull herself up short. They faced each other, hovering, eye to eye, wing to wing, exactly matching in size and height. "Am I right, Ambassador?"

T'sha dipped her muzzle.

Br'sei deflated, breath and energy flowing out of him together. T'sha wondered how long it had been since he refreshed, since he had been home, since he had flown with his own family. Who were they? She didn't know, and her ignorance shamed her.

"Tell me what I can do to help you, Ambassador," he said.

So many responses filled T'sha at that moment that she did not know which to choose. She was almost grateful when her camera tapped her postarm, interrupting her. She looked down and she saw only crust, wrinkled, rust red and yellow here for the most part.

But what was that dark spot that crept forward so slowly?

All but forgetting Br'sei, T'sha dropped down for a better look. From the taste of the air, she knew Br'sei followed her flight.

As she descended, the speck resolved into one of the New People's transports crouched on the crust directly below her.

She was about to rise again, automatically, to avoid detection when the transport flashed a bright light.

Startled, T'sha fanned her wings. The transport crawled a little northward, then stopped.

"What are they doing in there?" Without waiting for an answer, T'sha dropped down a little closer, even though the pressure became uncomfortable this near to the crust.

The transport crawled away a little further and stopped.

T'sha stretched her wings and flew until she was almost directly over the transport again.

It crawled out from under her, and T'sha flew after it. It kept going.

"They want us to follow." Br'sei's words startled her with their light touch.

He was right. They were trying to reach out. They wanted her to come with them, somewhere. A thrill of fear and eagerness ran through her. The New People were trying to talk to her. Was her particular person in there? The one who had stood so still, watching her during the rescue? Was this her doing?

"Br'sei." She turned to him, now knowing what he could do to help, although it was a long way from what she'd initially believed she would say. "I need you to go back to base. Don't tell anyone what you've seen here."

"Why not?" he asked mildly.

T'sha looked back over her wing at him. "Because it is possible there will be some objection to what I am going to do next, and I don't want to be stopped."

Br'sei held himself still. "What are you going to do?"

"Find out what the New People want." T'sha did not wait to see if he moved or not. She gave her will up to the wind and let it propel her. The transport saw her movement and began creeping forward again.

T'sha flew directly over the transport, working hard to keep herself from getting ahead of it. They moved so slowly, these New People, creeping across the folds and ripples of the crust. What was that like to feel the crust constantly under your hands? To know its composition and texture as intimately as any of the People knew the winds?

Curiosity spurred her forward, accompanied by a childlike fear that someone would see her and stop her game.

One of the living highlands approached, thickening the air with its scents, making T'sha's skin quiver reflexively with the anticipation of rich life, although there was none to absorb. The transport underneath her skirted the highland carefully as if afraid to get too close. Maybe they were. Frozen as cold as they were, who knew what the heat of a highland meant to them?

Beyond the highland, the crust was a tapestry of trenches and ragged valleys. In a small, irregular cup cut by some ancient lava pool waited another transport. The transport she'd been following pulled up beside its twin and stopped.

T'sha stayed where she was, and so did they. Immobile. Waiting. For what?

"Camera, descend and report," she said in the command language.

The camera extricated itself from her posthand and closed its umbrella. It dropped down until T'sha lost sight of it against the blacks and grays of the old lava flows. She banked in a slow circle, forcing herself to be patient.

At long last, the camera, its umbrella open, began to rise again. Abandoning caution, T'sha dropped to meet it. She grasped it in both forehands, turning it over until its replay eye faced her.

"Show me," she ordered.

In the bowed reflection of the eye, she saw the transports, standing still and patient. She saw a clear box, very like an isolation box, sitting on the crust. It was connected by tubes and wires to one of the transports. A low, perfectly straight, silver tunnel also connected it to a slight rise in the crust.

As she looked closer, she saw that inside the box was a sphere, and inside the sphere . . . was a New Person, rendered in shades of red.

It wasn't the bulky, shelled creature she'd seen walking around, but those had been protective coverings of some kind. No, this was a New Person, stripped to their essence, or nearly so.

It was a biped. Its torso was not so angular as the protective covering made it look. Its skin was soft, and it looked to be wearing some gentle skins or cloths. It had hands, a head, and, unmistakably, eyes. They were small, almost alarmingly so in that flat face, but those were indisputably eyes, looking out at her. It had one forehand raised up. In greeting? Perhaps. Why not?

Underneath the New Person's feet were more images, also all in red. Why red? Could they see no other color? T'sha ordered the camera to concentrate on the lower images. The surroundings vanished as the camera recalled what she needed.

The first image was discreet clusters of shining balls. One, two three, five, seven. Interesting. Communication through numbers? Maybe. A good idea. How could the New People know how much she knew about them? Numbers were concrete, hard to mistake, and easy to understand. She chuckled to herself. Oh, clever, New People!

The second image was another sphere. Inside it glowed a star, with its surrounding planets. Despite the strangeness of it being represented in red and white, she recognized it instantly. Of course. The New People had eyes. They would see as the People did and create images they could recognize. This was the New People's star system, with their world picked out in a red-and-white swirl, orbiting just beyond New Home.

It was as clear as the air around her, as alive as a wind from the highlands. The New People did want to communicate. They really were reaching out. She could not refuse them.

"Mustn't be rude, after all." She told her headset to send her voice on to the base and find Ambassador D'seun.

Silence descended while D'seun was located. T'sha looked at the camera's image again and at the New Person raising their hand. Did they name themselves? What was this one called? Was it male or female? Some other gender T'sha had no name for? Was it the one she had spent so much time staring at? What did it think when it looked at her? She wanted to know everything immediately. The necessity of waiting made her itch.

"Ambassador T'sha, where are you?" came D'seun's voice. If his voice was anything to go by, he was puffed up with anger again.

She gave him her coordinates, and from the resounding silence, she knew he recognized them. She said nothing. She
waited for him to ask.

"What are you doing there?"

"I was led here. The New People are trying to communicate."

Silence again. T'sha chose to interpret it as stunned disbelief.

"This is significant," said D'seun dryly.

"Yes it is. I need you and yours to gather together everything
you've got on how the New People communicate so we can
find a way to answer them."

"What . . . we . . ." he stammered.

T'sha swelled, although there was no one there to see. "We
can delay this no longer, D'seun. I know you have been observing the New People closely for a long time now. I've seen
your specialized constructors." She looked down at the waiting
transports and their viewing station. "The New People have
tried to speak with us and are waiting for us to make some
kind of reply. I will not disappoint them. You can help, or you
can force me to tell the Law Meet about exactly who here has
overstepped their commission."

Stillness and silence. The wind buffeted T'sha, urging her to
motion.

"How did they try to communicate?" he asked, finally. His
voice was small and tight, as his body was right now, T'sha
was sure.

"Visually. They have created a display with images." The detail was very fine for all its lack of color. She could see the New
People had five fingers on each hand, that they had crests of
fine, long tendrils on their heads, that the elbows of their fore-
arms bent in two, maybe three places, depending on how you
counted.

"Effective. We're not certain they hear as we do, but they can
see the same wavelengths we do." She heard the rustle of movement. "They have a written language. We have been working on
deciphering it and have made great progress, we think."

"Good," she said firmly. "Then you can come and interpret."

"T'sha, we must report this to the Law Meet."

"As soon as we have something to report we will. We must address them now. They are waiting for us."

Yet another silence. "You are pleased with this, aren't you?"

T'sha hesitated, clutching the camera a little too tightly. It squeaked, and she eased her grip at once. "It is what I wanted, yes. I am not pleased with how I've gotten it. You must come here now, D'seun."

She heard him whistle, low and disapproving, but in the end he said, "Very well. We will be there soon. Good luck, Ambassador T'sha."

"Good luck, Ambassador D'seun." The connection died, and she was left alone with the New People waiting below her.

Vee sat in the copilot's chair on board Scarab Three, which looked exactly the same as Scarab Five. Helen Failia sat in the pilot's chair as if it were the most natural place in the world for her to be. Adrian Makepeace and a woman named Sheila Whist had brought them down, but they were both in the back now, running diagnostics and suit checks and generally keeping themselves out of the way.

Through the main window, Vee watched the sheltered holotank with its trio of images—her own picture, taken from her image gallery, a set of prime numbers, and a miniature of the solar system with Earth highlighted. She'd been frustrated by the lack of color, but lasers were, by definition, monochromatic, and if they were going to make the one-week deadline, they had to work with what was available.

The tank connection was one of the biggest jury-riggings she'd ever built. The lasers' beams had been directed out of the Discovery through two ceramic-metallic tunnels. One for writing, one for display. The display screen consisted of some of her best films on a refrigerated platform between slabs of doped quartz.

It looked like somebody had set up a view screen in the middle of a desert.

The pressure wasn't the real problem. Years of oceanographic mining had resulted in the creation of pressure-resistant materials and provided collateral research on the effect of pressure on a whole world of substances. The real problem was the heat. The entire communications station had to be constructed so it wouldn't vaporize out there.

"How are we doing?" came Josh's voice through the intercom. He and his assistants, Ray and Heather, were down in the Discovery with the laser, making sure the Cusmanoses' machine worked and stayed working.

"No change." Vee craned her neck so she could see the circling black dot the scarab's cameras showed as a sparkling, golden, winged alien. Vee had wanted to fly the scarab straight to their base and get them to follow along, but Helen had nulled out that idea. She worried the aliens might take it as a threat or a challenge of some kind. So Scarab Ten had gone out on the ground and flashed lights.

It had worked, though. One of the aliens followed Scarab Ten back from wherever they had found it. Then it had dropped a little jellyfish down. The jellyfish had hovered over the holotank and shot back up to its owner. Since then, the alien had stayed where it was, tracing circles in the shifting, leaden sky.

Waiting.

"How are things down there?" Vee asked Josh, to keep the conversation going. Waiting and watching were starting to get to her. She oscillated between wonder and an involuntary fear that she couldn't make go away. *This kind of thing is tough on the sensitive artist's stomach.*

"No change here either," answered Josh. "But I'll tell you what. If we're going to keep this up, we need to terraform this room. I've got sand in my eyes."

"Ouch." Vee grimaced in sympathy. Not being able to touch your own skin was definitely a design limitation in the hard-suits, and when Josh had locked himself into his, there had been bags under his eyes.

Neither one of them had gotten a full night's sleep for a week. They'd spent the entire time in his lab trying to find ways to make this work. They had cannibalized half-a-dozen survey drones and simulated eight different kinds of protective covers and cooling systems before they found one that looked like it would work.

Their setup was that it not only had to function under conditions that were literally hellish, but it also had to be flexible. They had to be able to write and rewrite the images and do it quickly with minimal help from a computer. They had put so much work into the hardware that there had been little left for the controlling software. Vee would be typing in most of the commands by hand and most of those commands were recorded nowhere but in her own head.

There were going to be so many bugs to work out of this system that it wasn't funny. The biggest was that the whole lash-up was computer controlled from inside the scarab. How would the aliens be able to answer?

"Let me know when you're going to start making demands on this thing," said Josh. "I am not happy about some of these connections."

"Will do," Vee told him. Josh had a camera of his own down there. He could see what was going on. He just wanted some contact. Vee couldn't blame him. In fact, she was kind of glad.

"Coffee?" Dr. Failia asked Vee, reaching for the thermos stowed in the holder on the pilot's chair.

"No thanks," said Vee. "I'm wound up so tight right now I think caffeine would tear me in two." *And you didn't think to stock any tea for the trip, did you? Where are your priorities, Vee?*

"Ah, youth." Helen unscrewed the thermos and poured herself a cup. "You need to learn to relax."

Josh chuckled on the other side of the intercom. "Forgive me for saying so, Dr. Failia, but the only reason you're offering around the coffee is because you can't stand to sit in silence anymore."

"Tact," said Helen, sipping a cup of the thick, black liquid, "is another thing that comes with age."

Vee smiled. Josh had a good sense of humor, and he could dish it out and take it with equanimity. She liked that. She liked him. It felt good. He'd gotten out of her way like an old pro when her ideas had run ahead of her explanations and she'd just typed furiously, bringing the simulation up to speed, or had raged, unfairly, she knew, against his lab preparation because they didn't have the specialty parts she needed.

Good guy. Steady. A friend. Just what they'd need when . . .

A dark blur flew over the volcano's rim.

"Heads up." Vee leaned forward, squinting at the sky and ignoring the camera. "They're coming in."

The kite rode ahead of the winds, guided by a competent mind. T'sha resisted the urge to turn loops in the sky to say "Over here, over here." They knew where she was, and they were heading there at full speed.

"We will meet down beside the transports, T'sha," D'seun said through her headset.

T'sha whistled her assent.

The dirigible slowed its forward progress and descended toward the crust. T'sha pulled in her wings and deflated, settling further and further into the thickening air. There was no real wind this far down, just faint strugglings in air that was so solid you could perch on it. It was grossly uncomfortable, but T'sha had done plenty of deep work in her time. She could accommodate herself to it.

The New People's transports still waited side by side. They made an amazing amount of noise, all high squeals and long snores. But if they were speaking to each other, T'sha could make no sense out of it. A piercing metallic smell surrounded them, reminding T'sha sharply of the scents in the World Portal complex.

D'seun launched himself from the dirigible's gondola, leaving Br'sei, D'han, and P'tesk to drop the moorings and wrestle out the toolboxes.

D'seun didn't even acknowledge T'sha. He flew straight to the New People's display. He hovered around it for a long time, looking at the images from every possible angle.

T'sha glanced at the transports. What were they doing in there right now? Were they pleased? Bored? Worried?

"Grow the viewer," said D'seun to the engineers. "Make sure it faces the transports, not this screen. I don't know if this thing can see."

The engineers flew to obey. While Br'sei tore open a dish of growth medium, P'tesk opened the stasis cover on a box of seed crystals. Br'sei laid the seeds into the jellylike medium. The seeds responded instantly, fusing and replicating until the jelly swelled up out of its dish, forming a glistening bubble. The bubble grew until it was nearly the size of the New People's screen. P'tesk poured the neutralizer into the dish. Br'sei rooted a works box onto the side, running through the standard checks. The crystal was good. The medium was adequately conductive. No flaws in structure.

D'seun, meanwhile, pulled two cortex boxes out of the portable caretaker. He weighed them in his forehands and put one back. He laid the one he selected onto the works box, letting its sensors reach into the works and twine around the neural net. D'seun fanned his wings and backed away.

He spoke rapidly in the cortex's command language. T'sha was not surprised to find that she did not understand a word of it. The crystal lit up and a set of symbols printed themselves across its surface. D'seun looked toward the transports and the New People's screen.

"What are you saying?" asked T'sha.

"I am stating our purpose," D'seun said. His voice was slurred, suspicious. "Now we will see what they will do."

Inside the scarab, they watched the aliens arrive, watched their transmitter grow as if by magic, and saw bright-red letters coalesce inside it.

WE SERVE LIFE.

Vee had to swallow before she could force any words out. "It appears," she said slowly, "that they've been watching us a lot longer than we've been watching them."

"So it would seem," agreed Josh. "Now what?"

Vee looked to Dr. Failia. The older woman had set her coffee down. She watched the aliens, her hands on her knees, immobile and yet at the same time incredibly alive. Every line of her body sang with eagerness. She was looking out onto something magnificent.

Vee knew exactly how she felt. She thought of the portrait

file waiting in her briefcase. She'd have to start all over. She didn't do their beauty, their grace, their sheer *otherness* justice, not by light-years.

Dr. Failia cleared her throat, coming back to the everyday acknowledgment of her fellow human beings reluctantly.

"Well, since they're chatty, let's try the basics. Ask who they are."

"Cross your fingers over your connections, Josh." Vee's hands hovered over the keys while she remembered how they had this all coded in. Mentally crossing her own fingers for the solidity of their improvisation, she typed in a set of commands. The introductory images vanished and the holotank showed the words, *Who are you?*

The aliens stayed as they were. Helen reached across the command board and punched up the zoom on the camera. Now they could see the muzzle moving on the smallest of the group.

The words shifted inside the glass bubble to read *The People.*

"Well, that's helpful." Vee almost giggled. She swallowed. Too much wonder obviously had similar effects on the human psyche as too much fear. "First contact. Complicated stuff. How about I try a more detailed question?" Without waiting for an answer, she typed in a new set of commands. Their screen read:

I am Doctor Veronica Hatch. What is your name?

More conferring between the aliens. One of them, whose feathered crest was mottled crimson and ivory, flapped its wings restlessly. The smallest turned toward their screen and spoke again. More new words.

I am Ambassador D'seun Te'eff Kan K'edch D'ai Gathad. With me is Ambassador T'sha So Br'ei Taith Kan Ca'aed. We are ambassadors of the High Law Meet of the People. We have with us our engineers and assistants. Are there others with you? What is your purpose?

"Loaded question," said Josh.

Vee paused with her hands over the keyboard. "Can I ignore it?"

Helen raised her eyebrows. "I don't think so."

Vee nodded, chewed her lip thoughtfully, and typed.

With me are Doctor Helen Failia, Mister Adrian Makepeace, and Miss Sheila Whist. In the underground chamber are Doctor Joshua Kenyon, Mister Ray Sandoval, and Miss Heather Wilde. We are from Venera Base, which is a research colony for the people of Earth. She added a few extra commands. The pictorial diagram of the solar system reappeared with arrows and labels.

"Now may not be the time to get fancy," remarked Helen.

"Now is exactly the time to get fancy," shot back Vee. "One picture, one thousand words, you know? How are we doing down there, Josh?"

"It's green and go in here." His voice was both hushed and strained. Vee could practically feel his excitement vibrating through the connection.

The aliens flapped and hovered around the new scene shining in the holotank. They came within centimeters of its quartz surface but never actually touched it. Their control was incredible. Part of Vee's mind was already designing the movement codes, trying to work out how to show them to the rest of humanity.

The words in the alien's bubble changed.

Are you ambassadors? Do you speak for the New People?

Vee looked quizzically at Helen.

She puffed out her cheeks. Vee could almost hear her rehearsing different answers. "I don't think we do." She sounded slightly disappointed. "But we know who does."

We call ourselves human beings. No, we ourselves do not lead, but we would like a message to take to our leaders. "Since I don't think we can take them—" added Vee.

"You can be tactful after all," murmured Helen. "I'm impressed, Vee. Would you do me a favor, please, and get the big question out of the way?"

"Right." Vee knew exactly what she was talking about. She typed and the screen responded.

What are you doing here?

We serve life, answered the aliens, no, the People. *Life helps life.*

This time Vee didn't bother to check with Helen. She just typed.

We don't understand.

Three of the People had retreated from the screen. They perched in the contraption of sails, struts, and cables that had brought them here. It looked like a cross between a box kite and the old Wright brothers' airplane. Smallest, Ambassador D'seun, etc., and Crimson-and-Ivory remained by the bubble, which probably meant Crimson-and-Ivory was Ambassador T'sha, etc.

The ambassadors seemed to be having a discussion. They leaned close together, muzzles almost brushing each other. As they spoke, their bodies swelled and shrank. Was that their breathing? Or a way of showing emotion? Dominance maybe? Even this far down, where the light was gray instead of clear, they sparkled. The black lines on their bodies and muzzles stood out sharply. Maybe they were tattoos. Wouldn't that be a good one? If what humans had in common with aliens was body art?

A decision seemed to have been reached. D'seun spoke to T'sha and then the screen. Their spherical screen relayed the words.

We wish only community and cohabitation with the life of this world.

"Oh, my," murmured Vee. She typed.

You are colonizing?

D'seun pulled his muzzle back momentarily before he spoke again.

We do not know that word.

Vee considered a moment. Definitions had never been her strong suit. She was aware of someone standing close behind her, of warm breath on her ear. She typed.

You are moving People here? You are going to live here?

Yes.

"Oh, my." Vee's hands went suddenly cold.

Helen touched her shoulder. "I think it's time to bring in the U.N."

"Yeah," said Vee slowly. "I think you might be right."

"I'll go back up with Scarab Ten." Dr. Failia straightened up.

"I'll contact Mother Earth myself. Ms. Yan should be able to call together an emergency meeting with the C.A.C."

Vee turned to look at her. "Shouldn't this go straight to the Secretaries-General?"

"Bureaucracy will have its way." Helen's smile was humorless. Vee watched her eyes. She was calculating something, planning, working the variables. "It will get to them soon enough."

"Whatever you say," Vee said with a shrug. That was not her field, and she didn't particularly want it to be. "What should we do here?"

Helen was silent for a moment. She watched the People, hovering like living kites out in what Vee knew Helen thought of as her world. "Keep them talking."

"Dr. Lum gave me permission to visit the Cusmanoses," said Grace to the security guard outside Kevin Cusmanos's door. She held out the screen slip with Michael's authorization and seal on it.

"Right, Dr. Meyer," said the very thin, very brown man. "You can head on in." He touched the override pad.

The suite door swished open. Kevin looked up, startled, from his seat at the dining table. Derek was sitting in a strangely forlorn-looking chair in front of where the desk used to be. They'd hauled all the communications equipment out in preparation to turn Kevin's home into a cell. It had been Ben, of all people, who had talked Michael out of keeping them locked in Venera's minuscule brig.

"They're going to be manhandled by the yewners soon enough," he'd argued. "Let's at least let them wait for it in comfort."

"Hello, Kevin. Hello, Derek." Grace held up the pair of brown bottles she carried. "Brought you some beer."

"Thanks." Kevin got up to the take the bottles from her. He'd changed over the past week. It was as if the fire had gone out inside him, leaving behind nothing but cold resignation. Grace thought she knew the cause. Whatever he thought about the Discovery and how it came to be, Kevin believed heart and soul that he deserved to be punished for what had happened to Scarab Fourteen.

Grace turned her attention to Derek, who hadn't moved since she came in.

"Hello, Derek," said Grace again, gently.

Derek did not respond.

Kevin eyed her uneasily, but she waved him away. "It's all right, Kevin. I don't blame him. He's angry." Grace sighed. "I'm sorry you got caught up in this, Kevin."

Kevin's just slumped into his chair at the dining table. "It was my fault."

She nodded. "Among others. We were all in danger. There was so much to lose . . . at the time it seemed like a good idea." *If either of you knew how long, how hard I tried to find another way, you'd understand how desperate the situation really was. I tried everything else first. It was the only way.* "I got so damn tired of being ignored."

"Ignored?" Derek looked up. Sudden, raw hatred filled his eyes. "That's why you talked me into this? Because you didn't want to be ignored?"

And you just didn't want to lose your job, you spoiled child. She didn't say it. "Seems pretty stupid now that we've got real live aliens to talk to. No one's going to give a damn that I spotted their traces first."

"Well that's just too bad," growled Derek.

"Okay, Derek," said Kevin wearily. "You can't blame her for what you did."

"The hell I can't!" Derek snapped. He stabbed a finger at Grace. "It was her idea! If she hadn't—"

Kevin stood up slowly. His brother matched him for height, but Kevin's shoulders were far broader. He loomed over the smaller man. "You didn't have to do one damn thing," Kevin told him slowly. "She didn't have a gun to your head. You did this, and I did this. We got caught, and Bailey Heathe got killed because of us!"

"Because of you," grated Derek. "Don't try to bring that one down on me!"

Grace stepped between them, putting her back to Kevin before he could react. "My lawyers will get you out of this," she told Derek firmly. "You and your brother."

"They'd better." Derek didn't take his gaze off his brother, but he backed up a few paces. "Because we are not going to rot in a jail on Mother Earth alone, understand me?"

"You will not go to jail." Grace turned a little so she could see them both. "I'd better go. Kevin, try not to worry. It'll all be okay."

Kevin looked from Derek to her. "I hope you're right, Dr. Meyer."

Neither of them said good-bye. Grace walked out. Her stomach knotted up on her as she passed the guard stationed on the door and started down the busy residential corridor.

They would not go to prison. Grace watched her own feet as she headed for the stairs. They would drink the beer she'd brought, tonight, or perhaps tomorrow. They'd drain all the bottles contained.

Then, sometime within the next week, they'd die. By then they'd have eaten over a dozen meals and their buddies from the scarab crews would have brought them at least as many beers. The traces in their guts would make it appear that they had died of severe food poisoning. Her bottles would have long since been recycled and it would be next to impossible to say where the contagion had come from. The kitchens and food processors would have a bad week while they were turned upside down, but that couldn't be helped.

Organic chemistry was useful for so many things.

No, Derek and Kevin would not go to jail. There was so much work to be done. No one would ignore her anymore; no one would tell her that her work might reflect badly on Venera as a whole. There was one person left who might connect Grace's name to the fraud, but that one had so much to lose that she would not risk it. Grace was certain of that.

Grace lifted her head as she started up the stairs and found she could meet the gazes of the people she passed quite easily.

There was important work to do. She had to be free to do it.

Chapter Thirteen

Ben paced his office, trying to be patient. He had one of the few private spaces on the administrative level. The dampeners in the walls meant he couldn't hear the continual buzz and bustle going on outside. Sometimes he dropped them. He liked being around people. He did not like being shut up and alone, but there were things for which he needed privacy.

Like the transmission he was waiting for.

The office did have a real window, allowing him to see the cloudscape with its continual whorls and ripples and flashes of lightning. So different from Mars or the Moon. Those were static worlds. What motion there was, humans brought. Venus though . . . Venus was alive in its own right. It still had a beating heart under its volcanoes, and it still shifted and shrugged its crust, even without plate tectonics.

He could have spent his life studying this place. He could have given himself up to the world the way Helen had if there hadn't been other considerations.

He glanced back at his gently humming desk. Anyone running a systems sweep would think he was busy processing satellite data with the new criteria of observing the aliens (Holy God, those aliens!) and their artifacts. What he was actually doing was looking for a transmission signature. When his scanner found it, the transmission would be routed straight to the desk without having to go through Venera's usual exchanges and checks.

It wasn't something he liked to do very often. Michael and Michael's people were very good at what they did. Trying to get around their security measures was a chancy business at best.

Venera was alive with activity, speculation, and wonder. Everybody wanted their chance to go meet the neighbors. Michael was going to have to forcibly restrain Grace before long. They tried to tell her the board's consensus was that there should be only a limited contact team. Just for now, of course, until a good understanding had been established with the People.

Ben shook his head. They couldn't tell her the real reason only one scarab was being kept down there. He'd guessed at that reason and had told Helen his guess in private. Her silence had been enough to tell him he'd guessed correctly.

The Venerans needed to talk to the aliens. They needed as much information as they could get. Every bit of information they controlled was an edge on the C.A.C. But if anybody made a damning mistake, they needed to be able to say to the U.N., "It was your people who did that, not ours."

For the first time in a long time, he'd agreed absolutely with Helen's strategy.

His desk chimed. Ben was beside it in two long strides. The screen cleared and Frezia Cheney looked out at him.

"Paul." It had been so long since he'd used that name on a regular basis that it felt as if she were talking to some stranger. "Your word's been spread. Much to the chagrin of the yewners, may I add." Mischief sparkled in her eyes for a moment and then faded away.

"I hate to have to say this, but no one else is even close to ready for a succession attempt, distractions or paradigm shifts notwithstanding. They're going to have to let the chance pass. We're feeling the loss of Fuller here. There's no unifying voice anymore. There's no one person to talk to." She paused and shook her head. "The demo at the shipyard hasn't even managed to unite the Lunars."

Ben grimaced. That "demo" had been a stupid idea. When he'd caught a whiff of what was being planned, he—or Paul, rather—had protested to everyone he could and had been ignored.

But apparently he was not being ignored anymore. "I think

uniting us is up to you, Paul. The only way the wave is going to rise is if Venera takes the place of Bradbury and makes the break. With an example to follow, the squabblers will be able to shut up and drive, if you see what I mean." Her mouth twisted into an ironic smile, but her eyes still gleamed. "It's not that men make history; history makes men. If you can show us the way, we can still free the worlds."

The message faded out. Ben, moving more on reflex than any conscious thought, wiped the file and the record of receipt. Then he released a search agent into the system to see if there were any ghosts or records he'd forgotten and wipe them too.

The only way this is going to work is if Venera takes the place of Bradbury and makes the break. Ben sat back and ran one hand across his scalp. *If you can show us the way it can still happen.*

If you can show us the way.

Alone? Venera alone? Without help, without friends; at least, without friends who had declared themselves. Once they broke, they could maybe count on Bradbury and probably Giant Leap.

But then came the problem, the old, old problem. Mother Earth still controlled the shipping between planets. The tacit threat had always been that if any colony tried to become self-governing, Earth would simply stop transports to and from the colony, isolating the world. No food, no spare parts, no replacement personnel, nothing. Even Bradbury with its mixed industry had felt the pinch after a while. How much worse would it be for Venera? Venera manufactured nothing but research reports. They could not survive alone.

But Venera wouldn't be alone. Ben straightened up, one muscle at a time. Venera had neighbors. Neighbors who could fly from world to world as easily as a yewner bureaucrat could fly from republic to republic. More easily.

What if the Venerans set up one of their portals between Venus and Mars? Between Luna and Venus? The colonists could move between the worlds without any interference from Mother Earth. Earth's transport and communications monopolies would be shattered. The one sure control they held over the colonies would be gone.

If Venera could make a deal with the aliens. If it were Venera that spoke, not the U.N.

If it were Venera that spoke.

Venera, meaning Helen. Ben stared out at the clouds. Helen would never abandon the U.N. To do so would mean abandoning Yan Su, who had stood by her for so long.

No. He corrected his thoughts. *Helen would never betray the U.N. unless the U.N. betrayed her, betrayed Venera, first.*

If that happened, all bets were off. Helen would do anything she had to so that Venera would survive and be free to do its work with its people free to live their lives. She'd even make a deal with aliens.

An idea formed in his mind, one slow thought trickling into his consciousness at a time.

There was a way. He held it in his hands. He stood a very good chance of pushing Helen over the edge. All he had to do was lie to the U.N. about what she knew and when she knew it.

Ben leaned back in the chair as far as it would let him and scrubbed his face with both hands.

All he had to do was be the one who really betrayed Helen.

He'd been on Luna when he met Helen. He'd successfully left the name Paul Mabrey behind and found work as a geologist for Dorson Mines, Inc. As such, he supervised more databases than humans, analyzing rock and soil samples and looking for useful deposits. It was a job. It bought food and shelter and paid the taxes so he could breathe and drink, but it meant nothing.

He'd been in one of the public caverns. He'd just bought coffee and fry cakes for breakfast. He'd been sitting on a hard little chair, staring at the walls and thinking how much he missed the Bradbury gardens. The Lunars had covered their gray rock with vines. Morning glories and wild grapes made a living wallpaper and warred with the rambler roses and raspberries in providing color and scent. Pretty, but not the gardens. Empty, second-rate. Cheap. Like his job. Like him.

"Dr. Godwin?"

He looked up. A woman stood by his table, plainly dressed in a blue blouse and matching trousers. Her graying hair was bundled into a knot and pinned in place with wooden pins. Her eyes sparkled and her entire attitude said she knew why she was alive.

"Yes?" said Ben, wracking his brain to see if he should know her.

"I'm Helen Failia. I've been looking for you. I need a geologist who knows comparative planetology and volcanology." She dropped into a spare chair without asking. "For Venera Base on Venus."

"Oh?" was all Ben could think to say. Venera was half-built, half-occupied, and some said half-baked. It was a pure-research colony, the first in decades. No one believed it could last. The science currents predicted its death year after year. But somehow, Venera never quite laid down.

"Our staff is thinning out. We need to get some fresh blood in. Someone who can dig hard into the work." Which told him why her staff was thinning out. She didn't have the money to pay them what the mining companies could. Which also explained why she was willing to recruit someone who only had a few, very obscure papers to his credit. Papers he'd spent the past three or so Terran years carefully salting through the stream. Helen, he would learn, always had an eye open for a good bargain. "I've read your credentials. Your postdoctoral work is brilliant. You've got an eye for the unusual, and you don't mind hard work. Which is perfect for Venus." She didn't just smile; she beamed. Ben couldn't help thinking of Ted Fuller. On a good day, when things were going well, Ted radiated the same light.

Ben drank his bitter, cooling coffee, trying to sort out his thoughts. This was definitely not what he'd been expecting to hear this morning. He'd been expecting another day of trying to convince himself he'd made the right decision, that this life really was better than the one he'd abandoned, or would be very soon.

"Venus is open territory," said Helen, leaning on her elbows. "You can't throw a stone without hitting something new. You'll have complete freedom to direct the research. Anything you want to look at, it's yours."

Risky. It had the chance to bring him to public attention, and public attention could be the end of the line for someone hiding behind an alias.

He looked at the coffee in his cup. He looked at the vines covering the gray walls. He looked at the people around the table—miners, students, engineers, all buzzing about in their separate lives like bees and meaning about as much to him. He looked back at Helen, and in her dark eyes, he suddenly saw some hope. Hope of a real life, a better life, one with meaning and purpose to replace the purpose that had been ripped from him by the yewners and their troops.

"I'd have to hear about the base," he said slowly. "The facilities, the package you're offering, and so on."

"Of course." Helen picked up his coffee cup, sniffed its contents, and made a face. "But first you have to get some real coffee. On me. Come on."

He'd followed her without question. Into the Lunar coffee bar, down to Earth, out to Venus. He'd followed her for twenty years through funding fights, mission fights, personnel fights, and charter fights.

Ben swiveled his chair and watched the clouds outside the window. They swirled and flowed together like his thoughts. They had predictable currents, he knew, and if you worked long enough, you could map their movements and understand how each little particle fit into the greater flow.

He'd never even tried to tell Helen about what had really happened to him all those years ago. Helen would not have understood that what they were doing on Mars was real, even more real than the research, or building Venera into a sustainable colony that would outlive both of them. What really mattered was shaking off Earth's grip. What mattered was freedom. Right now, Mother Earth could tell them to do anything, anything, and they'd have to do it. They had no choice. Mother Earth owned them, their lives, and their homes. Helen never saw it that way. Helen thought she called the shots. Helen thought she was in control.

She wasn't. Mother Earth was bigger, more forceful, and more determined than even Helen Failia.

Ben turned back around to face his desk again and started typing.

Helen had to be shown the truth.

"Good luck, Ambassador D'seun," said K'est as D'seun glided through its windward gate. "Ambassador Z'eth is in the public park. She asks that you meet her there."

"Thank you, K'est." D'seun flew swiftly toward the park. He struggled to keep his senses open to the dying city—the bare bones, the air rich with forced nutrients, yes, but also filled with desperation. A thin veneer of life that was all that lay between K'est and true death, and all the citizens knew it.

This is what I fight for, he told himself. *We must prevent any more living deaths like these.*

D'seun's first impression of the public park was that it was bigger than his whole birth village had ever been. Bone, shell, ligament, vine, and tapestry outlined a roughly spherical labyrinth of arches, corridors, and pass-throughs. Flight became a dance, here. Wind became song, and the voice of the city guided him through it all.

"What am I interrupting here?" asked D'seun as he gave himself up to the drafts of the wind-guides and let them carry him through a corridor of story tapestries.

"Ambassador Z'eth has called a hiring fair," replied K'est.

D'seun dipped his muzzle. Such things had been rare once, but with the massive numbers of refugees and indentures that circled the world, the ones who held the promises were gathering more and more frequently to review the skills they held promise to, and to exchange those skills and the persons to better serve the cities and the free citizens.

Conversations touched D'seun at every turn, about medicines, about refugee projections, and the health of the canopy. Adults and children, both free and with the hatchmark of indenture between their eyes, passed him on every side. Tentacled constructors and spindly, broad-eyed clerkers trailed in their wakes.

Finally, the wind-guides opened out into a pearlescent chamber that could have easily held two or three hundred adult females. The voices of a quartet rang pleasantly off its walls. Here and there, clusters of ambassadors and speakers hovered, deep in conversation with each other. The archivers hovered in their own clusters, off to the side, waiting until they were needed.

Z'eth herself was easy to spot. She drifted from cluster to cluster. She'd listen to a conversation for a moment and then move on to the next. D'seun could not feel any words from her. She just listened.

Good. Perhaps she'll just listen to me.

Perhaps the city spoke to Z'eth, or perhaps she was just waiting for him, because as he flew through the portal, Z'eth lifted her muzzle and rose above the conversation where she hovered. D'seun flew quickly to her, deflating just enough to make sure his eyes were below hers.

"Good luck, Ambassador Z'eth," he said as they touched hands. "Thank you for agreeing to see me. Please accept a guesting gift, which I found on my journeys." As he spoke the formal words, he held out a palm-sized eyepiece. It lifted from his palm and hovered between himself and Z'eth. Inside, a delicate, biped drawn in shades of red raised her hand in greeting.

"Lovely!" exclaimed Z'eth. "One of your New People, is it not?"

"It is, Ambassador." He did not even attempt to pronounce the name they called themselves by. "They are what I have come to speak with you about."

Z'eth lifted herself and closed her right forehand around the eyepiece. "The members of the High Law Meet speak of nothing else. Their cogent method of contact with Ambassador T'sha has convinced many that they are a whole, sane people and should be treated as such."

"I wish to urge you, Ambassador Z'eth, to believe no reports from Ambassador T'sha and her followers." D'seun spoke earnestly, but softly. The touch of his words was for Z'eth only. "I see the tapestries they weave to show the New People as whole beings, complete in intellect and soul who live intricate lives and wish to exist with us in community." He swelled as far as he dared. "This is not true. They do not know even the first principles of life. Community with them is impossible."

Z'eth's crest ruffled and spread. She touched her muzzle to his, and D'seun felt all her gentle mockery. "You are so certain, Ambassador, you must have been paying close attention to them."

"Very close, Ambassador." What did it matter what she knew? Either he would succeed, in which case she would be with him, or he would fail. If he failed, nothing else mattered. New Home and Home would both be lost.

"Your attention has been closer, I think, than your commission allowed, and for much longer," Z'eth went on.

"Yes," agreed D'seun. He had been supposed to supervise the seeding of the world and leave. He had left, but when he had returned for a monitoring stint, he had left behind some special tools. Each monitoring stint after that had brought him new data. He had all but mortgaged his future for the analysis of it.

"And you have shared none of this illicit information with the Law Meet?" Z'eth inquired. "How discreet of you. Why have you kept this to yourself?"

"At first, I feared T'sha and those like her would fear the New People." He aimed his words right at Z'eth, not wanting her to miss a single one. "So I kept what I knew a secret until I knew how the New People could be controlled or eliminated." Preferably eliminated. New Home had to be kept pure for life the People created and understood. "But, instead, she has fallen in love with them and their dead things."

"Are you so sure they need to be controlled?" For the first time, the mockery left Z'eth's voice. "Why not let them flourish beside us?"

Revulsion crawled across D'seun's skin. "You do not know, Ambassador. They surround themselves with death. They bring nothing living with them. Their homes are dead, their shells are dead, even their tools are dead. They are ghouls, Ambassador, billions of ghouls who live in ignorance of even the basic ideas of spreading life. Can we permit ghouls to wander the winds of New Home with our children?"

Z'eth pulled her muzzle back in thoughtful silence. D'seun held himself still, trying to muster the patience to wait out her thoughts. He could not rush her. She had influence that went beyond wealth. If he could turn her from her patronage of T'sha, T'sha would be toppled. Everything depended on this.

"Ambassador, I seek a promise from you."

"I assumed." Her crest spread out even further, as if it reached toward every conversation and promise being ex-changed in her dying city. "And what would you pay for this promise?"

"My children, when they are born, will belong to your city on New Home," said D'seun. "They will serve your city until they are adults."

It hurt to say it. It hurt to know that it had to be this way. He had been indentured in his tenth year of life, when K'taith suc-cumbed to one of the first of the new rots. He had always sworn to the souls of his unborn children that they would grow to adulthood free.

But he had to break that oath. He had nothing left to promise but those children, whoever they were and whenever they would come to be. He could not permit the New People to spread their death further across New Home.

"A rich promise, and a risky one," Z'eth mused. "You may not find a wife willing to go along with it."

"I will find a wife who will," said D'seun, firmly. He had to.

"You sound most determined." Z'eth dipped her muzzle. "What promise do you want?"

"You will be elected to the Law Meet of New Home." D'seun drifted as close to her as he could without touching her. "There is no question of this. I have heard the proposed rosters in the Meet. Your name is on every one. You will be the most senior of the ambassadors, the leader there as you are the leader here. I ask that you promise to follow my lead when we must deter-mine the final disposition of the New People."

Z'eth swelled, just a little. *What are you thinking, Ambas-sador? What future do you taste?*

Her gaze drifted from him and passed over the shifting crowds that filled this beautiful chamber in the center of her slowly dying city.

"Thank you for your promise, Ambassador," she said. "It is rich and would bring my city benefit."

Hope swelled D'seun's skin; then he read the tilt of her head and the spread of her wings and knew what was coming next.

"But even if I accepted," she pushed herself closer to him, "I could make no guarantees of your success. T'sha is not the only one in love with the New People. There are many in the High Law Meet who are enchanted by their words. My influence is great, but I am not certain it is that great."

"But, Ambassador." He thrust his muzzle forward, touching her skin, breathing out his urgency with his words. She must understand, she must. "We cannot predict them; we cannot understand or control them. There must be nothing on New Home that we cannot control; otherwise life will rebel against us and bring death and imbalance, as it has to Home."

Z'eth backwinged sharply. "Ambassador, I think you have been too long away from the temples to speak so. We serve life, and in return life serves us. That is the way of it. Life does not attack us, nor do we attack it."

Abandoning all caution, D'seun swelled to his fullest extent. "We serve the life we know. We do not know the New People, or their life."

"You will calm yourself, Ambassador," murmured Z'eth. D'seun shrank down instantly. Z'eth remained silent for awhile, and D'seun had to concentrate on each small motion of his wings to keep himself in place.

"If I took your offer," she said softly, her words brushing so lightly against his skin he had to strain every pore to feel them, "I could promise only that I will vote with you regarding the disposal of the New People on New Home. It could be no more than that."

Cautious, controlled, very Z'eth. It would be an expensive promise. But Z'eth would not go into any such vote alone. Even if she exacted no promises from the other members of the New Home Law Meet, her vote would sway others yet unpromised.

And he might be able to swing a few votes himself, especially if he could find a way to silence T'sha.

Was it enough to break his vow to his unborn children?

The New People will corrupt us. They will take our world from us, as the rots have taken this world from us.

New Home must be for the People alone, or they would all die. He hovered alone, surrounded by death and life, and he was the only one who understood what it really meant.

His understanding had come to him the day his village, K'taith, had died. He'd huddled under his mother's belly up-wind of the village and listened to the speaker and the ambassador telling them that the village could no longer care for them. Its bones were too brittle; its skin and ligaments could no longer heal themselves. Their presence was hurting the village. It had asked for death, to be disassembled and its few healthy parts put to use elsewhere. The vote would be taken to see if the citizens would honor that wish, of course, but, said the speaker and the ambassador, they could not believe that anyone who loved the village would insist it continue in pain and helplessness it could not bear.

The vote was taken, and all free adults voted to let their village's suffering end. D'seun had just watched the discolored walls and the limp, tattered sails. He felt the wind against his own skin.

The wind that fed him had killed the city and taken his freedom. He knew that instinctively. Everyone knew what happened when their village died.

He had seen it then. There was no balance. The life that killed his home, his future, did not in any way serve him. The People were not strong, they were weak. Life did not serve them; it hated them. It planned against them in its wildness. It left no niche for the People to fill. Life on Home was closed utterly to them.

Oh, he'd mimicked the proper words and ways of thought. He had no wish to be declared insane, but he had known it all to be a lie.

Then he had spread his wings in the pristine winds of New Home and he saw how it could be. Life built by the People, life that truly did serve them because they laid down every cell and commanded how it should be.

If they permitted death to flourish there, they would never create this new balance. Life would once again cease to obey them and the death the New People lived in would take them all.

He saw the truth. He tasted it. He touched it every day, but T'sha remained numb and had convinced the others, even his hand-picked team who had promised to him so freely.

And there was nothing he could do.

Was there?

If Ca'aed were ill, if a quick rot took hold there, T'sha would have to see the truth. T'sha was not so far gone that she did not love her city. She spoke of it with fondness and concern, despite her tricks with Village Gaith.

Or if she would not see, at least she would no longer be able to interfere. She was not Z'eth. Without the wealth of her city, her ability to make promises would be gone, and with it her influence in the High Law Meet.

No. D'seun huddled in on himself, glancing furtively around the hiring fair as if his very thoughts could have touched those flying past him. *This is insane. To take life, to give nothing back, to treat life as raw materials (that did not happen, it did not. The New Person was dead. Dead).*

But if what I do ultimately serves life, our life? If T'sha's resistance and lies are broken, the truth can be heard. The danger the New People represent can be fully understood then. Yes. Yes. That is the way it is, the way it will be.

There were so many ways a city might sicken, even a wise and ancient city like Ca'aed. Especially when passing by a living highland when the winds were so thick with life. Even the most careful of welcomers and sail skins could miss something, say a few spores transferred from a quarantine that was no longer life-tight? Such things happened every day and could be made to happen again.

It serves life, for it allows the People themselves to live. Yes. Yes.

Z'eth was waiting for his answer. Waiting for him to decide whether her promise was worth the expense. It was. Oh, yes, it was. Life would grow from death, and in that way life would serve life.

"Call us an archiver," he said to Z'eth, his words steady and weighty. "I will accept this promise. My children will serve your city if you follow my vote on the disposition of the New People on New Home."

The smell hit Michael first—the sour acidic reek that he could taste in the back of his mouth. Then came the sight of Kevin and Derek, side by side on the white beds with soiled sheets, surrounded by a battery of monitors and tubes trailing limply into various injectors and samplers, all of which sat in an eerie silence.

"Sorry to haul you out tonight, Michael." Antonio Dedues, Venera's chief physician, stuffed his hands into the pockets of his traditional white coat and didn't look at Michael. Antonio's gaze was on the corpses in their beds with the useless, attendant machinery. "But you've got to witness the death certificates."

Michael swallowed hard against the smell and found his voice. "What happened?"

"It looks like food poisoning." Antonio came back to the present, jerked his chin toward the doctor's station, and walked Michael away from the sight. "Hey, can we get those two taken care of please?" he called to Jimmy Coombs, one of the nurse practitioners, who was passing by with a pile of screen rolls in his hands. Jimmy nodded and Antonio continued gently herding Michael away from the unpleasantness, something doctors got a lot of practice at, Michael was sure.

"Looks like?" said Michael, keeping his voice pitched low. He had no idea who was in the infirmary right now.

"They both came in about three o'clock complaining of fever and stomach cramps."

"I was notified."

Antonio nodded. "Symptoms got treated, and they got worse. Workup got done and by then we had a massive systemic infection." Antonio motioned him into the monitoring station. The place had so many different monitors and command boards, it looked like mission control for a major spaceport, and all the numbers and plots made about as much sense to Michael.

"The infection all but ate the broad-spectrum stabilizer we gave them while we were trying to isolate the bacteria and tailor an antibiotic to hit it," said Antonio. "There's only so much we can keep on ice around here." He frowned at the cabinets across the hall as if he wanted to blame them for what happened. "We did find the bug and get the antibiotics into them, but it was too late."

"But it wasn't food poisoning?" pressed Michael. He was still reeling. They were dead. Dead of a simple bug, something that should have been treatable in five minutes but wasn't. They had been good men, they had been idiots, they had been friends, they had been criminals.

They were dead.

"If it was food poisoning, where are the other patients?" Antonio swept his hand out. "We've shut down the galley level, of course, and we're going through and doing a sanitary inspection. You got the call on that too?"

Michael nodded.

"But nothing's turning up. We haven't got the autopsy yet, so I can't say for sure what they've been eating, but from what your people say, it wouldn't be anything that another couple hundred people hadn't swallowed." Antonio looked up at him. "Do you want me to say it?"

No, and I don't want to say it either. "You think they were poisoned."

Now Antonio nodded. His pockets bunched and wrinkled as he clenched his fists. "By someone who was very smart and very stupid."

Michael waited. Poisoned? Murdered? Who . . . but he knew who. It was the other person who had helped create the Discovery. They didn't want to be implicated, so they'd killed the men. God! This was not something that could happen. Not on Venera, not now. This was something out of the twentieth century.

"Smart because they were able to successfully cultivate a strain of bacteria we couldn't neutralize immediately. Stupid because in conditions like Venera's, where the food comes from limited production sources, there's never just two victims of a poisoning outbreak."

"How hard would it be to cook up this . . . bug?"

Antonio shrugged. "With access to a lab and a decent chemistry and medical database and a strong stomach, not very."

"Strong stomach?"

Antonio's smile was watery. "Even the unprepared food the galley sells has been sterilized eight ways to Sunday. The easiest place to get bacteria from around here would be your own waste products."

Michael hung his head, torn between disgust and black humor. "I should have thought."

"No you shouldn't," Antonio assured him. "Holy God knows I didn't want to."

"Yeah." Michael lifted his gaze again. "Look, I'll need the autopsy as soon as you can get it to me, okay?"

"Okay." Antonio glanced around at his monitors. "All this and we still haven't got the immortality programs up and running. Grandma Helen know yet?"

"Not yet." She knew about the galley quarantine, of course, but not about the deaths. Mother Creation, she was already walking on the edge with the C.A.C. meeting coming up. What was this going to do to her? "I'll tell her." *I don't want to, but I will.*

"Okay," said Antonio gratefully. "Thanks."

Michael left to the soft sound of Antonio's voice readying his autopsy team to find out what exactly killed Derek and Kevin. He walked down the corridors without really seeing them. The main lights were dimming toward twilight. The base was on a twenty-four-hour Greenwich time cycle, and now it was late in the summer evening.

Someone had deliberately committed a murder. This was not a fight, not a horrified and angry somebody who didn't mean to do it, "I swear I didn't. . . ." No. This somebody meant to do it. They had decided and planned and executed.

Now he had to tell Philip and Angela, and he had to tell Helen. He had to tell the whole world, all the worlds, that Venera was spinning out of control, that the arrival of aliens had made the place crazy, but not in any of the ways people had feared since the possibility had been raised all those hundreds of years ago. There were no riots, no religious revivals, no barbaric, tribal displays of aggression.

No. Just murder. This really had nothing to do with the aliens themselves. This had to do with petty, frightened humanity.

Michael stopped and rubbed his eyes. This was also nuts. Nuts. He had his work to do. He looked up, got his bearings, and headed for the staircase, the administrative level, and his desk.

It was midnight before he walked back through his own door. The light was still on. Jolynn sat on the sofa in front of the living room view screen, going over her endless series of teacher reports.

When she heard the door, she looked up and smiled, tired but beautiful.

"How twentieth is this?" she said as she swung her legs down so he could sit beside her. "The dutiful wife waiting for her husband to come home?"

Michael didn't answer. He took her in his arms and held her close. She returned the embrace, not speaking, just enveloping him with her warmth, her fragrance of soap and lilacs, and the strength of her presence.

"How bad is it?" she asked when he finally released her.

"Beyond bad." He pulled his cap off and tossed it on the end table. He told her about Derek and Kevin, dead in the infirmary, how the sanitary checks in the galley had turned up nothing, how he'd had to seal their room, quiz the people on guard, write it all up, decide whom to assign to the investigation, work out the announcement for general release into the base stream, and then go tell Helen.

"What did she say?" Jolynn asked.

Michael felt his jaw begin to shake. "That's the worst part. I'm not sure she heard me all that well. She was so . . . preoccupied with the C.A.C. report." He ran both hands through his hair, pulling strands of it free from the ponytail and not caring. "She basically told me to handle it, and I'm not sure I can."

Jolynn said nothing.

"It's not that they're dead," he told her. "It's that they were murdered by one of us. A Veneran, maybe even a v-baby. We've never had anything worse than a bad bar fight, and that was ten years ago. People come here to be safe. People come *back* here to be safe, and now . . ." His throat closed around the sentence. "Now, when the greatest thing that has ever happened to humanity is happening to *us*, we're killing each other. How the hell did that happen, Jolynn?"

She took his hand in hers. "Because we're being human, and some of us aren't very good at that." She stroked the back of his hand with her palm, a gentle rhythm, distracting him from the swirl of his own thoughts with the touch of her warm skin. "If we give into the belief that we are somehow better than the general run of people, it's going to chew us up and spit us out. That belief kills something vital, because as soon as you start believing you're better, you have to start proving everybody else is inferior. It makes you crazy."

"How would you know?" he joked tiredly.

"When I was on Earth, I went to the Baghdad ruins. Did you?"

Michael shook his head. "But you told me about them." Through her memories he saw the rubble, the dust, the rats, and the starving dogs nosing around the dust-gray skulls. He smelled the empty smell of desert encroachment and heard her whisper, "Look on my works, ye mighty, and despair."

"So I came back, to the world with the edges and the boundaries and its own history and Grandma Helen to make sure we never went crazy like human beings are wont to do from time to time." She shook her head. "Wrong again."

Michael let his head fall back until he was staring at the ceiling. "What do I do, Jolynn?"

"Your very best, my love," she said, enfolding him again in her arms. "Your very best."

Chapter Fourteen

Ca'aed first became aware of the wrongness as an itch. A small nerve bundle at the base of one of its lower northwest sails (half-furled now to keep the course smooth and steady) itched, not painfully but persistently. Ca'aed concentrated on the patch. The air around it tasted fine. A silent command sent a runner to the spot to ingest a few cells and compare them with the healthy patterns it held inside. Normally, Ca'aed would have just had the itch soothed by a caretaker, but times were dangerous now and caution was indicated.

Another itch, this one deep and nagging in Ca'aed's digestive veins. A small cramp formed around the itch.

Worry stroked Ca'aed's mind. What caretakers were in that area? Ca'aed felt and Ca'aed looked.

"Indenture T'elen," said Ca'aed. "A review of the digestive veins near you. There is a break in flow."

T'elen was responsive and competent. She bore her indenture well. Ca'aed tried to take care of its indentures, make their servitude easy, but some could not flow with their service. It understood, but it needed indentured and free people to live, as the people needed their city. All had to work together. Life served life.

Ca'aed watched T'elen as she located the swelling in the vein. T'elen smelled it carefully, touched it gently, checked with the interior antibodies, injected an anti-inflammatory, which eased the cramp but not the itch, and removed some cells and antibodies from the needle into a microcosm of her own design. Ca'aed knew T'elen hoped to make some promises based on the new microcosms to shorten her indenture and felt strangely pleased that its discomfort might help prove their worth.

A sharp spark of pain cut through Ca'aed's primary thoughts. The city isolated the spot. One of the sensor roots that tasted and tested the canopy to find the best harvest points. A blister swelled painfully on the outer skin, squeezing the pores closed and pinching the delicate papillae.

Worry pressed harder against Ca'aed's consciousness. It pulled out from several conversations with citizens and speakers and put as much of the traffic on its own behavior as it could. Ca'aed withdrew its thoughts into its own body that stretched across miles of wind and tried to understand what was happening.

Muscles contracted smoothly, hearts circulated the gases and chemicals, timed the electrical pulses, intestines filtered wastes, its own and its peoples, veins guided potentiated and unpotentiated neurochemical flows, and pores regulated diffusion. All good, all smooth, all as it should be, except there, and there and there. . . .

Ca'aed looked out onto the body of Gaith behind its quarantine blankets, and worry blossomed into fear.

Ca'aed found its chief engineer in the refresher of his private home with D'cle, who was one of Ca'aed's adopted citizens and the chief's companion-wife.

Another cramp, this one along a muscle for one of the upper southwest stabilizers. The muscle contracted involuntarily and the stabilizer wavered.

"Engineer T'gen," said Ca'aed through his headset. "Alert. I am ill. I repeat, I am . . ."

Pain! It lanced up the sensor roots, straight into Ca'aed's primary cortex. Blisters, dozens of them, popping out of the skin like a burning fungus. Pain, wrongness, illness, pain . . .

The pain ebbed for a moment, and Ca'aed was aware that T'gen was calling all the engineers and indentures via their headsets. Ca'aed mustered its resources and tracked them down, circulating the call with its own voices. It routed images of the affected areas to the research houses and tracked the response. T'gen flew fast into the deep crevices and chambers near the center of Ca'aed's body, where the main antibody generators lay. The required varieties were not getting released; new growth might have to be facilitated.

Below, indentureds and engineers numbed the pained roots and began treating the blisters with steroid compounds. Relief blew through Ca'aed and opened its mind up again. It was able to alert the surrounding traffic that there would be interruptions, that all should return to the home ports. It found the district speakers, let them know what was happening and that it was all being attended to, but alerted them to keep in contact with the city and each other. Ca'aed set some of its voices in reserve, just for the speakers.

Now, inventory the position and health of the sails and stabilizers. Along with waste disposal, those were key to comfort of the Kan Ca'aed. They were near a living highland cluster, and pockets of warm air would cause unpredictable currents necessitating thousands of small adjustments, and everything had to be in health.

Ca'aed felt the first patch of gray rot blossom on its skin, and it took all the strength of centuries for the city not to scream.

Vee yawned hugely as she stepped, dried and dressed, out of the shower cubicle. A mug of opaque black tea appeared in front of her. The mug was attached to a hand, which had an arm, on the end of which was Josh.

"My hero," she said fervently. Grasping the mug in both hands she took a huge gulp, almost scalding her tongue. "Ahhh," she sighed blissfully. "Is she out there?"

"As always." Josh waved toward the front window. There was the holotank and the People's display device, which Vee had come to think of as "the holobubble." Next to them, waiting patiently on her perches, sat T'sha.

At first, D'seun had spoken to them, along with T'sha. The ambassadors were always accompanied by at least three others who were all called "engineers" and seemed to be responsible for looking after the kite and the translators, as well as making sure their imagers were holding up.

After the third day, however, it had just been T'sha.

Where are the others? Vee had asked the first time she'd woken up and T'sha had been out there alone.

A compromise has been reached, T'sha said. *D'seun has left me with the translators while he returns to speak to our . . . wait . . . colleagues.* T'sha still had to pause frequently to argue with her translator on interpretation. At first, Vee thought T'sha had meant that figuratively, but now she knew better. The things controlling the holobubble were, in some way, alive.

Why did you need to compromise on that? Vee had asked.

T'sha had inflated, just a little, a gesture Vee had come to learn meant a mild emotion, such as annoyance. A full inflation was full emotion, such as anger or happiness. Vee wondered if they played poker on Home.

It is politics, T'sha had told her, *and I think I should not discuss that yet.*

You have politics too, do you? asked Vee.

Yes, we decidedly have politics too.

I'm sorry.

T'sha deflated, sinking, and causing her crest to flutter around her wings. *So am I.*

T'sha's engineers had rigged her what Vee understood was their version of a tent—a couple of balloons floating up near the cloud line, where T'sha was most comfortable. They were held in place by long brown tethers that appeared to have rooted themselves to the ground.

It turned out that the People didn't sleep. Every few hours, T'sha would vanish to "refresh," a physical activity that Vee couldn't quite make out but seemed to combine meditation and afternoon tea. Each trip took about an hour. Except for that, T'sha was always there and ready to talk.

Mostly it was Vee who talked back. They talked about T'sha's older brother, who seemed to be either a contracts lawyer or a court recorder, and about her little sisters, who were still in school. They talked about Vee's five siblings, and her parents and grandparents back home, and about the costs and problems of caring for a family, especially when you were the one with the most resources. They talked about marriage as a basis for the family structure, and it turned out T'sha was expecting to have several marriages arranged for her all at once, which Vee found delightfully practical. She had a hard time explaining courtship, romance, love, and individual, serial monogamy. T'sha thought it sounded like a lot of work.

They talked about seeing the stars, which T'sha had done only once in her life. She was fascinated to hear about living in a world where you could see them every night. They talked about cities, and Vee was stunned to hear T'sha speak about hers with the same words she used to talk about her family or her future lovers, until Vee remembered and quoted some old Sandburg poems about Chicago and New York. T'sha was fascinated by the poetry, and soon Vee was reading her Keats, Angelou, Shakespeare, Dickenson, and all the haiku she could dredge up. In return, T'sha told Vee stories of the ancient Teacher-Kings and riddles that had no answers, to which Vee replied with some Lewis Carroll and then had to explain what ravens and writing desks actually were. . . .

And on and on and on. They showed each other pictures of their worlds like proud grandparents showing off images of the latest addition to the family. Thanks to Josh putting himself through serious sleep deprivation, the humans had added two new lasers to their projector and they now had full color capabilities. T'sha asked Vee to show her things that were beautiful, and Vee did her best—great buildings, fine statues, forests, the Grand Canyon, and then she found that many times she had to explain what was beautiful about them.

T'sha showed her Ca'aed, the canopy, the clouds thick with things that might have been fish and might have been birds, and Vee did not have to be taught that these were beautiful.

For everything she learned, Vee was left with a thousand more questions. It felt like the only thing she knew for sure was that she liked this winged person who flew through a world that would kill Vee dead, and still had brothers and sisters and a home she loved, and a wicked sense of humor.

It was dizzying. It was magnificent. It was exhausting. Vee slept like the dead at the end of her shifts and was only vaguely aware of what else was going on in the scarab.

Vee snagged a piece of toast off the breakfast table, earning a dirty look from Sheila, whom she smiled at as she breezed by. She plunked herself into the copilot's chair, toast in her mouth and tea in her hand.

Good morning, T'sha, she typed, one-handed.

Good luck, Vee. Vee had quickly given T'sha her nickname after they had established that the long form gave the People's translator trouble.

T'sha seemed agitated this morning. Her body shrank and expanded as if she were breathing heavily. She shifted her weight on the perch that had been set up for her, and her wings twitched even though they were folded neatly along her back.

Is there something wrong? typed Vee.

Politics, replied T'sha. *We are on the verge of an important poll in the High Law Meet. Vee, I have worked on a scene I wish to show you. Something of Home. When you have seen it, I will ask you some questions and I will then take your answers back to the Law Meet. Will you watch?*

Of course. She wanted to add, "I'm all eyes," but she wasn't sure what T'sha would make of the metaphor.

T'sha's words faded, leaving the bubble clear and empty for a moment. Then a blur of color filled the bubble like smoke. The blur resolved itself and Vee saw another Venus.

But this one had life.

The bubble showed her an island made up of swollen roots and leaves covered with translucent gold and silver blisters. Green tendrils that might have been vines or blades of grass waved in the wind. Light, white feathers protruded from clusters of seeds, or maybe they were little mushrooms. They all hooked together as if hanging on for dear life. A nearly spherical slug crawled along one of the ash-colored branches only to get sucked up by something that looked like a cross between a jellyfish and a kingfisher.

This is the canopy, right? asked Vee.

Yes, came T'sha's answer. *The canopy is below the clear. It is a complex tangle of life which, with the living highlands, supplies all the nutrients that we need to live and thrive. The plants intermingle and grow out from each other creating, what . . . wait, islands of vegetation that support both fliers and runners, which live on the canopy as you do on the crust and never lift themselves from it.*

Vee glanced up at T'sha, trying to find words for the sheer wonder of what she saw, but T'sha was deflated on her perch, smaller than Vee had ever seen her, so small that her sparkling gold skin hung in wrinkles and folds around her frame. She was gazing at the image in the holobubble.

This is a construction from old records, read the text. *This was what we think it might have looked like several thousand years ago when the canopy was little more than loose islands floating on the wind. This is what it looks like now.*

A solid, verdant carpet, green and gold, red and blue, and brown. Broad, bubblelike leaves reached up into the wind from a solid mat of intertwined roots. A series of six-legged, what? Reptiles? Or birds? The local equivalent of chickens, maybe? Whatever they were, they picked their way between the leaves, sticking their beaks into bubbles here and there and draining them dry. But large patches of this field, with its one kind of "bird," were twisted black or limp brown.

I guess death and disease look the same no matter where you go, was Vee's first thought. Her second was, *Wait until Isaac gets a look at all this.*

Vee saw T'sha sagging next to the image, and details from the past few days' worth of conversations clicked into place. *You don't build things—I have that right? You grow them or breed them?*

Mostly, yes. T'sha shook herself, inflating a little, like a person trying to shake off a malaise.

And if they're alive, they have to eat, so they drain off the same stuff from the air that you do?

Yes. T'sha dipped her muzzle, an affirmative gesture.

And so you cultivated the most useful stuff in the canopy and in the clouds to thicken the soup in the clear which nourishes your living infrastructure, and you've overtaxed whatever the canopy eats?

Again, T'sha dipped her muzzle. *That is one of the things that is happening. Another is blights. Huge portions of the canopy are dying, and we cannot stop them.*

Vee nodded to herself as she typed. *Monoculture. We've had that problem on Earth too.*

T'sha inflated a little further, hesitating before she spoke. *It is more than that. Some of the symbiotes and the living infrastructure made more efficient use of the . . . soup than the food crops. The tenders are actively killing the crops. We have lost the balance and have not yet recovered it.*

Vee felt a twinge of sympathy. Imagine if the ladybugs stopped eating the aphids and turned around and ate the grain? What could anyone do?

So your world is dying?

Dying? T'sha flapped her wings as if to drive the word away. *No. It is changing. The change will be violent, and the outcome is uncertain. We cannot predict what the new balance will be like or how well it will support us. The most viable solution heard was to use the World Portals our technicians were experimenting with to find another world where we could spread a controllable life base and transfer ourselves. We could wait until the pace of change on Home slowed down, and then we could return, possibly reserving the New Home and . . . wait . . . allow one world to lie fallow and stabilize while we lived on the other.* T'sha turned her gaze directly toward the scarab. *This is our case, you understand. This is what we wish to do here. We wish to spread life. We will take no more than we need. Do you understand?*

Maybe the urgency was imagined, but Vee felt it nonetheless. Part of her was aware that someone had come to stand behind her and read over her shoulder. She thought it was Josh, but she didn't turn to make sure.

Wait, she typed. *You can't transfer an entire population from one world to another every ten years or so.* On the other hand, who knew? T'sha had shown her an image of the portal they used to transfer from Home to Venus, but she couldn't explain how it worked. Vee could give her no words to help out. This was so far up the line from the world Vee knew that there was no way to talk about it. They needed a quantum physicist or something down here.

We would not perform the transfer every ten years, T'sha's new words said. *It would be every three thousand.*

Vee whistled. *You think in the long term don't you?*

T'sha froze. Startled? *Is there another way to think of life?*

You'd be surprised. Vee licked her lips. *Look, T'sha, I think you should know there are those in the government on Earth who are not going to be very happy with the fact that you've started colonizing one of our worlds without asking them first.*

One of your worlds? T'sha grew and shrank uncertainly for a moment and then settled down, small but not sagging. *Then this IS your world?*

Yes, replied Vee, wondering at the emphasis.

T'sha's muzzle opened and closed a few times as she watched the holobubble. Finally, new words appeared.

How is it yours?

Vee pulled back a minute. As she did, Josh leaned forward. She felt him before she saw him. She glanced back, looking for suggestions.

"Be careful, Vee," he said. "I think we're probing close to a nerve here."

"You too, huh?" Vee shook her head. "Okay, let's go for honesty." She typed, *I don't understand.*

T'sha swelled and rattled her wings. Impatience? *How is it yours? What do you build here? Where do you live? How do you use this place? I must be able to speak of legitimate use.*

Josh looked down at her and shrugged. Vee felt a chill sinking into her. Josh was right. There was a nerve under these words, and she had to find a way around it. *We have our base, Venera, here.*

Again, T'sha rattled her wings. Her crest ruffled and smoothed as if it were breathing. *But your base does nothing. It does not expand, it does not build or grow, it does not spread life.*

Vee hesitated and suddenly wished Rosa were with her. Rosa was the one who could manage a room full of hostile board members. Rosa would surely be able to give the right answers to one alien. Actually, Vee wished there was anyone in this chair right now except her.

We have always considered the planets orbiting the sun ours. They didn't belong to anyone else.

Even the ones you do not use? They are yours? Now Vee couldn't see T'sha move at all. The ambassador just hung there, like a holograph of herself.

The idea has always been we'd find a use for them eventually.

No answer came back. Vee licked her lips and tried again.

I'm not saying this is right, T'sha, but it's an old habit of thought, and it's going to be hard to break.

No answer. T'sha's muzzle pointed toward the sky and her wings spread wide. Vee sat frozen with her hands hovering over the keys. *What do I do? What do I do? What made me think I could pull this off?*

All at once, T'sha froze. Vee saw her mouth move, but nothing new appeared on the translator. This had happened a couple of times before. T'sha was getting a message from her colleagues over the spidery headset she wore. Vee sat back and glanced up at Josh. His face was tight with worry. She knew exactly how he felt.

Outside, T'sha swelled as if she sought to drink in the whole world.

I'm sorry. I'm sorry. I must go. I . . . there is word my city is sick. Someone will come speak to you. I must go.

T'sha launched herself into the air, rocketing into the distance. The dirigible overhead detached itself from the tent and began to follow.

Vee lowered her hands onto the command board. "Good luck," she murmured.

"Her city's sick?" said Josh.

Vee nodded, watching after T'sha until she vanished over the edge of Beta Regio. "Her city's alive. It's . . . it's like a friend." She turned her gaze toward the sky again. The horror of the idea seeped slowly into her mind. The city was a friend and the city was sick, maybe dying. It was too enormous to be really understood all at once, and it overlaid all the previous conversation, where they scrabbled for ideas and understanding and came up empty.

Friends were dying, families were dying, and they needed someplace safe to go. That place, they had decided, was here. Their only question was whether the humans were here first.

And T'sha wasn't so sure they were.

"Josh," she said, watching the empty perches outside. "I think the easy part is over with."

T'sha rose from the World Portal into the miasma of metallic odors and coughed hard, contracting spasmodically around herself.

When she was able to spread her wings again, Pe'sen was beside her. "There's a dirigible waiting for you. Let me guide you out of here."

T'sha brushed her wing against his in thanks. "Quickly, Pe'sen."

Pe'sen led the way, calling ahead the securitors and the portals to clear the way. The metallic walls and struts passed by in a blur. All T'sha saw was the dirigible's open gondola. She shot inside, barely hearing Pe'sen's call of "Good luck!"

The dirigible already had its orders. It closed up and lit its engines before T'sha even had time to grasp its perches. She rocked badly as the dirigible shot forward, but she didn't care. She was on her way.

"Ca'aed?" she ordered her headset to carry her voice to her city. Her stricken city. How bad? Maybe not so bad, maybe just a panic, an exaggeration. Ca'aed was strong, Ca'aed had survived so much.

"T'sha?" came Ca'aed's voice, strong, but strained. "Good luck, Ambassador."

T'sha's teeth clacked involuntarily. "Good luck, my city. I'm coming to see what all the fuss is about."

"I'm not sure I can let you near me, T'sha."

Fear twitched T'sha's bones. "I'm your ambassador, Ca'aed. You cannot deny me."

"I can't endanger you ei—" The word cut off.

"Ca'aed!" shouted T'sha. *Life of my mother, life of my father, what is happening to you?*

"Evacuation," said Ca'aed. "We must call for evacuation. I am alerting the safety engineers. Do not come here, T'sha."

T'sha did not answer. She ordered her headset to find her birth mother.

"T'sha, you are returning?" came her anxious voice. "There is trouble—"

"I know Mother Pa'and. Listen to me. You must organize the family. The safety engineers are being called. Ca'aed says you need to evacuate."

"Life of my mother . . ." breathed Mother Pa'and.

"I know, I know, but we can't let this get away from us. We are a million and we may all be ill. A quarantine shell is a priority, but even before that we must keep everyone from scattering. Spread the word. Everyone must stay together. We cannot let anyone flee. Do you understand?"

"I understand Ambassador." Mother Pa'and's voice was firm now. "We will do as you say."

"Thank you. Good luck." *Hurry, hurry, hurry,* she thought to the dirigible. *I need to be there!* But she could hear the whine of its engines and taste the ozone and electrochemicals. It was already straining to reach greater speeds, sacrificing smooth flight to plow straight ahead. She could ask nothing more of it.

She did not even ask it to open its inner eyes. She did not want to see Ca'aed growing in the distance. She did not want to see its people, her people, swarming around it like flies. She would see that soon enough. She had to concentrate, call the speakers, call the archivers. The city's records had to be stored and saved.

A million people. A million to be quarantined and examined and provided for, even as Ca'aed itself had to be quarantined, examined, and provided for. She alone could make promises for her city. She needed to know what her city had left to give.

If Ca'aed should become sick now, you will have nothing left. Z'eth's words dropped into her thoughts. T'sha shoved them away. It was not that bad. She had not been that profligate. Surely not. They had caught this in time. There would be damage, yes. There would be expense, but they were a million strong and they loved their city. They were united and they had acted promptly. Their city had not let them try to keep quiet and hide this illness from the world. They would call in help from their neighbors. It would be all right.

The dirigible banked sharply and slowed. Its portal opened and T'sha shot out into the open air. She saw her city spreading before her, and her body collapsed.

Directly in front of her, heavy, fungal blotches filled the deep crevices of Ca'aed's coral walls. She could taste them with her whole mouth. Her throat and skin tightened against the sickness. The wake villages were already being brought around to the leeward walls. The safety engineers hovered with their tools, draping the villages in the gauzelike strainers to keep out contagion, if that was possible. Shells were being lifted from Ca'aed's body and orderly flight chains of people filed into them. As they filled, the shells were wrapped in strainers and tethered together with bloodless ligaments. The people were closed inside to wait for the doctors, to wonder if the sickness had spread from their city to themselves.

It was so orderly, it was very nearly a dance. The enormity of it dived straight to the center of T'sha's being and left her stupefied. Her family was in there somewhere. Mother, Father, her little sisters, her brother . . . Oh life and bone, brother!

"Ca—" she began, but she cut herself off. She could not rob Ca'aed of any of its concentration. She instead ordered the headset to find her brother on its own. A cluster of dirigibles flew the speaker's flags. She turned her flight toward them, beating her wings against the wind until she felt her bones would break.

"Ambassador!"

The voice came to her own ears, not her headset. T'sha saw a solid red crest spread on the wind and recognized Deputy Ambassador Ta'teth rising above the dirigibles. She put on a burst of speed and flew to meet him.

"Ambassador," he gasped as if he'd been the one flying so fast. "I am glad you are returned. We've been doing our best—"

"How bad is it?" T'sha cut him off, fanning her wings against the buffeting wind. She could smell the disease from here, cloying and sweet, just like the scents that had surrounded Village Gaith. The flies would be descending soon.

"Bad. The engineers are trying to keep up, but it is spreading too fast, in too many places."

"How did this happen?" T'sha demanded. Ta'teth dipped and shriveled before her outburst. T'sha cursed herself and dropped until she was level with her deputy. "I'm sorry, Ta'teth. I'm sorry. I do not blame you. But does anyone know what happened?"

Ta'teth recovered his size. "The best theories are from the indentures from Gaith, and they are very serious." T'sha grit herself against her impatience. Ta'teth was also scared. Ta'teth loved Ca'aed as she did. He was doing his best. "They think it is a new kind of virus."

"But that's a fungus!" retorted T'sha.

"No," said Ta'teth. "It's cancer."

"What?" The word was out before T'sha could stop herself. Cancer? How could that be cancer? A virus might cause a cancer, yes, but not like this.

"They think . . ." Anticipation of his own words made Ta'teth shudder. "They think it is a new strain of virus that has managed to take advantage of the People's close relationship with the cities. They think it replicates in sections, part of it in the people, part of it in the segments of the city's anatomy that are chiefly animal. The virus sections lie dormant in the hosts, mimicking, they think, familiar nutritive elements. They possibly even infect the monocellular nutritives and through them infect the hosts. The dangerous phase does not start until two or more sections of the virus are combined, possibly in the presence of an additional chemical stimulus—"

"In such a place as in the city's bowels."

Ta'teth dipped his muzzle. "Then it replicates furiously, devouring its host and releasing the undetected spawning segments, working too fast to be completely stopped or destroyed."

T'sha did not deflate. She felt paralyzed by Ta'teth's words, frozen as cold as a New Person. "It is a good theory. Is it being tested now?"

Again, Ta'teth dipped his muzzle. "They are hunting for viral DNA segments now and trying to map its life cycle."

"And we might all be carriers?"

"Yes," murmured Ta'teth. "Of portions of the disease, at least." He swelled and shrank. "There might be more than one strain."

The words sank into T'sha and she shivered, releasing old memories. What is the nature of life? went the first riddle in the story of Ca'doth. Three possible answers—a stone, a shell, the wind. A stone because life is strong and underlies the whole world. A shell because life contains and shelters what is precious. The wind because it is everywhere and cannot be stopped.

It is everywhere and cannot be stopped. "Have you told Ca'aed?"

Ta'teth collapsed in on himself. "No. I didn't think . . . I . . ."

T'sha flew over him, brushing her fingers against his crest. "No shame, Deputy. I'll do it now."

T'sha flew past the chains of her people being evacuated to the isolation shells, past the engineers with their flocks of tools surrounding them, between the walls patched with this strange, sweet cancer that mimicked a fungus so well. She knew where she wanted to be. There were eyes beside the main portal. Pretty silver eyes, which watched the winds and the world. She wanted to be there when she told Ca'aed.

"My city?" T'sha hovered before the city's eyes, each one as big as a whole person.

"Ambassador?" murmured Ca'aed.

"You are very ill, Ca'aed. They think it is a new virus." Slowly, carefully, she repeated what Ta'teth had told her.

The eyes remained focused on her, drinking her in as if she were the only thing in the world. Sorrow swelled T'sha's body. She wanted to wrap the city in her arms and hug it to her belly as if it were a child. She wanted to carry it away from here to somewhere safe, where the winds were wholesome and it could be fed and healed. But there was no safe place, not in any latitude. The whole world might be infected by now; they had no way of knowing.

"You must cut it out," said Ca'aed.

"What?" blurted out T'sha.

"This theory is sound. I run it through my minds. It holds, life of us all, it holds. They apply anticancer treatments now, and they have some effect, but they will take dodec-hours, and we do not have the time." Ca'aed paused as if gathering its strength. "You must cut out the affected sections of my body. You must isolate them, burn them if necessary. If my body is spreading infection, it must be stopped."

There was no room in T'sha for further horror. She would not permit Ca'aed's words to enter her. "No, a quarantine—"

"Will allow me to stew in my own disease," interrupted the city. "This way we may be able to save at least my conscious-ness and keep the worst of the infection out of the wind." Its voice was calm, collected. But T'sha still heard the fear.

Cut? Cut my city . . .

In front of her, a ligament snapped, the ends flapping into the wind.

"I am the shelter. I am the shell," said the city, giving the old words of the unity chant, the one T'sha had recited every year when the city passed over the First Mountain.

"We are the bone. We are the embryo," responded T'sha in-stantly.

"I preserve you."

"We preserve you. Life serves life."

"Life serves life," replied the city. "Cut out this disease from me."

Every bone in T'sha's body clenched. Cut out the disease. It was barbaric but effective if the anticancer treatments weren't working fast enough. Cut down the sails, cut out the homes, cut through the parks, the windguides, the promise trees. . . .

Life and bone, the promise trees, and I've heard nothing from T'deu. Suddenly, there was no question inside T'sha about where her brother was. He was deep inside the infected city, trying to save the beauty and intricacy he had dedicated his life to nurturing. Who knew what he carried inside him by now?

The safety engineers would have to keep him quarantined even from the other citizens.

Oh, my brother! And I cannot even go to find you now.

"Are you speaking to Chief Engineer T'gen of your remedy?" T'sha asked Ca'aed, her voice barely a whisper.

"I am. He resists. Do not let him."

Memories. A thousand, a million memories of a world that grew and changed, of life, and family and ambition, worry and debate, flight and stillness. Through all that there was only one constant—Ca'aed. Her ancient city, her soul's home. "No, I will not let him resist."

"I am ready."

"Stay ready." T'sha turned from the city walls and flew toward the isolation shells. It was not engineers she needed now but harvesters with their saws and hooks and pruning sheers. She needed to lead them deep into their city to places the engineers would numb. She needed their nets, their patience, and their precision. Ca'aed might be gutted, but Ca'aed might be saved.

But only if they were fast enough, only if they were right. Otherwise, they would be doing nothing but killing the city a piece at a time.

T'sha closed her mind against the thought and flew.

CHAPTER FIFTEEN

Yan Su sat in front of the full membership of the Colonial Affairs Committee of the United Nations. Their hearing room was something out of another age, with a crystal dome and green marble floor, polished wooden trim, benches and tables. All around the walls, gold leaf picked out the words of great sages from throughout history, messages of tolerance, patience, long thought, and calm.

Calm especially, she needed that today. She surveyed the committee, all twenty-two of them. She was number twenty-three. She had kept her appointment by hook, crook, and means that did not always bear the light of day, but she had kept it. Now, though, her colleagues all watched her with hard eyes and skeptical faces.

Nothing was eased by the fact that the holotank in the center of the crescent bench was activated to show the three Secretaries-General—Kim Sun, Avram Haight, and Ursula Kent. They sat in their conservative clothes and comfortable chairs with desks in front of them that had tidy rows of screen rolls laid out for convenient reference. The Secretaries looked cool, detached. The souls of worldly reason, they waited to see what the committee brought to light.

From the beginning, Su had known the events on Venus would end up here, and she had thought she'd be ready to speak about them. But now that she was here, she was no longer sure. She had faced down the committee before, but never had her prepared speech seemed so . . . absurd. She was used to arguing civil rights, articles of incorporation, land ownership, and mineral exploitation rights. She was not used to making announcements of discoveries. Especially not like this.

Su glanced at the representation of Helen Failia, who sat next to her in another holotank. The real Helen was in her private office on Venera, wearing an assembler rig and watching the proceedings through her wall screen. The image beside Su sat as still as a stone, except for her eyes. Grim exhaustion still hung about Helen from dealing with the sudden deaths of the Cusmanos brothers aboard Venera, and those tired, determined eyes scanned the members of the C.A.C. They looked for the members' reactions and tried to judge what Helen should do or say next.

The initial announcement about the contact with aliens had already been made. Now that the committee had sufficiently calmed down, it was time to move on and give them something else to chew over.

Su didn't give Helen the chance to do or say anything. Speed-of-light delays could be so useful at times. Su just cleared her throat and spoke with a confidence that had more to do with political experience than honest belief. "I would like to take this moment to say that Dr. Failia and the governing board for Venera Base were quite right in bringing this situation to our attention immediately. This is a diplomatic event unparalleled in human history, and as such, it deserves to be addressed with immediate and undivided attention.

"We must not," Su went on, "no matter how much our imaginations want to revert to old stories of invasion and attack, forget for a moment that our first indication that these . . . people existed was when they performed a rescue of seven human beings. Let me say that again. They rescued seven human beings. Seven human beings whose lives would have been lost if not for the selfless intervention of the aliens."

Screen rolls rustled and Patrick James, a fat, florid committee member with a thatch of yellow hair looked up. "What about the eighth human being? The report says the scarab had a crew of eight."

"Yes," said Helen's projection when the question reached her. "The eighth crew member, Bailey Heathe, was killed in the initial accident. His remains were not recoverable." She did not glance at Su. Helen had told Su why the remains were not recoverable. They had agreed that that particular revelation should be left for later, if it ever needed to be brought out at all.

Secretary Avram Haight, a needle-thin man with pallid brown skin and his hair cut short under his black cap spoke. "Have these . . . People . . . said what they are doing here?"

This was going to be tricky. Su and Helen had worked on the wording for an hour and agreed that Helen, as the one from the scene, should deliver it.

"They are interested in surveying the planet," said Helen.

"Just surveying?" Even through the holotank, Su could feel the weight of Secretary Haight's gaze. "This is an exploratory team?"

The question traveled to Venus. Screen rolls were shuffled. Eyes glanced around the room, measuring reaction, guessing intentions. Su's gaze met Edmund Waicek's and saw nothing there but cold hostility. Frezia Cheney had been as good as her word, and Edmund's spinners were now all in a scramble, re-explaining his every statement against the colonies, trying to salvage the impression that his judgment was sound and unbiased. There was even some careful talk of a conflict-of-interest hearing. Very careful, but there it was.

Every little bit helped. Some people were finally beginning to get the hint that a completely anticolonial viewpoint was no longer flying with the entire population of Mother Earth.

Finally, Helen's answer reached the hearing chamber. "No, Sir, it is not just an exploratory team," she said. Her voice was calm, but Su could see how tightly she held herself. "They wish to assess the possibility of establishing a permanent colony on Venus."

Here it comes. Su held her breath. But the explosion did not happen. Instead the committee just murmured and whispered. Even Jasmine Latimer, who went in for shouting and pounding the table, blanched only slightly.

Maybe we can pull this off. Maybe it won't have to be a circus.

"Dr. Failia." Secretary Kent unrolled a screen and swept the

gaze of her overlarge blue eyes across it. "What are the Venerans doing now?"

Again the speed-of-light delay stretched out. Helen's image
sat at Su's side, making motions Helen had made six minutes
ago. *Does Edmund know I raked his background back up?* Su
found herself wondering. Probably not, or she would have felt
the backlash by now. No, her campaign to keep him busy appeared to be working.

*At least something is. Keep your focus, Su. This is not about
Edmund; this is about Venera.*

Helen's image spoke. "We have asked members of the U.N.
investigative team to establish communication with the People." Helen had her hands folded together in front of her. Su
tried not to notice her white knuckles. The statement was only
a minor stretch. Dr. Hatch was a team member, and Dr. Kenyon
was not really a Veneran. "The People seem quite willing to
talk."

Secretary Kent looked down her long nose at Helen. "Has it
been made quite clear that no one on Venera has any power to
negotiate any kind of treaty?"

When that question reached her, Helen answered with
forced patience. "Yes, Secretary Kent. Everyone is aware of
this."

Su minutely adjusted the table microphone. "Dr. Failia decided to address the C.A.C. immediately because Venera lacks
trained mediators, linguists, or diplomats at this time. A new
team needs to be assembled as soon as possible." Several of
the committee members nodded in approval, but everyone else
seemed to be waiting for the word from on high. The faces of
the Secretaries were not revealing.

"It is very clear we need a new team," said Secretary Sun. He
looked like a young, vigorous man with a full head of black
hair, a round, open face, and eyes that rivaled Secretary Kent's
for their size. Su had once heard an estimate of his yearly bill
for med-trips and body-mod. There were counties in North
America that didn't make that much in a year. "What we want
to establish here is that Venera Base has not overstepped its

bounds." Secretary Sun looked directly at Helen. "Why are you still allowing your people contact with the aliens?"

More waiting. Su's fists tightened until her nails pressed painfully into her palms. Too much waiting. It was stretching her thin. She had waited for Helen to contact her, even after she had found out there were aliens. She had waited for Mr. Hourani's answers to all the questions raised by the shipyard bombing. She had waited for each and every one of her questions to reach Helen sitting up there alone in her Throne Room as they tried to work out a strategy for coping with a miracle so huge that Su's mind shied away from contemplating it.

"The people establishing contact with the aliens are not my people," said Helen. The gaze from her image met the gaze of Secretary Sun's image without hesitation. "They're yours. The optical specialist you sent us, Dr. Veronica Hatch, has taken charge of the communication project."

Su wondered what Dr. Hatch was going to say when she heard how Helen worded that particular fact.

"She did this without your permission?" Like Secretary Kent, Secretary Sun had perfected the art of looking down his nose. Su supposed it was something that came with high office.

Images stared at each other while their physical bodies shifted in offices continents apart. *And here we sit with these illusions, waiting to pass judgment on each other. Stop it, Su. You're being ridiculous.*

Helen's image spread its hands. "I was directed by the C.A.C. to cooperate fully with their team in all matters pertaining to the Discovery. Communicating with the People to determine if they built the Discovery and for what purpose it was built, seemed pertinent to the Discovery."

Silence, except for a few coughs and the rustling of fabric and screen rolls. Su suppressed a smile. They'd scored a touch with that one, but it was a long way from a telling blow.

"Forgive my ignorance, Dr. Failia," Jasmine Latimer glanced at her colleagues and the Secretaries, as if seeking permission to speak. "But how is an optical specialist helping to communicate with the aliens?"

Helen cocked her head, looking intelligently interested, an expression Su had seen her use at a hundred cocktail parties.

The question reached Helen, and her answer returned. "We have so far been unable to establish whether the People can hear on frequencies we use or whether they hear at all. They do, however, have eyes that are similar in construction to human eyes. Because of this, Dr. Hatch speculated that we might be able to communicate visually."

"So," said Jasmine. "Dr. Hatch is teaching them English?"

Helen held her interested pose. The question went out, the answer came back. "We've had to teach them very little."

The words were out of Helen's mouth before Su could do anything. They had already been spoken six minutes ago. There was no way to censor them or talk over them. They were spoken.

"We are perfecting the communication hardware," Helen's image went on. "Dr. Hatch is working on a holography display that will give us both mobility and a full range of communications options."

Su did not crumple in her chair, but she wanted to. *Too late, too late*.

"Just a moment, please, Dr. Failia," Secretary Kent interrupted by raising her hand slightly. "Would you please elaborate on that earlier point. You had to teach them very little? About what? About English?"

Helen kept her expression admirably placid. Su felt certain that she spent the whole long time delay inwardly kicking herself.

"The People seem to have a facility with language," said Helen. "They are picking up English rapidly."

"Dr. Failia," said Secretary Haight sternly. "How long do the aliens say they've been on Venus?"

For the first time, worry lines creased Helen's forehead. "They haven't said."

"Have you asked?" Secretary Haight reached for one of the rolls on his desk and opened it. "Wait." He held up a hand, but his attention stayed focused on the roll. "Let me change that question. How long have you been aware of their existence?"

"For ten days," said Helen. Her voice was still calm, but Su could hear the strain creeping in around the edges. "As soon as we learned they were there, I contacted Ms. Yan and asked her to arrange this session."

"I wonder. " Secretary Kent laid her hands, one on top of the other, on her desk.

"About what, Secretary Kent?" asked Su.

Secretary Kent blinked her huge blue eyes. "Your people were so resistant to having a team of U.N. observers come to Venera Base. It was almost as if you were afraid the team would see something you did not want them to see."

At last, Su saw a chance to step in. "The only reason Venera Base did not want the U.N. team on Venus was that they were concerned about possible interference with an ongoing scientific investigation of the first importance. The team members were unknown quantities and the Venerans had no say in their selection." *Well, little say,* Su added silently. Now was not the time to bring up Helen's lobbying efforts or Su's own covert maneuvers.

"And yet," said Secretary Sun, "there are these reports that the Discovery was in fact fraudulent." He gestured to the rolls on his desk.

Helen hesitated, visibly gathering her inner resources. Su answered for her again. *Save your voice, get your bearings, Helen.* "The investigation of the Discovery is ongoing."

"And I understand from this report that the Venerans are making use of the laser that is part of the Discovery in order to communicate with the aliens?" Secretary Sun sounded overly innocent, as if there was nothing behind his question but honest curiosity.

All at once, Su saw where the questioning was going. For the first time in her whole political career, her mouth went completely dry. She felt the eyes of her colleagues on her, Edmund Waicek's most of all. *I missed it. I had all the facts in front of me, and I completely missed this interpretation. Oh, Mother Creation . . .*

"It is part of the holography system, yes," came Helen's answer. She hadn't seen it yet. Or maybe she had. These words were six minutes old. Maybe it had dawned on her by now.

"Convenient that it was in working order, isn't it?" said Secretary Kent. "And just what you needed?"

Cut it off, Su. Su leaned forward. "Secretary, fellow committee members, we are all aware that when a complex occurrence is scrutinized, the separate events rarely add up directly. Loose facts can be stuffed into any number of boxes." *Heaven knows I've done it often enough, and there's enough going on here that you could find an interpretation to fit every need.* "What is before us now, and what must remain before us, is that for the first time, we are speaking to another intelligent species. We must send a diplomatic team to properly welcome them and begin formal contact."

"A diplomatic team will most certainly be sent," said Secretary Haight. He sounded far too righteous for Su's liking. "But there are one or two other background matters that need to be cleared up first. The first is this photograph we were sent."

Photograph? The photo appeared on Su's desk screen. A copy sped toward Venus. Su, suddenly afraid, looked down at the black-and-white satellite shot that caught the alien's portal.

Su's heart thudded once, hard. *Where did they get that from? They shouldn't have that.* The room was tense, silent. Su realized they were waiting for Helen to receive the image. Su looked to the holotank and saw the representation of her old friend trapped inside, almost as if it were Helen herself who sat in that clear cage. The image looked down, and focused, understood what was before it, and Su saw no possibility of explanation appear on Helen's tight, distraught face.

"According to the satellite record," said Secretary Haight, "this picture was taken over a year ago. That's well before the original Discovery was announced and certainly well before you saw fit to report to us that you had met aliens in your personal backyard."

They had plenty of time to study the confusion on Helen's face, how her jaw began to work back and forth, how she had to struggle to still it, the way her hand trembled as it lifted to brush one white lock of hair back behind her ear.

But, in the end, Helen lifted her gaze and spoke firmly. "I am sure you are aware that our satellites record thousands of hours of images in a single year. We do not have the personnel or the computing power to analyze all of them carefully." She glanced down at the photo's caption and her voice took on an added measure of calm assurance. "This was not of an area under active study. It bears a close resemblance to a land feature known as a 'tick.' Like the vast majority of all our satellite imagery, it was filed for later study."

"But you must see it from from our point of view, Dr. Failia." Secretary Kent had a smile on her face. She was once again, all innocence, all righteousness. All for the cameras and public record. "This looks a little strange."

"A scientific inquiry is not a political or legal inquiry, Secretary," Su said smoothly. "Particularly from a privately funded project. The researchers must concentrate on areas most likely to yield interesting or useful results. As Dr. Failia said, this"— she gestured at the photo—"appeared to be a common Venusian land feature. Nothing to excite additional inquiry. A review of Venera's work practices can certainly be arranged for another time. What is most important now—"

"Is that we understand exactly what our position with regard to these aliens is," said Secretary Haight, cutting Su off. "And to do so, we need to know the truth about how long the Venerans have been in contact with them and exactly what they've been negotiating."

When the question reached her, the color drained from Helen's face. "And when we have established this, then what?"

Secretary Haight looked at her as if Helen had just missed something glaringly obvious. "Then Venera Base will be placed under the direct control of the Colonial Affairs Committee, which will oversee personnel assignments and all other requirements pertaining to the alien dialogue."

The words crept the long, slow way to Venus. Helen's face remained frozen and paper white. "I see," was all the reply that returned.

"You are not being accused of anything yet, Dr. Failia." Secretary Kent's voice was soothing, almost sweet with reassurance. "We are merely asking for clarifications."

"I see." Without another word, Helen's representation vanished.

Su stared at the empty box, along with everyone else. She looked mutely up at the Secretaries and the committee and then back at the box.

"A recess, please, Secretaries, committee members." Su got to her feet. "Surely there's been an outside interruption in communications from Venus."

The Secretaries gave their assent. It was still being seconded as Su turned and hurried out of the chamber, the sounds of her footsteps echoing off the marble walls.

What does she think she's doing? Su ground her teeth as she marched across the lobby. *This is not productive. She could be cited for contempt. She could be arrested. . . .*

What if she doesn't care?

Su staggered and caught her balance against a marble bench. She sat down heavily, as if pushed bodily by her thoughts.

This might have done it. They had attacked Helen's integrity, her management of her people and her world. It might have been enough. After all the work and the caution and the planning, this confrontation might have pushed Helen over the edge into rebellion.

Su took a deep, slow breath. "Oh, Helen," she whispered. "Oh, Helen, my friend, be careful."

Michael watched as Helen slowly, deliberately, removed the assembler rig goggles and set them on her desk. She blinked at them a moment before she could make herself look up again and focus on Michael and Ben.

"That," said Michael mildly, "was probably not extremely productive. They're going to haul you down there for contempt."

"Then they are going to have to come and get me." She pulled the gloves off, one finger at a time.

"Helen . . ." began Michael. A cold sensation crept through him as he watched her eyes. This was not Helen angry. This was not even Helen furious. She had gone past those emotions into some new world, and he wasn't sure how to pull her back.

"No." She swiveled the chair and stabbed a finger at him. "No. We're finished with them." She stood up a little bit at a time, as if all her joints protested the move. "They are not taking our world away from us."

"Amen," whispered Ben. Michael whipped around to stare at him.

"That's not the word I'd use." Helen smoothed her scarf down. "Michael, someone here sent the committee that photograph. I want you to find out who."

"Does it really matter?" Michael spread his hands.

"It matters!" Helen began to shake. "The U.N. is about to take Venera away from us and one of our own people is trying to help them!" Her fists clenched involuntarily.

Michael licked his lips. "Okay, Helen. I agree, we need to know who sent that picture, but just so we can head off a complete takeover. We can tell the C.A.C. somebody's been spreading lies and then they'll—"

"And then they'll still conclude we are even more out of control than they thought we were and come up with a few extra security people," said Helen bitterly. "It's done, Michael. Whatever spin can be put on that photo, it's not going to change anything. They are coming and they are taking over." She smoothed down her scarf. "I just want to know who it was so we can keep them out of the info loop. Start with Grace Meyer. She might just have done it to see me out of here."

"Helen, we don't know—"

"Then find out!" Helen's fist slammed against the wall. "That's your job!"

"All right, Helen, all right," said Ben. "We'll find out for you. Don't worry about it."

"Good. Good." The tide of her more-than-anger subsided in her a little. "While you're doing that, I'm going down to the surface to talk to our neighbors. We're going to need them. Ben, have a couple of pilots meet me in the hangar, and warn Josh and Vee I'm coming down."

She left the office without looking back. Michael stared after her as she walked down the stairs and began crossing the farm, with her shoulders hunched and her hands knotted.

He turned to Ben. "What are we going to do?"

Ben shrugged. "I'm going to send a message to Dr. Hatch and Dr. Kenyon. I assumed you were going to start checking out whether Grace Meyer gave the C.A.C. that photo."

Disbelief flooded Michael. "Ben, she's over the edge. She doesn't know what she's doing."

"Yes, she does." Michael could practically hear the *finally* Ben added in his thoughts. "She's saving her home, and she's asking us to do the same."

Michael's hands fell to his sides. *You're on your own now, Michael,* whispered a voice in the back of his mind. *He's gone with Helen or taken her with him.*

"All right," he heard his own voice say. "But you'd better hope I don't find out you sent that picture."

Ben's jaw tightened, just a little, but he said nothing. He just turned and left, following Helen's path across the farms.

Michael rested one hand on the windowpane and tried to think, but before he could sort out what had just happened, his phone spot chimed. Michael touched it to take the message, a little relieved.

"Code 360-A," said a recorded voice.

Michael swore under his breath and rounded Helen's desk. It woke up when he touched the command board and he shuffled her icons until he got the security overview and entered his own passwords. The desk took a reading of his fingerprints and let him in.

360-A was unauthorized access to com archives. Yes, there it was, the serial number. It didn't use Venera's ID system. Probably a briefcase jacked into the system for somebody's fishing expedition. Probably Stykos and Wray trying to get their story out. Maybe Peachman, but he didn't seem like he had the expertise, although he certainly had the love of publicity. They'd tripped one of Michael's bugs, and it had pinged their case and dumped the report for him.

He couldn't really blame them. Somebody had to try. In their place he'd have done the same. Maybe he could have Helen talk to them again. He glanced toward the door. Or maybe not. Helen was not at top form right now.

So, where are you? He typed in the appropriate commands. The answer appeared a split second later.

The infirmary? Michael frowned. *Who'd . . .*

Michael swore again, loudly this time. He tossed down the command to shut the intruding case terminal out of the com files and ran out the door.

By the time he reached the infirmary cubicle, Angela and Philip had their briefcase packed away, and they both had the nerve to look affronted.

"What the hell were you trying to do?" Michael demanded in a hoarse whisper as he touched the control for the cubicle's sound dampener.

"You've been holding out on us, Michael," said Phil. "You've got this base bugged into the middle of next week, and you didn't think you should tell us about it."

"I showed you all security measures pertaining to the Discovery," said Michael slowly, enunciating each word. "I gave you every authorization—"

"You've got a private copy of every single conversation that goes on on this base," croaked Angela. "E-time or face-time. Wouldn't the good citizens of Venera like to know about that? Does Grandma Helen even know?"

Of course she does; she approved the design. Michael didn't say that. There was nothing he could say. The files existed. Gregory Schoma had created the programs and done the wiring. Michael had never needed to resort to them for any case he'd supervised, but they were there all the same. Everyone more or less expected message logs to be kept, but message texts? Usually written permission had to be obtained before private e-mail could be stored. Venera was very proud of its privacy regulations.

But what was he going to say to these two? That he didn't approve of those copies? That he'd never used them? He'd never erased them either.

"If you'd told me what you were looking for," said Michael, "I'd have given it to you without the hackwork."

"Would you?" Philip lifted his eyebrows. "I want to believe you, Michael, but—"

Michael waved his hand to cut the other man off. "I'm not going to play Prove-It-To-Me with you. What do you want? If I've got it, I'll give it to you."

"Who faked the Discovery?" asked Angela.

Michael blinked. "Derek and Kevin Cusmanos. They confessed."

Angela shook her head gently. For the first time since entering the cubicle, Michael found a moment to wonder if she was still in pain. She still had plenty of tubes and monitors taped to her bare arms.

"They didn't do it alone. You know that, Michael," she said. "You're not stupid and you know the people around here much better than we do." Her voice took on a rasp. Philip drew a glass of water from the dispenser and handed it to her. She sipped. "So who else faked the Discovery?"

Michael weighed his options. He could stall, he could lie, or he could be straight with them. He didn't really like any of the choices. At last, he said, "I don't know."

"Was it Dr. Failia?"

"What?" The word jerked Michael out of his slump. Angela didn't bat an eye; neither did Philip.

"She has complete control of Venera's financial records," said Phil. "The base is her whole life, and it was about to die. People around here worship her. They'd start a war if she asked them to. It would not be hard for her to funnel the necessary money down to the Cusmanos brothers so they could do the deed."

"No," said Michael.

"No, you know she didn't do it, or no, you don't want to believe she would?" Philip looked down his nose at Michael. "You're a v-baby, aren't you?"

Anger rushed through Michael's veins. He clamped his jaw shut around the words that wanted to tumble out.

When he was certain he had control of his voice, he said, "There are some things Helen wouldn't do, even for Venera."

"Are there?" whispered Angela. "There are two dead men

next door to us, Mr. Lum. Who else on this base would people kill or die for?"

They were trying to anger him, trying to get him to doubt what he knew. It was a good tactic, and they played it out like the pros they were. But a tactic was all it was, a game, a way to try to turn him against Helen and Venera. That was all.

"The Cusmanoses died of food poisoning," lied Michael, slowly, reasonably. "We found a whole batch with the same contamination and have closed the brewery. It was bad luck."

"It was dead convenient," said Philip. "And you're being deliberately obtuse."

Michael just smiled a little. "And you two are completely objective and did not get sent up here with any agenda at all. The C.A.C. just wants what's best for the planets. Am I right?"

"Come on, Michael." Angela rolled her eyes. "You're too smart for this."

Michael nodded again. "You're right. I am."

He left them there and made his way back to the main corridor and joined the flow of life that swirled through Venera, all day, every day. This was his home, his place, his life. He knew its upside, and its underside. He knew what the people sheltered here would and would not do.

The yewners were used to chaos. They were used to looking for rebellion and conspiracy and greed. They weren't used to people being happy. They didn't understand. This was another world. His world. He would not let them turn him against it.

He would not.

After Michael stormed out, Philip got up out of his chair and closed the cubicle door.

"Well," Angela said mildly. "I don't think he's going to be able to kid himself for more than three days, maybe four, tops."

Philip shook his head and returned to his seat. "Less than that. He's good people, at bottom. He knows where his own lines are, and they've been crossed."

"They've been erased." Angie fell back on her pillows. "If we're right."

"You've got to be kidding? How could we be wrong?"

"We could always be wrong." She let her head flop toward him. God, it felt good to have those earphones off. "We've got more simulations than direct evidence. One good lawyer, and we're suspended for negligent harassment and God knows what else."

"Won't stay that way." Phil picked a spot at the tip of her fingers that didn't have any tubes sticking out and patted it. "I just wish we could have got to him before the Cusmanoses had to die."

"Yeah," Angela coughed. Phil practically jumped to hand her the water. She smiled as she took it. " Thanks."

She drank. It tasted good. It felt good going down. The pain was almost gone. She couldn't believe how good it felt, just to move an arm under the sheets and not have it feel like hot sandpaper. To be able to turn her neck freely, to not have every sound screaming straight through to her brain. "I wish we could have told him we know about the C.A.C. accusations. That might have pushed him over."

"Now, now, we don't want him to know how many of his landmines we did get around." Phil looked at the door thoughtfully and fingered his beard. "We might be wrong about how long it takes him to come around. I want a back-up plan, just in case."

"Let's get to it." Angela pushed herself up a little higher on her pillows. Work felt good. Working was easier than thinking about what was waiting outside the walls. Aliens. Living creatures, intelligent creatures right here, right next door to Mother Earth, and they'd saved her life. Saved all their lives.

And Helen Failia might have known about them for years. She might have defrauded to keep her secret. She might have killed. She was definitely in contempt of committee.

And right now this woman, this maybe-murderer, was controlling all human contact with these new people. That could not be allowed to continue.

Chapter Sixteen

"This is ridiculous." Vee shoved her briefcase back on the scarab's kitchen nook table. "Why don't we just fly over there? We know where they are."

"Maybe because we've been told to stay here?" suggested Josh.

"We haven't been told anything lately." Vee glanced toward the main window. The perches and the holobubble sat there in the gray twilight, unattended. Naturally, they'd been out to take a look at it all, and they had good measurements and great pictures, but they had completely failed to elicit any response out of the nobby "cortex box" at its base that functioned as translator.

"Not to mention that if we left," Josh went on, "we wouldn't be able to talk to any of the People we met." He waved his hand at the plans for the modified survey drone they had been hashing out on the briefcase screen. "This is a long way from finished."

Vee and Josh were working up simulations for a mobile communications drone which used parts scavenged from survey drones and his lab. The problem was, of course, that while the drones had all kinds of recording equipment attached to them, they had zilch in the way of projection equipment.

Vee found herself wishing she could talk to Derek Cusmanos. He'd done such a job on the laser in the Discovery, they could use him now. She shook her head, a little sad, a little angry, a little confused. First he'd blown his talents on a fraud, then he got caught, then he went and died from a bad batch of yeast.

How did you even start to deal with something like that? Especially when you were the one who helped catch him in the first place? Guilt, cold and unfamiliar, took hold, and she set it aside with difficulty.

"We don't need to talk to them; we just need to let them know we're still here." Vee chewed her lip thoughtfully. "T'sha said they have politics. Maybe the local bureaucracy is having a hard time deciding on a replacement for her. If we showed ourselves, it might be a motivator."

"It might be seen as a sign of aggression. We really don't know that much about them, Vee." Josh was trying to be reasonable. He was even succeeding, but Vee wasn't in the mood for reason right now.

"We know a little. We know they're ready to talk." She pressed her fingertips against the tabletop. "We know they have a hierarchical social infrastructure, and we know they really want to settle this planet because their own is in trouble." She met his gaze. "Personally, I think it'd be a bad idea for all concerned to let them talk too much about that in private."

Josh watched her thoughtfully for a long moment. "Plus, you're bored, right?"

She smiled her patented number-fourteen vapid smile. "You know me so well."

"Mmmph," snorted Josh, exaggeratedly unimpressed. "Unfortunately, I'm not the one you have to convince. Adrian!" he called up the corridor to the pilot's compartment. "You hearing any of this?"

"I'm trying not to," Adrian called back.

"All I'm suggesting"—Vee stepped into the aisle where she could see Josh at the table and Adrian crouched in front of the pilot's chair, checking the inventory in one of the storage cupboards—"is that we fly in, showing that we are in fact still here, and come back. It's just to start things up again." God knew they weren't having any luck appealing to Venera. Supposedly Helen was talking to the C.A.C. today, but no one upstairs seemed to be willing to tell them how that was going, if it had happened yet. That, even more than the empty perches out-side, was making Vee nervous.

"Look," Adrian straightened up. "I'm not sure I want things to start up again, all right? I'm even less sure I want to have to explain to the governing board that I helped start them."

"Dr. Failia's last orders to us were keep them talking," Vee pointed out. "We're currently failing in that assignment."

From his face, Vee could tell she'd scored a hit. "I don't think going into their camp was part of what she had in mind," said Adrian.

"Keep them talking," repeated Vee. "Which we currently are not doing." She folded her arms. "If the U.N. wants to know what our current status is, what are we going to tell them?"

Adrian's shoulders sagged. He looked past Vee to Josh. Josh shrugged. "I almost hate to say this, but she's right. If we have to give an update, it's going to be lean."

Adrian turned away and carefully slotted his inventory roll into its rack. When he faced them again, his expression was grim. He was remembering the crash, Vee was sure. He was re-membering the aliens carrying away the body of copilot Bailey Heathe. They still didn't know why. Vee had been reluctant to ask the question. Okay, Vee had been afraid to ask the ques-tion. She wanted the aliens to be . . . good people, understand-able people. She'd been unwilling to compromise the image she was building in her mind.

Going to have to get over that and fast, Vee, she told herself. *Or you are going to be no good to anybody.*

"If we do this," Adrian said, laying the emphasis heavily on the first word, "we do this quickly. We go in, we fly a couple of circles to let them know we're still around, and we come back. That's it. Okay?"

Vee nodded soberly, covering her private triumph. Finally! Something to do besides sitting around and watching the world blow by.

"I'll go inform Sheila of our new assignment." Adrian slid past Vee, heading for the rear of the scarab. Sheila had proba-bly heard every word and decided to keep out of it, something she was very good at. Vee hadn't been able to get more than two words out of the woman since they'd dropped down. Vee suspected she was withdrawing from the utter strangeness of what was happening around her, which Vee could understand intellectually but not emotionally. How could you not want to know everything there was about the People? How could you not want to find a way to make friends?

Especially since it sounded like they were determined to be neighbors.

Had anybody else thought about that? Everyone had seen the transcripts of all the conversations, but had they really thought about it? The People were coming. No, they were here, and they were here to stay. They planned to transform Venus. Had anybody really thought about what that meant?

Adrian came back up the aisle followed by Sheila, her mouth pressed into a thin, straight line. Another thing she wasn't happy about. Vee turned to Josh, who just shrugged again, as if to say, "It was your idea."

I'll buy her a coffee when we get back. It seemed to be the official beverage of Venera.

"If you two could strap down please," said Adrian as he settled into the pilot's chair.

"Right." Vee patted Josh's hand. "Come on, back to the cocoons."

Josh didn't say a word until they were both strapped in and their couches' indicator lights all shone green. Then he turned his head toward her.

"What if they say no?"

"What?" She lifted her head just a little so she could see his whole face over the edge of the couch.

"When we show up, indicating we want to talk some more. What if the People say no?"

"Then we'll know." Vee let her head drop and focused on the view screen. "Anything's better than not knowing."

Through the intercom, she could hear Adrian and Sheila running through the preflight checks. The tourist-guide banter had completely vanished, and Vee found herself missing it. It had made her feel they really were a united team, that they all agreed this was something worth doing. Maybe she'd been kidding herself, but that was how it felt.

"I hope you're right," said Josh as the scarab lifted off the ground. The soft hum of the flight engines crept through the walls. On the screen, the twilight landscape of Venus sped by under the scarab.

"Are you afraid?" she asked.

Josh was silent for a moment. Then he said, "Yes. I wish I weren't, but I am. I mean, I was there. I saw them rescue Scarab Fourteen too. I've sat here and talked with T'sha, and she's civilized and curious, and incredible, and I'm scared to death of her and everything she represents." He licked his lips. "They might be stronger than we are . If they decide they don't want us here, there might not be anything we can do. But at the same time, I don't want anybody else thinking that way, because I'm afraid somebody down at the U.N. is going to do something really stupid, like decide we don't want them here under any circumstances."

"Oh, good." Vee gave him a watery smile. "I thought it was just me."

They lapsed into the silence of their individual thoughts. Venus continued to slip by underneath them, twilight deepening into darkness. The wind rocked the scarab gently, just to make sure they didn't forget it was out there. Vee knew where they were going. They had detailed satellite images of the portal now. But what would they find when they got there? Was T'sha there, or was she still with her sick city? Vee thought that was likely. If T'sha had come back, she'd surely have returned to talk with them. Unless something or someone had prevented her. . . .

No, there was no reason to believe that. Except that the People had politics too. Politics made human people do strange things. Who knew what it made aliens do?

"God and Mother Creation," came Sheila's stunned voice through the intercom. "They're everywhere."

Vee's gaze jerked to her view screen. It showed nothing but the Venusian surface, glowing brightly in the darkness. She unsnapped her straps and struggled to her feet.

"You're not . . ." Josh stopped himself and undid his owns straps.

Swaying with the rocking motion of the scarab, they both made their way out into the main corridor. When Vee could see what lay outside the main window, she stopped dead in her tracks.

The people soared and wheeled in the night like birds, but they had none of the random motion or simple, obvious purpose of birds, and they glowed. Each one of them was a shimmering, living flame. Those flames rode the winds surrounded by clouds of their shining jellyfish. They tied new, big, shimmering white bubbles to their established base. They launched silver-scaled dirigibles into the air. They hovered, staying still relative to their base in knots of twos and threes, probably talking earnestly. They lit the night with their very presence, and Vee knew deep inside she'd never forget the pure beauty and wonder of this one moment, no matter what happened next.

What happened next was that they were spotted.

A trio of People broke away from the others and dived toward the scarab. Sheila's hands convulsed on the wheel.

"Wait for it," said Adrian, gesturing to her to relax.

The People pulled up sharply in front of the main window, close enough that Vee had to squint against the light they radiated until her eyes adjusted. She could see their muzzles opening and closing and their flexible lips covering teeth that looked like a forest of tightly packed toothpicks. Their shining wings rippled minutely in the wind, each centimeter of skin adjusting itself to keep them from being blown away. Their jewel-colored crests spread wide. What were they for? Stabilizers? Sensory organs? She hadn't asked. It seemed like she hadn't remembered to ask anything important.

But, God and Mother Creation, they were beautiful.

One of the People drifted forward from the others, until its (his? her?) muzzle floated a bare centimeter from the thick layer of quartz that separated the humans from the outside.

"Isn't he one of T'sha's engineers?" Josh traced the air with his finger, indicating the interlocking circle pattern on the underside of its wings. The tattoos stayed black, despite the surrounding light. The effect was startling.

Vee nodded. *They never told us the engineers' names. Why?* But he did look familiar. She stepped forward, leaning between Adrian and Sheila, and looked straight into his eyes.

Do you see me? Do you know me?

Outside, Semi-Familiar swayed from side to side, as if he were taking the measure of the window. Adrian seemed torn between working the controls to keep them steady and staring at the People to try to guess what Semi-Familiar might do. Semi-Familiar circled the scarab. He flew above and underneath. He peered into the rear hatch window. He hovered a long time beside the treads.

"What's he doing?" demanded Sheila all of a sudden.

"He's an engineer," Josh smiled. "He's saying, look, here's a cool new machine. How's it fit together?"

Vee managed to stifle her laugh. But Josh was right. That would be the first thing an engineer would do.

At last, Semi-Familiar returned to the main window, and he stayed there for a long moment, doing nothing but looking in at them, not quite touching the window while his fellows talked—maybe argued—behind him.

Finally, he backed away, drawing almost level with his companions. He said something, and they responded by lifting their muzzles, and deflating and reinflating. Agitatedly? Approvingly? She could tell nothing from their eyes.

Semi-Familiar flew off to the northeast a little and then darted back. He repeated the move several times.

"I think he wants us to follow him," said Vee.

Adrian's hands clenched the wheel and then released it. "Okay," he dragged the word out like a sigh.

"I am officially protesting this," said Sheila. "I end up like Heathe, I'm coming back and haunting the hell out of you, Makepeace."

"You end up like Heathe and I'll deserve it." Adrian adjusted his controls and eased the stick forward. The scarab flew gently after the Person they thought they recognized.

Their passage did not go unnoticed. The People swarmed

around them, thrusting their glowing muzzles toward their windows, and peering inside the scarab with their silver eyes.

"Keep out of the damn way," breathed Sheila, but it was more like a prayer than a curse.

They did, barely sometimes, but they did. They were born knowing what was needed for flight, and they did not interfere with the scarab's wing or block the forward path. They did swoop in wide circles all the way around the transport and hover alongside, keeping pace with the machine easily.

"I swam with the dolphins once, in Hawaii," said Josh. "That was like this, only, this is more . . ."

Vee nodded, understanding perfectly. She remembered the time her mother took her and her brothers and sisters to a butterfly atrium in St. Louis. She'd stood still in the middle of the garden, sweat and humidity soaking her clothes, while butterflies fluttered all around. The little blurs of color appeared here and there, holding still for a moment before taking off or landing, according to their needs of the moment. She'd felt herself to be in the center of a whole new world, one that belonged to butterflies instead of people.

That feeling came back to her now, impossibly magnified.

Now the portal spread underneath them. Vee hadn't been prepared for how big it would be. It must have been at least a kilometer across. More. It stretched out until the darkness hid the far edge in her sight. The support struts hunched up like mountain ridges.

The air at the portal's center trembled, and the scarab vibrated in response. Adrian gritted his teeth and eased the scarab backwards and up. He glanced at Vee as if he wanted to tell her they were leaving now, but he didn't say anything, and Vee silently thanked him.

Outside, Semi-Familiar stopped, fanning his wings to keep his place. Another Person rocketed up from the portal's edge. This one had a blue-and-white striped crest that Vee definitely recognized.

"Ambassador D'seun," she said. Josh nodded once.

D'seun swelled up in front of Semi-Familiar, and whatever he was saying, he was saying it fast and there was a lot of it.

Up until then, Vee would have bet nothing could make her take her eyes off the People, but, beneath them, the center of the portal began to glow.

A net woven of strands of pure, white light formed in the massive portal. The strands thickened and strengthened until they became a sheet of light that twisted and folded, and Sheila and Adrian were shouting at each other, and the scarab was backing away and the world clenched itself up for a minute and a whole flock of shining golden bodies shot out of the center of the portal like a living fountain.

D'seun turned his back on Semi-Familiar. *We have to find out what this one's real name is.* The ambassador swooped down into the center of the arrivals. They lost sight of him among the others wheeling and diving in the twilight air.

Semi-Familiar looked over his shoulder at them, trying to send them some message they had no way to understand, and followed Ambassador D'seun down into the flock of newcomers. His arrival stilled them, and they fanned out in an uneven sphere around him.

"Scarab Three, Scarab Three," called the intercom. Everybody jumped. "Scarab Three, where are you?"

"Not where we're supposed to be," muttered Sheila.

Adrian shot her an aggravated glance and opened the radio. "We're doing a reconnaissance on the aliens, Venera. Everything's okay. What's up?"

Or maybe they're doing reconnaissance on us. The newcomers were heading their way, fanning out like geese, if geese fanned in three dimensions.

"Dr. Failia's on her way down to the Discovery site. She wants to talk to the People for herself. Is your ambassador back?"

The latest crowd of People surrounded them, hovering, peering and talking, unheard and uncomprehended, to each other. One large, bright Person with an amethyst crest hovered alone in front of the main window. The wavering tattoos around its muzzle matched both D'seun's and T'sha's.

"I think we've got a new one, Venera," said Vee.

"Then bring them back with you, but get back there. Everything's blown up, and we need to sort out what they're doing here."

"Roger that, Venera," said Adrian, fervently. "We're on our way back."

"Okay, kids," said Sheila as she and Adrian worked the controls, banking the scarab in a wide arch. "Time to play follow the leader."

"That was the New People?" asked Z'eth, both wonder and amusement filling the air between her and D'seun.

D'seun dipped his muzzle. "Their engineers, rather than their ambassadors. No ambassador would have been so rude." He could not believe Br'sei had brought them here to disrupt the welcome he had planned for Z'eth and the other ambassadors, to display the New People before D'seun had a chance to say *anything*.

"I would have thought they'd be bigger," mused Ambassador P'eath. "From your description, Ambassador D'seun, I was expecting monsters."

"Should we follow them?" piped up Ambassador K'ptai. "They only have a single working station for communication. Is that not correct?" She turned an eye toward D'seun.

"That is correct, Ambassador K'ptai," he said, deflating a little in deference. "I was hoping we could take counsel first so that you could be fully conversant with the current status of New Home. . . ."

Z'eth overflew him, gracefully, with plenty of distance. "Perhaps we can hear what the New People say and then what you say. It is rude to keep even mere engineers waiting, surely."

The whistles of assent buffeted D'seun from every side.

"I hardly think we need a formal vote here," remarked Z'eth. "Will you lead the way?"

D'seun forced himself to swell. "Of course, Ambassadors." Well, let the New People show them. Let the ambassadors see what he had seen. It would happen. It could not help but happen. The ambassadors were not fools, not like Br'sei. They would see the truth.

Besides, he had Z'eth's promise. With that secured, all would be well.

All the dirigibles that were not out with the engineers and surveyors were quickly summoned, including the one D'seun had been using since the beginning. It knew its way perfectly by now. It needed no prompting to take them across the plain and over the Living Highland 76 to where the two transports waited, low and gleaming in the dim twilight.

The dirigibles slowed, reaching out their anchors to each other so they made a waiting chain while the ambassadors spilled from the gondolas. The ambassadors swam against the thickening air to hover just above the crust, circling around the transports and the communication screens, peering closely at all they saw. The air rippled with their excited commentary.

Only D'seun came immediately to hover beside the perches T'sha had left behind.

The translator, activated by his presence, read the words that appeared on the New People's screen along with the familiar image of Engineer Vee. Now though, instead of shades of red, she was many colors—cream and pink and gold in coverings of pale blue and green. The New People's engineers had been busy.

"Ambassador D'seun?" The translator's clear voice cut through the swirl of exclamation. "Good luck to you and to everyone who has accompanied you."

The words touched the circulating crowd of ambassadors and reminded them that the formations in front of them were not just some growth on this strange crust. The ambassadors arrayed themselves in a politely interested tier, all facing the transports. Ambassador Z'eth came to hover directly beside D'seun.

Lest I forget who is senior here, thought D'seun. *I forget nothing, Ambassador. You will understand what I am doing, soon.*

"With me is the Law Meet of New Home," said D'seun to the translator. "They wished to hear you speak on matters pertaining to this world on which we find ourselves. Is this you to whom I wish good luck, Vee?" *Let it be seen that I am civilized and polite. That I am a whole person.*

There was a pause while the translator displayed the words for the New People and they formulated their response.

"Vee is here, but does not speak. I am Helen Failia. I am the ambassador for Venera Base." The image of the New Person on the screen shifted slightly and became smaller, rounder, more wrinkled, and a little darker, with a more abbreviated gray crest. This image too raised both its hands in greeting.

Finally they see fit to send someone we can truly speak to. "Good luck to you, Ambassador Helen."

"Ambassador Helen," spoke up Ambassador Z'eth. "Forgive me if I do not observe necessary ceremony, but the Law Meet is assembled here to seek an understanding of your claim to this world." D'seun reformulated her words into the translator's command language.

Words appeared under the New Person's, Ambassador Helen's, feet. The translator read the words out.

"Our claim to this world is that we live here. Before we came there was no life at all on Venus. Now, there are ten thousand of us in Venera Base. Four thousand of those were born in that base and have no other home. Our work is the study of this world. That study gives us both individual reward and our means of exchange with others of our kind. Without it, we have no home and no purpose to our lives.

Behind and above, D'seun heard the rustle of wings and skin. "Now, there," said K'ptai, "is an answer that is neither greedy nor insane."

"Such a difference to deal with an ambassador," said D'seun, his voice carefully neutral. He spoke to the translator. "Then why is there no life beyond your habitat? Why have your people not expanded in the last eighty years?"

A pause. "You have been watching us for that long?"

"We have been working with New Home that long. We needed to see what your claim to this world is."

"And because you do not recognize our claim, you will throw us off this world?"

K'pta froze. "Is that what they think? That *we're* insane?"

Ambassador Z'eth swooped a little closer to the translator. "We make no claim on anything used to support and maintain your life or the lives of the other New People on this world. These things are yours and are acknowledged as such without question."

New words appeared on the screen. "I understand you wish to make this world your home?" read the translator. "How will you do that?"

D'seun looked to Z'eth for permission to speak, but it was P'eath, Ambassador for Ba'detad in the Far Southerns, who came forward to answer, swelling her aging body as she did. "We have already established that this world is capable of supporting the life that supports us. If, and only if, no one else has a valid claim to this world, then we will attempt to establish a biosystem." She waited while D'seun translated between her and the tools. "If the biosystem takes hold, then we will birth settlements for our people and we will live here while the changes on our home rebalance themselves and we can again live there. When we are gone, this world will be left as fallow to rebalance itself." P'eath had proposed the original idea of New Home. She carried her pride of that accomplishment like an extra tattoo on her wings. But her vision extended no further than finding a new world. She did not see the wider implications of allowing the New People to remain here.

"What about the rest of the planets that orbit this sun?" asked the translator for Ambassador Helen.

"We do not need them," said Z'eth without hesitation. "They will not help us spread life."

"What about us?" The image gestured toward the clouds. "The humans here on Venera? While you are . . . spreading life, what will you do with us?"

"Ambassador," murmured D'seun to Z'eth, keeping his words light as pollen. "Do not answer. Make no promises. There are consequences here. . . ."

But if Z'eth heard him, she gave no sign. She kept her gaze fixed on the communicator.

"Community is a resource," said Z'eth. "One which we hope you will provide for us. You have studied this world for a long time and we hope you will share your knowledge with us."

No, no. There can be no community here. This world must be ours alone. They cannot be controlled, cannot be predicted. I hold your promise!

"In return," said Z'eth, spreading her wings to show their scope and the canopy of her tattoos to the New People waiting in their shelters, "we hope we can help you." No one questioned her right to speak or her words. D'seun's gaze swept the assembled ambassadors, and he wondered how many of them owed promises to Z'eth.

The image of Ambassador Helen bobbed its face several times. "This all sounds very good, but what assurance can you give us that you will not change your position later, when there are more of you here?"

That was a tricky question. It raised implications of sanity. If the People were insane, they'd lie. But there was no way to prove sanity in advance. After a moment, Ambassador P'tkei descended to within the translator's range and spoke. "What assurance would you accept?"

There was a long pause, even after the words had been fed to the translator. "Good question."

D'seun fluttered, inflating and deflating rapidly, angry at this show of understanding and aware his anger was absurd. They would betray themselves soon enough. This was a thin shell. It would crack. "This world was declared New Home by the High Law Meet. Since then, miles had passed under us both and we have done nothing but debate your status and save your lives. If we were insane, as you fear, and meant to destroy you, would we not have done so already?"

Another pause. Were they debating over there? Or were they just trying to understand?

At last, the answer came. "I can accept this."

"Then we have our understanding?" said Z'eth. "You agree this world is ours to make our new Home?"

"Yes," said the translator. "To you, this is New Home, and together we have community. You will help us if we need it, as you helped the others in the scarab that crashed?"

"Life helps life," said Z'eth. "We will do what we can."

"Our situation here is not easy." The image of the ambassador seemed to shrink a bit. "There are those with whom we disagree about our rights to this world, and consequently yours. They might attempt to cut off our supply routes from the other worlds. We may be forced to ask for a great deal of assistance in maintaining ourselves here."

Hope and fear burned together inside D'seun. There was clear acknowledgment that this was New Home. That would relax many of the ambassadors at his back. But there were words in this delectation that would raise the questions he needed openly debated. Here was the first crack in the New People's shell.

D'seun opened his muzzle to speak, but Z'eth spoke first. "This is our world, together. We will of course help you."

Ambassador Helen's image raised its hands again. "Thank you, Ambassadors all. We will talk more in the future. Hopefully our engineers can find a way to make this easier."

"I am certain they can." Pride swelled Z'eth. She hadn't heard it, then. That was all right. He would make her hear.

"Good-bye, then," said the words beneath Ambassador Helen.

"Good luck in your life."

Z'eth a apparently resisted the urge to trumpet her triumph, but she did spread her wings to the assembled ambassadors. "We have them. We have this world. Clean and clear, it is ours."

"But we still have a problem," said D'seun, deflating humbly.

"Ambassador?" Z'eth shrank to something close to her normal size.

"The other New People. Their distant family on their other world." He swelled and lifted his muzzle, making sure his words touched all the Law Meet of New Home. "Did you not hear the ambassador? They are willing to dispute the clear and legitimate claims to this world, when they have no counterclaims in place. They are insane."

Vee watched D'seun and the other ambassadors spread their wings and rise gracefully into the sky like a dream of golden birds.

"I cannot believe you did that," she whispered harshly to the command board. "Holy God and Mother Creation, I cannot *believe* you did that!"

I can't believe I let you do that. Vee looked down at her own hands on the command board. Helen Failia once again sat in the pilot's seat.

"I didn't do anything," said Helen, firmly. "I just made sure we had backup in case the C.A.C. tries to force us to do things their way."

"Didn't do anything?" Vee stared at her in complete disbelief. "You just got an alien race involved in a pissant bid for revolution that they can't possibly understand. You called yourself an *ambassador*, for God's sake. Do you know what that means to them? It means you speak for a whole city, that you have the right to make decisions for an entire population!"

"I do speak for a whole city," replied Helen.

"Did Michael and Ben know what you were going to say?" asked Josh from his position in the back of the cabin. They'd rigged up a monitoring station in the Discovery so that he wouldn't have to leave the scarab to keep an eye on the equipment.

"They knew." Helen nodded once. But she did not, Vee noticed, look at either of them.

"Did they approve?" inquired Josh.

Helen turned and gave him an icy glare. "That is none of your business."

"The U.N. could be doing anything," said Vee hoarsely. "They could be planning an embargo. They could be sending in soldiers!"

"Maybe." Helen's voice was flat and practical, just like the expression on her face. "That's their problem."

Vee got slowly to her feet, her hands shaking with rage. Josh scraped his chair back a little, and she saw his expression urging her to caution. She didn't care. He didn't get it. None of them got it.

"You idiot!" she rasped at Failia. "You stupid, bloody-minded, idiot! If we get them involved with this, they may decide the Terrans are greedy or crazy. Do you know what that means to them?"

"No." Helen regarded her calmly. "And neither do you. Sit down, Dr. Hatch."

"And remember who I'm talking to?" shot back Vee. She swept out her hand. "How could I forget? I'm talking to a woman who is willing to get an entire alien race involved in her stupid little pissing games!"

Helen's face flushed a dark purple, even though her voice remained soft and calm. Her gnarled hands clenched the seat's arms.

"Dr. Hatch, thank you for your help in facilitating communication with the People. I think, however, you had better be aboard the shuttle which will be returning your colleagues to Earth."

Josh laid a hand on Vee's shoulder. He opened his mouth to start to say something.

"No, Josh," said Vee, coldly. "I think you'd better distance yourself from me." She met Dr. Failia's gaze without blinking. "I think I'm a very bad person to be near right now."

But if you think I'm going to let this happen, Dr. Failia, think again. Think hard.

They held their ground, staring each other down. There was no way for her to win here, Vee knew, and her only exit options lacked dignity. *But a display of petulant vulnerability now might be beneficial later on.*

God Almighty, Vee you have been doing this for too long.

"They shipped all the dissenters out of Bradbury too." She whirled around and stormed down the central corridor and into her cabin. The door swished shut behind her. She wished it would slam.

Vee dropped onto the edge of her couch and pressed her fingers against her temples. *Think, think. This has to handled. You can't let them do this to T'sha. To the world. To everything.* A sad realization came over her. *Nobody even asked about T'sha. We don't know what's happening to her.*

She stayed like that until she heard the door swish open again. She unfolded herself. Josh stepped over the threshold and let the door close behind him.

"How's life outside?" she asked lightly.

He sat on the edge of the couch facing her. "Helen's calling up to the base to say mission accomplished. Adrian is going a little nuts checking and rechecking the soundness of the scarab." He glanced at the door. "I think he really does not want to be here."

Vee laughed, once. "That makes two of us." She looked down at her fingertips. "What are you going to do?"

Josh sighed and looked around the cabin, a little bleak, a little annoyed. Vee sympathized. This was a lousy place to be having this discussion. Neither one of them could stand up straight. The crash-couches weren't comfortable to sit up in. Her shoulders ached and she bet his did too, and who knew when Helen was going to come walking through the door to see what they were conspiring about. The whole situation stank.

"You know what's the worst?" Josh asked suddenly, as if reading her thoughts. Vee shook her head. "That I can't win. If I go home, I'm turning my back on what might be the most important thing that's ever happened to humanity. On the other hand, if the Venerans start anything, you know the propaganda machine on Mother Earth's going to paint Venera as a bunch of mindless Fullerite rebels. So, if I stay, it'll look like I'd rather be with traitors and aliens than my friends and family." He glanced at Vee and shook his head again. "It'll look like I'm a traitor."

"I know," she said. "It's pretty much a disaster." She reached up and pulled her veil off, picking out the pins and dropping them into her lap. "Maybe the smart thing is to leave it to the disaster makers."

Josh's mouth quirked up. "You don't mean that."

She shrugged. "Not really." She wound the scarf through her fingers. It was real silk, a blazing paisley pattern. Amber, her next-to-youngest sister had bought it for her, for some birthday or the other. "What's going on here, it's stupid. If I can stop it, I have to."

"Because it's stupid?" he said quizzically. "Not because it's right, or wrong, but because it's stupid?"

He looked incredulous, and she supposed she couldn't

blame him. It sounded hard, even to her. She searched herself for an explanation. "You know why I do my act? My Vee-the-Temperamental-Artiste act?"

"I have a few ideas." Josh leaned back on both hands. "Most of them have to do with getting attention."

Vee waved his words away with the end of her scarf. "When I hit college, the beauty fads had cycled back around to tall, skinny, and pale." She spread her arms wide. "Ta-daa. Suddenly, and for the first time in my life, I was it. I was the ideal. As a result, I had people sidling up to me and saying"—Vee leaned forward and gave an imaginary person a confidential nudge—"'My dear, wherever did you get yourself done?' I'd say I'd never been 'done.' This"—she gestured at her torso—"was just me. They'd look smug or sour, and not one of them would believe me. So"—she shrugged—"I started telling this long story about this bod shaper in the Republic of Manhattan and how much physical therapy I had to go through after he added ten centimeters to my height, and how he'd died last year in a boating accident, and I was just devastated because what if I needed to get short again. . . ." She dropped her voice back to normal. "Nobody with a brain believed me for a second, but the ones without a brain. . . ." She tightened her hands around the scarf. "Right and wrong can be difficult, but stupidity is easy to spot, and this situation is brimming with stupidity."

The corner of Josh's mouth twitched. "Must be a nice view from up there."

"Maybe." Vee looked at the door. It remained closed. "Will you help anyway?"

Josh dropped his gaze. A dozen different kinds of indecision played across his face, one after another. Did he have family on Earth? Vee wondered. She didn't know. She'd never asked. She'd accepted the appearance of a bachelor researcher, without ties to bind or to anchor. The realization hit Vee hard. She'd become so used to being judged by her surface appearance, she'd somewhere started doing the same with other people.

And here was the one person of unquestioned substance in

this whole gigantic mess, and he might be about to slide through her fingers.

Josh sighed, interrupting her thoughts. "I will help. I think we'd better start by talking to Michael Lum. He's the steadiest member of the governing board, and has the fewest political interests."

Gratitude rushed through Vee. "Thank you," she breathed.

Josh studied her, looking for what she had not said. Maybe he found it. She hoped he did. She hoped there'd be a chance to say it later. "You're welcome." His smile was small, but it reached his eyes. "What do we do now?"

Vee considered. Much to her relief, ideas sparked quickly to life. "You need to go out there and make obeisance. Make sure she knows you're still on her side so you can keep working on the mobile com drone. We may need to be able to talk to the people without interference." She gave him a wry grin. "Nobody's got you down as a troublemaker yet. You'll be able to work the system more easily than I can."

"All right." Josh uncrossed his legs. "While I'm working behind the scenes, what are you going to do?"

Vee grinned at him. "Make trouble."

"Ambassador Helen has with her own words condemned the New People's distant family as insane." D'seun flew with the Law Meet over the New People's transports and his words were heavy with assurance. "They would hold back the spread of life if they could. Do we permit New Home to grow in the presence of this threat? Do we refuse to do our best to help this life with which we now share our new world?" *This life which cannot survive without its distant family, unless they turn to us, and then we will have the control we need. Yes, all could still be made right.*

"Do we know that this is the best?" countered bloated K'ptai, overflying him without regard to rank. D'seun might be younger, but he had been an ambassador longer than she. "Our understanding is still incomplete."

"Helen is an ambassador." Z'eth steered her path between

D'seun and K'ptai. "We must agree that her words are more accurate than any engineer's could be."

"Ambassadors, Ambassadors." P'eath lifted herself up until it seemed as if she would touch the clouds. "We are not children playing about the edges of our village. These are not appropriate questions for the open air. We must return to our debate chamber, crude as it is, and make proper consideration of all matters there. Our haste is unseemly. We have not examined all the evidence." But D'seun did not miss the way she glanced up at Z'eth as she spoke, almost as if she were seeking permission to be reasonable.

"There is one question we might think on as we return, however," said D'seun softly, lifting himself up so they would all feel his words. "The New People require raw material from the world they call *Earth* to maintain themselves. We have many records of this fact. The distant family is threatening to withhold this. Do we deny our neighbors access to the raw materials they need to survive and spread their own life because an insane family stands in their way?"

Silence spread across the wind. D'seun flapped his wings, taking himself outside the quieting circle of ambassadors and saw what he expected. They all looked to Z'eth. Could they all owe Z'eth? Had she brought every vote with her? And she had promised her vote to him.

If that was true, it was done. Even if T'sha returned this minute, she could not ruin what he grew here. The New People would be contained or destroyed. The health of New Home was assured.

D'seun swelled. All was finally well.

Helen watched the People filter into their dirigibles and depart. She felt empty, as if somehow drained of purpose.

Not surprising, I suppose. I just gave the world away. She brushed her hair back behind her ears and tried not to hear Vee's accusations ringing in her ears.

The radio crackled to life. "Scarab Ten, this is Venera Base," came Tori's voice.

Helen leaned forward and touched the Reply key. "This is Scarab Ten. Go ahead, Venera."

"I'm glad we got you, Dr. Failia. There's a message here incoming from Earth, and they won't talk to anyone else on the governing board."

Won't talk to anyone else? Is it Su? "Can you send it down?"

"It'll be audio only, but yes, I can."

Helen pushed herself up a little straighter in the chair on pure reflex. "Okay, Tori, put it through."

"Everything okay up here, Dr. Failia?" Adrian's head poked around the corner from the analysis nook.

"Fine." She picked a coffee cup up out of its holder and stared at the dregs in the bottom. "It's just the C.A.C. calling to tell me I'm in contempt, I'm sure." *Or to find out what I think I'm doing, at the very least.* She tried to remember whether the cup was hers or not, and couldn't. She put it back.

"Helen?" said the voice from the intercom. "This is Su. I have Secretary Kent with me. You've raised a great deal of concern with your . . . abrupt disconnection from the committee meeting."

I'm sorry to have to drag you into this Su. "Good afternoon, Madame Secretary Su."

Venus spread out in front of her. Beta Regio lifted itself out of the ragged plain. The plateau was the color of ashy coals in the twilight, but with bright ribbons of lava lacing its side from the volcano that forced itself up from the tableland's edge. It steamed and smoked in the wavering air and would continue to for centuries to come.

Unless, of course, the People wanted to do something else to it. Could they stop a volcano? They could travel instantly across light-years, and they were talking about transforming an entire world. What was one volcano compared to all that?

"Dr. Failia," came Secretary Kent's voice. "I'm not going to turn this conversation into a total farce by informing you that you've been charged with contempt of a governmental committee."

I'm so glad.

"What I am going to tell you is that in accordance with the

articles of incorporation for Venera Base, you are being removed as head of the governing board."

"By whom, Madame Secretary?" asked Helen.

The time delay dragged out. Helen watched the smoke of the burning mountain. She remembered her first glimpse of the volcano. She'd been dropped down with Gregory Schoma in a very crude version of what would become a scarab. Theirs was more like a cross between a turtle and the original lunar rover. It was cramped as hell, they were strapped in to the point of suffocation, and despite the shielding, despite the scrubbers, despite everything, the cabin still smelled strongly of rotten eggs.

Helen hadn't cared. No one had ever been below the cloud layer before. Oh, they'd sent some probes down, but never a person. They were first, and they'd see . . . they'd see . . .

Then had come that moment when the blanket of clouds had parted and she looked down and saw what they'd been guessing at and arguing over for literally centuries. She saw the mountain lifting above the rugged tableland with lava running freely down its charcoal slope.

"It's alive!" she had shouted to Greg, delight making her foolish. "It's alive!"

"You can help keep this process as smooth and open as possible," Su was saying. *Did they give you a script to read from, Su? This doesn't sound like you.* "We will need to consult closely with your people about their experiences and the data they've gathered thus far on the aliens."

"No," said Helen.

Alive. Almost no one seemed to understand what that meant. This world still had a living heart. It wasn't broken, like the Moon, or burned out, like Mars. It had fire, it had air, it had earth. There was even water, if only just a little in the heart of the clouds. It had all the ancient elements, the only world that did, aside from the home world herself. It was Earth's neglected twin, but because they couldn't mine it or build on it, no one cared.

"I beg your pardon?" came Secretary Kent's astonished reply.

"Your people will not be consulting with my people. Your people will not be allowed to land."

No one cared how beautiful this world was, how rich and vibrant, how much they could learn about the origins of their own home from this mysterious and fiery place. No one at all cared what she might have to offer.

Except the people in Venera, and now, the People.

"Helen. Be very sure you understand what's going on here." Su again, sounding much more like herself. "You are not being given a choice. The *Golden Willow* will be leaving in two days. It has a complement of C.A.C. diplomats and support staff, as well as a full company of peacekeepers to make sure that this transition goes smoothly and to advise in case the aliens become overtly threatening." Su paused to let that sink in. "If you try to break your charter, all flights to Venus will be halted. There will be no transport of goods or people between Venera and Earth. All satellite support will be shut down. You will not be able to speak to any of the other worlds. You will be completely cut off." She spoke the last words slowly, making sure Helen heard each and every one.

Su was trying hard. She was a good friend, and she genuinely cared. A sort of colonial mother hen was Yan Su.

"It doesn't matter, Su," sighed Helen. "This little call is just for show and we both know it. The Secretaries and the committee are going to do what they are going to do, and so am I." She cut the connection.

Take good care of my world, she thought toward the vanished aliens. *You're all we have now.* She got to her feet. She didn't want to have to shout at Adrian, but they needed to get back in the air. There was still Venera to consider, after all, and it looked like Venera was going to be put under siege.

CHAPTER SEVENTEEN

Michael glanced at the clock on the living-room view screen. 4:05 a.m. Not a time anybody should have to know about. There should be a rule that everybody was allowed to sleep through four in the morning. Because when you were awake at four in the morning, you felt like the last person alive in the world. In any of the worlds.

He'd kissed the kids good night hours ago, running through the rituals of tooth care and storytelling on autopilot and hating himself for it. Even Jolynn had gone to bed at last, not saying anything when he didn't join her. He'd just lie there, staring at the ceiling, all his thoughts running circles. They both knew it. They'd been there before, although not quite under these circumstances.

In four hours, Helen would be taking off from the surface to come back home. In less than that, every single person aboard Venera would have heard what happened between her and Secretary-General Kent. Half of them already knew before they'd gone to bed. It was the only subject being talked about in the Mall, in the labs, up and down the staircases, and along the halls.

She'd come back tomorrow, and then what?

The lights would come up to full morning, and he'd still have Bowerman and Cleary trying to get into the base system and calling him a hypocrite. He still wouldn't know who killed Derek and Kevin. He didn't even know who sent that picture that Helen had decided was a direct attack against her and Venera.

Or rather, he might know. He just didn't want to look.

What if it were Ben? Without Ben's urging, she might give up this whole revolutionary idea. Maybe she was just grasping at the straws he held out. Without him, Michael could talk her out of this.

But he'd have to do it quickly. He'd have to have the evidence in hand when Helen got off the shuttle. He couldn't give anybody time to think.

Which meant he'd have to open Schoma's com files.

Well, maybe he'd nursed this particular secret long enough. He was expecting everybody else to take responsibility for their actions in this farce; he had to be ready to take on his.

Once he'd shown Helen what a mess they were really in, they could call Yan Su in on their side and hash out a compromise with the U.N. Then he could find out who had taken Derek and Kevin's lives, and everything could get back to the way it was supposed to be. Well, mostly. They'd still have the aliens to deal with, but at least the human order would be restored.

Right then, alone, in the silence and the darkness, the human order was all Michael cared about.

D'seun had never seen an experiment house as crowded as Tr'es had managed to make hers. Yards of encapsulated holding racks made a stiff net strung wall to wall and floor to ceiling.

The net left no room even for one person to stretch his or her wings. Tr'es climbed clumsily from rack to rack with her recorder bobbing through the air behind her. The racks were full of specimen spheres and microcosms that held the raw materials from both the New People they had acquired. Most of them, D'seun saw, were solutions of various colors—red, blue, yellow, gray, even a deep greenish purple. There was a skull, recognizable mainly by its eye sockets. Tr'es's tools had separated it neatly into plates, exposing the wrinkled gray matter underneath. It was remarkably compact. Tr'es had told him it was the major nervous center. The New People, it seemed, thought with only part of their bodies.

"Good luck, Ambassador," said Tr'es, climbing over the near-est rack, carefully not touching the spheres encasing the raw materials, D'seun noticed. "How can I help you?"

D'seun held onto the threshold with one hand to keep him-self in place. "Good luck, Tr'es. Your work is going well?"

Pride swelled the engineer up until D'seun thought she would burst. "There is such a wealth of material here, Ambas-sador. We lost next to nothing this time, because we had ap-propriate stasis containers and microcosms ready to hold the materials." She spread her crest out. The individual tendrils brushed the racks surrounding her. "It is a vision of an entirely different way of arranging and spreading life. But"—she went on excitedly before he could speak—"there are some shocking familiarities on the molecular level. This may be confirmation that life is patterned, not random. That the life we see is as it is because this is *the* working template. . . ."

D'seun clacked his teeth at her enthusiasm. "Engineer, while I sympathize with your eagerness to reshape our notions of the nature of the universe"—she shrank in on herself, abashed—"are you aware of the nature of the debate happening in the Law Meet?"

Her crest ruffled. "I had heard, Ambassador."

D'seun dropped himself directly into her line of sight. "It is becoming increasingly likely that the distant family of the New People will be declared insane. We need to know if you have found anything in terms of a molecular solution, should we need to separate out their raw materials."

Tr'es stilled and shrank. "Insane?"

D'seun dipped his muzzle. "One family of them may be."

"A deep shame that they let this happen to themselves." Her words barely reached him. "They are so elegant, so complex."

"Perhaps because of their complexity, they were unable to prevent this tragedy," suggested D'seun. The words felt good as he said them. After all, how much damage had the People themselves done because they didn't understand the true com-plexity of Home? But New Home was a simple world. They would be able to control what they did here. No more cities would die under their hands.

Tr'es's gaze drifted from specimen to specimen. "There are several possibilities," she said slowly. "Like us, they actually live in symbiosis with all manner of monocellulars. There is a particular one. . . ." She clambered through the racks, climbing over and under them without regard to orientation.

We have to get this child more room, thought D'seun idly. *Surely we are not that pressed for resources.*

She stopped by a specimen microcosm full of a hazy gray solution. "I found it in some of the orifice membranes. It seemed to be doing no harm, but when I cultured it in some tissue and bone samples, it seemed willing to feed on whatever it found, very like a wild yeast. I think it maintains a balance in the New Person's body. But that balance can be tipped, by, say, increasing its concentration in the body or possibly a chemical trigger that would turn the benign strain virulent." She paused again, studying her brew. "It uses the chemicals trigger method naturally, so that might be the course to follow."

"Could you pursue that line of research?" asked D'seun, swelling slightly. "If we need it, we will need it soon." He gazed around her ordered chaos. "I will see you are granted help and more space."

"Thank you, Ambassador." There was gratitude in her words, but still she deflated where she clung. "Are they really insane, Ambassador?"

"Some of them are," he said, kindly. He could tell her more later, if that became necessary. "Only some. As are some of us."

"Then it will be a kindness to the rest if we do this." One of her forehands hovered over the specimen sphere.

D'seun was tempted to clack his teeth at her piety, but he did not. Even after all she had seen, Tr'es still believed that life truly did help life, on all levels and in all ways. It was one of the qualities that made a good research engineer. If she needed to justify what she was about to help do to the New People in order to work well and quickly, he would willingly help her.

"A true kindness, because the insane family is threatening to cut the sane off from the resources they need to live." That startled her. She had not heard this part. She stared at him, horrified. D'seun dipped his muzzle. "It's true. You'd best get to work, Engineer."

"Yes, Ambassador." She started speaking in a command language so specialized, D'seun understood only one word in three. A number of tools detached themselves from the caretakers inside the crystalline racks and began creeping toward the gray-filled microcosm.

D'seun left her to her work.

New Home's world portal had no securitors, no recorders, no gates. But it had no privacy either. The entire base knew when it was in use and exactly who was going through. Br'sei had spent the past dodec-hour engineering a need for fresh monocellular templates, because there were still some mutations around Living Highland 98 that he didn't like the look of and he did not want them to work their way up the chain when there was a chain for them to work their way up, of course.

He had not asked Ambassador D'seun for permission to return to Home. He had asked Ambassador K'ptai instead while she was on the way to the grand debate D'seun had called. She had quickly granted his request and vanished into the new debating chamber that his people had grown for them.

For now we have ambassadors again, and we must do nothing without their official notice, thought Br'sei as he waited in the center of the portal for its light to reach for him. *Oh yes, we all have a voice, and we all have a vote, but what does it mean, unless those who overfly us all approve?*

They were bleak, cynical thoughts, but he did not even try to disperse them as the portal's light enfolded him and carried him back to Home.

T'sha had been an engineer. T'sha saw the patterns of life. T'sha would not let this happen without a hearing.

T'sha did not owe D'seun her future.

Br'sei rose from the light into the vast metal cage of struts and supports that held the World Portals of Home. The technicians fluttered and fussed about drain of generators and danger to delicate connections. Br'sei apologized to them all and flew out of there at the lowest possible height to show his shame at

having put them through any trouble. It was quicker than trying to assert his rank, and the whole sky knew he'd had
enough practice at humility lately.

Out in the open air, he returned to his proper size and flight
path. Several public-use kites were moored to the portal cluster's chitinous outer frame. Br'sei picked the closest and settled
himself onto its perches.

"Take me to Ca'aed," he said in the kite's command language. "The flight is urgent."

But the kite hesitated. "Ca'aed is under strict quarantine. I
cannot take you there."

Br'sei pulled his muzzle back. Of course. Ca'aed was ill. In
all his turbulent worry and need, he'd almost forgotten why
T'sha was no longer on New Home.

*I have flown in a dead world too long. I've forgotten what it
is to be part of the greater balance of life.*

But nothing had changed. The debate on New Home was
forging ahead, whether Ca'aed was sick or well.

"Take me as close as you can," Br'sei ordered the kite.

The kite's ligaments trembled, but it was a lawful order and
the kite could not refuse. It unfurled its sails and tails and lifted
itself free of the mooring clamp.

The canopy sped away under them, filling the wind and Br'-
sei with rich life. He felt pleasantly dizzy drinking in the living
air, but he could not make himself relax. He kept watching the
colors rushing away underneath him, looking for gaps in the
canopy's growth, or worse, the telltale grays, browns, and
blacks that indicated an untended patch of disease.

How sick was the world? He was not sure anyone really
knew anymore. Oh, they made reports and projections, and
filled microcosms with guesses. But no one really knew.
D'seun thought he did. But then, D'seun thought he knew the
New People were insane and needed to be killed. Br'sei
might even have believed him if he hadn't seen them for himself and if he hadn't known how early D'seun had reached
that conclusion.

Br'sei no longer had any doubt that it was D'seun who was

insane. Could it be proved, though? That was the question. Br'sei owed D'seun so much. . . .

If D'seun were found insane, then Br'sei owed him nothing. But if insanity could not be proved and it was Br'sei who made the accusation, then D'seun could take him into court, denounce him for malice, and seek his indenture.

Br'sei had been indentured before. He wore the marks of it. He'd sworn it would not happen again. Not even for something as important as this.

I am a coward. Br'sei shrank in on himself, but he did not tell the kite to change direction.

At last, the kite slowed its flight. "This is as far as I may go," it said, furling its wings and banking away.

Br'sei looked to the southwest. Warning beacons floated in a tidy net in front of the kite, each barely a thousand yards from the other. They seemed to be guarding nothing but the busy, healthy canopy, though. He heard no sounds except for the wind. He tasted the currents, and they seemed clear. On the horizon sat a single gray smudge, which he supposed must be Ca'aed.

A warning net this far out? No one was taking any chances. The situation must be very bad.

Br'sei lifted himself off the perches. The kite quivered and breezed away before he had even cleared its tendons. Br'sei rattled his wings, uncertain whether to be amused or worried. Regardless, he flew toward the warning net and felt his skin begin to prickle from the currents it sent out.

"Attention," said his headset automatically. "You are approaching a quarantined area. Please select an alternate path."

"Quiet," ordered Br'sei. "Find me Ambassador T'sha. Tell her I am waiting at the quarantine boundary."

Silence stretched out around him, except for the distant noise of the wind through the canopy. No one came, no one went. He was used to solitude and emptiness but not in a world where he could taste life. It was eerie.

He strained the wind through his teeth. His engineer's palate had lost some of its sensitivity but not too much. He cataloged the flavors and sensations in his mind.

His headset remained silent. Br'sei searched tastes and scents for the rank sweetness of disease and found none. Good, perhaps this was an overreaction. There had been so much illness that it was better to be safe, especially if some vectors remained unidentified.

Eventually, the headset spoke. "Good luck, Engineer Br'sei. This is speaker Pa'and. Ambassador T'sha cannot answer you now. I offer my help."

Br'sei beat his wings impatiently, but kept the emotion from his voice. "I have come from New Home. There is an emergency. I must see Ambassador T'sha."

Silence for a moment and then, "There is an emergency here too, Engineer."

"I know." Br'sei dipped his muzzle, although there was no one to see except the warning beacons. "I am an engineer. Perhaps I can help."

Silence again. "I thank you for your offer, Engineer Br'sei, but if you enter the quarantine, I cannot promise you will be allowed to leave it."

Br'sei hesitated, fanning his wings uneasily. Well, he would find his way back when the time came. Without T'sha, D'seun would have no opposing voice on New Home. It would become his world.

"I will come in. I may be able to help."

"I would thank you for your help," answered Speaker Pa'and. "I have sent the entry command to the quarantine net."

While Br'sei watched, four of the beacons faded from green to brown. He darted through the gap. On the other side, he took his bearings on the gray smudge on the horizon and beat his wings until he found a soaring wind to carry him forward on its back.

Br'sei had been to Ca'aed many times. As an apprentice, he had been required to study in each of the twenty-four ancients, where life had grown layer upon layer for more centuries than anyone could accurately count. While he explored the depth and breadth of its body, he had talked to the city. He'd found a kind of openness in Ca'aed that was sometimes lacking in the other truly old cities. There had been contentment there, beyond duty and pride, and kindness. He'd briefly considered asking for adoption, but his own birth city needed free citizens so badly that he never had.

The horizon distortion began to clear, and Ca'aed came into focus. Something was wrong, though, and Br'sei couldn't quite make it out. He strained his eyes. He saw the gold shadows of the citizens flying about their business. He saw the wake villages, but why did they look like they were being towed by their people?

What am I seeing? Br'sei angled his wings to find more speed in the wind.

Voices touched him. The faint voices of people called to each other through the air. Between them came the strong voices of the city, directing, arguing, reassuring. Under it all, Br'sei heard pain. Pain restrained with great strength, but it was there.

At last, his eyes resolved portions of the panorama in front of him, but for a long, agonizing moment, his soul refused to believe his eyes.

He saw a gleaming white bone, as broad as his own torso, laid bare to the wind and a cluster of people layering it over with something pink and translucent.

He saw six people rise from the city with a quarantine net held between them. Inside the net hung something misshapen and patched with gray.

He saw that what surrounded Ca'aed were not its wake villages. Those hung in the distance, like children afraid to come too close. These were great segments of coral wall, tangles of muscle, tendon and ligament, sections of skin and flesh gone colorless with fungal tumors, air sacs, intestines, veins, even a heart. One of the city's huge, precious hearts hung, blackened and distorted, in a quarantine blanket with a flock of tools inside the blanket, and a flock of engineers outside.

They're cutting the city. Life and breath, they're cutting *the city*. Horror drew his bones together.

The delicate perfume of disease touched him, and it was all Br'sei could do to keep going.

As he drew near the very edges of the furious activity, a female flew toward him. For for a moment, Br'sei thought it was Ambassador T'sha. But as she reached him, he saw she was older than the ambassador, although they shared a coloring of crest and skin. She and T'sha were birth family though, that much was clear.

"Good luck, Engineer Br'sei." She raised her hands in greeting.

"Good luck, Speaker Pa'and," replied Br'sei, reading her tattoos.

They touched hands, but Br'sei could not keep his gaze focused on her. It kept skittering over her back to the surgery, the desperate butchery, of Ca'aed.

"I didn't know," he murmured, shrinking in around his apology.

The speaker just dipped her muzzle. "How could you, Engineer? But perhaps you see now why the ambassador cannot speak with you."

Br'sei lifted his muzzle. Sounds and scents filled him—strained voices, blood, rot, pain, the sounds of knives in flesh and saws in bone. He could not escape it or turn away.

I should leave, or I should help. Ca'aed was one of the first cities, an ancient life, a good soul with irreplaceable memories and knowledge locked inside it. He should not be scheming to take away its ambassador at the time she was most needed.

Even knowing that, he spoke. "Let me see the ambassador, Speaker Pa'and. I swear to you, this is not a small thing. It affects the entire future of New Home and it needs her voice. Our future, our hope, Ca'aed's hope, needs her voice."

Speaker Pa'and pulled back. She fanned her wings to rise a little above him. Br'sei worked to hold his bones still.

She will refuse. She will not believe me. Tension sang through Br'sei's soul. *I will have to go back alone.*

"She is consulting with some of the other speakers and the archivers," said Pa'and. "I will take you to her."

"Thank you," replied Br'sei fervently.

Pa'and gave him no answer. She just turned on her wingtip and led him a long a curving path around and over the edge of the ruined city. People dived in and out of its body, calling to

one another. Br'sei saw engineers, harvesters, and conservators, and dozens of others whose tattoos he could not make
out, all borne up by hard purpose and fear as much as by the
wind underneath them.

*They do feel the death. They will not say the word to them-
selves, but they feel it.* Br'sei kept his muzzle closed and followed the speaker.

Around a bulbous outcropping in Ca'aed's wall, Br'sei finally
saw T'sha. She hung swollen between the city and three males,
as if she sought to protect Ca'aed from their approach.

"We cannot promise them any of our people until all the
vectors for this cancer have been analyzed," T'sha was saying.
"We can promise them full and free use of any knowledge their
people discover, and surely there are some futures they'd be
interested in."

One of the males deflated. Br'sei thought he might be a
brother, for he shared his colors with both T'sha and Pa'and.
"We've spread the offer of knowledge too thin, Ambassador.
It's losing its value. We are going to have to offer people or, at
the very least, skills."

Frustration ruffled T'sha's crest. She turned toward the male
speaker. "What volunteers have we . . ." The sentence died
away as she saw Pa'and and she saw Br'sei.

"Your pardon," said T'sha to her advisers. She rose above
them and flew to meet the new arrivals. "Engineer Br'sei, what
are you doing here?"

No words came. What was he doing here? What had driven
him to the heart of this disaster? For a moment he honestly
couldn't remember.

"A moment please, Speaker?" said T'sha to Pa'and. Pa'and
dipped her muzzle and soared away to the cluster of waiting
males.

She was exhausted, Br'sei could see that at a glance. The
color had run from her skin, leaving her pale and gaunt as if
she could not inflate herself fully anymore. Her words felt brittle against his muzzle as she spoke.

"Tell me what has happened, Engineer."

Br'sei deflated. "Ambassador D'seun is trying to convince the

New Home Law Meet that the New People should be turned to raw materials."

He expected an explosion, but it did not come. She just settled lower in the air as if she had lost all strength and only the wind kept her from falling. "Openly now? What changed?" She looked up at him, sorry and tired, and too full of these things to be afraid.

He let himself drop until his eyes were level with hers, and he told her how the New People came to the base as the ambassadors arrived and how they spoke with each other and all seemed well, until D'seun . . . until D'seun . . .

"Until D'seun and his words overrode whatever the New People actually said." T'sha brushed her wing past her eyes. "Life of my mother, Br'sei. He'd have them kill a whole world full of people?"

Br'sei dipped his muzzle.

"And they're listening?" A spark rose in her, burned, and swelled her skin with its heat. "No one has called this what it is?"

But Br'sei noticed even she did not say the word *insanity*. "There are promises involved," he told her. "I haven't tracked them all yet."

"Ambassador Z'eth." T'sha turned her face to her ruined city. Its miasma of scents and voices washed over her.

She stretched her wings to their limits. "Why?" she whispered to the wind and the pain and the ruin. "Is it my greed? Did I destroy the balance of our lives?"

"No." Br'sei pressed closer, making his words strong and heavy so she could not mistake them. "Not yours, D'seun's. You have to go back. You have to tell them what's happening. They'll listen to you. You're—"

"I'm what?" she whirled to face him, and he felt a dare in her words. "I'm nothing, Br'sei."

"You're an ambassador," he said evenly. "One of their own."

She dipped her muzzle. "An ambassador who tried to do everything at once, who tried to compass worlds, and now her own city is dying because of it."

Br'sei shrank under her words. He couldn't help it. "This disease is not your fault."

"Perhaps not." She fanned backwards. She was shrinking again as the spark within her faded away. "But it is my responsibility."

Br'sei felt his bones go absolutely still. "You will not come back? You will let the New People die?"

"Are they children?" she asked bitterly, dismissively. "Have they no ambassadors to speak for them?"

"Yes, they are children." He swooped closer. She could not do this. She could not turn away and leave him, leave *them,* he corrected himself, alone to face the insane and the greedy. "They do not understand what their words mean to us. I am sure of it."

T'sha drew closer, until her muzzle touched his. "What changed your mind, Br'sei? You were not so sure of them when you and I went to view their city?"

Br'sei held size and place. "I had not met them then. I had not seen them for myself." He pressed his muzzle even more tightly against hers. "You were an engineer once, Ambassador. You understand how deep the roots of our instincts sink. You know what it is to feel the balance, the wonder of new life that is sane and whole. You've brought such life into the world with your own work. There have been moments when you just *knew* that this was good and it would work." Now he pulled away and spread his wings. "I looked at them when they came fearlessly to meet us, and I just *knew.*"

For a moment, he had her. He could tell by the shine in her eyes and the angle of her wings and the taste of the air near her skin. But in the next moment she had swollen, and risen, and turned away.

"I will not leave my city."

All the air left Br'sei at a rush. He had lost. They had lost. He had tried to bring protection for himself and the New People, and that had failed.

Now what? he asked himself, but he already knew the answer, and it frightened him.

"There is nothing I can say then." He spoke his words to her wings and crest. "But, you must forgive me, I am going back. I am going to warn them. Maybe they can defend themselves, maybe not. But life helps life, and I must do what I can."

He banked around and flew away. There were still the quarantine checks with their bother and worry to get through, but he would deal with that. He had to. He was all the New People had now, all New Home had. Himself, alone and afraid.

In some small part of his soul, he hoped to feel the touch of T'sha's voice against his back, but it did not come.

Chapter Eighteen

"Scarab Ten approaching the runway. Welcome home, Scarab Ten."

Tori's words reverberated through the P.A. From the internal speakers, Michael heard a tinny reproduction of the cheers filling the corridors.

At the sound, his fists clenched until his knuckles turned white.

Michael remembered being selected for the governing board. He remembered reading the notice on his briefcase screen, leaping up, yelling like a fool, and dancing Jolynn, who was then six months pregnant, around the apartment.

Gregory Schoma had retired and moved back to Mother Earth. Helen and Ben between them had decided that his replacement should be someone born on the station. They had noticed the prestige schism growing between research and nonresearch personnel. That was a problem all outposts had dealt with since the first permanent settlement in Antarctica. They had also noticed, however, that a growing number of the nonresearch personnel were native Venerans.

That did not suit either of their visions for the base. So they looked for a Veneran who would be acceptable to the various funding groups and found Michael Lum. Veneran-born, Earth-educated, a talented administrator, trained by Schoma himself, and married, with a baby on the way.

"I know," he'd told Jolynn, when they'd collapsed breathless on the sofa. "It's partly a face appointment, but that's okay. Just think what I can do from up there. Think about it! I'll be doing the security and infrastructure maintenance, but I'll be constantly meeting with Bennet Godwin. Access to Dr. Personnel himself."

From the beginning, Ben had shown concern for the issues Michael raised. Ben had listened. Ben had worked with him to improve the base's on-site education facilities, had worked to get Terran equivalencies and Terran accreditations for Venera's schools. He'd worked quietly to see that the details of tech and maintenancer jobs were publicized to those children so that they could be someone important to the well-being of their world, rather than just a janitor.

And Grandma Helen had smiled on them all, and it had been good.

And now? Michael's knuckles ached. Now he had opened the files he swore he was never, ever going to use. He had his people looking at Grace Meyer as a murderer and Ben Godwin as a traitor, and he didn't know what to do.

He heard the faint rumble of the hangar airlock cycling for the scarab.

"Airlock open, you're clear for the hangar, Scarab Ten," announced Tori.

Michael had seen Tori take her post at flight control this morning. He'd done high school equivalencies with her. She was a cynic. She took nothing at face value. But at that moment, she had looked like she had seen a miracle, or at least a really fine illusion.

She wasn't the only one. The whole base had turned out to welcome Helen home. Somehow, her trip down to talk to the aliens had traveled through the rumor mill and become a Historic Meeting of Peoples to Reach a Great Accord. Everyone had heard about Secretary Kent's conversation with Helen, along with one version or another of its unveiled threats.

A copy of the transmission had even shown up in the base's public stream. Michael suspected Ben was responsible for that. Ben was responsible for so many things.

You wait, he thought toward the man standing tall, and strangely serene, at his side. *What will you do when she finds out you are the traitor?*

Michael and Ben stood in the passenger clearing area, watching on the wall screen as the hangar doors parted and the scarab, its cermet hide scarred and pitted from use, rolled in between the silent rows of machinery—shuttles on the left side, the other scarabs on the right. It slotted itself neatly into the empty bay.

"Extending ramp," said Tori as a walkway stretched itself toward the scarab's airlock. It wasn't all that hot out there, and the pressure was almost exactly one atmosphere, but the combination of CO_2 and hydrogen sulfides was not healthy to breathe for very long.

There followed a series of rumbles and whooshes familiar to anyone who had traveled in space, as more airlocks opened. Then, Helen Failia, looking as straight-backed and determined as ever, marched down the narrow connector.

"Welcome home, Dr. Failia," announced Tori over the intercom.

Helen looked only a little startled. "Thank you, Tori," she said in the general direction of the open intercom. Then Helen faced Michael and Ben. "A full welcoming committee, gentlemen?"

Ben practically beamed. "It's not just us." He swept a hand toward the intercom. Helen's eyebrows rose as she identified the rushing noise as voices and exclamations.

"Well," she said, sounding slightly pleased. "We'd better not keep them waiting."

"Helen." Michael quickly sidestepped into her path. "There's been a couple of developments you need to know about, right now."

Helen frowned, but Ben scowled. A dark-red flush crept up his neck. ·

"Okay." Helen glanced around. There was a small lounge off the corner of the clearing area for the occasional passenger who came down sick and dizzy from the transitions between weightlessness and full gravity. "Gentlemen . . ." She gestured for them to follow her.

But movement caught his eye, and Michael glanced back toward the connector. Josh Kenyon and Veronica Hatch walked out into flight control. Veronica caught Michael's eye and lengthened her stride.

"I'd like to talk with you," she said as she brushed past him. Then she set her jaw and headed for the hallway, shouldering her way through Helen's crowd. Michael looked back again at Josh. Josh simply nodded and turned away, vanishing back into the scarab for reasons which he obviously did not feel like sharing.

Deal with that later. Michael hurried to catch up with Helen and Ben.

The three of them crowded into the lounge, with its small table, a couple of chairs, and an old-fashioned fainting couch. Helen walked to the back wall, turned around, and folded her arms.

"Well?"

Which first? Michael thought of the cheering crowds and the recording of Helen's conversation with Mother Earth.

"We know who sent the photo to the C.A.C."

Helen took a deep breath and expelled it slowly. Michael couldn't help glancing at Ben. He'd gone ghost white, and Michael smiled inwardly with a kind of grim triumph.

Helen looked from Michael to Ben. He saw the realization come to her. Her face shifted, the expression turning from impatience, to shock, to disbelief, and finally to sorrow.

"No, Ben. You didn't."

"I'm sorry," Ben spread his hands. "I . . . I wanted you to see what Mother Earth really planned for us. It was the only way."

"Trying to push us into a revolution was an answer?" demanded Michael. Ben looked regretful, but not at what he'd done. He was only sorry he'd gotten caught. "I'd hate to hear the question."

Ben just shook his head. His color was returning, and now he was a little too pink. "You did hear it. You just weren't listening."

Which didn't even deserve an answer.

Helen collapsed into one of the chairs. She pressed her forehead against her palm and huddled in on herself as if she were cold or frightened. Michael didn't blame her. He'd felt the same way when he saw the files. Ben wasn't who he'd pretended to be all these years. He had lied and manipulated them all from the start. This was just the latest in a long series of deceptions. Michael wasn't even sure it was the worst.

Michael opened his mouth to tell Helen, but she lifted her head. "Well, it doesn't really matter," she said.

Michael choked. "What?"

"We need Ben." Helen got to her feet. "It would have come down to this sooner or later anyway. I need you both to keep Venera working."

"I'm with you Helen," breathed Ben, all sincere loyalty.

"Holy God!" Michael swung around to face him. "You! She doesn't even know who you are!"

Helen stayed still, swaying a little on her feet. *She must be exhausted,* thought Michael. *Or just stunned. Maybe that's good. Let me show her how bad this is. Shock her back to her senses.*

"His name is Paul Mabrey," said Michael, looking straight at Ben. The pink tinge to his skin faded, then darkened, until he turned red with what? Shame? Anger? "He followed Fuller through the Bradbury Rebellion and then disappeared under cover of an alias, leaving the Paul Mabrey identity as one of the sharpest clip-outs our two U.N. security drones say they've ever seen." Ben's eyes narrowed, just a little, and Michael wondered what he was thinking. It didn't matter. "He used you, Helen. He used you and Venera."

"No." Ben scrubbed his scalp. "Never. Not until the yewners threatened to take us over. Helen, I just wanted Venera to be free."

For the first time in his entire life, Michael saw Helen look her age. She stepped slowly and carefully around the table and stopped when she reached Michael's side. She laid her hand on his forearm, and he felt the dryness of her skin, and the deep grooves in her palm.

Grandma Helen looked up at him with her dark eyes. "It doesn't matter Michael," she told him. "We've already taken the first steps and we can't turn around." She squeezed his arm, and continued past him toward the door. Ben flushed even darker with triumph.

No, no. I will not let it go like this. Michael had control of his voice again. "First steps?" he demanded of her back. "And we're standing on, what? Fraud? Murder? Grace Meyer murdered Derek and Kevin to keep them from tagging her as one of their bosses. Are you going to say that doesn't matter?" He strode forward until he was beside her, at least partly in her line of sight. "They were Venerans, Helen. They were born here. They expected you to look out for them." His hands flailed helplessly in the air. "Are you going to let them down?"

That stopped her. She stood there, just on the edge of the door's sensor range. Michael's heart hammered hard in his chest. She had to listen to that. She had to.

"Give Grace to the yewners," she said. "They can take her down to Mother Earth for prosecution."

"Helen!" Michael cried. No other word would come.

"No, Michael," she said softly. "It's too late. The U.N. wants to take the world away from us. We are not going to let them."

She stepped forward. The door swished open. She walked through the empty staging area and out into the crowded hallway beyond, with Ben right at her heels.

There was nothing Michael could do but follow along.

By the time he got to the corridor, the noise was deafening. People lined the sides of the staircase three deep. Applause, cheers, and cries of "Welcome home!" showered down on Helen from all sides.

As Michael and Ben trailed behind, Helen descended the stairs. She shook hands, clasped arms, waved, looking for all the world like a politician or like royalty. She had been both in her time, without the titles, but with the jobs, and she was milking that experience now for all it was worth.

Helen turned off the staircase when they reached the Mall. The entire place was jammed. Parents held their children on their shoulders. People whistled through their teeth and waved as Helen worked her way through, laughing and trying to shush the crowd, shouting she had something to say.

A space cleared in front of them. Someone shoved a table

forward. Ben saw what was coming and held Helen's hand while she stepped up on a chair and then up onto the table, turning it into an impromptu dais with himself and Michael flanking her like an honor guard.

Now, Helen's arm-waving could be seen, and silence spread out from around her like a wave. She looked small up there, but pride gave her stature. Pride and confidence. Helen knew exactly what she was doing, or at least she thought she did. Michael glanced at the public screens and there was Helen. Someone had been on the ball and gotten the cameras going.

"You have already heard that I cut the line on the C.A.C.," said Helen, loud enough to be heard over the ambient noise of the gathering. "Now I want you to hear why."

Yes, tell us why, Grandma Helen, thought Michael as he felt his neck muscles tense.

"I did it because they were about to remove from us the one right we have always had. The right to conduct our lives, our work, as we see fit. They intend to tell us what to think about the new race of people who have come to our world. Our world, not their world. They have not spoken with these new people. They have not listened to them. But we have. We know that they are scientists and explorers, just as we are. They are looking to make new homes for their people, to carry out their work and live their lives, just like we were when we created Venera forty years ago. Their world is in crisis, and they want only to alleviate that crisis.

"This is what we heard. This is what we told the C.A.C. How did they respond?" Helen spread her hands as if amazed at the wonder of it all. "They told us we knew nothing. We didn't count. Our research, our expertise, our collective experience meant nothing, nothing at all, because we were not politi-cians." She stressed the word *politicians* like most people stressed the word *bastard*.

"The politicians from Mother Earth, on the other hand, have determined that our new neighbors are dangerous, despite the fact that those neighbors have done nothing but watch us until lives were in danger. Then they intervened and saved all those who could be saved.

"But that doesn't matter. The politicians of Earth have de-cided our neighbors are dangerous, so dangerous they are. Be-cause we do not agree, because we know that judgments must be based on facts, on the evidence, not on rumor and fear, the yewners are going to invade our home, push us aside, and tell our neighbors that they must leave or die."

She paused for breath. No one moved. No one murmured or stirred. She had them. They heard her and they understood. Only some of this had actually been said out loud by Secretary Kent, but the people around her accepted Helen's expansions without question.

Cold fear reached inside Michael's mind.

"To make good on this threat, they need Venera. They need our home, our equipment, the products of our sweat and our vision. They need our minds, our experience, and our inspira-tion. If we deny them Venera, if we deny them ourselves, they cannot threaten the murder of the only other intelligent species humanity has ever met.

"I cannot, I will not, order anyone to cooperate with this aim. I can only say I will not permit this invasion. I will not permit this usurpation of everything I have worked for. I will stand alone if I need to, but I still stand, here." She stabbed her finger toward the floor. "On this deck which I helped build, in this place that I helped, that you helped, bring to life. No one is going to take it away from me and use it for murder, or threat of murder. No one. Ever."

The cheer was deafening. It rang off the walls and the ceil-ing and reverberated through the deck. It surrounded the peo-ple who thrust fists into the air, hugged each other, stomped their feet, clapped hands, babbled out their agreement. A few, a very few, Michael noticed, stood stock still, their eyes cast down and their faces pale. A very few had the good sense to stand in the presence of that speech and be afraid.

And you? he asked himself as he watched the storm of en-ergy and anger pouring out around him. *She's doing it. She's starting her own little dictatorship right here. Look at it. The first steps have already been taken. What are you going to do about it?*

Michael searched the crowd for familiar faces, looking to see what friends and colleagues were doing. A shock of fear ran through him. He couldn't recognize anybody. They'd been transformed out of all recognition by their excitement, by Helen.

I can't even see Jolynn. Where's Jolynn?

Helen held up her hands for silence. It took a moment, but the crowd quieted down and turned its attention fully on her again.

"This is not going to be easy. This is not going to be without risk. The C.A.C. is sending up the military to take Venera from us. They've threatened a trade embargo and a complete communications shutdown. If we're going to resist, we're going to be placing ourselves and our children in danger.

"I do not want anyone at risk who does not believe in what we are doing. I do not want any children at risk at all. The *Queen Isabella* enters high orbit tomorrow, and they will take with them anyone who wants to leave.

"We only have a few days to perform an evacuation and set our defense plans into motion. Fortunately, we only need a few days. I want everyone to consider their lives, their needs, and their beliefs and then make up their minds. No judgment will be cast on anyone who wants to leave. If you cannot support us honestly, then you are better off elsewhere, and we are better off with you elsewhere."

Silence. Some shuffling feet and rustling cloth and a few coughs, but mostly profound, attentive silence.

"Finally, let me say this. Our new neighbors have promised to help us. We are not alone in what we do. We will never be alone and at anyone's mercy again."

Another cheer, just as deafening, just as prolonged, and just as transforming. Michael looked from Helen, who looked grimly satisfied with her work, to Ben standing beside her. Ben's face was flushed, but not with anger. This time it was with an unfamiliar excitement, as if he were looking forward to what was coming next.

Suddenly Michael couldn't stand it anymore. He turned on his heel and walked away. He didn't know if Helen or Ben looked after him. He didn't care. He was barely aware of the touch of bodies against him as he pushed his way toward the stairs. He had to get out of the hall, away from the crowd of strangers around Helen.

Where is Jolynn?

The residential corridors were empty. Everyone who hadn't crammed into the Mall was in their rooms, he supposed, watching the spectacle.

Stop. Wait. Michael made himself halt. He stood there, hand on the wall, feeling the slight padding of the soundproofing under his fingers, as if it would keep him grounded and remind him where he really was and what was really going on.

Jolynn is at home. She's with the kids. Everything is okay. He took a deep breath. *You need to work out what you're doing. Are you just following along, or are you going to make your own plans?*

Like talking to Veronica Hatch about the possibility of useful action?

He barely knew Dr. Hatch. There were a thousand other people he would have rather had on the tip of his mind right now. But she was outside it. She didn't have the visceral connection to Venera that almost everyone else here did. Even more important, she'd actually talked to the aliens. She was on the front lines of the whole mess, at least when it came to information, and information was what he needed if he were going to explode Helen's inspirational speech.

He redirected his steps, up one level and around one of the inner corridor rings until he stood in front of Dr. Hatch's guest quarters. The door scanned him and opened automatically.

You were expected, he thought as he went inside.

Dr. Hatch sat cross-legged on her bed, doing something with her briefcase. She looked up as he came in but did not look surprised.

"That was quick," she said, shutting the briefcase down. "Thank you for coming."

Michael nodded and took a seat on the desk chair. "What did you want to talk about, Dr. Hatch?"

She met his gaze, and he knew what she saw. She saw fear

and she saw anger. She probably even saw disbelief at the display he had just witnessed. How had it happened? How had it gotten so bad so fast?

"We need help with a little espionage," said Dr. Hatch.

"We?"

She nodded. "Me and Dr. Kenyon." Dr. Hatch leaned forward, resting her elbows on her knees. "We've got to talk to the People, without your friends on the governing board knowing about it."

"We do?" Michael's eyebrows lifted.

Dr. Hatch frowned, hard. "Look, the People don't know what they're getting dragged into. They haven't been told. It sounds like we're asking them for more rescue help or maybe a technology exchange, not help dealing with an invasion. We're playing games with them. It is not fair and it is not right."

"What the aliens think is the least of our problems," said Michael, remembering the crowd cheering Helen on. Helen didn't know what was really going on. She hadn't heard him the first time. That was the only answer. He could walk in there and show her again what Ben had done, what Grace had done, and then, and then . . .

And then what? She'd be alone in the Throne Room, with him, and what would he say to her then? How would he stop this, stop her? What if he said the wrong thing and she decided he was a traitor and should be put on the ship as well? Would she think to send Jolynn and the boys with him? Would he have to ask to be allowed to remain with his family?

Michael didn't know if he could stand that.

I can't believe I'm even thinking like this. Holy God, what's happening to us?

"What the aliens think is the least of our problems, is it?" Dr. Hatch was asking as she raised her own eyebrows, in mockery of his own expression, Michael suspected. "This is all happening because of the People. Because the People came here. Because Helen and Ben think they have the People's support for what they're doing. Without the aliens—" she waved her hand—"poof! Nothing happens, except the exposure of a little well-perpetrated fraud."

"So what do you want to tell them?" asked Michael. "Sit back while we sort this out?"

"Essentially." Dr. Hatch dropped her hand back onto her knee. "They understand politics. If we tell them this is a political debate that needs to be resolved, I think they'll give us the time."

"This is a little more than a political debate." *A little more? Who am I trying to kid?*

"Let me talk to them," said Dr. Hatch, low and earnest. "Let me get them to talk to you. Together we can at least try to pull them out of the equation. Without them, Failia and Godwin will have to deal with the U.N., because without the People, Venera cannot make a real stand."

Michael chewed the inside of his lip and turned the idea over in his mind. Hatch and Kenyon. Josh he had known for years. He was steady, quiet, uncomplicated. He did his work and he went home. Dr. Hatch acted like a fool some days, but she was the one who spotted that the Discovery was fraudulent.

"It's a good idea," he said. "It's worth a shot. But I've got to tell you"—he tugged on the end of his pony tail—"I'm not sure how much I can help you right now. I'm not sure about a whole lot of things."

Veronica nodded, all the bluster and kidding gone from her face. "Just help me not get thrown out of here. I'll take care of the rest."

Michael searched her eyes for a moment. She meant it. She wanted to stay, and he wanted . . .

What do I want?

He wanted to talk to Helen. He wanted her to see what she was doing, to herself, to Venera, to everybody and everything. But he didn't know if she would hear him anymore or if she ever had. He saw the flush in her face as she addressed the crowd, as she finally made Venera truly her own. How could he reach past that? How could he make her hear?

God, God, God, what am I going to do? Jolynn, Chord, Chase—I can't risk them. If I can't make her hear, what do I do?

The image of Jolynn's golden-brown eyes flashed in front of his mind's eye, and he knew. There was one thing that might still reach Helen, and if it didn't work, well, the *Queen Isabella* would be right there.

The engineers had grown a debating chamber for the Law Meet, but there had not been time to grow a very big one. The pink-and-cream shell was barely big enough to hold all the ambassadors who hovered in the air, finding still pockets between the currents of the distracted wind.

Eighteen ambassadors had been assigned to New Home. Each of the twelve specialties was represented, along with six seniors to act as administrators. D'seun knew only a handful of them, but that did not matter. He held Z'eth's vote. The rest would follow along with them as soon as the formal debate was over with.

D'seun hovered near a speaker box improvised from some of Br'sei's lacelike cortices and a frame of stiffened ligaments shielded by nothing more than sail skin. Through the light gaps in the shell's side, he could see the joyous activity of the newly arrived engineers. Surveying expeditions were being set to ride the major latitudes. All the living highlands needed to be located and tested. The winds had to be gauged and mapped, along with as many of the cross-currents as possible. The wind seed that had sprouted needed to be analyzed in terms of growth and evolution so it could be determined what could be best layered on top of it.

So much work, so many minds and souls needed. So many complications, but soon those would be lessened. While all his colleagues listened, the speaker box pulled the record of Z'eth's last conversation with the New Person, Ambassador Helen, and repeated it smoothly. Hearing it again, it sounded no better.

"There are those with whom we disagree about our rights to this world, and consequently yours." The box used its own soft, unimpressive voice to repeat Ambassador Helen's words, as it had no reference for how she really sounded. "They might attempt to cut off our supply routes from the other worlds. We may be forced to ask for a great deal of assistance in maintaining ourselves here."

The final words died away and D'seun expanded himself,

body and wings. No matter what promises he was certain of, he was an ambassador with a case to present.

But before he could begin, Ambassador T'taik rattled her wings. She was from the Calm Northerns, like T'sha, and had the red-and-white crest and burnished bronze skin to prove it.

"Ambassadors, I ask you to keep in mind two things," T'taik said. "The first is that this engineer, Vee, has made no promises or exchanges for representational power among her people. She is just an engineer, trained in the use of tools, not of words. This Ambassador Helen is basing all she knows of us on potentially inaccurate information. This may have led to a poor choice of words. Second"—she raised her hands—"T'sha was in a similar position. Despite her title and power to promise, she is only very new at our work and it may be she misrepresented herself. Ambiguity can be seen for example—"

D'seun ruffled his crest and broke across her words. "You are too hard on our colleague, Ambassador. Her words made the situation abundantly clear. The New People are obviously composed of several different families. The ones who are our neighbors and offer us community are one group, and they are, probably, sane. But these others, this distant family, are not sane. They are greedy and seek to stop the spread not only of life, but of their own offshoots."

T'taik swelled at his words. "Ambassador D'seun, you have been so ready to condemn someone as greedy or insane during this undertaking, I wonder at it."

D'seun shifted his weight on the perches. "I have. I have been overzealous in my desire to claim this world as New Home. I admit this. If the Meet wishes to poll the members about my fitness to give opinion on this issue, I will not argue the question."

It was a good strategy, and one that D'seun could be confident of winning. The ambassadors debated it briefly and the question was soon called. The consensus was that D'seun recognized his overzealousness and would not be denied a voice and vote in future.

"It must be acknowledged, however," said Ambassador D'tran, "that an engineer, someone responsible for building and creating, must know what uses the resources of the world she lives on are being put to. If the New People have a legitimate claim here, why did she not say so? T'sha did make that point clear in her previous conversations." T'sha's last conversation with Engineer Vee had also been played for the Law Meet.

"We do not know for certain that Ambassador T'sha's words were completely clear," replied T'taik. "The New People are not cortices. We cannot read their imprinting to be certain the information has been properly received."

They are listening to her, D'seun felt his bones tighten with worry. *How could they be listening to this?*

"It may be that you are both right."

D'seun turned gratefully to Ambassador Z'eth. A stray breeze blew past, carrying the touch of Z'eth's words on it as she spoke.

"It may be that this New Person, Engineer Vee, did not properly understand what she was being asked and so improperly transmitted and translated that information for her ambassador. It may also be that she is in fear of a family of her people that are insane. Which of us could clearly speak of such a thing to strangers, whose motivations we do not know?"

Z'eth beat her wings twice, lifting herself up over the center of the Meet. "So my first belief is that we need much more time to speak with Ambassador Helen, Engineer Vee, and any other New People who present themselves."

No, no, there is no more time!

"However," Z'eth went on, "if the distant family of the New People is found to be insane, we need to ask what should be done about them."

"Clearly, they need to be prevented from interfering with the New People and New Home," said T'taik. "Their means of transport should be fairly easy to identify and disable."

T'sha must have sent T'taik to speak in her place. That was the only answer. What promise lay there? He had not had time to research this all as thoroughly as he should have. If they listened to this now. . . .

"I say that's not enough, Ambassador T'taik." Ambassador P'eath, who, like D'seun, was a refugee from the Southern

Roughs, inflated her body fully. "When has any insane being been allowed to exist as more than raw materials to build a sane future from?"

T'taik dipped her muzzle. "That is the way it has been, yes. But we have it from Engineer Vee that the New People do not have the same views of how to deal with insanity."

"They would allow insanity to live? To grow in its own way and risk smothering sanity?" P'eath extended her wings. Relief lifted D'seun's body. "With respect, T'taik, it sounds as if our neighbors may be slightly insane themselves."

"Is difference insanity?" inquired T'taik mildly, letting her crest rise as if in surprise. "If it is, we are in great trouble, because the Equatorials and the Northerns will be at each other's throats in the civil courts again."

A general whistle of assent, and some clacking muzzles in chagrin and amusement. Disquiet filled the pockets between D'seun's bones. He looked to Z'eth, who made no move to silence the words. What was she waiting for? Why was she permitting this to continue? She had promised! He had agreed to give her everything he had. He should put an end to this right now, call for a vote and end this display. . . .

The chamber portal opened. All the ambassadors fanned their wings, turning themselves to see what this interruption was.

It was Engineer D'han, shrunk so small he was almost cringing as he floated through the threshold.

"Ambassador, forgive me, but . . . Ambassadors," he stammered, beating his wings and bobbing his head, looking for a friendly face. "We have a translation of one of the last transport-to-base transmissions from the New People. . . ."

Several crests ruffled quizzically. "The New People exchange patterned radiation, as I have told you," D'seun reminded them. "Most of it heads off into the vacuum, but some of it passes between their base and their transports on the surface. We have been monitoring and translating it since they first began, although it is still slow going because it is so tangled with their command languages. The practice greatly improved our speed of communication when we were finally able to speak to them."

"Thank you, Ambassador." Z'eth dipped her muzzle to him and then she dropped herself to D'han's level. "What do they say in this translation you have made?"

D'han seemed to have pulled himself together. His size normalized and his sentences smoothed out. "They say the distant family is insane."

The chamber erupted. Questions and exclamations buffeted D'seun, but even so he swelled in triumph. Now the debate was over. Now they could move.

Z'eth rose up high, spreading her wings and swelling her torso to its fullest extent. "Ambassadors! Ambassadors, please!"

Did you know? D'seun gazed up at Z'eth in awe and admiration. *Did you time this entrance?* She might have. It was well within her skills to delay a message just a little so it might be used to bind the Law Meet together whether they were promised to her or not.

Stillness settled slowly. Z'eth fell back beside D'han, who looked a little dazed now. "How is the distant family insane, Engineer? Tell us exactly."

D'han's gaze darted around the room, amazed to find all the ambassadors pinning him down with their attention. "The distant family says they are sending a force to New Home. They will cut the New People off from the resources of their world and force them to comply with the wishes of the distant family."

"Well then." Z'eth whistled and lifted her muzzle to the entire Meet. "It appears the New People have ended our debate for us. We cannot permit the insane to overrun the sane."

As the whistles of agreement filled the chamber, D'seun's soul swelled.

At last, he thought. *At last. This world will be ours and the New People will be ours or they will be raw materials to serve us and our life.*

At last.

CHAPTER NINETEEN

Crowds thronged in the corridors outside flight control. Children clung to their mother's tunics or their father's arms. Teenagers slumped against the walls, torn between looking tough and being uncertain. Whole families stood around and sorted through bags, trying to make sure everything precious had gotten packed.

Five thousand people—half the base—had decided to stay and sit out whatever the U.N. was going to put them through. A whole five thousand, and Helen was grateful for each person.

But according to the note in her desk that morning, Michael Lum was not one of them.

The crowds parted around her, saying hello or just looking guilty as they did. Helen still had to crane her neck, searching for a truly familiar face amid the crowd that suddenly all looked alike to her.

At last she spotted him. He stood patiently with his wife and their two children. He had one arm around Jolynn and one hand on his older son's shoulder. Jolynn rested both of her hands on the shoulders of the younger boy and looked straight ahead with a kind of grim determination, as if she could make the line move by sheer willpower.

Helen's name rippled through the crowd as she marched up to Michael and his family.

"Good morning, Michael," she said. "Good morning, Jolynn. May I speak with your husband?"

"Certainly, Dr. Failia." Jolynn shuffled backward a fraction of an inch. She and Michael exchanged a look Helen couldn't read, and she felt an irrational stab of annoyance run through her.

Michael said nothing, just crossed to the other side of the corridor a half-step behind Helen. She had to pivot to face him. When she did, she saw his face was full of the gentle humor that had characterized him for so many years.

"I take it you got my resignation," he said.

"I did." She nodded once. "I do not accept it."

"Helen." He dropped his gaze to the floor. "You're going to have to."

A hundred emotions flooded through Helen—sorrow, betrayal, loneliness, desperation. She had no words, no words at all. He was a child of Venera. He was everything they had worked for.

"This is your home, Michael" was all she could think to say.

"And that is my family, Helen." He stabbed a finger at Jolynn, who had her arms around Chord and Chase. "Whom I love. Now, you've got this great idea about saving the world from the madness of Earth and that's fine, but you're doing it by creating more madness."

"I am trying to put an end to—"

"To what?" Michael threw up his hands. "Our stability? Our safety? How many lives is this glorious ending worth? We've got two dead already, Helen. I will not stand around and watch the body count rise."

Helen felt her chest constrict until the pain ran down her arms. She could not lift a hand against his words, which struck her like blows. She could barely think. Michael, Michael who had gone away and returned to become one of the people she trusted the most in all the worlds. How could he say this to her? How could he abandon Venera?

"Do you have any idea what's about to happen?" she asked him coldly. "They are not just coming to end any independent research, any good science we might ever do; they are coming to decide what all of us are going to do with the rest of our lives." She stepped up close to him, trying to fill his world with her words. He had to understand. He had to. "And what about the aliens? Do you really think the U.N. is going to let them build a new home here? The yewners are coming to rob us and them of the future, of our future."

"Our future?" Michael's voice cracked sharply on the second syllable. "Our future based on *what?* Murder? Deception? Wounded pride? Don't you see what you're doing?" He swept out his hand. "You are demanding that the people of Venera give up their lives, their freedom, their futures, their families so you can keep your pretty toy. At the very least, you are going to prison. You might manage to get killed if the U.N. troops decide to come in shooting, and if you don't stop this disaster right now, you are taking five thousand people with you."

"What's happened to you Michael?" Helen searched his face, looking for something she could understand. "The only way we're going to lose is if they divide us. By leaving, you are going to let them walk in here and take whatever they want to, without understanding what's really at stake, without caring—"

"You just don't see it anymore, do you Helen?" His hand swept out, encompassing the corridor, the crowds, the whole of Venera. "You don't care what anyone does or who they really are." People were starting to murmur, starting to stare. Michael didn't seem to notice. He stabbed a finger at her. "All you care about is your vision and your pride, and your pride is Venera!"

Helen's fists clenched. This was not happening. Michael could not be leaving her. Not when she needed him.

"If you've got a problem with me, you take it up with me. But right now—"

"If I have a problem." Michael barked out a short, sharp laugh. "That's almost funny."

Helen's whole body trembled. "Why are you doing this?"

He met her gaze without hesitation. "Because I will not leave my family to help you start a war." He shook his head. "You need fanatics to help you now, Helen. I'm sorry to say you've got them."

Fear sent another spasm of pain through Helen's chest. "I don't need fanatics, Michael. I need you."

"No, you don't." He shook his head sadly. "You want me because I'm a v-baby and I fit your picture of what Venera ought to be. You've lost your ability to see what it *is*."

"No," said Helen softly, firmly. "This is not about me. This is about Venera's survival." She gripped his arm, as if she could transmit understanding from her flesh to his. "This is about the U.N. This is about the People flying through the Venusian clouds, looking for New Home."

This is about you abandoning your position and your responsibilities.

Helen met his gaze and held it. "If you won't fight for your home, for your people, maybe you should go." She released him and stepped back.

Even through her anger, she saw how the years of life and service weighed him down, pressing him into the deck and demanding he remain there. "I was going to stay, Helen, I really was, but I can't." He stretched both hands out to her, pleading. He was still so young, really. Younger than she'd been when she first flew through the clouds of Venus. He'd given his heart to so many things. He wanted to do right, but with so much to love, how could he see clearly what was most important?

"I can't stand what's going on here," Michael was saying. "Grace was the last straw."

"Grace . . ." Helen felt the blood drain from her face. "She'll be punished on Earth."

The look he gave her was pure, stunned disbelief. His hands came up as if he meant to strangle the air between them. But his fists closed on emptiness. "Earth," he breathed. "Mother Earth can't be trusted. Mother Earth is the villain. But Mother Earth gets to decide how to punish the woman who killed two of our own." He looked back at Jolynn and his children and shook all the years of his service off. "Good-bye, Helen."

Helen just stood there and stared. Michael reached his family just as the line began to move again. Michael picked up his bulging satchel. Jolynn wrapped an arm around his waist, almost as if she meant to pull him along if he faltered. He put his arm back around her shoulders and together they and their children walked onto the shuttle.

Helen's balance rocked. Her knees buckled and she had to put one hand on the wall to steady herself.

"Dr. Failia?" said someone timidly. "Are you all right?"

"Yes, yes." She pulled herself upright. "I'm fine."

She turned away from the crowds that were working so hard to get away from what was coming and started down the stairs to the Throne Room.

She did not have the luxury of time to mourn Michael's leaving right now. No matter what else happened, Venera still needed taking care of. Venera needed her. Venera could not betray her. She would not give it away as she'd been forced to give away Venus.

Venera, at least, at last, was hers.

CHAPTER TWENTY

T'sha nestled against the central heart of her city. She felt the ticking and timing of its valves and sacs underneath her body. Above her swarmed clouds of flies so thick they blotted out the sight of the clouds, and she could barely hear the rustle of her own skin under their triumphant buzzing.

All around her Ca'aed was dying and the flies had come to celebrate. She could smell nothing anymore but the scents of the rot. There was nothing to hear except the flies, and the wordless mewlings and keenings as the pain became too great for its smaller voices.

"Stop," Ca'aed had said, how many hours ago? T'sha didn't remember. Maybe it was only a few minutes since. She didn't know. "There is nothing to be done. Stop."

They had fought the disease with knives and shears. They had fought with monocellulars and antibodies and killer viruses. Its people had fought hand, wing and heart, and it had not been enough.

Now their city, exhausted and in agony, asked to be left alone.

T'sha had sent all the engineers to the quarantine shells, but she herself had descended into the exact center of the city, where she could touch the deepest part of its ancient, ravaged body.

Let the cancers take me too. She sent the thought freely onto the wind. *Don't leave me here alone with nothing but my failure.*

"I remember when we grew the first park," said Ca'aed. Its voice shook. It sounded old.

"Tell me." T'sha nestled closer.

"I was so excited. I had spread out far enough that it was quite a flight sometimes for the people to get out to open air. So we were going to make a place just for gathering, just for dance and beauty in my heart. I think I drove the engineers to distraction. I insisted on testing every graft myself for its strength and vivacity." Ca'aed stopped. "I don't remember their names. The engineers. They were so patient, and I don't remember them."

"That part of you was probably removed," said T'sha. "It's not your fault."

"Ah. Yes."

The city fell quiet for a moment. Under her torso, T'sha felt one of the heart sacs collapse, and it did not swell again.

"Tell me about the New People," said Ca'aed. "I want something different to think about."

T'sha stirred her wings. "They are very different from us," she began hesitantly. "They do not fly naturally. They spend long stretches of time doing this thing they call *sleep*, where they lie down in darkness and are still. At this time, their whole consciousness is changed from one state to another. It is part of their refreshment cycle." She paused. "I admit I do not quite understand it."

"It sounds frightening," said Ca'aed.

"It is natural to them," T'sha reminded the city. "They speak of sleep as if it were another place. They say 'We go to sleep.' I found it a little easier to think about that way. It made it a journey they must undergo."

Ca'aed thought about that. "Yes, that is a little easier." The muscles under T'sha cramped and smoothed, and one of Ca'aed's other voices gasped. "Tell me how they live on their world," its main voice asked.

Vee's pictures soared through T'sha's memory. So strange, so different, but spoken of with such pride and delight. "They live on the crust of their world where the air is the thickest. It is so cold there, they have great pools of liquids filling the valleys that they call *lakes* and *oceans*. Vee lives in a city on the edge of one of these lakes. Their cities stay in one place," she explained, "and the New People travel to them, as ambassadors do to the High Law Meet."

A whole world of High Law Meets, T'sha remembered thinking. *How grand that must be.* "She says her city is an ancient place, encompassing revered centers of science and learning. Its people are great engineers and merchants and have been so for centuries. She spoke of the lake it sits on and how it sparkles blue and silver in the sunlight, and how it has a wealth of legends that belong just to it."

"Then they do love their cities?" asked Ca'aed.

"Yes, very much." T'sha rubbed her muzzle back and forth against Ca'aed's skin, as she could not dip her muzzle pressed so close to the city. "They write poems about them and tell each other stories of their greatness." She paused again, remembering. " 'Come and show me another city with lifted head singing so proud to be alive, and coarse and strong and cunning.' Vee told me that was written about her city."

"I like that," said Ca'aed. "And their cities love them?"

"No," said T'sha as gently as possible. "Their cities are not such as they can return the love."

"What a great thing it is," murmured Ca'aed. "To be able to love even that which cannot return your love."

T'sha had not thought of that before, but the idea felt comfortable inside her. "Yes, it is a great thing."

"I heard Br'sei when he came."

A cloud, thick with the smell of illness drifted across them. T'sha coughed. "I'm sorry, Ca'aed. I did not mean you to." *I thought you too distracted. I should know better than to underestimate you, even now.*

"Will you abandon the New People?" asked Ca'aed.

T'sha stiffened. "I cannot be with them and with you. You are my city."

"You cannot choose which life you serve," whispered Ca'aed. Its heart labored unevenly as it spoke. T'sha lifted herself until her skin just brushed Ca'aed's skin. She could no longer control her size. Her body shuddered and wavered to the uneven rhythms of Ca'aed's last heart.

"I must choose," she said.

Something stank, thick, rank, and choking. She could sense it in every pore. The flies landed on her wings to taste her flesh, and she lacked the strength to shake them off.

"Perhaps I am not dying," whispered Ca'aed. "Perhaps I am going to sleep."

"Perhaps you are."

Ca'aed's heart spasmed. It jerked twice. Another foul cloud rose around T'sha, and the heart lay still.

T'sha settled slowly onto the still skin that covered the heart. She could not move her wings or even her bones. Around her she heard sounds of collapsing air sacs and loosening muscles.

She heard herself moaning.

But she did not hear Ca'aed. She would never hear Ca'aed again. Her mind clutched at the last few words, drawing them deep into her soul. All the words she would ever have. There would be no more. No more, ever.

You cannot choose which life you serve.

What a great thing it is, to be able to love even that which cannot return your love.

T'sha rose from her city's silent heart. She swelled herself, aware she was exhausted, but no longer caring. She beat her wings until her body caught the soaring wind and she shot out of the city's body.

She saw no one. She heard nothing. She was aware only of where she must go and what she must do. There were vague voices somewhere, calling and arguing, but they meant nothing. All the meaning was in Ca'aed's words. Those and her body were all T'sha could call her own now, and she could not forsake them.

Vee had thought that seeing the People through a wall screen, in the familiar surroundings of Josh's lab, would lessen some of the impact. She was wrong. They were just as grand, just as golden, and just as awe-inspiring in their aerial dances.

Well, the camera's working, she thought.

This was the test flight of the new drone they had dubbed "His Ambassador's Voice." Vee and Josh stood beside a desk in Josh's lab, surrounded by dismantled lasers and survey drones. Josh had the specialized keypad for flying the drone in his hands, and Vee had her briefcase with its image catalog and updated software open and jacked into the drone controls. A tangle of cables held them together. It was probably symbolic of something.

The fly-by drones were already remote controlled. They used the communication satellite network that ringed Venus to send their signals back to Venera, so they were natural candidates when Vee and Josh began to think about a mobile communications device.

The problem had been, as ever, mounting a projection device that wouldn't melt or be crushed.

Their reworked drone was a big, blocky confabulation that only stayed up because it was supported by Venus's atmosphere. Most of the size was a consequence of the insulation and housing for the projection laser and the last sheet of Vee's film. The drone didn't fly so much as lurch, but that was all right. It moved. Now they had to see if it could speak.

Through the drone's camera they watched a flock of the People's attendant jellyfish scatter in all directions. A trio of people floated up to look into the main window, close enough that Vee could see their tattoos clearly. She spotted the interlocking circles on their wings. These were all engineers, but she couldn't see Br'sei among them.

"Your turn," said Josh softly.

"Right." Vee licked her lips and pressed the Send key to execute the commands she had waiting.

A strip at the bottom of the screen lit up with the message that was, hopefully, at this moment being displayed on the film right next to the camera.

Good luck. We would like to see Ambassador T'sha or Ambassador D'seun, please.

One of the People broke away from the others and dived toward the base. The other two stared at the drone, each other, and their vanishing companion.

"Think they got the message?" asked Josh dryly.

"Looks it. Can we hover here?"

"After a fashion. Nothing like them." Josh worked the stick and the keyboard for a moment, and the drone slowed its flight. The propulser readouts that appeared on the desk crept up from green toward yellow. Josh hit a few more keys and they faded again. The view on the camera bobbed unsteadily up and down, but it stayed where it was.

"You'll be up for Adrian's job next," remarked Vee.

"You couldn't pay me enough to do Adrian's job." The sourness in his voice told Vee that Josh was thinking about Kevin, and the exodus that was going on over their heads, and whatever might be coming next. She touched his arm, but he didn't look at her.

Two People rose from the base. As they got closer, Vee was surprised to see the Engineer Who Looked Familiar beside the stranger. He carried a lumpy, mottled gray-green package clutched in his hands.

He did not stop level with the others. He kept going until he was almost on top of the drone. His muzzle and tattooed wings blocked out the rest of the view.

Vee sucked on her cheek and typed. *Hello, Engineer. What is your name?*

The engineer stared at the message and then looked straight at the camera lens. He raised both of his forehands, a greeting gesture, Vee remembered T'sha saying.

The lumpy package the engineer carried turned out to be a knotted ropelike thing with several objects clinging to it. Without looking down, he ran his hands over several of the objects, and Vee realized that most of the time the People couldn't see what their hands were doing.

What must their hands be like? Are they more sensitive? Less? Do they have more senses than the five humans have?

"I think he's about to make a few improvements," remarked Josh.

"Oh good," said Vee. "Always room for improvement."

The engineer plucked something off the rope and spread it on the drone's hull. It was silver skinned and glistened. It spread out tendrils that gripped the hull as tree roots would grip a stone.

Josh typed quickly, bringing up status readings that flashed past on the deck. Vee couldn't understand half of them, but they all shone green. Whatever their engineer was doing out there, it wasn't hurting their experiment.

The engineer pulled a clear disk off his rope and nestled it in the center of the tendrils. Then he took what looked like a balloon filled with pinkish jelly and settled it on the disk. The bag swelled, puffing up as if being inflated by an invisible pump, until it became a perfect sphere about the size of Josh's head. When it stopped growing, the engineer pulled a small white box with a grainy surface that reminded Vee of unpolished coral and slid it next to the sphere. He backed away with one stroke of his wings. Words appeared inside the sphere.

Good luck. I am Engineer Br'sei. Is this hybrid harming your transport? Is your visual field blocked? This hybrid should function down to the freezing point of, wait . . . water. Will that be cold enough?

"Good luck? Good lord," laughed Vee. The thing clinging to the drone looked ridiculous. It looked like a child's clay masterpiece surmounted by a pale-pink crystal ball.

It's probably an incredible jury-rigging, she thought.

"Everything's still green," reported Josh. He looked at the conglomeration again. "Doesn't block too much of the camera."

The hybrid is not harming our transport. The temperature tolerance is more than adequate. What is its range? Vee typed out the new message.

At the moment, the hybrid is limited to vocal range, came the reply. He shifted his weight. Embarrassed? *I must ask you to feel these words,* Br'sei went on. *Ambassador T'sha is not here. She is trying to save the life of her city. If she were here, she would surely tell you that you need to warn your families. D'seun is trying to get you all declared insane.*

"What?" said Vee before she remembered that Br'sei couldn't hear her. She typed her question.

What?

"The Law Meet has determined that your distant family is in-

sane. We are finishing the means to separate their souls from their raw materials.

"Distant family?" said Josh.

Vee's heart thudded once, hard. "They mean the Terrans." The words almost choked her. She typed,

You are going to kill the Terrans? The people on Earth?

Br'sei dipped his muzzle. An affirmation. *They say the Terrans are insane. The sane and the insane cannot live together.*

"Josh," croaked Vee. "I think you'd better go get the governing board."

But Josh was already gone. Vee typed. Her hands had gone completely cold.

What are they going to do?

The words spelled themselves out in front of Vee's eyes. *A monocellular to be launched through the portal. . . . A chemical trigger that would turn a benign monocellular life form in the human body into a lethal strain. . . . Deaths within hours. . . .*

"Holy God and Mother Creation." Vee could barely control her hands anymore. She couldn't encompass this. Earth. They were going to wipe out the human race. They were going to kill everyone.

Everyone.

No, Br'sei, the Terrans are not insane. They're different. We disagree, that's all.

Br'sei swelled a little as he studied the words. *They did not threaten to cut you off from the resources you need to live? We misunderstood?* She thought he might be hopeful.

What is misunderstood is the reason for it, Br'sei. "Come on, come on, you have to understand this!" *It is an internal conflict, nothing more.*

Br'sei did not respond. He pulled back, and D'seun swept into the camera's view followed by a Person Vee did not recognize. D'seun spoke to Br'sei, swelling his body and flapping his wings as if to shove Br'sei aside.

Br'sei spoke.

I am asked if I think I am now an ambassador, read the screen. *I am asked—*

D'seun dived at him, beating him away with his wings. Vee saw his skin tear open, freeing wisps of vapor. Br'sei fell back under the attack, shrinking and dropping as he did.

Stop! Stop! Vee typed frantically. But he did not stop. He drove Br'sei backward. His wings smashed against the display bubble, tearing it open. It flopped sideways, spilling out a pink fog that dispersed into the clear air.

Vee looked down at the torn bubble and up at the strange members of the People. The one who had arrived with D'seun spoke to Br'sei's companions. One of them vanished.

Vee didn't stand still to watch what happened. She had to tell somebody. Warn Earth. Who? How? The communications were blocked by Michael. But Michael had left. Had he thought to turn the blocks off before he went?

Vee shoved the drone controls aside and began typing so fast and hard her fingers screamed in protest.

Rosa, Rosa, Rosa, be there, be there, be there. Vee grasped the edges of the desk and leaned over the screen, gasping for breath around the panic that filled her throat. Would it work? Could she open a line? What if she couldn't?

She glanced up at the wall screen. Br'sei's friend had returned with a string of lumps. A tear ran down Vee's cheek.

The desk screen cleared, and Rosa's concerned face looked up at her. "What's the matter Vee?"

Vee almost laughed. There was no time. "Rosy, listen to me. I haven't got any time to explain. There are live aliens on Venus and they have decided the Terrans are too dangerous to live. They're launching a virus or something like it through their portal. They're going to try to kill the Terrans, Rosa. All of them. If we can't stop them, it's going to be soon." On the other screen, the Person had new tendrils spread out on the drone's hull and had produced another pink bag. "Rosa, you have to tell the U.N. They have to figure out a plan. I'll try to get more information through as soon as I've got it."

The delay ticked by, and the pink bag grew. Her manager's face went white, then gray.

"Vee, you don't mean this—"

The new pink bag was a full bubble outside the wall screen now. The stranger beside D'seun spoke.

I am sorry you had to witness that, Engineer Vee. Br'sei does not speak for the People. I do. I am Ambassador Z'eth.

Vee bit down hard on her lip. "I mean it Rosy," she whispered, wiping at the tears on her cheeks. "Call Yan Su. She'll confirm what I'm telling you about the aliens. Tell her about the virus. I'm doing by best, but . . . Please, call my family. Tell them they've got to get off Earth, go to Luna. Give them my account access, but you and they have to get out of there. I've got to go." She cut the connection and it felt like her heart was torn in two.

Ambassador, she typed with her cold, trembling fingers. *This is Vee. The people of this world do not want the Terrans dead.* Rosa would not stay on Earth. Rosa would get away. They couldn't kill her family. Mother, Father, Gramma, Grampa, Kitty, Lois, Tom, Amber, Auden. Rosa. Nikki. Everybody.

No, no, no, they would not die. She couldn't let them. She had to think of something to say. She had to think of *something. They—*

You are not an ambassador, replied Z'eth. *You cannot say what your people want.*

"No, but tell her *I* can." Vee jerked around. Helen and Ben hurried into the room with Josh on their heels.

"Thank God." Vee wiped at her cheeks and stepped away from the board, letting Helen take her place. She bumped against Josh, who just laid his hands on her shoulders. She leaned against his chest, drinking in his warmth.

Helen's hands shook as she lifted them to the command board.

I am Ambassador Helen, Ambassador Z'eth. Good Luck. I am asking you to stop whatever plans you have for the people of Earth. Let us talk. Let us explain.

Ambassador Z'eth swelled. *Ambassador Helen, there is nothing to explain. We have your own words condemning the Terrans as insane. They seek to cut you off from the source of your life for no reason.*

Helen took a deep breath. The trembling in her hands stilled for a moment. *Ambassador Z'eth, please, try to understand. We don't think they're crazy. We think they're wrong, but there's a difference with us.*

I understand that, but it is not only a question of what you think, replied Z'eth. *This is now our home too. You promised this world to us, and we must protect ourselves.*

Josh's hands tightened on Vee's shoulders. Vee clenched her fists. She had to do something. She couldn't just stand there shaking like a frightened child. She had to do something.

There was nothing she could do. Nothing at all.

Yes, read Helen's new message. *But not like this. There are six billion people on Earth, Ambassador. Most of them have nothing to do with this. Most of them don't want a war. They just want to go about their business.*

Z'eth's crest lifted. *Then why are they permitting this? Why has there been no poll?*

"How fast can you explain representative democracy," whispered Vee. She couldn't help it. Josh just held her close. He understood. Oh, God, he understood.

Ambassador, surely you do not believe there is only one right way to do things.

Z'eth swelled even further. She was enormous. It looked as if she meant to fill the whole world. *No right way can involve submitting to greed.*

"Damn you!" Helen's fist thumped against the desk. She typed.

We are not submitting. Listen, please, listen. Helen's whole body was shaking now. Ben shoved a chair behind her, but she did not sit. Words spilled out of her fingers onto the screen.

Once, our only world was Earth, but there were too many of us living there and we needed too much to support our lives. Earth was choking on us; it was dying. We moved out to fresh worlds to seek the space, the minerals, the power that we needed to live and keep our world of Earth alive.

We spread to our Moon, and to a world we call Mars, as well as this world of Venus. Before we came to these places, there was no life at all here. We spread our life beyond the confines of our own planet for survival yes, but also because we found those other worlds beautiful and we wanted to know all of their wonders and secrets.

It is true that even after all this time the colonies like ours still need Earth to live. But Earth also needs us. The people of Earth are trying to stay alive. Without the colonies the world will choke on itself again.

They fear that because of you they will lose us. They are trying to prevent that. But we need them and they need us. If we took the colonies from them, they might die. If you take Earth from us, we will die. You will kill us all. Is that spreading life?

Vee's breath caught in her throat. They'd have to listen to that. That was their own language. They'd have to understand that.

Ambassador Z'eth glided closer to the screen, filling the world and blocking out options.

It is you who do not yet understand. You will no longer be forced to depend on your insane family to survive. This is our world now, and we will help you and make sure you live.

The implications of Z'eth's words reached inside Vee and squeezed her heart.

"Jesus God," whispered Josh. His arms trembled even as he pulled her closer. "We're going to be another experiment for them. They're going to use us. . . ."

Movement in the corner of the screen caught Vee's eye. A familiar shape, beating its wings so fast she could barely see its markings, but she knew its color and its crest.

"T'sha!" Vee broke away from Josh and thrust her hands onto the keyboard.

T'sha! They're trying to kill Earth! Her family's names ran through her mind, blocking out everything else. *There's six billion people down there! They—*

The message line went dead.

The screen went blank.

Vee lifted her trembling hands off the keys. "What happened?" she whispered as she backed slowly away. "What happened!"

Ben came up to Helen's right side and touched a few keys. When he turned, his face was paper white. "It's the satellites. They're down. The U.N.'s started their attack."

"NO!" screamed Vee.

Beside her, Helen's mouth opened soundlessly and she clutched Ben's arm. In the next moment, Helen Failia slid to the floor.

While T'sha watched, the message faded from the New People's display. The tool foundered in the air and began to sink, gathering momentum as it fell.

D'seun did not move to stop it. Neither did Z'eth. T'sha darted down and grasped the cold, clumsy thing without thinking. It burned all her palms, and she shrieked, but she kept hold of it. Br'sei swooped after her and grasped one of the thing's extensions, pulling it toward a construction shelf where it could rest.

"A malfunction, apparently?" said Z'eth overhead.

Her hands stung, but T'sha ignored them. She rose to meet Z'eth's gaze.

"Ambassador, did you not see their plea? We cannot do this thing."

"Why not?" asked Z'eth, her crest lifting as if she were genuinely surprised. "We have declared them insane. This world is ours, and we have every right to protect it from insanity. There is nothing wrong here, Ambassador."

T'sha stretched out hands and wings to Z'eth "Please, Ambassador, this cannot be done. It is wrong, *wrong*."

Z'eth rose over her, her voice sad, but stolid. "I have given my promise, T'sha. What can you give me to change that? This is too much; there are too many ties. I cannot just break my words because you wish things were other than they are."

T'sha shrank. She had nothing, nothing except Ca'aed's last words, and Z'eth would not accept those. "You must stop this. You know it is wrong. D'seun is insane!"

Z'eth's muzzle lifted. "That doesn't matter!"

No, you did not say that. You could not possibly have said that. But D'seun hovered behind Z'eth, swelled to his fullest extent, pride and triumph filling the world. "How can what is right not matter?"

Z'eth flew so close to T'sha that she could not even see

D'seun. "Because D'seun is also right! We need this world, and we need it now. Not fifty years from now, not twenty. We are dying T'sha. Your own city, T'sha, how does it do?"

A moan burst free from her. "Ca'aed is dead."

For a moment they were all silent and still. T'sha's wings folded over her eyes, and she wished she were dead with her city. She had failed. She was nothing. The New People would die as Ca'aed had died.

Her wings fell away from her eyes and she looked up at Z'eth hovering in front of her.

"I am sorry." Z'eth brushed her muzzle against T'sha's. T'sha could barely feel it, her skin was so contracted. "But if we do not create our life here, in just a few years, all the cities will be dead. What good will sanity and right be then?"

"What can I promise you to change your words? What can you be seen to accept that is worth the lives of the New People?"

D'seun rose from behind Z'eth, a great cloud lifting up from the horizon. "Ca'aed is dead, T'sha," he announced, as if he savored the words. "Your people must be indentured so their children will be adopted by what cities still live. You have nothing left."

T'sha looked at him and hated what she saw. Greed and insanity and the terrible power of both. But he was right. He was right and she could not dismiss his words. What did she have to promise Z'eth? Nothing. Z'eth had given a promise to D'suen, and T'sha had nothing with which to counter that promise. She had Ca'aed's last words and her own wings and that was all. . . .

Her own wings. T'sha jerked her muzzle up to stare at Z'eth.

Her own wings. No one had made such a promise in centuries, but it was still legal. It could still be made and accepted and it was the richest offer, the final promise of all.

T'sha swelled to her full size. "My life, Ambassador Z'eth."

"What?" Z'eth pulled her muzzle back.

"My life," T'sha repeated. "I give it to you as promissory. If you do not kill the distant family, my life is yours. Not your city's. Yours."

Z'eth's whole body tensed. "That's a very old-fashioned idea, Ambassador."

"It's still legal." *Life of my mother and my father. . . . Oh my sisters, my brother, forgive me, forgive me.* "And it's all I have left."

"T'sha." D'seun thrust his muzzle at her. "Why are you doing this?"

T'sha rounded on him. "Because there is nothing else I can do, D'seun! No matter what the New People said for themselves, no matter what you heard, or saw, you wanted them gone. You have blocked me at every turn, and raw materials and soul are all I have left!" She shrank in on herself and sank down until her belly touched the thickening air and she could fall no further. Memories of Ca'aed and all its beauties filled her. If Z'eth agreed she'd never have a home again, never fly anywhere without orders. Gone, everything would be gone.

But she had to make this work. The New People were not insane. Vee was not insane. "My life, Ambassador Z'eth. You will have a promise such as no ambassador has had in two hundred years."

Z'eth hesitated. "The teachers do not favor such promises."

T'sha swelled yet again. Every tendon, every pore strained to the fullest. "My city is dead. Yours is dying. I can promise nothing to it. We have only each other."

"No!" cried D'seun, flapping his wings as if he meant to strike T'sha. "Ambassador Z'eth, I hold your promise. You will follow my vote about the disposition of the New People."

"The New People on this world," Z'eth told him. "On this world only, and you have already argued they are sane." She turned her back on him and swelled her body until her size matched T'sha's. "If we do this, we must truly do this. I cannot turn around in a year, or two, or ten and set you free again. This will be a legal, binding promise. You will be enslaved to me, and I will use you as such."

T'sha glanced over Z'eth's wing and she saw Br'sei there, hunched in and shrunken. His skin was torn. Something had happened, and she could not ask him what. She had meant to repay him for all he had done to help her, but if this worked,

she would never be able even to make a promise of her own
again. All that she had, all that she was would be Z'eth's until
her soul flew away free, to go to *sleep* with Ca'aed's perhaps.

T'sha dipped her muzzle.

"Done," said Z'eth.

"Ambassador!" shouted D'seun.

"It is done," said Z'eth calmly. "And it is not done." She faced
D'seun. "Do you wish to protest, Ambassador? How many
promises do I hold for you, D'seun? What shall I call in first?"

T'sha swelled, even as she felt her future slide off her skin
like wisps of cloud. No husbands, no wives, no children of her
own.

Nothing left at all, except six billion of the New People who
were free to prove what they truly were.

"It will be worth it," she said to Br'sei, knowing they would
be her last free words. "It will."

A voice nibbled at the edge of Helen's hearing and tugged at
the comfortable blanket of darkness. She did not want to hear
and she did not want to wake up. There was nothing to wake
up to.

"Helen, come on, Helen, you can't leave it like this.
Helen . . ."

Can't leave it like this? Can't leave what like this? She'd have
to wake up to find out. Helen strained for a moment, but, grad-
ually, her eyelids fluttered open.

At the sight of Ben's frantic face, memory flooded back, the
New People, the threat to Earth, to them all. . . .

"What's—" she croaked.

"It's okay, Helen." Ben smoothed her hand. "You're in the infirmary. It's going to be okay."

Another voice. "The New People have given in. They're not
going to kill Earth." Veronica Hatch, that's who that was. "They
sent up a balloon to tell us so."

Helen coughed. "Get to the shuttles. Tell Michael, tell the
yewners." She squeezed Ben's hand as if to drain his strength
into her. "Tell them we give in too. Get them back here."

"No, Helen, it's all right," whispered Ben anxiously. "The New People relented. There's no need—"

"Do it." Her head fell back against something soft that had been placed there.

Don't you see? she wanted to tell him. *We were wrong. We were seeing only in terms of ourselves, our futures, our pasts. We didn't see in terms of worlds, in terms of time and all the lives that are connected to ours. We thought, I thought, Venera was all there was, all I was. I was wrong, I was so wrong, and Michael was right. We have to make peace now. We have to remember how much more there is to us than just what we've done here.*

"He'll do it," said Veronica firmly. "Trust me."

I do, Helen closed her eyes. It would be all right. She'd get better. There was work to do, for Venera, for herself, and for all the human beings for whom this would now be a point of new beginning as they reached out to the People, came to understand them, taught the People about the breadth of humanity so both sides could truly understand their neighbors.

It all began now.

Epilogue

Yan Su's apartment was two stories above the main deck of U.N. city. Her small balcony faced west and let in the magnificent colors of the sunset over the waters. Standing by its rail, she could even see Venus shining peacefully in the darkening sky. No matter how hard she looked, she couldn't see any sign of the chaos going on up there.

When she had received Rosa Cristobal's call telling her about what the aliens had decided, she had stood frozen in place for several long seconds. Then she called the Secretaries-General. They in turn had put every single satellite on high alert to try to detect whatever missile the aliens would hurl at Earth to launch the virus, carefully ignoring the fact that the aliens could probably just make it appear anywhere they pleased. They spread the word to every major disease-control center on the planet. Every doctor who could be reached by the long arms of government bureaucracy was awake and on alert.

They waited, Su waited, in the darkness of her own apartment, frightened both by the magnitude of what was happening, and her own inability to do anything at all about it.

Then nothing happened.

Su looked down from the stars. Below her balcony, she could see a familiar figure crossing the deck.

She gripped the wrought-iron railing and watched Sadiq Hourani present himself to the door of her building for identification and admittance. The swish of the door was lost under the roar of the ocean waves, but she did see him enter.

Be here any moment.

She felt strangely calm. She had a fair idea what had brought him to her door this late at night without calling ahead, but somehow she could not get herself to fear it.

Perhaps I believe I deserve whatever comes.

She walked back into her living room. The room was comfortable, even a little luxurious with its thick, Persian carpet, the carved tables, and vases of fresh flowers. The balcony's etched glass doors glided shut behind her. As they did, the front door chimed, and its panel showed her Sadiq waiting in the hallway with his endless patience.

Su took a deep breath. "Door. Open."

The door did as it was told, and Sadiq walked into the foyer. He looked tired, she thought, and a little sad.

Well, they had been friends for a long time, and this had to be something of a disappointment for him.

"Good evening, Su," he said, walking forward. "I'm sorry for calling so late—"

"There's no need for you to apologize to me." She waved his words away. "Won't you sit down?" Su gestured toward one of her low, faux leather sofas. "I don't see why we should stand on ceremony after all this time. Can I send for some coffee?" It was astonishing how easily she fell into the hostess role. Then again, she'd had a great deal of practice at play acting.

"No, thank you." Sadiq remained standing. Su smoothed the hem of her long, rose tunic under her as she sat. She looked up at him, not weighing, calculating, or judging, just waiting to see what he had to say. She always tried to avoid planning her next move until she had all the required facts in her hands. That was one of the things that had made her so good at what she did and helped keep her at her post for so long.

Sadiq sighed, and she saw actual indecision on his face. She imagined he wanted to be angry, to let righteous rage fill him up and carry him through this, but it wouldn't come.

"Why did you do it, Su?"

She raised her eyebrows and curled up the corner of her mouth. "I have a busy schedule, Sadiq. Which 'it' are you talking about?" She thought she knew, but she wanted to be certain.

Sadiq bowed his head and folded his hands behind his back. He looked at the pattern of the carpet, burgundy and gold, so many knots all tied together to make their own pattern. A nice metaphor. "I've been having an extremely interesting chat with a feeder named Frezia Cheney, who let slip some facts about a conversation she had with your son, Quai. Quai, in turn, told me you asked him to set up a stream corporation called Biotech 24 so it could donate money to Grace Meyer, who, we now know, was the brains and funding behind the falsified Discovery on Venus." He looked at her. She sat very still, trying to keep her face impassive. She mostly succeeded, but she felt her eyes widen slightly.

"How did you get Quai to talk to you?" she asked softly.

"I told him about your surveillance on his private mail."

"Oh." Su dropped her gaze. So here was the payment for that. Her heart swelled with love and sorrow until her entire chest tightened, but she couldn't blame her son. No, she could not blame him at all.

"There is even an implication"—Sadiq moved just a little closer—"that you and some of the Venerans have known about the aliens for years." He spread his hands, appealing to her. "Why, Su? What were you doing?"

Su smoothed the fabric of her tunic across her knees. She reached out and minutely adjusted the small jade-dragon carving on her coffee table.

"I thought," she said, drawing her hand back but not lifting her gaze from the sinuous reptile, "that I was creating an unprecedented opportunity for the colonies to gain political capital."

Sadiq sank onto the sofa, facing her. "Tell me," he said.

She touched the spines on the dragon's back, gingerly, feeling their needle sharp tips dent the skin of her fingertips.

"Grace Meyer sent me an agitated message three years ago. It seems that while searching for her UV absorber, she found a satellite photo of what looked like an alien artifact. She was telling me rather than Helen Failia, because she did not like Dr. Failia and wanted to go over her head."

"Do you know the source of this feud?"

Su smiled thinly. "It seems Dr. Failia was unwilling to actively seek funding for Dr. Meyer's projects. Dr. Failia was afraid that searching for life, which had failed so many times before in so many more likely places, would make Venera look silly and spoil its ability to get serious funding and serious attention. Dr. Meyer never forgave her." Su shook her head. "And we think the in-fighting in the legislature is bad."

"So, she gave you this photo and told you her theories—" Sadiq prompted.

"And I asked her to keep them both quiet for a while." Su pushed at the dragon so that its focus shifted from looking directly at her to looking at the wall past her right shoulder. "At first, I didn't believe it could possibly be what it looked like, and I also did not want public ridicule to fall on Venera.

"Grace said she would do no such thing, however. She was tired of having her work suppressed, she said. She was ready to sign off in a huff, when the idea struck me." She rubbed her palms together.

"Suppose there were aliens on Venus. Suppose they made contact, not with the government of Earth, but with Venera base. Venera would have the chance to do what no one had ever done. It would have a first that could not be taken away from it. A colony with a contact that not even the C.A.C. could take away, no matter how hard they tried. It might even lead to a successful independence bid. One without bloodshed this time." She looked up at him. The sadness had deepened on his face. "The C.A.C. is never going to let the colonists go. Their status as second-class citizens has become too ingrained and in some ways too convenient. I came to believe that to get full civil and human rights restored would take a revolution, but not a bloody one, not like Fuller's." She smiled softly. "If anyone could make it work, it would be Helen Failia, I was sure. Her people were so loyal to her.

"I added in the fact that Grace wasn't going to keep quiet. She wanted her recognition, and she wanted it now, and I started getting ideas.

"I suggested we create what became the Discovery." She turned her hands this way and that, examining the backs, the nails, the deeply lined palms. "It was brilliant, actually. I was very proud. It served to focus public attention on the colonies. It raised all sorts of questions about Terran rule from places other than Bradbury, and it got the scientific world to take Grace Meyer seriously. Grace found help from some of Venera's many underfunded departments, and I found there were plenty of places between Earth and Venus to hide the money they used for the construction." She smiled at her hands. "Actually, except for gold for the laser, it was quite an economical operation."

"I see," said Sadiq.

"It also got the Venerans actually looking for aliens. I felt if the news came from anybody on the base other than Grace Meyer, Helen would have an easier time of things."

Sadiq turned away. He paced slowly over to her balcony doors and looked out onto the night.

"Tell me what you're thinking," asked Su.

He shook his head slowly. "So many years of fighting. So many years of a single goal in mind—equal rights for the colonies. It blotted out everything else, even the stunning wonder of meeting another form of life, other minds from other worlds. Everything was just there to be used. Nothing could be left alone to just happen." He turned around and his eyes were shining a little too brightly. "I'd hoped you were above that."

"I'm sorry." Su clasped her hands together. "What do we do about this?"

"I don't think there's anything else to do." Sadiq turned back toward her. "The story will be breaking soon, and your attempt at a bloodless coup killed two men. I'm sure that will keep you busy enough."

Su bowed her head. "I am sorry, Sadiq. It looked like the only way to break the C.A.C.'s hold on the colonies."

"I'm sure it did." He paused. "Do you know, Veronica Hatch tells me that one of the People's ambassadors sold herself into slavery to save us all."

"Did she?" murmured Yan Su. "What a fine thing to do for strangers."

"Yes." He looked down at her. "I wonder if we'll ever be able to show such a fine thing to them."

He left her there and walked out the door. Su sat where she was for a while. Then she rose and walked back onto the balcony to breathe the salty night air and look up at the sky. She did not know, after all, how much longer these privileges would be hers.

Daylight had dwindled to a patch of gray on the horizon. The gentle yellow streetlights had come out, lighting the deck and dimming the stars overhead.

Su turned her face to the evening star.

"Thank you," she whispered, hoping somehow her words would touch the stranger who had saved them all. "Thank you."